BEINGS

BEINGS

A NOVEL

ILANA MASAD

BLOOMSBURY PUBLISHING
NEW YORK · LONDON · OXFORD · NEW DELHI · SYDNEY

BLOOMSBURY PUBLISHING
Bloomsbury Publishing Inc.
1359 Broadway, New York, NY 10018, USA
50 Bedford Square, London, WC1B 3DP, UK
Bloomsbury Publishing Ireland Limited,
29 Earlsfort Terrace, Dublin 2, D02 AY28, Ireland

BLOOMSBURY, BLOOMSBURY PUBLISHING and the Diana logo are trademarks
of Bloomsbury Publishing Plc

First published in the United States 2025

ISBN: HB: 978-1-63973-700-0; eBook: 978-1-63973-701-7

Library of Congress Cataloging-in-Publication Data is available

2 4 6 8 10 9 7 5 3 1

Typeset by Siliconchips Services Ltd UK
Printed in the United States by Lakeside Book Company, Harrisonburg, VA

To find out more about our authors and books visit www.bloomsbury.com and sign up
for our newsletters

Bloomsbury books may be purchased for business or promotional use. For information
on bulk purchases please contact Macmillan Corporate and Premium Sales Department
at specialmarkets@macmillan.com.
For product safety–related questions contact productsafety@bloomsbury.com.

To Mike, who kicked this whole thing off,
and to Micha, who unknowingly helped finish it

Safe journey, space fans,
wherever you are.

—Stephen Hill, host and producer of *Hearts of Space*

"It is not that I have no past. Rather, it continually fragments on the terrible and vivid ephemera of now."

—Samuel R. Delany, *Dhalgren*

Words change depending on who speaks them;
there is no cure.

—Maggie Nelson, *The Argonauts*

This is how I like to imagine them:

Sitting in the sky-blue Chevy Bel Air, he behind the wheel with both his hands on it, a man who took driving seriously, who understood that the weight and speed and thrust of a car are as full of latent danger as a bullet nestled in the chamber of a gun, and she his trusting passenger, not only willing but also eager to shed responsibility in favor of frivolity, which in this moment meant keeping the little dog, Dee, curled on her lap while her eyes freely roamed the landscapes flying by, endless woven tapestries hanging on either side of the black asphalt corridor. It was a cold autumn night in 1961.

They knew how to be quiet together, these two.

But not always, nor even frequently, for each was brimful with thoughts and opinions, and it was in their particular natures to take pleasure in vocalizing these. Both, moreover, had learned long ago when and where to stay silent in order to preserve their own sense of dignity, not to mention their physical safety, and had spent quite enough time keeping their mouths shut and faces impassive even as they yearned to contradict, correct, or at the very least challenge the record in rooms full of white men. Together, then, there was no need for self-imposed muzzles.

Among their earliest joys, these mutual funnels of sometimes suppressed speech, tornadoes of words twining round one another as they sat up late at night in those early days, when he was still married to his first wife and she was trying very hard not to appear to wish it were otherwise.

In those white wicker chairs on the porch of the boardinghouse where they first encountered one another, his family slumbering, they talked about everything under the moon, he offering her cigarettes first, until his case ran out and she told him to hang on a minute and dashed to her room, all five feet of her, elevated another one and a half inches by her sensible, black, thick-heeled shoes. He knew he desired her when she returned unshod, a half-full pack of smokes in her small hand for them to share, but this was nothing new nor particularly alarming, only a measure that he was as much a man then as he had been at thirty and twenty-five and eighteen and sixteen. Desire, anyhow, did not always lead to divorce, so he lit her cigarette that first night and lit one himself and they continued discussing the state of the world and the wrongs they saw in it, and if sometimes she said the kinds of things that he heard in rooms full of white men, well, they were alone on a porch together. Later, after he had divorced his first wife, they were alone in motels together, until, eventually, they were alone under her own roof as often as he could get a weekend off work and then, finally, once they had married and he got the transfer to Boston and moved in with her, they were alone together in the home that was now theirs, shared, and when it was just the two of them, he felt fully within his rights to contradict, correct, and at the very least challenge her ideas. He noted that first night that she did not flinch like other small white women might when he did this, but rather leaned forward as if to shorten the distance between her eardrums and his mouth, her eyes a little narrowed either with the effort of listening or from the smoke.

There was intimacy in this shared silence too, now, only months after he had moved in with her, his second wife, to whom he was, too, a second husband.

. . .

They had set out from the Canadian border some hours ago, and it was now after midnight. She wished this brief, belated honeymoon would not end, but there was a storm coming and they had not brought enough money with them for a third night at the motel. She hoped her husband did not blame himself for this. The weekend was his idea, a welcome and romantic surprise, sprung on her when he returned from work in the morning just four days before. Oh, she hoped he was not in a bad mood. He got mad at himself sometimes, a quiet anger like parental disappointment, his expression similar to how she imagined he must look at his boys when they were naughty or got low grades at school. He held himself to such high standards, became annoyed when he had missed a turn on Route 3 an hour or two ago. They doubled back and stopped to ask for directions at a restaurant, had ended up eating there, too, and the moist slice of chocolate cake she had gotten sat in her stomach, its weight welcome, sweetness still lingering in her mouth. She shuffled nearer to him on the bench seat—Dee slunk off her lap to the floor in response—and leaned forward to kiss the fat knuckle of his thumb. He did not like taking his hands off the wheel except to shift, especially when it was as dark as all this, which she knew, and so she nuzzled her forehead against his shoulder, just once, quickly, and moved back. He smiled, eyes still on the road, and she knew he was all right.

He was indeed in good enough spirits, although distracted. He was tired, and the hamburger he had eaten hoping it would give him energy had instead made him lethargic, his eyes heavier now. He should have had a coffee, but his ulcer had only recently subsided and he was limiting himself to three cups a day, none later than 5 p.m. He tried to fix his mind on something. The radio was off. It had begun emitting too much static, that gray shuffling noise, in the twists and turns of the highway making its way through the White Mountains. He did not wish to engage in conversation with his wife; he was too tired to feel intelligent, and the road was dark, demanding his concentration. He knew he instinctively glanced at her when they talked in the car and the margins were narrow on this road. It was better not to risk it.

His mind turned over the events of the weekend, the good food and the music, the Negroes he had noticed in Montreal and how surprised he was, never having considered that men of his race might live in such a strange, somewhat exotic place, all that French. Silly, he realized now, driving, as of course Negroes lived all over the world. He had friends in the service who told him about Negro Frenchmen and even Germans, although they had had a bad time of it during the war. He thought again about a conversation that he occasionally found himself having with certain men over the years, a talk that always went the same way, about how they noticed themselves, sometimes, thinking about things as if they were white, with the same advantages handed to them and thus the same ease of bestowing judgment upon others. As if the way white folk talked and lived, their innocence or, more commonly, their willful ignorance or outright racism, had permeated something in them. He and his wife had recently attended a scientific lecture about the blood–brain barrier, a set of selective cells in the brain that form a semipermeable border that only some substances can penetrate. That was what it felt like: the prejudices he saw all around him doing just what they should not do, what he wished he could prevent them from doing, and jumping the blood–brain barrier.

> *Before we go any further, I want to acknowledge my choice of racial terminology, which in my era is outdated and offensive. But the couple did not live in my era, and this is their story, the couple's. For their time, and specifically their generation and class, the use of the term <u>Negro</u> was widespread and politically correct. Younger people, students and activists mostly, were just beginning to reclaim the word <u>Black</u>, but this wouldn't achieve widespread acceptance and popularity until the end of the decade. Not until the mid-2010s did it become consistently capitalized in written media. I've chosen to use the terms contemporary to the couple in order to avoid anachronisms.*
>
> *Language changes. What is widespread or preferred or acceptable changes from one era to the next. The language I use in my asides—preferred and respectful in my era—may well read as old fashioned, rude, or downright bigoted by the time anyone reads this.*

His musings were interrupted by his wife asking him to look outside, at the bright star near the moon. Was it moving? He glanced up, puzzled. It did seem as if a speck of light was slightly farther from the bright moon every time he took his eyes off the road. Surely there were no satellites orbiting above New Hampshire, but perhaps, he ventured, one had drifted off course.

She kept watching the speck grow brighter, wondering if it was a trick of their own progress that made it seem to move. The moon hung like a big, beautiful lamp that night, drowning out many of the stars nearest it. The sky looked for a moment like the pictures in a storybook she had read when she was a child, during the days when her mama had limited her to one a day because no one had time to go to the library as often as she wanted, and there certainly was no money for books, not even before the Depression. The book was loaned by a neighbor, children's stories about the constellations. She remembered so few of them now, but she had for a while begged her mama to stay outside after dark on weekend nights with a small flashlight so she could look up at the stars and down at the book and try to find which constellations lived in the sky above her. There had not been any moving stars then, never, except when one fell, lucky, and she would make a wish. But the roving light she saw now, one hand nervously fiddling with a blue earring, seemed to be going much too slow to be a good luck charm and too fast to be a star at all.

At her feet, the dog was whining a little. Dee was a good dog, well trained, did not make a fuss when she needed to go to the bathroom, and never went on the floor at home or in the car, but just asked quietly, like this, whether her needs could be attended to. So her owner asked her husband to stop the car, for the dog, but also so she could look at the light, and see if it really was moving.

.   .   .

He stood outside the car, smoking, while his wife walked the little dog down a stretch of highway. He kept looking back and forth up the road, worried that a trooper might come by or a policeman or just a driver out late and bored and looking for trouble.

She took the cigarette out of his hand and smoked it and called him a sleepyhead, for he had not noticed her coming right up to him with the dog, not until she touched him. He could be like that, lost in thought and space, and she thought him almost too handsome in this stoic state. She loved his smile too, of course, even if his teeth were fake. They fit well and looked very natural on him, so that most people did not know.

He stretched once more and put an arm around her shoulders, asked if the dog was all right now, and she said yes, so they climbed back into the car. She settled herself and Dee as he pulled back onto the road. The cold night air and the little walk had refreshed her, and she looked out the windows with renewed interest.

There it was, the same peculiar light movement, and she began to track it again, the comfortable joy of a moment previous turning liquid inside her, sharpening into nervous curiosity. She pointed and asked her husband to look again, and told him he was being ridiculous if he thought the growing light could possibly be a star or even a satellite, so much farther away would it have to be then.

He raised his eyes cautiously. No, she was right, it could not be a star, and he said so, told her that he had made a mistake, that it was simply an airplane on its way to Canada. Yes, he soothed himself as he kept driving, it was just something regular like that, no need to get excited. The turns were getting sharper, and he wanted to pay attention, for there were too many stories in the newspaper of cars crashing in these mountains, usually when a driver was drunk or fell asleep at the wheel. He did not want to become an item in the paper, and he did not want such a pleasant trip to be ruined by his inattention, by his wife's fixation on this perfectly ordinary airplane.

Still, he wished now to see another car, anyone who they might be able to shine their high beams at to say hello to, maybe even stop for a moment to ask if they, too, were seeing the persistent moving brightness overhead. He knew better than to be spooked just because it was dark, but his wife's nervousness was putting him on edge. She had her face right up to the window on her side, he noted, keeping watch, and just as he was about to say something coolly reassuring to her, to himself, he heard her gasp and instinctively hit the brake pedal. When he looked out past his wife, he saw the Canada-bound light, bigger now, as if the plane's altitude were dropping—which could not be, it had many miles to go before the next airport, why would it be descending already?— and he saw it shudder in stillness that seemed entirely unnatural and change course, no longer northbound, passing them, but reversing entirely from its former direction and heading south. Toward them. After them.

Unnerved, he pulled the car sharply into the next rest area he saw, a little clearing with picnic tables and some trees and what looked like an outhouse tucked sheepishly far back. He got out, and she followed.

She sensed he was rattled, her husband, and that he would not admit it. He had his superstitions, everybody did, whether they copped to it or not, but still, he was a man most often inclined to take the rational route through things. He believed, or tried to believe, that reason would prevail, that he could reason his way into people's hearts, into legal justice, into equal protection under the law. He was a man who liked to learn, who fiercely sought out experts on matters he did not understand, whether in books or lectures or TV and radio broadcasts. She loved him for this, and for much else, but she also thought his cerebral bent could be rigid, limiting, and in this moment knew she simply must shake him out of his stubbornness, for she was beginning to get really frightened now and told him that whatever he wished to call it, it was still there and it seemed now to be following them, and even worse, now that they had stopped, it seemed to be closing in on them.

He shook his head and lit a cigarette for her, handed it over, and lit another for himself. He insisted again that it was a commercial liner, nothing else, but she asked how that could be, since she had never heard of a passenger airplane with a destination reversing its course in the middle of its journey like that. Preposterous. She was right, he knew this, and was glad now that his boys had not come with them on this trip. When he was first imagining the vacation, on his long shift four nights before, he allowed himself an expanded fantasy, one where his former wife could be reached in time, where she would allow her sons to take a day or two off school and take this trip with them. The boys liked his new wife, perhaps because while she was not as fine a cook as their mother, she did allow them dessert every night.

His boys would have become excited by this roving light. Or perhaps not, but only because they both would have been asleep in the back seat this late, after 11 p.m. already. His mind conjured the cozy image of the smaller one leaning his head on the chest or shoulder of the bigger, and another option, of them curled up, toe to toe, sharing the blanket that was always folded in the back seat, just in case the car ever broke down in the middle of the night or in winter and he had to wait until morning for someone to drive by and give him a hand or a ride to the nearest gas station to call for help.

Of course, this image of his sons was foolish; they were teenagers now, one still in high school, the other due to start college in the spring. Yet he always pictured them as younger than they were, missing the prepubescent boys who gave their affection freely, who had not felt the need to posture at manhood.

It was thinking of them, his sons, that brought another idea to mind, one that was so obvious that he almost laughed in relief as he exhaled.

They had visited him for two weeks over the summer—Philadelphia was nearly a six-hour drive away, a longer bus ride because of all the stops, and so their summers and Christmas were the only occasions he expected to be able to see them for an extended period, a reality that constricted his heart when he let himself dwell on it, as he sometimes did during the long nights at work, and which made him desperately unhappy in a way that caused him to nearly, if not quite, regret all his actions of the last few years—but when they had last visited, they did what they had sometimes done when they were younger: went plane-watching. In Philly, he had taken them to the road near the airport, and they would make a game of guessing where the planes were going and listing all the things they knew about the state or the country they were imagining as its destination. He taught them how to tell what designs on the tail belonged to which airline.

As he stamped his cigarette out, he told his wife it was a Piper Cub, surely, some hunters flying around in it who must have stayed out too late and gotten lost and now could not see very well in the dark and were trying to make contact with the nearest air traffic control. But she told him it was not hunting season, which was true, although they could be poachers, of course, and perhaps they were flying at night like this because their flight had never been approved in the first place. She also told him she could not hear any noise, and a Piper Cub would be making some, especially one flying lower, nearer. He suggested the wind might be carrying the sound away; his wife raised her brows at him. The night was still.

She remembered the binoculars she had meant to get out of the car before and hurriedly retrieved them, handed them over to her husband. He put the strap over his neck; her mouth twitched. She had made fun of him just days earlier for doing the same thing at the Niagara Falls, which they had gone to see on their way to Montreal. He had said the binoculars were expensive. Such a careful man, she thought lovingly even as she teased him for his overabundance of caution, tickling him and making him drop them from his eyes over and over.

Now she watched his face as he looked up, his mouth widening as he squinted. Her heart was pounding, for she had a suspicion, but not one she was willing to voice quite yet, especially not as her husband, who had seemed so relieved only a moment ago, became increasingly agitated. He hated not knowing things, did not take well to the unexplainable. He would think her ridiculous for even considering it. Her sister had seen some years ago one of those unidentified flying objects people spoke about sometimes, more so back then than recently, she thought, and her sister had a good head on her shoulders, children, a husband, a nice home, and plenty to be taking care of without inventing silly stories. So, yes, she had believed her sister, what her sister had seen, while her rational husband clearly had not, although he claimed to be agnostic on the topic. She knew she should not bring this up now, not when he handed her the binoculars with a slightly shaking hand and lit another cigarette from the butt of the last one.

She brought the lens up to her eyes and was disoriented for a moment by the view of the stars, but then saw it—there!—flying in front of the moon. She could see its shape silhouetted at first, but she kept with it and soon saw some colored lights go on and off along the sides. It sped up and she lost it, then found it again and noticed it was slowing down as it passed in front of the moon once more. Because she was prepared this time, she focused closer on it and could see its shape, longish and curved, with narrow bands of flashing lights, red and amber, green and blue. She asked her husband if he could see them too and he repeated that it must be an airplane, it had flashing lights on it like they did, and when she interrupted to ask where its tail was, where its wings were, he said it clearly was not a commercial airliner or a hunter's private vehicle but rather a military plane of some kind.

She suddenly realized, as she handed the binoculars back to him, that their little dog was sitting at her feet and shivering as if cold or terribly afraid, much like when they arrived at the veterinarian's office, the site of shots and other indignities. Taking pity on the sweet thing, she brought Dee back into the car, soothing and shushing while she waited for her husband, who was taking another look at the sky, cigarette hanging between his lips.

As he watched it, he wished again for some other nighttime driver to pull off the road, bear witness to this matter. He had read once about the phenomenon of folie à deux and was frightened to think that he and his wife might be going mad together. As he watched the plane—or whatever it was, for he had to admit that he had never seen any aerial vehicle change directions as fast as this one did, nor had he ever heard of any that could change altitude or speed as abruptly—he strained to hear something, anything, other than the soft rustle of leaves from the trees sheltering the picnic tables in the clearing nearby or the crickets singing in the grass. He had turned the car motor off, and although he could hear its mechanical clicking as it cooled, there was no whir from above, no slight buzzing, not even a hum. He had the distinct notion that the flying vehicle, which was moving back and forth still across the moon but seemed unwilling to go off in a direction that would take it away, away, away, was looking back at him.

Watching him?

Ridiculous.

No, he had to shake himself free from such nonsense. He got into the car and told his wife they really should hurry on so they could get home. At this rate, he grumbled, with all the stopping and starting, they would get no sleep at all. He repeated that the thing outside was likely a military plane, perhaps something they were not even supposed to see, and maybe that was why it was sticking close to them, to make sure that they would not talk about it. His wife asked how anyone that far away could possibly know what they were going to do, and besides, they could pull off at the nearest gas station and make a phone call and whatever it was flying up there would not be able to stop them. He gripped the steering wheel tighter and suggested that perhaps they were playing games with them, then, some air force hot-shots that got their rocks off by trying to frighten gullible women in the night. He knew at once that his voice was too loud, that he had given away his own fear, and regretted his lost temper. He hoped she took his anger as part of his usual ambivalence about the military, in which he had served, and which had torn his face open and killed too many of his brethren both here and abroad. He was a patriotic man, proud of his service, but he could not always put away his conscience, that voice that asked what good it was, fighting wars, especially wars that had nothing to do with them.

They drove, uneasy with one another in a way that felt new and vaguely itchy, as if their bodies were wrapped in sackcloth rather than their sensible garments of cotton and silk. He knew the car was going far too slowly for his stated impatience to get back to Portsmouth, but neither he nor she mentioned it. She kept her eyes fixed upward, through the windshield, occasionally leaning against the side window. Cannon Mountain was ahead, a looming shadow with a bright peak, the lights of the eatery and tramway terminus looking like a Christmas tree in a dark room, only the angel still switched on.

When the moving light disappeared behind the mountain's silhouette, he pulled the car over again, breathing a little easier, waiting silently with his wife to see whether it would appear again. He hoped terribly that they would soon be laughing at this strange tension, attribute it, quite rightly he thought, to their tiredness and the long trip, their eagerness to be back home.

She clutched the edge of the seat as he got back on the road, her breaths a little shallow with anticipation. She had to admit that she was excited, even eager to experience something out of the ordinary. She desired this even after a trip that was as out of the ordinary for the two of them as it could be, for it was their belated honeymoon, and while neither of them was in their first blush of youth, nor was this her first marriage or his, it was still special to be alone with her beloved for days at a time without the imposition of work or friends or civic duty. She wished fervently that this could be enough; it was all she had ever really and truly wanted, to be desired by a faithful man and be his intellectual comrade and make a life together that was as unselfish as they could make it while also enjoying the fruits of their labor every once in a while, as when they had been sent that wonderful photograph of President Kennedy, signed by his own pen, thanking them by name for their work stumping for him in New Hampshire.

They breathed together as he drove, the dog panting a smile up at them. For a few quiet moments it seemed like whatever had been happening was now over.

But it wasn't, of course. If it had been, I would likely have known nothing about them. The vast majority of us, after all, know little to nothing about the vast majority of us.

It was not over, he realized, a pulsing pain beginning to throb in his gut. The bright object came out from behind the mountain as they surpassed its breadth, and rather than returning to its earlier position directly above them, it remained to their right, dipping lower than ever so that it was obscured on and off by the trees.

They passed a small sign, illuminated by the high beams, that directed interested tourists to take a right for Flume Gorge. Flume. It sounded like a conflagration, a sudden and violent plume of fire, and he gripped the wheel harder. There were few lights on the narrow, curving highway. He slowed further, distracting himself with the sensible fear of a speedy driver coming round the bend without care and plowing into his wife's pretty car. Fluming.

She watched for the bright object, a thrill trapped in her throat. She said nothing when they drove right past a motel, VACANCIES lit up in neon above a single yellow square. She imagined the night manager inside, feet on the desk, trying to stay awake with the paper or a small TV set. How glad the clerk would be to have the night's boredom interrupted! But they did not have enough cash with them for a room, and besides, as frightened as she was, she wanted dearly to see what would happen next. Her whole body tingled with the fear, the adventure. She could not believe any real harm would come to them. Nothing so very bad had ever happened to her, even though many things had threatened to over the years. She had survived diphtheria, two bouts of pneumonia, a likely unnecessary appendix removal—the doctors were all so hot for appendix removals in the '30s—and she believed in some quiet corner of herself that she was a little bit blessed, that God watched over her safety.

Around the next bend, the trees thinned out on the right, and when she looked through the binoculars again, she felt the early stirrings of what, much later, she would recognize as awe: the thing above was huge, round. She could clearly see now two rows of lit windows. Her heart raced. She told her husband he must stop and look, he must, and reached for his arm, tried to convey the urgency she felt, the need to share this moment. It was like nothing else he had ever seen, she told him.

They were in a stretch of emptiness just south of Indian Head, a kind of summer campground where two imitation wigwams sat empty in the middle of the clearing. He could picture his boys, when little, running in and out of the structures, could imagine them playing war games, holding sticks and yelling Bang! at each other, or mingling with the children of other families and putting together an impromptu baseball team. But it was dark and deserted now, cheerless, and she was still clutching his arm. He stopped, to humor her, and took the binoculars before getting out.

He left the car running and leaned against its soft, comforting vibration. The plane that was not a plane hovered at an angle a hundred yards away and maybe two hundred yards up, a treetop's worth above those standing silent and tall below. His wife demanded to know if he saw it, her voice shaking. He was scared too. He knew planes well enough. He was a rational man. He understood that there were things the military did not share with the populace, but this—this hovering silence, bladeless, wingless, its lights all wrong—it seemed to be far beyond the capabilities of what he knew of modern engineering.

The thing swung over the road from one side to the other, and he followed it through the binoculars, his mouth dry. Small fins silently emerged from its sides, each with a red light at its end, and the two rows of curved and lit windows tipped toward him, as if the thing was looking at him, at them. He leaned in to shut the car off and walked away, crossed the rest of the road, walked onto the dewed grass as if compelled; he had to get nearer, had to see it better.

In the car, his wife bent over to pet their dog with a trembling hand, murmuring nonsense comfort words to it, to herself. When she sat back up, she fully realized just how spooked her husband must be, because he had left the vehicle right in the center of the road, between southbound and northbound lanes. Anyone coming from either direction might smash right into them. Worse, the man took the darned keys with him. So while she could not move the car, she could keep her eyes peeled, watch the road while her husband watched what she was beginning to allow herself to call a UFO, at least silently. She would call her sister tomorrow morning, once she had slept.

In turning her head back and forth between the front and back windows of the car, her gaze caught something moving. Her husband. His figure blurred into the darkness and density of the trees, the field he was crossing, the shadow cast by the now enormous object above him. He looked so very small beneath it.

She screamed his name, and the dog yelped at the sudden loudness of her voice. He probably could not hear her, she realized, so she slid over to the driver's side, to the open door, and called out for him again, again, again.

Whether or not he registered a sound in the distance, he would never remember later. He was too focused on what he saw above him through the binoculars. There, behind the windows, were a dozen figures crowded together, all wearing uniforms, black and shiny. They did not look quite right; something was wrong with their skin, with their eyes, those eyes that seemed to meet his gaze. For a wild moment, he felt he had the upper hand—after all, they did not have binoculars, so surely he was seeing them much more clearly than they could see him.

All at once, they stepped away as if called by something, someone, and moved to a wall full of lights and buttons behind them, which reminded him of a telephone switchboard or an electrical panel. Only one figure remained at the window. The husband's fingers moved, trying to focus the lens on that face, a face he could not reconcile with anything he had seen before. It seemed to be getting closer, the face, the craft, descending. He felt powerfully that something terrible was about to happen.

That he was going to be taken.

Captured.

In a panic, he turned and ran to the car. Get away, get away, get away, he must get away, he thought, his entire body shivering despite the mild still air, even as he sprinted faster than he had since basic training. His bowels shifted in him, his heart raced, his ulcer pulsed. He heard his wife shouting for him, saw her coming out the driver's side. She slid back in and babbled as he thrust himself into the car, put it in gear, and started driving, but he could not register any of her questions, so full was his head with the word run, so full his mouth with the word capture.

I

Now

A strand of fairy lights has finally given up the ghost and the new shadows look menacing, unfamiliar. The Archivist unplugs, replugs, but the strand doesn't mend itself. The orange-shaded floor lamp will have to do. They refuse to use the overhead fluorescents when alone. Too cold. Too impersonal.

It's time for them to leave, but where they are feels more like home than the blank white box housing their possessions, one of four rooms in the apartment they share with three other adults they are not related to by blood or friendship. They've been meaning to put something on the walls, decorate those empty expanses with some color, but it's not like anyone else is ever there; there's no one to impress, to make comfortable.

The Archivist blinks. They've been staring at the glow on the old speckled tile for some time now. Habitually, they look back at their desk, their screen, and scan the new messages in their inbox. Two are unimportant, another is irrelevant, and a fourth is a follow-up to a query that came earlier. A correction: the name of the woman whose papers are being requested is spelled without an *a*. Phyllis Egerton, not Eagerton. The Archivist dutifully makes note of this; finding the writer's box is the first task they're going to tackle tomorrow.

One more time, they click Refresh, because there is comfort in the archive's after-hours quiet, because their mother has been texting confused and confusing dispatches again, and because stuffing their aching body into a sweater and coat and scarf and hat and gloves feels overwhelming. A new email pops up; subject line: Aliens. Although they know they shouldn't, that they've given their underfunded, underpaying workplace enough of their time, they open it.

It is addressed to them, specifically, which is unusual. Normally, they are simply To Whom It May Concern or Dear Sir/Madam to the scholars and doctoral students utilizing the archive, serious people whose formal education vastly outranks the Archivist's, who has attained their position due to early luck, on-the-job learning, and a willful competence.

This email, though, comes from an intern at a production company that's working on a documentary examining otherworldly visitors to New Hampshire, where UFO sightings and experiences with extraterrestrials are, apparently, not uncommon. The intern has identified the Archivist as one of the children who attended Slopeside Elementary in 1996 and witnessed a strange event that received some media attention at the time. If the Archivist would be willing, the intern writes, the documentary's producer would love to ask them, on camera, about what they saw.

A YouTube link is included at the bottom of the email, and the Archivist clicks it, baffled. They did attend that school for two years, but the video's title is KIDS SEE SAUCERS IN NEW HAMPSHIRE SCHOOLYARD '96, and they're certain there's been some mistake.

But then there they are, their child self, nine years old. They're sitting on a picnic bench, squinting against the sun as they talk to an interviewer. Their wispy hair hangs limp around their round face and they have a tooth missing, visible as their small mouth moves silently, a microphone appearing and disappearing beneath it. The Archivist watches, half convinced it's finally happened, they've truly lost touch with reality this time since they can't hear anything but the hum of the computer fan. No, they're not hallucinating, they realize. The video is muted.

They ex out. They don't want to hear themself or know what that child is saying. It's too weird. Too disturbing.

On their way back to the apartment, swaying with the movement of the train, their spine curves and their head droops, their body echoing the question mark filling their mind.

Why don't they remember that interview? Why don't they remember any of it?

June [unintelligible], 1961

Mon petite Rosa,

It's been barely a month since graduation and that's about all the French I remember. Boy, aren't you glad you didn't do a language? Useless stuff that doesn't stay stuffed in my brain. Maybe if Misyur Smith had anything of the dashing Frenchman about him I would have retained more. (Probably not.)

Are you surprised to hear from me like this? I think that hiding this letter inside a catalog inside a manila envelope was a stroke of genius, if I do say so myself. At least it will have been if it works and doesn't fall into your mother's hands. If so, then I'm toast, so please write back quickly and tell me I'm not, will you? I won't say too much in this letter, though, just to be safe.

I bet you've been worrying. I'm all right! And before you get in a tizzy, yes, I telephoned home when I knew Mother would be out so Papa knows I'm safe, though I wouldn't tell him where I was. He's resigned to it, you know. Mother is another story. I thought she'd be glad I'm gone, but Papa said she's heartbroken. I told him he meant "furious," and he laughed, so I know I'm right.

There's so much I'd like to tell you, dear, but I have to be patient. If Mother finds out I've written with a return address and everything, she'll probably make Papa drive to Boston to get me back. Imagine if I was a boy and enlisted in the military without telling her? I bet she'd come right to the barracks and shout louder than any drill sergeant could until she made them give her rebellious son back. Maybe not, actually. She'd probably be proud and crowing about it to everyone. "Oh, Phil is in the <u>service</u>, don't you know!" Ha! Well, I'm not a boy, more's the pity. Mother's stuck with what she's got. Or not got, as the case may be . . .

I swore to myself that I wouldn't write so much about her. I guess you could say I'm still steamed about everything.

Write soon, dear, care of the YWCA, 40 Berkeley Street, Boston. (If you're reading this, Mrs. Fowler, I can promise you that Mother won't find me there if she comes looking!)

Love always,
Phyllis

July 5, 1961

Dearest Rosa!!!

I was so relieved to receive your letter. Now I can tell you everything. And you must tell me more in your next. You will, won't you?

You know how everything started, of course, or should I say how everything ended. I suppose Mother has burned all my books by now. I tried to convince her not to, I told her it was bad precedent, and she couldn't speak for how insulted she was that I invoked the Nazis. How dare I speak of such things, my uncle Norm died a war hero, et cetera et cetera. Lucky your stash wasn't found! Anyway, I had to leave after that. I know you didn't believe I'd actually do it, but here we are. You asked how I'm getting along, money and things, and what about college.

Well, let me tell you something, old girl—I guess I've already been to college, since I was nearly editor in chief of the school paper and its first girl ever to make managing editor. I didn't tell Mr. Cote (that's my new boss) which school, and he assumed I meant college, I'm sure of it. (He barely glanced at my résumé.) Why should I correct him? I was telling the truth! He also believes that I'm twenty-one and not nineteen.

I'm telling it all backwards. Let me start again.

When I got to Boston, I stayed in the YWCA for a few days. They took me right in, and I became one of a fascinating group of women. Some were older women who'd fallen on hard times, some had very young children with them and, I suspect, bad husbands they'd run away from. Some were like me—new to Boston and getting on their feet. The residence is integrated, would you believe it? I feel very modern living in a city with so many different kinds of people.

I didn't loaf around for a second. Papa gave me some money before I left (Mother doesn't know and hopefully never will), but he didn't have very much. Last year's bad yield, and then the coyotes . . . I knew I needed a job as soon as I got here, so I was up late my very first night looking at help wanted ads. There were all sorts of things that I could have tried for, but I found one that I thought suited me especially well: proofreading copy at the Boston Traveler. It's a Herald paper that comes out in the evenings.

I called and made an appointment to come see about the job, but when I arrived this dumb cow of a secretary barely looked at me. Even when I told her my name and why I was there! When she went to tell Mr. Cote, I saw she was leaning forward (so the neck of her dress opened a little) and doing that blushing thing and laughing too loud. So I thought, naturally, that Mr. Cote must be an awful scoundrel. He may yet turn out to be, but so far I don't think so. He doesn't pay her flirtations any mind, anyway.

I waited so long that I was just in the middle of asking the cow—fine, her name is Enid—where the ladies' was when he came up behind me and, I'll never forget this, he told me, "No time for a piss now, busy day, busy day." I wasn't sure whether to laugh or be embarrassed. (Or should I have been offended? What do you think?) But it didn't matter because he wasn't really looking at me, he was already turning away. So I followed him to his office, and he had these stacks of paper everywhere and little placards sitting on top of them, like KENNEDY and SOVIETS and THE PILL and NEGRO RIGHTS. I guess that's how he keeps some kind of order in what was otherwise a sty worse than your brothers' room.

He told me to sit wherever so I found a corner of a chair, and then he offered me a cigarette. He smokes your brand! I took one even though you know I don't like it so much, but it was nice having a little taste of you there. It gave me strength. (Now I'm doing the blushing!)

Anyway. He gave me this typed-up article and a red pen and told me to proof it while he went to get coffee. He offered me that, too, and I told him I didn't drink it, and you know what he did? He came back with a cup for me anyway, with lots of milk and sugar, and told me I better have it because I'll need it soon enough. I took that as a good sign, and ever since I've been drinking a small cup every day because it seems like the thing to do when you work at a newspaper. Don't mock me! I never told you it was silly to try out for cheerleading, did I, when you said it was the thing to do? I can just see your face reading that. All right, you can mock me a little . . .

I made fast work of the article, you know I'm a whiz at that sort of thing, and I guess I impressed him because he hired me on the spot. I heard later that he was desperate since the last two girls didn't work out and there was a man before that who had been there for years and made a big fuss about wanting a bigger salary and they couldn't or wouldn't give him a raise. I guess that's why they started advertising for girls, thinking we'll work for less without a fuss. If only they knew! For now I'm very grateful to have a job that I rather like, even if my head does ache by the end of every day, squinting at all that smudged copy. Sometimes, when the girls in the secretary pool are short staffed, I help with typing too. My eyes certainly get tired, but that's what the coffee is for, I suppose.

So there you go! I'm a lady with a job and am now settled in a little furnished room all my own. (I printed the return address on the envelope, but keep it somewhere safe? Or memorize it? I'll omit it next time, just in case. I don't want Mother to demand your folks interrogate you.)

I'm saving up for my own typewriter now. I would have brought mine from home, but it was just so heavy . . . So I'm writing my stories longhand again. It took a while before I had the time and energy, because I didn't have any place to be alone at the YWCA and then I was getting used to the work, which really is exhausting, not to mention depressing, sometimes, reading the news all day long. Speaking of, can you believe that Hemingway died? They say the gunshot was accidental, but I don't know, I've heard rumors that say different . . . What do you think?

Less morbid: I've enclosed a story I wrote last week. I know you've said they're good enough to publish, and since moving and being all independent and adult like this I'm feeling very brave, so I've decided that I will send one to Fantasy and Science Fiction one day. I haven't yet, but I will. Tell me what you think of this one? My favorite line is the first: "Estelle thought she'd like men better if she were a man herself." Of course, then she manages it and . . . well, I'll let you read the rest. Originally, I thought that Estelle would become a man by drinking a potion, but then I thought it would be better if there were a device that enclosed a person inside, like a womb, and that was how the person changed. I think my descriptions of the inside of the device are rather good. They gave me shivers, anyway.

I've stayed up too late now and I'll pay for it in the morning, but c'est la vie. Why does French always come back to me when I'm writing you?

Love always,

Phyllis

2

Now

The Archivist dreams of silver capsules, shiny black uniforms, and wakes with a dry tongue and a sense of dread. They're up and swallowing their prescribed pills before they realize their alarm hasn't gone off yet, that the sun has only just begun to rise. They've been woken by something else: a thunking coming from their window, which is open a crack behind the ratty curtain, white with pink embroidered flowers, left by the room's previous tenant. Too tired to be spooked, the Archivist draws it back, half expecting to see a would-be intruder sheepishly scrambling down the fire escape. Instead, it's a skinny hairless cat, its wrinkled, triangular face staring in unabashedly, pawing at the windowpane, which is loose in its frame.

They are about to open the window and let the poor thing in out of the cold when a woman crawls into view holding a thick wool hat with a bobble dangling from it. She shakes it at the cat, who doesn't move, and then puts the hat back on her shaved head and pulls a bag of treats out of the pocket of her oversized hoodie and opens it. The Archivist taps on the window and she startles, the bag falling onto the metal slats, treats scattering, some dropping to the ground below.

—Oh my god I'm so sorry what the fuck, the woman says in a rush, shading her eyes and trying to see in.

She has a gold nose ring, and the rising sun glints off it. The Archivist slides the window up, apologizes for scaring her, asks if the cat belongs to her. They don't ask if she's English, because she sounds it, and they don't want to be obnoxious.

—Yes, and the asshole decided that this morning was a great time to give his mum a heart attack. I only opened the window for a minute.

The Archivist nods, not sure what to say next. They've always been bad at this sort of thing. Interacting. They're keenly aware, too, of the scent of coffee on the woman's breath. She's so close they can see a leftover clump of mascara on the lashes of her left eye, what looks like a toothpaste stain on the zipper of her hoodie.

—Anyway, the woman says, sorry about this little dude. I hope he didn't wake you.

—It's okay, he's cute, the Archivist finally manages.

—I think so, too, but he freaks my flatmate out. People hate naked cats. Yes, mate, she says, that's you, you're naked.

The cat is now butting the woman's hand, demanding pets, and she takes the opportunity to grab hold of him firmly. She apologizes again and scoots backward on the fire escape to the window open to her own apartment next door.

The whole interaction took two, maybe three minutes, but the Archivist is pretty sure it's the closest they've come to having a conversation—out loud, anyway—in several days. At work and with their roommates they mostly keep to themself, monosyllable when necessary. They close the window firmly, try to shake off the almost unbearable intimacy of speaking to someone so early in the day, so near where they sleep.

· · ·

On the way to the archive, they encounter a different, more accustomed, intimacy. Their body is pushed and shoved onto the train in the morning rush, their space invaded by elbows, backpacks, a stroller, the wet nose of an inquisitive dog held in someone's arms. It is a blessing, this crush, the irate and hurried sleepiness of the general public preventing their body from being the subject of glares, assessments, confusion, or the raised eyebrows of recognition.

Normally, this is also when they most vividly come up against the musky, damp, buzzing reality of other people. It's the most they're touched by others. But the scent of coffee on the neighbor's breath and her golden-brown eyes meeting theirs with ease stick with them today. To be looked at, to be seen, however fleetingly, is to exist.

On occasion, and as the drives into the White Mountains became ever more regular, it presented and represented itself: a curious mood gripping them. They did not speak for long intervals, and neither wondered why the other was quiet, as might have been the case elsewhere. They had said all they could say on the matter and, even as they tried to retrace their steps from that confusing night, they wished dearly to pretend that these jaunts up and down Route 3 were merely a married couple's weekend outings. They often camped for one night somewhere in Vermont, or farther north, just across the border, and in the busyness of setting up their tent and starting a fire, their silence broke, and they chattered to keep the darkness and what it might hold at bay. Sometimes, when they built a large enough fire, or later, when summer came, they made love under the stars, their bodies safely earthbound and, for a while, mercifully unconscious of what might lie above.

> But no, I am telling it out of order, aren't I? I can't help it. I am trying to tell you a story about things that actually happened, whether you or I believe them or not, but I am sidetracked, time and again, by imagining my way into their mundanity.
> Let's call it what it is: I am making things up.
> With a purpose, though. Which is to convey the truth.
> Well.
> A truth.

Before the frequent drives started in earnest, then:

They went back to work, of course. Life does not stop, even when the utterly unexplainable occurs. It had not stopped when the stock market crashed and their families found themselves facing true poverty despite having never invested in any stock that was not alive and kicking over milk pails. It had not stopped when the little man across the ocean—as she thought of Hitler, incredulously, in later years—began terrorizing his own countrymen and then others' too. It had not stopped when their own nation joined in the war against the little man and his goose-stepping toy soldiers. It had not stopped when she had been ill, and ill, and ill again, or when she dropped out of college to marry, or when her first husband stepped out with one mistress after another while she cared for his three children from his prior marriage. Life had not stopped for her second husband when his jaw had been torn open while he was in the army, long before they met, of course, or when he suffered through many surgeries to put it back together, nor when he faced the indignity of learning to use false teeth as a young man who had never thought to doubt his right to the original set. It had not stopped when he and his first wife began to argue, or when they went to counseling, or when they divorced, and it did not stop when he fell in love again and had to learn to live without his sons. There was nothing, really, that could stop life from continuing on, except for its opposite, and even then, it went on for everyone else.

So the couple resumed their regular lives, but they did not forget, although the husband wished to. Indeed, he insisted that he would, no matter what she said to the contrary. There were other things to worry about, after all. His X-rays came back with reassuring results, but his ulcer kept returning. Their little dog, Dee, became ill, first with a fungus, and later with a respiratory infection that kept recurring, and whenever the dog began a fit of labored breathing, the wife would pet the long, beautiful fur and try to reassure Dee as she had once stroked the backs of her three stepchildren when they were sick and allowed her such closeness. When the husband saw her caressing the animal, he thought not of his wife's stepchildren, who were now adults living on their own, and whom his wife felt insecure about, for although they had spent nearly fourteen years under her care, she was not their biological mother.

No, when he saw her on her knees in the living room, murmuring to the dog as if to a child, he thought of the tenderness she showed his own children, and sometimes, wistfully, he imagined the ones they might have had together if only she had not been barren.

Just when some time had passed, after Christmas and New Year's, the couple was reminded, forcibly, of what had occurred. Whether they wanted to or not, they had to face it once more.

> *I am leaving things out. Things I do not understand or that I cannot dramatize for you. I have limitations, despite all my research. Or, perhaps, research is all I am good for.*
>
> *But here are some things worth knowing about what happened after that September night in 1961: The husband and wife called the nearby air force base to report their sighting. Two men who worked for IBM—they were merely UFO enthusiasts, but the husband and wife seemed overly impressed with their employer—caught wind of the encounter and met with the couple; both wife and husband, in reconstructing what had happened, realized that while, yes, they had arrived home later than expected, in the dawn hours, they also could not remember the full extent of the night prior.*
>
> *They recalled everything up to the terror he ran from, and they recalled a series of odd sounds occurring in the car, once, then twice, and they remembered feeling drowsy and safe, which did not make sense at all. The time it would take to drive home from where they were when he saw what he saw above the field was half what it took them to actually arrive. But this was so uncomfortable to consider, to reckon with, that although they accepted it as fact, they tried as best they could to put it aside.*
>
> *Well.*
>
> *He tried, anyway.*

It happened on a day when they were driving through the White Mountains. It was one of their early journeys, before silence began to reign. They set out with the intent of returning to where they had been, but instead, not truly wanting to relive it all, they enjoyed the scenery and relaxed after their long workweek. They hiked a short way up a trail accessible from one of the highway rest areas and found a clearing in which to spread a blanket and share their picnic lunch. They took turns reading and dozing. Full of food and hot coffee from a thermos, bundled up in sweaters and long underwear and thick socks, the sun shining on their patch of dry ground, it felt almost like spring.

Almost, but not quite. Soon enough a chill set in and they had more coffee to warm and wake themselves, and, laughing and panting, raced each other down the trail to the car. He lost, burdened by blanket, basket, and thermos, but was glad to let her run ahead, her weekend pants endearingly bulky, her face exertion-flushed by the time he caught up and kissed it.

On the drive back, he remembered why they had come to this region and remarked loudly on some trivial aspect of the scenery, eager to forget again.

She had not forgotten, though. There were days when she had a nagging feeling, as if she had left the stove on or neglected a bit of paperwork, and she had recently taken to staying at work an hour late, going over case reports, worried that something was awry. But today, the unscratched itch was quieter. She saw how happy her husband was, so she let him forget and allowed herself the pleasure—which still took her breath away sometimes, when she paused to count her blessings—of feeling joyful and safe in her marriage.

They arrived home tired, but in the comforting way that accompanied a good day's activity, hungry for a warm dinner. The porch light was off, which was odd, but each assumed the other had forgotten to turn it on before they left that morning, and perhaps this was true.

She unlocked the back door and stepped into the kitchen, her hand shooting out to flick the light switch. But then she stopped, and he had to say her name and touch her arm before she took another step into the room.

The kitchen table, white, rectangular, was piled high with dry, dead leaves. Some had bits of red or gold clinging to the edges. At first, it felt like magic, as if a leaf pile for children to jump into had been transposed from its proper place outside in autumn to their kitchen in the dead of winter. But then it began to feel very wrong, all this dead plant matter in the middle of the neat room with the mint-green refrigerator and lemon-yellow cabinets and white countertops and checkered linoleum.

She murmured his name, dazed but a little relieved. The other shoe had dropped. This must have been what she was waiting for, she thought, for something else strange to happen so that she could stop doubting the reality of that night.

He reached for the pile, and although she let out a little cry, he did not stop. He touched one of the leaves, took it in his palm: curled and brown, spine curved in on itself like an old man he knew in Virginia as a boy, a man who had hurt his back hauling cargo on and off ships and could no longer work, who spent his days drinking the pain away in the bar, face collapsing over the years, becoming lined and exhausted. The husband made a fist, crushing the leaf, then looked at the residue and sniffed it: dusty life snuffed out.

The wife dithered, asked what he was doing, what he was thinking, and instead of responding he took a heavy rolling pin from its place on the counter and the big kitchen knife and began a tour of the house, stepping quietly in case the intruder—surely, there must have been an intruder—was still there. He found nothing and no one, and the windows were all shut and locked, none broken.

In the kitchen, she ventured closer to the table, less scared now that her husband was checking whether anyone was in their house, and she began, first gingerly and then with gusto, to sweep the leaves onto the floor, faster and faster, so that some hovered in the air for a fraction of a moment, buoyed by the gusts she was creating. There, at the bottom of the pile, she saw a glint: a pair of earrings, blue, her own. She realized they had been missing since the night of the UFO. She remembered having put them on in the motel room that morning, remembered even performing her nervous habit of playing with them in the car, but had no recollection of removing them at home. Now here they were, returned. The same pair, it must be, because the back of one of them was bent, bent because she had taken a pair of pliers to it, a regular practice as her right lobe hung closer to her scalp and the earring clasps often poked at her soft skin there.

When he returned, the leaves were everywhere and the door was still open, welcoming in a cold wind. She stood bent over the table, looking like a witch, her mouth ajar, her head down, the bone at the base of her neck in stark relief, the leaves rustling with the draft. He shut the door, and in the quiet stillness that enveloped them, he put down the knife and rolling pin and came to hug her from behind. He asked her what was wrong, why she put her earrings there, and she told him no, these were the ones she had worn, and apparently lost, that night. He did not ask what night she meant. She felt his grip tighten as he asked her if she was sure, absolutely sure.

She was.

She pulled away and said she would put them in her jewelry box and could he start cleaning up please. She averted her face, scrunched with the failing effort to keep from crying. In their bedroom, she put the earrings away. She wanted them out of sight, but also felt she could not get rid of them. It was unclear to her why she was still crying.

Silent, the husband swept the leaves up. He took leftover meatloaf out of the refrigerator and turned the oven on. He checked the doors and windows again and picked the phone up once or twice, intending to call someone—the police? the base? or was it his ex-wife's soothing voice he wished to hear just then, a woman who had known him since he was a knobby-kneed teenager and she a taller, more refined one?—but set the receiver down without dialing. When the food was ready, he brought the plates into the living room and called for his wife to come join him, Jackie Gleason was starting. When she did, her face looked fresh, as if recently washed, and he knew she must have been crying. He gave her a plate and turned to the tube. They would not speak of what happened.

It was not the last strange incident. If only it were, maybe everything would have gone all right. Maybe they could have moved on, given time.

Evening, weeks later. He was at the South Postal Annex, sitting at his keyboard alongside Mike, Robby, Gordon, and Ed, craving a cigarette. The envelopes kept coming, sliding toward him on their tray, each with its individual handwriting and smudges, each requiring his full attention so he could type in the relevant code that would send the letter to the correct bin. It was tedious yet absorbing work, so he did not notice the commotion downstairs until Gordon tapped him on the shoulder and asked if he wanted to go smoke and see what all the fuss was about. He nodded, hearing the men below shouting for others to come look, come look, and made sure his conveyor belt was paused before getting up. He stretched, grabbed his jacket from the back of his chair, and followed Gordon down the rattling metal stairs. Whatever was going on, its timing was perfect, he thought, as he pulled a cigarette out.

A few dozen men crowded at the picture window that faced the train tracks. They were quiet now, and when he joined Gordon near the back of the clump, he saw why. Low in the sky was a sun that had already set, an orange orb that could not be the moon.

Could it?

It moved. It turned on its side, making a slit of its light, and then blinked out of existence. A loud cry went up, the men protesting its disappearance like a fumbled pass in football, followed by excited murmurings as they discussed what it could have been. He heard the words they tossed around, <u>flying saucer</u> and <u>Russians</u> and <u>trick of the light</u>, then took a deep drag of smoke and started back to his station. Gordon followed, asked if he had ever seen a thing like that, and he barked out a forced laugh and said no. No, of course not.

When he sat back down at his keyboard, he was grateful to note that his hands were still more or less steady.

· · ·

Another night.

They had been out driving, winding through the White Mountains, when they spotted a car stopped alongside the road. There were figures all around it, blue jeans and letterman jackets, and she stared at them, her hand clutching the door handle. She noticed he was slowing and told him sharply to drive, to drive fast and go, now, go, and he did, alarmed, thinking she saw some danger lurking among them, although when they passed, they could both see it was simply a gaggle of teenagers whose car had broken down. Four of them were gathered near the trunk, laughing and smoking, while a fifth and sixth were bent under the hood in front. Poor devils, he thought, but when he looked at his wife, he saw she was white as a sheet. When he asked what had frightened her so, her eyes welled up. He did not press.

· · ·

And another.

On his way to work, he saw a police roadblock stopping every car as it came through. His ulcer pulsed painfully inside him, and although he told himself that there was probably an escaped criminal or a car thief or maybe even a kidnapping, and although he knew he had done nothing wrong, still, the mere sight of the blocked road and uniformed men sent him into a panic. He had never been arrested before, had avoided that particular humiliation, which was not to say he had not been stopped by officers of the law before and asked questions they had no business asking. Still, he thought he would not be arrested on this night, either, since he was a civil servant and wearing his work uniform, was mild-mannered and had a strong-toothed smile, and was lighter-skinned than some; he hoped all this would protect him. Yet something about their uniforms, the glint of their flashlights catching on one another's belt buckles or wedding rings . . . It reminded him of something, somewhere, sometime else.

Since there was no one behind him, he reversed and began driving home. On the way, he stopped at a payphone and called in sick with food poisoning.

His wife was getting ready for bed when he came in. He explained that something about the roadblock had scared the stuffing out of him, and she embraced him, tightly. She was glad to have him home and pulled him to bed with her. It had been some time since they had made love at night, their schedules normally so opposite, and it had been even longer since they had done so with such ferocity. His body felt vital and alive with every thrust, with every high-pitched moan he evoked from her.

When they were each sated and satisfied, the sheets beneath them dewy with sweat, she turned over onto her stomach and he acknowledged the unspoken request and ran his fingers up and down the smooth skin of her back. So smooth, women's skin, he thought, a marvel of human engineering. He wondered whether they had developed such skin to pleasure men's fingertips, the way flowers' intricate coloring invited bees to stop and get nectar-drunk. She felt cold, too, her sweat having chilled in the cooling house, and she was so still that he had the mad idea that she had turned to stone under his touch.

But no. She had merely receded into herself, as she did sometimes when she was gathering courage. When she finally spoke, she felt him startle; he must have thought her already asleep. She told him she had had the dreams again, the ones that started after that night, that she suffered through alone while he was at work, her body thrashing into wakefulness. She told him what she remembered of the most recent ones, how frightening they were, and suggested lightly that they might finally go and see a psychiatrist for hypnosis treatment, as their new friends from IBM had suggested those many months ago when they first met. His fingers had stopped tracing shapes on her skin, and she feared he would say no again, but instead, he agreed, then turned away, bringing his knees closer to his body. She cuddled up to him, relieved, and slept soundly that night.

So it was settled. But until they found a psychiatrist, the couple wrote letters to friends and experts, including to a man at the National Investigations Committee on Aerial Phenomena (NICAP), and the wife began what would become a lifelong obsession, getting her hands on any books on the subject of unidentified flying objects as she could. Did she believe all or most of what she read? I suspect she did. That because of her early and enduring love of books, she saw anything written down in one as trustworthy, which meant that once she began looking for answers, she found them. She wasn't gullible, fanciful, or easily manipulated, or perhaps better to say that we are all gullible and fanciful and easily manipulated when we are vulnerable and searching for a way to explain our experiences to ourselves.

And he? Another way of dealing with hurt is shrinking away from it, avoiding its memory, attempting to dissociate it from one's lived experience. Isn't that just as natural, just as understandable?

I, for one, do not blame either one of them for dealing with the memories of that night and its aftermath in the ways that they did. They couldn't have known that in the future their actions would be scrutinized and dissected and examined for signs of deception, manipulation, and insanity on a national scale.

3

Now

———

There are many ways to be seen, and the Archivist firmly believes in the importance of witnessing the past through the detritus it leaves behind, more or less preserved.

Although they intend to look up Phyllis Egerton first thing, they end up spending several hours on various tasks given by their supervisor and colleagues who outrank them. The Archivist will never be promoted beyond the title of assistant due to their lack of formal education in the field, but they have been at the workplace longer than some of the others and know the ins and outs of the stacks better than anyone.

The stacks aren't as impressive as the name makes them sound; not for this archive, where the banks of shelves are not packed densely enough to be put on rails so they can slide up and down the room. Those are next door, where the library's bigger archival collections live. Here, in this grant-funded annex that is always on the verge of being shut down, the stacks are only the back two rooms of a squat repurposed office building, four tall, wide, and deep bookcases in each, on which sit rows of banker boxes and file organizers. The Archivist loves these rooms, plain as they are, and sometimes goes in at the beginning of the workday just to stand still with their eyes closed and breathe.

There's no time today, though, much of it spent fetching, carrying, and delivering items: newly arrived folders stuffed with papers; three coffees in the morning and afternoon from the chain on the corner; a set of forms for an elderly man wishing to donate his recently deceased husband's ACT UP pamphlets and related op-ed drafts. In spare moments, the Archivist accesses the online finding aid and searches for Phyllis Egerton's name. She's listed under the Lesbian section, her papers held in Box 23-G. There's no other information. The archive's materials are only partially digitized due to poor funding, lack of sufficient staff, and the general need to prioritize requests from patrons over slow-moving organizational projects.

During their lunch break, the Archivist goes to the stacks to retrieve Phyllis. The musty scent of cardboard and paper is exquisite. They inhale particles of dust that might once have touched the bodies and belongings of people living ten, twenty, fifty, one hundred years ago. Box 23-G is not large, nor very heavy, and they carry it back up to their corner of the office and stow it under their desk until they have time to investigate further. For now, the Archivist writes back to the academic who asked about her, tells him the files have been located, asks what in particular is he looking for.

They stay at the archive late again, this time not out of a sense of duty or enthusiasm for their work. Much more mundanely, they get lost down an internet rabbit hole.

It's a relief. They've spent the day trying not to dwell on the weirdness of the YouTube video from last night, their past self experiencing something they have no recollection of. They're not ready to return to the footage yet, but they begin to nibble around the edges of what it might be about. They start by looking up the production company the intern who reached out to them works for, which leads them to the list of other documentaries it's put out about various supernatural phenomena, all occurring in New Hampshire, which is apparently the company's special focus. There's one about the Woods Devil, a local bigfoot-like creature. Another is about the haunted Newport Opera House. A third is about a couple, Barney and Betty Hill, allegedly the first people to be abducted by aliens, at least in the United States.

The Archivist watches the trailer for that one. It looks cheap, lots of stock footage and cheesy animations of flying saucers and green alien faces, and a narrator who sounds robotic. They don't bother trying to track down where they might watch it. Instead, they find the Hills'

Wikipedia page, then the books written about them, the documentaries and podcast episodes and subreddits devoted to them, the TV movie and the lore and the fan art and the conspiracy theories and and and.

When their eyes begin to burn, they realize it's been two and a half hours, their head is aching with hunger, and they desperately need to pee.

January 1, 1962, just after midnight

Dearest Rosa,

Happy New Year! I miss you so much. I wish I could be with you and everyone else, building a bonfire and drinking punch that's definitely been spiked and roasting marshmallows when it gets so cold that everyone needs some sustenance.

There's so much to tell you, as always. For instance, I'm trying to make friends, but I'm not very sure how to go about it. One of my neighbors is a young Negro woman who must work the same hours I do most days because we're both on the T platform early each morning. We exchange nods and smiles and pleasantries about the weather but nothing beyond that, really. The first hurdle is to find out what her name is!

Since moving here, I've become so different, almost shy. You'd find it alarming! But I can't help it. It's still strange, all these months later, being here alone. There's so much happening all the time, but there's almost no one to talk to. My voice is probably shriveled up from lack of use. Do you remember how I shouted Billy down in that one fabulous argument we had in the newspaper office, about whether to run Milly's editorial supporting the Greensboro Four? What a little weasel Billy was. I don't know if I could yell at him now.

Anyway, I'll tell you more about Boston life next time. It's getting late, and I'm getting tired, so let me just tell you a little bit about the story I've enclosed a copy of here, which I'm really keen to hear from you about, because I think it's one of my boldest yet.

I've set it on Titan, one of Saturn's moons, and I think I'm going to write some more pieces that take place there. I'm becoming quite enamored with the little world I'm building. The heroine of this one is named Fiona Bridges, and she was raised in the Ring Region, which is what I'm calling Saturn's rings, which are made up of all these rocks and debris. I'm envisioning it as what counts for rural in space: there aren't many rocks big enough for habitation and they're few and far between and sort of volatile. So she grew up on Killian, which is a big carved-out rock in the Ring Region, and due to mysterious reasons that you'll find out, she's fled Killian for Titan, where she's hoping to make a new life.

. . . sound familiar? I didn't even think about it while I was writing, but when I was done, I wanted to give myself a good shake. Talk about lack of imagination! But I've come to love Fiona now and Titan, too, and even Killian, and I'm excited to write about them more. Tell me what you think of this adventure, won't you? I think I could try one of the magazines with it.

Yours, always,

Phyllis

June 15, 1962, late

Dear Rosa,

The headline of the day is MOM FOUND STRANGLED IN BACK BAY APARTMENT. She was 56, and it was done with the cord of her own housecoat. And right under that do you know what they printed? An advertisement for a figure-controlling girdle. Ladies, get strangled by some monster or strangle yourselves willingly! I didn't know whether to laugh or cry.

I also don't know what to say about your last two letters. First you tell me not to write you again, ever, and so I acquiesced, although really I wrote reams and then burned them all up in the sink. But then, not a week later, you've become enlightened because you've seen an analyst one time and he told you the only trouble is that you're repressed? And that we can still be very good friends?

I really don't understand it. Please tell me what "very good friends" means and whether you still love me. Don't make me beg you to be clear with me, Rosa. It's not like you, and it's mean, and besides, a "very good friend" would not act this way.

Yours, always,

Phyllis

September 1, 1962

Dear Rosa,

Congratulations on the start of your college journey! I'm kind of jealous, but maybe I'll go myself one day. I think you'll have a ball there, a blast, a real hoot—but won't you miss your new beau? Or maybe you've decided he doesn't matter so much now that you have your sights set on the next big thing to do? First, break a heart, then get a new boyfriend, then go to college and SHINE!

I'm sorry. I'm being bitter and mean, and if you've stopped reading by now I understand. But I have a big adventure to tell you about and so I think I will, even if you throw this letter away. I've shared some of it with my neighbor Molly, whom I'm becoming friends with, but there's parts I can't tell anyone other than you.

I've told you a bit about my boss, Mr. Cote. He treats me well, better than some of the girls who don't like the way I talk or dress. More's the pity for them, as I think a few are quite lively and could be good fun, if only they hadn't made the decision to dislike me for stupid reasons. (Boy, I am in a <u>mood</u> today, aren't I. Mother would say I must be getting my "monthlies" soon.)

Last night, Cote snapped his fingers at me and said to get my behind out of the office already. I never leave on time, because what am I going to do at home? Look at my empty walls? The narrow hard bed? The boring secondhand sheets I bought because they were cheaper than the patterned ones? Being an independent lady isn't the easiest thing, you know. I make all my own meals and bring my own lunch to work most days. Anything to economize. I left New Hampshire with so few clothes that I've been building my wardrobe ever since, and of course I need warm things and those are a pretty penny, plus rent, and the occasional hamburger for lunch when I try to socialize with folks at work so they don't see me as a cold fish. Besides that, there's taking clothes to the laundromat, and line drying the nicer things across my tiny living room so there's a wall of wet, dripping clothes I walk through anytime I go from the bedroom to the kitchen or back. And I still haven't gotten my typewriter. They're expensive and I haven't felt like writing recently anyway.

So all that waits for me at home, as I was saying, is my roommate, that silent thing that hulks in corners, sits across from me at breakfast, sobs late into the night, and doesn't even pay rent: Lady Loneliness.

There's a story there . . . Personified loneliness. I'll have to think about that. It feels good to have an idea. My mind's been so blank.

Back to my adventure. Mr. Cote told me to get going because it was Friday night, and he wouldn't leave until I got my purse and walked out with him. Bossy! Fitting, I guess. We're slowly becoming friends, I think. He's a bachelor, and he doesn't flirt with the women here, he really doesn't, not like some of the others who make ugly jokes and try to pinch our waists and backsides when we pass. Enid, the receptionist, still won't give up on Cote, by the by, but what can you do.

It was "hotter 'n hell" per Cote, the sun not yet set. I was about to say goodbye and head to the train, but he stopped me and asked whether I had somewhere to be or was I just going home to mope. I tried to tell him that I had letters to respond to (one letter anyway, a short one from you). He said those could wait and to be a sport and come have a drink or two with him.

He wasn't asking me out, that was clear. He was talking like a pal, you know? As if I were another fellow. So I agreed!

We took a different line than the two I'm used to riding. As usual, I stared at everyone quite unabashedly. There is always so much to look at here, and smell, and on a Friday night even more so. Smell? Yes, smell! There were laborers in the car who were still sweaty from their day's work and stank with it, and women doused in flowery perfume, and the reek of booze wafting up here and there though I couldn't tell from whom. Whenever I'm on the train I think about how much Mother would loathe it, which, of course, makes me love it all the more.

"You look like a kid in a candy store," Cote said quietly, smiling with those small yellow teeth of his. I'm sure he's quite right. He told me our stop was next, and so we started working our way through the crowd to the door (it was standing-room only, you see), and when we got there, I saw a vision. This woman on the platform about to come on just as Cote and I were supposed to be getting off. There was something gamine about her, her hair was cropped short and mannish and she was wearing suspenders like a man, and I don't think she was wearing a brassiere . . . I could see a faint outline of her nipples through the thick undershirt she was wearing. I've really never seen anything like her, and haven't been able to stop thinking about her since. I'm not sure if I want to look like her or get to know her.

She stared right back at me, though, and that gave me more pep in my step than I'd had in weeks.

Cote pulled me out and chastised me for acting like a tourist, standing in the doorway like that. But what could I do? I'd felt like I'd been punched. In a good way. Is there such a thing?

Of course, I shouldn't be telling you all this. You'll think I'm telling you only to make you jealous. And that may be a part of it, I confess, but Rosa, if we're really to be very good friends, then I can't hide these things from you, can I? I don't have many people in the world, and none who know me so well, and despite everything, I still trust you.

Cote led me to a bar he wanted to go to in Scollay Square, near the docks. It was a sailor bar, and it was pretty crowded and rowdy, mostly men on shore leave, I guess, which reassured me that I was correct and this wasn't a date. We sat with some friends of Cote's who work for the morning <u>Herald</u>, and after we ordered drinks, they talked shop and I listened with half an ear and watched the room.

Well, I got good and drunk. I was getting bored by their talk, but they kept ordering drinks, which made me feel very chipper and interested in everything again. If I closed my eyes and ignored the noise, I could smell sweat and beer and tobacco, and it reminded me of Papa and his shirts soaked in summer. With sweat, yes, and also with saliva from the goats and the cows who nip him affectionately. A funny moment of memory teleportation. (Say, now there's another idea to jot down . . .)

My fifth (I think) drink came from a man at the bar. The waiter pointed him out. Men pay some kind of attention to me fairly often, because I'm young and bright and dress all right and men are what they are, but no one has ever bought me a drink like that before, which made the man quite fetching to me, at least from a distance.

Mr. Cote told me I didn't have to drink it and I asked why. He said that the man might think I owed him something. "Well, do I owe you anything, since you've been buying the drinks 'til now?" I asked. He got all blustery, denying it, but one of his friends piped up and said something like, "Sure do, he wants you to keep coming with him so he has cover when he goes drinking." Cote was indignant, said he was just trying to look out for me. I think he was drunk as all hell.

His other friend called him Kitty and told Cote not to get his knickers in a twist, and I couldn't stop laughing for a while. When I recovered from my little fit, I told my tablemates that it was getting late and that I should say thank you to the nice man who bought me a drink before going home.

I felt very bold and pretty, which was likely the alcohol, but when I got closer, I saw the man wasn't very good looking. He was quite a bit older, maybe even Papa's age, his beard flecked with gray. He had some freckles on his nose that were sweet, but his lips were quite thin and not nice at all. He told me his name, Ray, and I told him mine, and he called me charming and put his hand on my knee, which I pushed off. I probably should have left then, but I didn't because he got me another drink and I was feeling a little wild.

He told me all about his job on a freighter and his time in Korea, and he showed me a scar on his neck where shrapnel had lodged and he'd nearly bled out. He didn't have a ring on, but he did slip up at some point and said, "Beth always says that I . . ." Honestly, I lost track of what he was talking about. He was very dull and asked me nothing about myself.

Eventually I realized that I could use Cote as an excuse to get away, but when I looked over I saw that he wasn't at the table anymore, although his fellows were. I thought he might have gone to the gents, so I waited, but he didn't come back and I didn't know his friends well enough to go sit with them. I was feeling miffed about Cote and a little bereft, I won't lie, but I told myself to buck up and stop feeling sorry for myself.

I told Ray I had to get home, and I was really quite drunk. He told me he would help, and he got me into a taxi, except he got in as well. Things start getting blurry around this point. He gave the driver an address that wasn't mine, and I tried to protest, but I was slurring my words. Ray put my head in his lap and pet my hair, which felt pleasant for a little bit and then didn't.

When the cabbie stopped, I told him again that we weren't at my place yet and he turned around and said something like, "Course not, sweetie, it's a motel. Listen, bub, she all right?" Ray must have said I was, but I started shouting. I don't remember what, just that I was very vocal and Ray got mean and then slammed the door to the cab and left. I told the driver my address and he took me home. The whole thing reminded me of that awful night with Vincent. Remember? When I officially lost my virginity? I was disgusted when I got home and cried and showered and vomited a few times and slept horribly.

I'm never drinking that much again. But it sure was an adventure, I guess.

Yours, always,

Phyllis

4

Now

The Archivist keeps hoping it'll come to them in a dream but it doesn't. The memory stays where it is: lost, maybe, or buried but still findable beneath a violent repression. The Archivist has listened to and read and watched too many debunkings of the theory of repressed memories to believe they can be recovered, yet they don't know how else to understand why they're unable to remember whatever happened at Slopeside.

They're still resistant to watching the video of themself. Whatever they see in it will color anything they might eventually dredge up. So they try not to dwell, secretly hoping that forgetting all about it will let them remember, but their brain, so far, isn't fooled by these tricks.

The Archivist fills their mind instead with their newest surely dead crush, Phyllis Egerton.

The academic who inquired about her hasn't written back, a not uncommon occurrence, but the Archivist nevertheless dove into her files and has become enamored of this woman. As they do with so many of the subjects in the archive, the Archivist feels Phyllis deserved, still deserves, so much more. They find themself mentally composing screeds they might send the academic, telling him off for neglecting her.

The intern for the alien documentary, on the other hand, has been following up relentlessly, once every other day. The Archivist has no real social media presence; they have accounts, of course, but they're set to private. They lurk rather than post and never got in the habit of using anything resembling their real name in their handles. But even though they don't have any information listed publicly, the intern manages to find and message them on one of the apps. He also tracks down their personal email address and contacts them there.

The Archivist is somewhat spooked by this, and even more so on the evening they find the third Just Checking In (This is Brett from DynamicDocu!) subject header in their inbox and read that the producer is really very interested in them. Brett claims the Archivist could be the star of the doc, that they're the perfect person to represent what UFO experiencers are really like: sane, employed, even politically progressive. Unnerved, they decide to have a cigarette about it on the fire escape. They haven't smoked regularly since college but find the occasional nicotine hit an indulgence they're comfortable with.

They've relaxed enough to let their eyes unfocus until the streetlights become fat orbs floating in darkness when the window next door opens and the neighbor with the cat, whom they've dubbed "Ava" in their head because she looks like an Ava to them, begins climbing out. The Archivist immediately stubs the cigarette's end into the wall and begins apologizing, face preemptively flushing with shame; surely, the neighbor will now avoid them.

—Nah, man, it's why I'm out here too, she says.

She shows the Archivist her palm, which is cupped around a rolled smoke and mini-lighter.

—S'a relief, honestly, the neighbor says, 'cause where I last lived I had to go all the way to the sidewalk when I wanted a fag after my shift because the lady next door complained about the smell, and like, who has the energy for that, you know?

—What do you do? Sorry, the Archivist adds, that's a really boring question.

—Not boring! Well, maybe if your job is. I'm a vet tech. Which can be dull, yeah, but I love animals and I've got a knack for soothing them so I like it.

—That's so cool.

She says nothing to this, just stares at her phone, preoccupied. The Archivist imagines what they'd say if she asked them what they do for work. They would explain about the archive, and if she seemed interested, they would tell her about Phyllis. About how, distracted by their regular work duties, they're only able to spend time with their crush in short bursts, and how they're currently poring over the first batch of Phyllis's letters, which they've digitized and are now making searchable. The computer does the first read-through and translates the image into accessible text, they'd explain, and then the Archivist goes over it again, correcting and adding what the program can't recognize, which is quite a lot. It's painstaking work; the letters are written on thin airmail paper in blue ink that's faded over time, the cursive legible but smeared. It's an intimate process, one the Archivist finds deeply peaceful.

Not that the neighbor would care about any of this. Why should she?

—Shit, she says, my mum's calling. My auntie's in hospital. Mum? Yeah, hang on. Maybe I'll see you out here again?

By the time the Archivist processes what she's just said, "Ava" is already gone, so they don't get the chance to say that yes, they hope she will.

They watch the sky go inky. A moonless and velvety dark spreads, contrasting with the street lamps and leftover Christmas lights still shimmering in some windows and on front lawns below. They should spend more time out here. It's beautiful.

They imagine what "Ava" might be doing next door while on the phone. Maybe she's making tea in that finicky way, with real leaves and a strainer, and trying to calm her mum down. Maybe she's crying, hearing about her aunt being rushed to the emergency room, the terrible accident she's had. Maybe she's pulling a suitcase out and packing frantically, knowing she'll have to return to her home across the ocean and never come back. Then again, maybe her aunt only sprained her ankle and "Ava" is already off the phone and is settling down to watch a movie with her roommate, a white man with a round face and a big red burn mark on his neck and square black glasses who the Archivist thinks must be in his forties. They were told, by one of their own roommates, that he's been the maître d' of a fancy restaurant for years and that his place is rent-controlled so he'll never leave. He used to live with someone else, a short, pinched-faced white woman with platinum-blond hair down to her waist whose teeth reeked of money, but that was probably a year ago or more, and then "Ava" moved in. The Archivist has always read the man as gay, can only assume that neither woman is a girlfriend, but they suppose they might be wrong.

Whatever "Ava" is doing, she's certainly not thinking of them. This is a problem they have. They want strangers to care about them. They want to care about strangers. When they try, and they do sometimes, something always goes wrong. So they don't do it often, not anymore, not with people in the real world, anyway. The fantasy is enough. It can be enough.

The Archivist shivers, and remembers why they don't sit here and watch the sky more often. Their hips and ass are aching from the cold, hard surface, its bumps and protrusions, reminding the Archivist that due to their genetic condition, they can never take even a moment's painless-ness for granted. When they come in, their lower back is so stiff and sore they can't stand fully upright, and even though they're alone, the Archivist feels embarrassed at moving like this, bent, their body behaving like it's decades older than it really is. They hate it. Their body. Its unruliness, its pain, its contradictions, the lumps of flesh they do and do not have, the constant, relentless discomfort. Not for the first time, they wonder whether they will ever have sex again. They don't feel attractive at the best of times, and at moments like this, they feel repulsive, monstrous.

They shouldn't be like this, shouldn't have a crone-like stance at their age. They should have figured out how to make it stop, and since they hav-en't, they're a failure, obviously, because they haven't tried hard enough. Even after the Archivist finally received an actual diagnosis last year, one that involved a mutated gene, most doctors knew little to nothing about the disorder and simply shrugged it away. Mostly, the doctors have, over the years, implied that the pain is all in the Archivist's head, that it's their own fault that they're sick, ugly, unfuckable.

A lifetime of frustration morphs into a furious grief that crests as they ball their hands into fists up and hit their thighs again and again and again, and they want to do worse, to return to the habit of sharp objects and blossoming blood, but they resist, and when the energetic rage filling them finally recedes, the Archivist falls into bed and out of their body.

They scroll through the usual things first, the ones that tend to help: videos of otters holding hands and ferrets eating eggs, elephants making friends with sheepdogs and cats taking care of piglets. But their inner voice, the one that berates them, in their mother's voice, for being tired and weak and inconvenient, isn't quieted.

After some deep breathing, they decide to try a different kind of distraction. They go to Reddit and start clicking through r/Abductions, r/UFOs, and r/Experiencers. They expect to pity the people posting there, to feel superior, to find solace in their own rationality. But as their eyes scan story after unlikely story, they let themself sink into the unfolding narratives: the guy finding out from his mom that the nightmares he started having after a recent spooky encounter in the woods had also plagued him as a child; the woman who, after having a stroke, claims to communicate with beings from another world; the teenager who thinks they might be part alien due to the skin disorder that leaves bits of them a scabby gray.

The Archivist wonders, at first, whether people invent things like this for the same reason they themself so desperately need to escape reality. They read deep into the night, shifting their phone, a patch of ghostly light in the dark room, from one hand to the other every few minutes to ease the cramps and nerve spasms. After midnight, something changes. They begin to question their own convictions, their concrete perceptions of reality. The accounts are too emotional, uncertain, and desperate for answers to be solely the products of bored trolls or overactive imaginations, and the Archivist realizes they've begun to give the stories the benefit of the doubt, to even find some convincing. They're reminded of their own attempts to describe their pain and its debilitating nature to white coats who wore sneers and had an eye on the clock. They wonder whether this is the first step toward remembering.

But when they fall asleep, they still don't dream of aliens, only of dancing with a person who tells them everything is going to be all right, that they, too, will get past this and leave something good behind. Faceless, featureless, the Archivist nevertheless can tell that the silhouette they're dancing with is Phyllis.

She worried. She worried about her husband, whose face seemed to have aged in the last few months, gravity sagging his cheeks. She urged him to go to the doctor again; he complained of headaches nearly every day now, and on weekends he sometimes lay in bed for hours, rousing himself by lunchtime but often wanting nothing more than to sit with his newspaper and read quietly, or, if he could stand the sound, sit at the dining room table and type up the letters he drafted by hand. She offered to do this task for him, since she was a better typist, always needing to file one report or another at work and forever writing letters, which, these days, were often to people who might help provide her with more information on what she and her husband experienced or at least confirm that neither of them was crazy. But her husband preferred to do the work himself.

He had borne his long commute to Boston steadily, as cheerfully as he could, for the better part of three years, but his body seemed, finally, to be reacting to his schedule, to the two-hour drive both to and from a standard shift—when he was not working overtime—and to needing to sleep during the day, if he got any sleep at all. He believed he would be fine if only he rested more, but that was exactly what his body would not let him do. He lay awake soon after dawn, listening to his wife move around the house as she prepared to go to work: the sharp whistle of the kettle on the stove cut short immediately, almost before it started, since she thought him asleep; the gentle murmur of water poured over a tea bag; the nervous tapping of her little shoes—he would never stop finding her small feet worthy of note—as she read the paper, which crinkled when she folded it; the muted metallic clatter of the toaster popping up and the scrape of a knife against the hardened bread followed by the three or four crunches, ravenous morning bites. Finally, the tinkling of her urine in the bathroom, the rush of a toilet flush, the rasp of her purse being pulled off the kitchen table on her way out, its metal clasp dragging along the surface, the rattle of glass panes as the door opened and shut, and the car engine rumbling to life before the grinding of tire against asphalt signaled her departure. He marveled, some mornings, at the thousand little noises a person made.

Other mornings, he felt his nerves, which he imagined as instrument strings, tightening and stretching and beginning to fray as every sound his wife made was amplified a thousandfold by his deep, aching desire for sleep. What would happen, he wondered, when they snapped?

It would be some time before he would be forced to reckon with what such a breakdown in his self-control would look like. Presently, his physician recognized that he was under a great deal of undue stress and referred him to a psychiatrist.

I fear I am going too slowly, keeping you from the good stuff. Shall I hurry it up? Or shall I try to reconstruct for you what he might have spoken to his psychiatrist about? Here are some things I know, because he recounted them later on:

I know he spoke of race, that is, of racism, but also of the complex nature of his family's history of Blackness and whiteness. A light-skinned great-grandmother on his maternal side was raised by her mother's—and thus, her own—enslaver in his household. By "raised" I mean that she was a servant in the home, caring for her white half sisters, a service for which she was rewarded—or, perhaps more accurately, very belatedly paid—with 250 acres of land for her and her husband. In one account, this husband was an Ethiopian immigrant and their farm prospered. In another account, it seems that this Ethiopian immigrant was on the paternal side of the family. Regardless, there is great emphasis in these secondhand accounts to understand, perhaps, why the husband was able to get along so famously with white people.

I believe that he did his best to accord others that which was undoubtedly, systematically, denied to him at various points in his life. I believe that he tried very hard to view everyone he met as a human being to be judged by actions and words rather than appearance, class, or caste. And I believe that the obsession with his proximity to whiteness reflects, rather, the anxieties of the white people in his life—and especially those who wrote about him—who needed to explain to themselves why this Black man was acceptable to them when so many others were not.

I mention all of this because his race is rarely discussed in the telling of the pair's fateful abduction, although the fact remains that he was an activist with the Portsmouth NAACP. It is unfortunately difficult to reconstruct what his precise work for the cause of civil rights entailed, for, as anyone who has ever been a part of an ongoing, long-standing fight for any kind of rights knows, much of the institutional work is unglamorous: research and information collection and coordination with larger networks and the organization of small, dull, practical matters like budgets and agendas and recruiting speakers for fundraisers and arranging travel for spokespeople and volunteers and dealing with the accounting ledgers so as to obtain reimbursements, and writing and editing and proofreading pamphlets and, and, and.

Few records remain of his work, or his NAACP chapter's work; in the couple's archives, it is the documents related to the abduction and its aftermath that reign supreme.

I believe, as I have stated, that what this married couple said they experienced that night must be taken seriously on its own merits. But I cannot help wondering: They were a Black man and a white woman alone in a car on a deserted road in the middle of the night in a sparsely populated, mountainous region. If they did come across another vehicle, and if that vehicle contained white men, perhaps armed, perhaps looking for trouble, and if those men accosted and violated and humiliated this interracial couple . . . Well. Would you want to remember such an event? Or would your mind, perhaps, wish to translate it into something else?

But no. Now I am straying too far. Now I am advancing theories. There are endless theories, of course, but my goal here is not to discuss them more than absolutely necessary. Besides, I have to wonder what such an imagined theory says about me, about the limits of my own imagination.

Where were we?

Ah, yes.

His psychiatrist.

It's unclear when he began to see this doctor. Summer of 1962 or early 1963? Regardless, he spoke in sessions about his childhood, of course, of being raised in a largely white neighborhood in Philadelphia, of his time on his uncle's farm in Virginia and how he wished to have stayed there, of being the target of occasional racist bullying in junior high and the tussles he sought out in order to prove himself strong and worthy of the other boys' respect, of teachers telling him he should not aspire to much for surely there was, as he put it, "no future for Negroes" in the professions he wished to pursue, of the racist hazing he both saw and suffered in the military, which he joined in the hopes that there was a future for him there.

One time, he mentioned to his psychiatrist the terrifying night in 1961. The doctor listened patiently to his brief detailing of the incident and asked whether he thought it had any bearing on his current frustrations, exhaustions, and physical ailments. He had not considered this question before, so eager was he to simply put away the night in question and leave it to his wife to collect the breadcrumbs along the path she seemed so intent on following. No, he told his psychiatrist emphatically. He did not believe that the night had any bearing on his current frustrations, exhaustions, and physical ailments.

He was not, when he said it, entirely sure whether he meant it.

. . .

The couple's minister was more open-minded than some, and one day invited them to give a talk at the church study group. The wife was eager to do so, having subscribed to the National Investigations Committee on Aerial Phenomena—or NICAP—newsletter, which told her of sightings all over New England. If there were other people seeing UFOs, then surely she and her husband were not mad. Moreover, since the newspapers did not report on the matter seriously, and since the military was instructed to feign disinterest in the matter—she had learned this from a friend of the minister's, a major—was it not brave to come forward and tell their story?

She had always felt very close to her ancestral history, full of rebels and truth tellers according to legend, from the earliest days of her family's refusal to follow the Roman pope during the Papal Schism to their later commitment to Quakerism to coming to the New World, where they were persecuted still and founded their own town, to their adoption of abolitionist ideals and actions some time later to her mother's proud unionizing activities and on through her own induction into the Inter-race Commission during her first stint in college and her current membership in and work with the NAACP, not to mention her job as a social worker in charge of child welfare, a position she had already, at this point, held longer than any of her predecessors, who apparently could not handle the stress of carrying such a caseload, let alone the pain and suffering and rage-inducing circumstances she witnessed on a weekly, if not daily, basis.

Yet, despite being progressive for her day, she was still of a particular place and time, and she had, like many a white American woman, her fair share of biases, prejudices, and the occasional stark obliviousness. Her family lore—which she would proudly repeat—painted the Indigenous peoples of the land they colonized as violent enemies of the peaceful Quakers. Years later, long after the events in these pages took place, she took an interest in—and spoke frankly about—theories that implied that ancient civilizations could not have come up with their mathematical, engineering, and technological feats on their own but were guided by visiting aliens.

Still, in the wife's mind, standing up to oppression and naming inconvenient realities was what made people heroes, and although she attempted modesty, she would concede to herself, privately, that she took rather well to such actions, and one such could be standing up in front of her minister's congregation and sharing the truth of what she had seen.

. . .

Her husband, however, balked at the minister's request. Although he liked the man as well as the church, he worried far more than his wife did about what people might think of him. He worried, too, about what telling such a tale would do to his respectability should the matter be shared further.

Reputation, he knew, was important, especially for his positions as legal redress chairman for the NAACP and as board member of the county's antipoverty program. Not to mention the ribbing he would get from the men at work if they heard anything about this.

But, as she reminded him over a dinner of fried fish at Yoken's on a warm Friday evening in September, he always told her that life was for living, not for worrying too much. He stared at his fork, angled up toward his mouth, crisp breaded fish flesh speared on it, and wondered when he had last taken his own advice. For a long time now, he had been doing little but worrying. There were, of course, moments of levity—tickling his wife when he happened to walk into the bedroom when she was in only her bra and slip, the tender skin of her belly too inviting to resist; joking with his colleagues when they took their smoking breaks together; even with his psychiatrist, occasionally, such as when he shared the story about the Christmas during the Depression when his parents pretended that there would be no gifts because Santa did not have enough fuel to come by their house, only for him to wake up in the morning and discover a modest pile of presents near the chimney and his father's feigned surprise as he yawned over his hot, bitter-scented morning coffee. But he felt, for the most part, a heaviness in his limbs, a pressure in his psyche. Perhaps it was his desire for secrecy, for privacy, that was constraining him so much. Perhaps he was trying too hard to be reasonable, sensible. Perhaps he should let in the strangeness of what had occurred and accept it as part of the narrative of his life.

So he agreed, and in the end, there was nothing so remarkable or stressful about the evening after all. Just as the study group had always been open to learning about other cultures, belief systems, and various approaches to the Divine, so that each individual among them may better understand both the world around them and the Kingdom of God within, so, too, did the members of the group listen to the strange tale of what the husband and wife had gone through that night without apparent judgment. They were thanked for sharing their experience, and afterward, when everyone milled about with small cups of coffee, grazing from plates of homemade cookies and jam tarts, no one treated him any differently, and they talked, as they usually did, of church committee work, of their children, and of books, movies, and television programs.

She was positively giddy afterward, for she enjoyed, he knew, being the center of attention. As they walked through the parking lot to the car, he slung his arm around her shoulders and asked whether she had ever wanted to be an actress. She laughed and told him she never had, though everyone else seemed to dream of it. Even if she came to it late—for she had dropped out of college when she was young due to a severe infection after her first year, and was hospitalized and operated on to remove a cyst clinging to her ovary and intestines, a procedure whose recovery time ate into her small savings so she could no longer afford the university fees or books—she was exactly where she wanted to be, in a career that allowed her to help people.

. . .

Things seemed quiet for a time. They were still driving into the mountains every few weeks, trying to figure out where they had gotten lost off Route 3, but so far had found nothing. Sometimes, she tried to describe her dreams to him again, to explain the uncanny feeling that they were not really, or not only, dreams but something else entirely.

But daily life continued apace. The husband requested a transfer to Portsmouth, and he finally received word from his boss that he might, within a year, have a much shorter commute. He did not want to wait that long, but it was easier to handle the drive when he considered it a temporary inconvenience. His wife was eager for him to work closer to home as well, and hoped that he might also return to day shifts.

Maybe I was wrong to tell you that it was that night in the White Mountains that changed everything for them. Maybe this, what I am about to tell you next, was the event that had the biggest impact on their lives:

One Sunday afternoon, when the trees were aflame with color, when pumpkins adorned every porch, when out-of-towners were easily spotted by their open-mouthed wonder at the fall foliage, two white women showed up on the married couple's doorstep. They seemed respectable enough, middle-aged, hair neatly pinned and makeup understated, and when they said they had driven all the way from a suburb of Boston to speak to the couple, the wife let them in.

They had read about the couple's experience in the NICAP newsletter, the women explained once the percolator was on and they were seated at the kitchen table. The couple had received a copy of this newsletter, too, but as it was not widely read by the general population, neither of them had worried about the exposure, although the husband wondered now whether they should have. It had only taken the women this long to come visit because they first had to consult with their bimonthly UFO study group to make sure that everyone was interested and then the two ladies had to find an afternoon they could take for themselves, which was difficult, they explained, laughing, what with their children and husbands having various plans and events that needed tending to.

The married couple exchanged a small, secret smile at this. Though he missed his children, and though she had long wanted a child of her own and had stopped taking any precautions once she and her husband were married, on the off chance that her womb was still viable, still, they both agreed that they had a lot more time at their disposal than friends and family who had children living with them. They always reassured each other that they would trade it all in an instant if only they could, but there was no reason not to enjoy it while they had it.

Eventually, satisfied with the polite sufficiency of their small talk, the women stated the reason for their visit: Would the couple join them at their next meeting—which would feature other eyewitness testimony and a Harvard astronomer's recorded lecture—and share some words elaborating on their extraterrestrial experience?

The wife glanced at the husband before asking the ladies how they came to join this study group in the first place. The women exclaimed that they should have said earlier that they, too, had seen things. One had witnessed a series of flashing lights in the sky on a bitterly cold winter's night two years ago, and the other had seen an orb not unlike what the husband had beheld at the post office the year before, a round golden light that seemed to shiver and shake and swerve and become a sliver very suddenly, as if a lunar eclipse had spontaneously occurred, which, of course, was impossible.

It was these two sane, normal, stout housewives' experiences that convinced the husband. Before his wife could speak, he reached a loose fist into the center of the table, as if delivering his verdict inside it, and rapped on the surface twice. They would attend, he said, and his wife enthusiastically added her assent, and the women soon rose to leave.

What was so remarkable about that afternoon? Nothing, really, except that it led to what happened next.

The meeting with the study group should have been utterly unremarkable, similar to the one at their church—speakers, a presentation, a short discussion, then coffee and tea and a table laden with grazeable snacks. Instead, they arrived and discovered the community center's recreation room completely packed. Every seat was filled and there were more people standing all along the walls. After a brief introduction from one of the women who had invited them, the couple was given the stage.

Only later would the wife realize that the meeting was not usually so well attended, that their presence was the main draw that afternoon. She stood nervously beside her husband, who spoke first, twisting a handkerchief between her short fingers. He was more accustomed to public speaking then, by far—his activism often involved giving educational or persuasive talks to local government officials, business associations, and donors—and she focused on his words, taking comfort in his voice, which he knew how to project well for a room of this size while still giving the illusion that he was speaking rather quietly, intimately.

His prior experience did indeed help him sound confident, despite not preparing a speech, having imagined that they would be speaking informally to a much smaller group. He explained his own skepticism, making it clear that he was not a fanciful man, and was pleased by the chuckles in the audience as he confessed that he thought his wife was being a tad excitable when she first tried to get him to pay attention to the strange object in the sky. He related the experiences as he recalled them, changing a detail here and there in order to maintain his dignity—he told them, for instance, that he had been laughing in disbelief, rather than shouting in terror, when he ran away from the large craft after seeing the beings through his binoculars—but he tried to be as accurate as he could. He ended with a sincere request for answers, if anyone happened to have any, for he was still deeply troubled by that night and his inability to explain it away.

When he gestured for her to speak next, she froze. What should she say? He had gone through it all. Should she repeat the details from her perspective? Should she decline to speak? But everyone, including her husband, seemed expectant, so she strode forward and tried to quell the quaver in her voice. She added details he had forgotten, such as Dee's shivering and the strange infections that later plagued the little dog. Then the wife was hit with inspiration. Her dreams! She knew without looking that her husband was frowning in his seat, but she hoped that her dreams might strike someone in the room as familiar. She described how one of the nightmares involved a dozen or so figures, very like those he had seen through his binoculars, standing in the middle of a road. She described how, in the dream, she and her husband were taken by these beings into a craft and separated, how they were each asked questions, and how she had been told that they would not remember a thing after. Finally, she explained that while she knew they were dreams, they had recurred for several nights and she thought of them still and believed they had to mean something.

There was a restlessness about the room once the couple had finished speaking, and some members left during the next presentation. Others spoke to them after it was concluded, to thank them or ask clarifying questions.

When they drove home that night during an early fall sunset, they agreed that it had been an overwhelming and unexpected afternoon. They also agreed to finally consult with a psychiatrist who could help them unlock the memories of what had occurred during those missing hours. The memories had not returned naturally, and they were both tired of speculation. If a professional could help, then it was high time to seek one out.

It was only some six weeks later that they first met the psychiatrist who would end up playing such a pivotal role moving forward. But imagine: What if they had been able to consult with him and attempt to heal from the trauma of that night and its following confusion and then . . . go about their lives?

But they would not be allowed to do that. For that meeting where they spoke, unprepared and put on the spot in front of a large group of strangers, was recorded without their knowledge or consent. And eventually, the recording found its way into the hands of someone a little bit like me: someone who wished to tell a good story.

Is that all I am trying to do, after all? Tell a good story?

5

Now
———

The Archivist has had it with the intern. They should have just responded to him earlier, said no from the start. But they didn't, which tells them something; their erstwhile therapist used to say they should pay attention when they couldn't make a decision, that their ambivalence might reveal their true feelings.

They no longer have a therapist; this was back when they had a girl-friend who was able to put them on her insurance, which was better than the kind they have now. But if he was right, then maybe some uncon-scious part of the Archivist wants to be in the documentary. Or wants to have something to say that's worth documenting, worth witnessing: by a camera, a crew, an interested audience.

.   .   .

When they get home from work, there is a stamped envelope addressed to them stuck in the handle of their bedroom door. Inside is a typed letter from the intern at the production company asking yet again for their response to his inquiry. The Archivist snaps. They write a sternly worded email informing him in no uncertain terms that they do not have any interest in being interviewed about the incident at Slopeside Elementary. They add that he should be ashamed of himself for per-severing to the extent that he has, and that if he goes any further, he could be credibly accused of stalking. Hands shaking, they hit Send and hope this will be the end of it, at least as far as the intern and his bosses are concerned.

What they don't tell him is how infuriating it is to be badgered about something they'd like to but cannot remember. It's as if they're being asked to re-create the illustrated and poorly spelled stories they used to crayon and staple together when they were little, booklets that their mother was always getting rid of whenever they moved, or when she decided she couldn't handle clutter, or when she was in a bad mood. The Archivist knows about these because their mother has mentioned their existence, but though they wish they could, they can't picture the pamphlets or what they contained, what tales their child self had imagined.

The Archivist also doesn't tell the intern how scared they've become; knowing they can be so easily found despite their attempts at having little to no online footprint makes them fear their mother tracking them down as well. Once, a long time ago, when they naively agreed to give her their address, she showed up with a duffel bag full of nothing but socks and underwear and said she had to move in because the feds were after her.

The feds had not been after her, but her weeks-long refusal to leave got the Archivist kicked out of the room they'd been subletting.

As they recall the incident, stress hormones flooding their body, they stare at a spot on the wall where they killed a mosquito last summer, just after they'd moved in. They'd left the bloody smear there rather than trying to wash or scratch it off. It was a badge of ownership, even though they don't own the room, only the items and things they do inside of it, and anyway, is ownership even something they aspire to when it is, under capitalism, nearly always a matter of bloody violence when you get right down to it? Why should they want to own anything but their own self, damaged goods that they may be?

Time blurs as their gaze fixes on the smear. Close up, it looks like the inside of a peace symbol, its spokes without a circle, but from where they are now, it's just a dot, noticeable only because they know to notice it. They jolt at the sound of the familiar door slam that occurs every night around now, announcing that their roommate who works nights is heading out. They move their cursor to light up their laptop screen and see the intern has written them back already. One line: You don't have to be such a bitch about it.

Well all right then, they think. Moments later, though, another email comes in from the same production company. It's from the producer himself, and in it he says the intern is going to be dismissed for his unprofessional approach, which the producer has apparently only just learned of. He asks the Archivist if they're willing to schedule a phone call so he can apologize for the intern's behavior and explain more about the project, its goals, its ethical concerns, and who among the Archivist's former schoolmates are already on board.

The Archivist doesn't know what to make of it. The email came too soon after the intern's. But they're curious about who from Slopeside Elementary has signed on to speak with the producer already, wonder whether he could put them in touch. Would they remember what happened if they could talk to someone else who experienced it?

For now, they want to get away from the screen and go out to the fire escape to smoke.

This time, unlike the last few, "Ava" is there. They haven't been trying to bump into her, exactly. But they haven't been avoiding that eventuality either.

—Hey hey, she says as the Archivist gets settled.

—How's your aunt? they ask.

They're proud of themself for remembering to ask her this.

—What? Oh that's so sweet of you to remember! She's all right. I mean, not really, but she's not getting any worse so there's that.

Should they say they're glad to hear it? Or that they're sorry? "Ava" doesn't let the silence go on long enough for them to figure it out.

—It's like, I just wish Mum wouldn't panic about it so much. What Auntie has isn't going away, there's no cure, and she's a champ about it, not that she should have to be, but like, Mum is always acting as if she's on death's doorstep and that's just not true.

—What does she have? the Archivist asks.

Too late they register the indelicacy of the question, but "Ava" doesn't seem to mind.

—ME/CFS, "Ava" says, it's a

But the Archivist cuts her off.

—I know. It's awful. I'm so sorry.

—You're like, maybe the second person I've ever met who knows what it is.

—For a while I thought I had it, but turns out my fatigue was from something else.

—Sucks, man, "Ava" says and sighs.

—Yeah.

Together, they sit in what the Archivist thinks of as companionable silence. The Archivist wonders what "Ava" would think about their predicament with the documentary, the memory they don't have of something that apparently did happen. Or that some childhood version of themself says happened. They imagine telling her about it, until "Ava" yawns and they catch it.

—Don't laugh, but I'm going to go to bed, I think. I've been keeping granny hours, she says.

—No judgment here. How's your cat, by the way?

—He's good! Thanks, mate. He's, uh, not allowed in my room when I open the window. What with past misbehavior and all. Anyway, good night.

—Night.

She called them mate, the Archivist notes. They're obviously not, really, but it's nice to think they might be, one day. Her mate. Britishly, that is. Her friend.

Before going to sleep themself, they pull up the YouTube video again. KIDS SEE SAUCERS IN NEW HAMPSHIRE SCHOOLYARD '96. They're not ready, not quite yet, but nearly.

March 3, 1963

Dear Rosa,

Congratulations on your upcoming nuptials. I cannot, of course, come to the wedding, since my parents will be there. You know I wouldn't be able to help myself if Mother said anything, and I'd give as good as I got and we'd make a scene and your happy day would be ruined. Besides, you've told me yourself how difficult the rumors have been to quash. I'm glad you're going to live in California with your new husband—surely rumors won't follow you there. I hope you finish school out west, since you were enjoying it and you have a mighty big brain, which is one of the things I've always loved most about you. I hope he treats you well and that you're happy.

(I do mean that, despite everything.)

Drop me a line when you reach California after your honeymoon?

Yours, always,

Phyllis

September 17, 1963

Dear Rosa,

Until you tell me otherwise, I'll keep writing, even if you don't respond. You sent such a short letter from Sacramento, and you didn't respond to the two I sent in reply, but the letters haven't been returned to sender, so they seem to have arrived somewhere. If you throw them away, so be it. I've tried writing in a journal and it's not the same. I bore myself. When I write to you, I can imagine you caring, even if you don't.

I also have no one else now. Molly, my neighbor (I think I told you about her at length sometime last year?), who's become a fast friend the last few months . . . She just got married, too, and last week she moved with her husband to Philadelphia to be nearer his family. I approve of her choice, not that she needs me to—her hubby seems kind and the way he looks at her, it's like she's the sun and he's Earth, orbiting her forever. It's good for a man to know how worthy his wife is. I hope yours knows how worthy you are.

Anyway, my efforts at making other friends haven't yielded much fruit. There are those I talk to often enough at work, and some of my neighbors and I say hello in passing, but other than Molly, Cote is the only one I can call a friend and he's also still my boss, which makes things somewhat difficult. People at work were talking about how much time we spent together, taking walks during lunch once in a while, and the whispers got to Cote so I've been seeing less of him outside the office.

I've tried going on dates too. But I'm usually so bored that I end up wishing I'd stayed home with my books and magazines. When I've liked the guy more or less, he's always wanted to touch and kiss and I find myself repelled. Bobby and I did plenty of necking in high school, and it was fine, if not very interesting. And then Vincent, well, I barely remember that. But I can't fake the motions now. I get nauseous, and a chill goes up my spine, and I want to run. I keep saying yes when I'm asked though . . . You see, I'm trying!

I've decided to see a psychiatrist like you did, Rosa. I am so lonely, and I don't know that I'll ever find someone else like you. Or like we used to be. I know others must exist, or else we'd never have found those books we loved to read together before daring each other into the many things we did. But I don't know where such people are. Maybe you're right and we were perverse. Maybe

I want you the way I want you because I'm sick. Or neurotic or crazy or whatever they call it. If that's so, I'd like to get well.

This is how I made the decision: Last week, I was taking a walk and saw a vagrant lady. Her pants were too short, and her boat shoes were too big, and I could see her delicate ankles. She was standing at the railing and talking to herself, or maybe to the seagulls that were dancing in the air. Her hair was covered with a cheerful yellow kerchief, but everything else she wore was rumpled and clearly unwashed. This blond gal with some runny-nosed children was nearby and I saw her stop a policeman to tell him in a whine that her children were "scared of the madwoman," although they didn't seem bothered, too busy fighting over a bag of old bread for the seagulls. But the policeman tapped his cap and walked right over to the vagrant lady. I should say she was a Negro, too, and I was scared to see what would happen next, so I left.

(Yes, I'm ashamed. I know I'm a coward. I should have stayed.)

I kept thinking about her, and wondering how she ended up where she was. She must have been loved once, right? I hope she still is. But she seemed so alone, so alone. And it made me question whether I was going to survive being as alone as I feel. I bought a plant a while ago and find myself talking to it. And I talk to the pigeons who nest outside my kitchen window. So, perhaps I'm also going mad. I don't want to end up like that vagrant. I feel terrible for saying so. I don't suppose she wanted to either. No one wants to end up on the street, right? Thus—my decision.

There is so much about this city that I wish I'd never seen, so much that tumbles around my head the way my clothes do at the Chinese laundry where they know to expect me every two weeks like clockwork. But I can't wring out the sights the way the dryer does my clothes. There is so much abundance here but so much waste and cruelty too. Do people always turn monstrous when stuffed together so close like this? Or is it my intimacy with the crimes and corruptions of the day, every day, that make me believe less and less in the goodness of humanity? A question for the shrink, maybe.

I've been working on a new story after the last three were summarily rejected. It's about a utopian planet called Egalitaria, a place where everyone has enough to eat, a place to live, and the ability to take part in their township's politics. By design, there are no cities on Egalitaria. Once a town grows beyond 5,000 souls, two dozen families are chosen by lottery to pack up their things and search together for a stretch of empty land to develop into a township of their own.

The story follows the daughter of one of these families. They travel and travel, trying to find a place to settle, but they keep coming across one town after another, wandering on and on, slowly losing hope that they'll ever find anywhere uninhabited. They eventually ask existing townships for succor and to be allowed in, but no one helps because it's not the way of their world. The caravan of families is supposed to be self-sufficient. But as they travel, they begin running low on food and water. People argue and violence breaks out among them.

The daughter listens to the adults at night. They're getting desperate and come up with all sorts of half-baked plans: waging war on a small township so that they might take it over; splitting the families off and going to different towns and claiming their caravan was attacked and they cannot, of course, found a town all alone as a single family; sending the children away to see if, without the adults, a town might take them in. The daughter begins to wonder whether the lottery that sends the families off is really a death sentence.

I haven't figured out the ending. I think the daughter might suggest an idea of her own—taking to the sea in a collection of boats and founding a floating town on the water instead of land, a town that might take in all who wander. But I'm not sure. Maybe, instead, I'll have the caravan do what human beings seem so intent on doing: kill all the residents of one township and take it over. Then the daughter will live with the shame of her parents' decision for all her days.

I'll tell you how it goes. The story, and also the shrink.

Yours, always,

Phyllis

November 28, 1963
December 1, 1963

Dear Rosa,

Sometimes, when I put on makeup, I feel like I'm making the bed: tucking all the corners in so my face is pleasing and inoffensive, neat and orderly, my eyelids fluffed like pillows with mascara and eyeshadow. I've always hated making the bed.

This morning I did my makeup especially carefully because I don't know what a shrink expects from patients, and I have bags under my eyes from the long days we've had since the assassination. It's been extras upon extras. But I made the appointment three weeks ago and I wasn't going to miss it. I'm committed to getting better.

On the train over, everyone was reading the newspaper, like they always do in the mornings. I really can't anymore. It's too much. Politics, spousal murders, cold war with the Russians, hot war in Vietnam, the KKK and police truncheoning, jailing, and killing Negroes for demanding fair treatment. Day after day I read through these awfulnesses, again and again and again, doing my job, and my heart aches. I feel useless, and worse, I know that reading about it all is nothing to experiencing it. So I look out the window on the T and try to appreciate this old city's architecture, which is very beautiful indeed. When I tire of that, I look at the people.

(I'm not complaining about my work, mind you. I like fixing the words on the page. It's soothing. It also feels like the only kind of fixing I know how to do. Is it good for anything? I don't know. But I have to hope that reporting the news matters, and that my part in it does, too, at least a little bit.)

Everyone on the train this morning was all bundled up against a bitter cold that hadn't materialized. It's been a bit warmer than it should be all over New England, but Bostonians haven't abandoned their coats and scarves and thick stockings under their skirts. Creatures of habit. I enjoy looking at everyone's clothes, the bold colors, the pastels, the drab utilitarian grays and browns and blacks. I don't think too much about how I dress because it makes me feel like I have clamps on my head that are rapidly tightening. But it's fun to watch.

Speaking of my head: I cut my hair quite short recently. It's easier to deal with, and looks pretty fetching!

When I found the office where the shrink was, I was confused at first because there was a store on street level, with TV sets in the window. Most were showing the morning news, but there were two low down tuned to cartoons. The Flintstones. I used to watch that show when I babysat Merle and Linda's toddler some Saturday mornings, remember? That feels so far away, so long ago. I guess it is.

A child ran up in front of me and pressed her face against the glass to watch Fred and Pebbles walk through a caveman grocery store. She glanced at her parents, who nodded and smiled at her, so she went back to the TV. I felt an ache then—I wanted that. I've always known I want to be a mother, to be a better one than mine. But I don't know if I ever will be. Because I'm broken, aren't I? I'm sick. If I can't make myself find a man, how will I ever have a child? Looking at that little family, I wanted so badly to just be normal.

Your mother must be writing you every day asking about grandchildren, right? For all I know, you're pregnant already. I hope you'll at least write to tell me if you have a baby so I can send it presents. Will you?

Anyway. I figured out that the shrink was on the second story and climbed up and rang the bell for M. IVERSON, PSYCHIATRIST, M.D., as the plaque read.

A prim and proper secretary opened the door for me, a nail file in her hand. She smiled and I tried to smile back, but it was probably weak. She must be 35 or maybe 40. She had those laugh lines near her eyes and around her mouth and some grooves on her forehead too. A radio was softly playing Trini Lopez, the same clapping and guitar I've heard a hundred times these last few months.

"Are you Miss Egerton? You can walk right on back there, hon," she told me, with a bit of a drawl. I wondered what a Southern belle was doing up North, and was on the verge of making up a whole little story about her in my head when I realized I was really going to see the shrink now. I was a bit early, but she said I was his first patient and not to worry about it. But I was <u>so</u> nervous, and I asked her, with a quake in my voice I hadn't expected, "What's he like?"

"Oh, honey, you're trembling!" she said, and offered me a cup of tea. She's a redhead, and while she was bustling around making the tea (there was an electric kettle in the corner just like mine), I had a chance to really watch her. She's quite beautiful. She was wearing a mint-green-and-white checkerboard dress that was tight around the middle, and her calves were thick and stockinged underneath, and she had these little white heels on. "Really, he's very nice, there's nothing to be afraid of," she told me.

I asked her where she was from, and she laughed and said, "Damn, been trying to get rid of this old twang for years. Just a little town in Georgia."

"It's groovy. Why would you want to lose it?" I asked.

"Well, people ask a lot of questions and sometimes a girl's gotta leave Georgia in Georgia, you know?"

She gave me the tea and also a shortbread cookie she'd baked herself, and it was so delicious it made me want to buy tins and bake those banana chocolate chip muffins we made in your mother's kitchen. I don't think I've baked anything since then, unless you count chicken, which I don't.

The Chiffons came on then and Alice—I finally remembered to ask her name—mouthed along with the first line, "He's a soft-spoken guy . . ." and pointed to the closed door where the doctor was. It's silly, but it did make me feel a little better.

It's getting late. I'll finish this letter tomorrow morning.

It's actually several days later. I've been so exhausted with work that I just couldn't muster up the energy to keep writing until now. I was telling you about the shrink. His room was sort of what I imagined a shrink's office would look like, heavy bookcases filled with big, thick, boring (probably) medical texts and a couch and an armchair. He shook my hand, warmly enough, and invited me to sit down on the couch, and we chitchatted for a little bit about how

I moved to Boston a few years ago and where I worked and the weather and Kennedy. (It's almost impossible to have any conversation these days that doesn't include the assassination . . . People on the T talk about it, the radio broadcasters mention it, the TV news I sometimes watch at the bar down my street goes on about it.)

Finally he asked me, very seriously—but softly!—what brought me there. I've heard you're not supposed to tell people what happens with your shrink, but I suppose you know what I talked about anyway. How you and I had an "unnatural" relationship. How I left home when Mother threatened to throw me out or have the Father give me an exorcism. How I look at women the way other women look at men. Or the way men look at women.

He told me—and this surprised me—that it's not unnatural to have curiosity about my own sex and that it's not uncommon for children and young people to experiment with one another. Did your analyst tell you that?

Then he asked me how I felt about men. I told him I'd lost my virginity when I was 17 if that was what he meant, and he asked me to tell him more about it so I did, a little bit, and then he asked me a question I confess I didn't think a doctor could ask.

"Did you enjoy yourself?"

He must have seen all over my face how revolted I was by the idea of enjoying what happened with Vincent, not that I remember much. He asked me some more questions and got the whole story out of me. He rubbed his beard in a way that I thought was very shrinky, you know, and asked whether I hadn't looked at men the same way since. I said yes, although that's not quite true . . . I went out with Bobby before, and Russel before that, and we necked, but I wasn't excited by that either. I never mooned over boys the way you and other girls did.

Then he asked me another question that really shocked me. I don't think I can write it down, even, it made me feel so queer. I told him that Mother said to never, never, ever do that because it's a sin . . . I didn't tell him that I ignored her sometimes, and I certainly didn't go into detail about what you and I used to do. It feels too private, too mine.

He told me there was nothing wrong with <u>that</u> either, though. Not you and me . . . me alone. I almost burst out laughing, imagining what Mother would say if she heard him. The horror! She'd be apoplectic. Anyway, he tried to explain very scientifically about natural sexual desires and needs, how they're evolutionary, like animals in heat rutting, et cetera, but I was squirming so much with embarrassment that he stopped.

I couldn't think what else to say, but then I remembered the little girl downstairs, and I told him that I want to be a mother and need a husband for that. It would be nice to <u>like</u> that man, of course. My parents once liked each other. I remember when I was little—I don't think I ever told you—I heard them <u>rutting</u> as the good doctor put it (I hate that word!) some nights, and Papa used to kiss Mother every morning and spin her around before going to do the chores. That was before Mother's miscarriages, before the two dead babies, my little brother and little sister, buried under the black willow tree a year apart. Before Mother decided that marrying a Quaker was a mistake, that she was being punished by God, Christ, and the Holy Spirit for letting her Catholicism lapse all those years. Before she decided that her only living child, me, was a disappointment, too bookish, too interested in Papa's farmwork, too impatient with church.

Now here's where it got interesting for me professionally, for my stories, I mean. He asked me if I'd ever heard of hypnosis. I thought immediately of <u>The Manchurian Candidate</u>, which I went to see alone last year, but he said it was nothing like that, that the movie greatly exaggerated and misrepresented the entire endeavor. He seemed pretty peeved, as if the film offended him, which was funny and reminded me of an argument I had at work once with Enid about science fiction being for little boys.

But he said that hypnosis can be used to put someone in a state of relaxation where they may access certain stressful or upsetting memories that the conscious mind is repressing. He thought it might help get at the root of my disinterest in the opposite sex, and that over time it might even help stimulate, via hypnotic suggestion, my interest in men. He told me that there are psychiatrists in England who have done some remarkable work to help homosexuals—!—live "perfectly normal, healthy social lives." That was exactly what he said. Perfectly normal, healthy social lives. He admitted there hasn't been much research on this, and it's been tried only on males, but he said the same principles should apply.

He also told me that some psychiatrists are beginning to believe that it's an incurable condition that can be managed only with lifestyle choices. Which sounds like a lot of work, to be honest.

For now, I told him I'm not interested. The idea of lying there, being hypnotized by this man, professional as he may be, is extremely unappealing. Honestly, the whole thing was strange, as if just being there was a kind of hypnosis. I felt very far away from myself during the appointment, as if I was watching myself having a conversation with him, this stranger asking me the most intimate things. It's funny, you and I used to talk about everything, everything, everything. Maybe I'm just out of practice. It's not like I have much opportunity to talk about myself like this most days.

Well, that's that. I suppose we'll see what comes of all this. I have a session later this week, but don't worry, I won't give you a blow-by-blow each time . . . I like telling you about new experiences, though.

I've also been thinking about how I might use hypnosis in my stories. I think I may explore my Saturn world some more and go back to Fiona and give her a few new adventures. Maybe she'll get hypnotized by an alien race? I'll keep thinking about it.

Yours, always,

Phyllis

P.S. Rosa, I also have to tell you this. I had never, not until the moment he said that word, thought of myself as a homosexual.

6

Now

For several weeks, the Archivist is pulled away from Phyllis's files by an exhibition the library is putting on and the reams of paperwork, press releases, and informational materials they are burdened with putting together. Once the display is finally set up in the foyer of the main building, they have some time to breathe, and are free, temporarily, to pursue their own interests once more.

When they are about halfway through going over the computerized transcriptions of the scanned letters in blue ink on airmail paper, the Archivist begins to sift through the rest of Phyllis Egerton's box to see if any of the apparently missing missives might have been lost within her folders. But no, the rest of the material consists of yellow legal pad pages filled with messy but legible print in thick black ink, some clippings, and a ream of typewritten pages. There is something familiar about the stories Phyllis has described, especially that one about a place called Egalitaria, but the Archivist doesn't have the time or the desire to scratch the itch right now. They haven't, for example, even googled her. Not yet. They'd rather get to know Phyllis privately before figuring out who she might have become in the public eye. There are many writers in the archive whose internalities the Archivist can never entirely access, their names too familiar, their writing too famous to exist without the public personae they cultivated. But Phyllis—she is still entirely singular, belonging to no one but herself and, perhaps, Rosa.

At home, the Archivist has a new preoccupation that has been keeping them to their small room even more than usual. Their roommates don't mention it, but the Archivist can tell, from the raised eyebrows they're greeted with on their way to the bathroom or kitchen, that there is some concern, or at least curiosity, as to what has increased their hermitage. Or maybe they're imagining it, giving too much credit to their roommates' attention.

A few days after the intern's last email and the producer's first one, the Archivist finally watched the YouTube video. They girded themself with comfort: a peanut butter and jelly sandwich, a glass of milk, the red flannel pajamas so warm they require keeping the window cracked in winter to justify wearing them. They made sure the sound was on, took a bite of the PB&J, and hit Play, and even though it was their own childhood face talking in the frame, the first thing they heard was a voice-over.

A strange case of what some are calling mass hysteria took place at a public elementary school in New Hampshire last week.

The Archivist's face disappeared and was replaced with B-roll of a low brick building with a sloped roof, tiled hallways lined with tall blue lockers, a yard with a sandbox and jungle gym and swings, the long empty stretch of green rolling hill behind it.

It was a normal Wednesday morning near the end of the school year and the children were out at recess with little adult supervision. As is custom, some of the children played at the bottom of the slope that gives the school its name, where some bushes and trees provide them with a natural playground.

The reporter came onscreen, a short pinkish woman wearing a skirt suit, her hair a professional bob, and began walking down the slope toward the camera.

Suddenly, just after the bell rang, about thirty children ran from this area toward the school, a few of them calling for their teachers, some silent and wide eyed. They told the adults a strange tale, a very strange tale indeed.

The reporter's voice went on, describing the children's claim that they saw something shiny peeking through the trees. When they approached, they found three large silvery orbs sitting on the ground and humming. An image of this, clearly a child's drawing, moved across the screen. The closest orb opened, and two short beings came out. They stared at the children, silent. Then the beings went back into their craft, which hummed some more and turned invisible. That was when the kids bolted back up to school.

A well-known child psychiatrist and Yale professor was dispatched to Slopeside Elementary the following day to interview the students and discuss what they saw. Those conversations were, of course, confidential, but some parents allowed their children to speak on camera for this special report.

And there was the Archivist again, a banner beneath them reading _____, *9 years old* and a gray-haired white man with John Lennon glasses sitting with them.

What did the person you saw look like? the man asked, the banner below changing to list his name and degree.

He was a alien, the Archivist's child voice responded.

All right, the alien. What did it look like? Can you draw it?

The camera cut to another drawing: vaguely triangular head, black eyes, lipless, two slits for a nose, body black beneath the neck.

Was it two different colors? the psychiatrist asked.

No, that's his clothes.

I see, okay, so it had on black clothing. What happened when you saw it?

He looked at me and I thought I should maybe look away but then I didn't.

You didn't?

I couldn't, I guess.

That sounds sort of scary, that you couldn't look away.

The child the Archivist once was considered this for a moment, then shook their head.

It wasn't scary? the psychiatrist asked.

No, it was okay. I knew he was good. He wasn't going to hurt me.

So you felt safe?

Yeah.

All right, and what happened then?

I told you before.

I know, I'm sorry that I'm asking you to repeat things. But now we have the cameras here and you and your mom agreed we could talk again. Is that all right?

Okay.

So can you tell me again now? What happened next?

Yeah, he told me that the planet was in trouble. That there's too much pollution and we're hurting it. The planet.

This being told you this in words?

No, with his eyes.

How with its eyes?

I dunno. He just did. He was a he not an it. Stop saying it.

The camera cut to another child now, a little boy with a black bowl cut and orange glasses whose name on the banner read *Jason, 5 years old.* He looked familiar, somehow. Those thick orange glasses, the silver cross necklace. The psychiatrist asked him similar questions and the boy gave similar answers with a younger child's vocabulary and a prominent lisp.

We need to recycle more, Jason said in closing before the camera cut back to the reporter.

What did these children see? Could this event have anything to do with a similar one that occurred in Zimbabwe two years ago, known as the Ariel School UFO Incident? Is this an episode of mass hysteria? Or did these children watch too much Captain Planet *and make up a wild tale to bamboozle their teachers?*

A teacher came onscreen next, a fat white woman with a high blond ponytail wearing a striped dress. Karen Walsh, according to the banner, an art teacher. She also looked familiar.

No, they're not making it up, she said, shaking her head so her ponytail swung cheerfully from side to side. *I don't know what they saw, but it was something. Half these kids never spend any time together, they're in different grades, they don't know each other's names or anything. Fourth graders don't talk to kindergarteners,* Karen said authoritatively.

Whatever happened here, the reporter said, now walking up the slope, *will remain a mystery, unless, or until,* and here she raised her eyebrows meaningfully, *these visitors from somewhere far, far away decide to return.*

The clip ended, leaving the Archivist underwhelmed. They'd expected it to trigger their memory, maybe even a flashback. They'd expected to have an emotional reaction, at the very least. Instead, they found themself curious and somewhat annoyed rather than spooked by their lack of recollection.

They started looking into the incident. But there wasn't very much to find, at least not easily. In lieu of learning anything else significant about their own experience as a child, they began to delve into the history of UFO sightings dating back to the late nineteenth century.

Mysterious lights in the sky in the early twentieth. The effects of the devastating wars and the atomic bomb on the phenomenon. The few strange encounters ordinary people claimed to have with aliens. Roswell, of course. Area 51. Finally, they found themself back at the couple they'd learned about on the night the intern first reached out, the first abductees, and that's where they've stayed since.

Now, the Archivist spends their evenings combing through another set of materials—the couple's—which they discovered housed in an archive at a university the next state over. They don't order everything, not all at once. They pace themself, a child given access to a cookie jar full of foreign treats, savoring each newly discovered flavor as it melts on their tongue.

Before the story went public, when it was still a private affair, shared first with a beloved few, then with the relevant officials, and finally, on rare occasions, with small self-selecting groups . . . and before it was tainted by money, that most powerful of fictional forces, and fame, and infamy, and the court of public opinion, this story was still one about trauma.

A little before eight in the morning on a cold day in January, the couple pulled up to the curb on Bay State Road, in front of an imposing row of brownstones. The husband put the car in park and rubbed his eyes. It was strange, coming into Boston on a weekend, and in the morning, no less, when he was so used to the city at night, to being home and in bed at this hour.

The wife patted his arm lightly and asked if he was ready, and he nodded and said he was. They got out of the car and walked up the steep old steps into the building and up another floor to the psychiatrist's waiting room, where they were greeted with a smile and a robust hand-shake and an offer of coffee.

The couple was anxious that day, fittingly, as anxiety was what the psychiatrist was hoping to treat them for. That and, of course, the memory loss, which the psychiatrist told them was a very interesting case, dual amnesia being quite uncommon. In their first meeting with him, they had explained the strange occurrences of that September night in 1961, and he had seemed to believe them readily enough, for he himself had seen something that he considered a UFO once or twice, although he would not speak of it further or speculate on what that meant or what it was. He agreed only that there were things that could not be explained. The psychiatrist did not consider himself a closed-minded individual, but he had some preconceived notions about the couple and what they had experienced, which perhaps he was aware of—and perhaps not.

The psychiatrist would see them each individually, and the entirety of January would be dedicated to conditioning the couple in the hypnotic procedure. The hypnotic state was believed to be a safe way to discover what filled the forgotten period of time. A theory aired by others was that the forgetting itself had been achieved by a process similar to hypnosis, and the psychiatrist, when the couple mentioned it, allowed for the possibility, although with some doubt, having never heard—outside of fictional representations—of anyone being put into a such a state without their will or knowledge, let alone being conditioned so well, successfully, and quickly that they obeyed the command to forget what they had just gone through. Even the most suggestible of people could not, the psychiatrist knew, be induced into forgetting two hours of their lives. Hypnosis, the psychiatrist would tell anyone who expressed doubt in his methods, was not magic, but a scientific process.

.   .   .

The psychiatrist's aims were these: first, to ascertain that both the husband and the wife were good candidates for hypnosis; second, to go over the couple's memories of that night in detail while they were in a relaxed state; third, to use hypnotic suggestion to induce the couple into recalling the events that occurred during the gap of time that night; and, fourth, and most importantly, regardless of what they recalled, to ease their anxiety, which had extended over the last two and some years, ebbing and flowing but always present.

As for the couple, the husband was eager still to put the experience behind him by learning the full extent of what occurred that night, facing it, processing it, and thus reducing its power over him; the wife, meanwhile, was most curious about how the contents of her nightmares were related to the period of missing time.

Hypnosis is still used all these decades later in therapeutic settings. It is still not entirely understood why it works on some people but not on others. Anecdotally, I have heard that it works best when its recipients want it to work, and the couple certainly wanted something to help ease their anxieties.

I should tell you, also, that what I know about the couple's treatment comes from their own accounts, yes, but also relies on the psychiatrist's writings as well as things he allegedly said to other people. And the psychiatrist, like everyone else in this story, has contradicted himself, which is to say that he, too, was a human being with an ego and a flawed memory. But this is not his story, and as a result, I have taken pains to trust the couple's accounts more than his.

The conditioning sessions went very well, and the psychiatrist discovered, in both husband and wife, prime subjects for hypnosis, so they were all ready, in February, to begin the therapeutic work.

The psychiatrist started with the husband, believing him to be the more rational of the two and less prone to flights of fancy, and was thus surprised to hear, under hypnosis, the husband explaining that his wife rarely became excited, rarely became emotionally involved in the same ways he did, and so when she insisted that he look again at the object flying in the sky that night, he knew to take her seriously, knew he must, even though he did not want to. This was a theme that came up again and again throughout his sessions: he did not want to believe what he was seeing, what was occurring to the both of them. He even begged to be woken up several times, but the psychiatrist, like a stern yet caring father, was firm in not allowing this deviation from the plan and kept him in the state of relaxed near-sleep, instructing him to feel calm, to feel no fear, to feel completely comfortable. Yet the husband wept terribly when he described feeling watched by the craft above. He shouted and screamed in true terror, reliving the moment precisely as the hypnotic state and the psychiatrist's instructions were urging him to do. He was especially fearful at the memory of a particular set of eyes, which he described as large, black, and slanted, which belonged to the one he instinctively knew was the leader, and which, when words failed him, he asked to draw for the psychiatrist.

Throughout the session, the wife waited nervously in the outer chamber, trying and failing to read, wishing she could hear something from inside, and when her husband emerged from the office, the psychiatrist assured them both that he would remember nothing they had discussed, but that if he did, he was to let the psychiatrist know.

As she put her book into her purse and shrugged on her coat, she watched her husband's face, noting the tearstains on his cheeks but also that he seemed steady, no worse for wear. Was he really this calm, this collected? Or was he putting on a brave show? She knew her husband was worried, more worried than her, about submitting to such a vulnerable process, but she also knew that he, more than she, was convinced of the necessity to heal. How could she explain to him, to the psychiatrist, to anyone, really, that she was not yet sure precisely how to feel about it all? Yes, she was anxious, and yes, she wished to know more, to understand more of what had occurred, but there was also something like elation sitting beneath her breastbone, a small bubble of wonder, something like awe. If indeed the craft they had witnessed had come from outer space, if indeed her husband had locked eyes with beings from another world, and if, indeed, even a tenth of the things she dreamed had really occurred during the period of missing time . . . Well! In that case, as frightening as it had been—and it was, as the violent pounding of her heart when she awoke from her nightmares could attest to—still, she had to admit that something extraordinary had happened.

One of the main criticisms lobbed against her is that she inflated and exaggerated, that she was excitable, that she simply wished to believe. That she was, in other words, a silly woman leaping at shadows and claiming that in them lay proof of ghosts. There is always the possibility that this is true, but I cannot ignore the sexism underlying the ways in which her actions have been interpreted.

Is it really so hard to believe that, in the face of the unexplained, in the face of the mysterious, in the face, even, of trauma, some human minds would prefer to find a way to read their experience as marvelous, miraculous, awesome? Consider Moses and his burning bush, for example. If you were to encounter a fire that sprang up suddenly in front of you, that did not spread or seem to obey the laws of nature as you understood them, and you began hearing a voice from within it, which was impossible, what would you think of it? Might you not also hear God?

On the drive home, the husband began to feel something was amiss. He was thinking about eyes, about eyes telling him something, but could not understand why or what it meant, and the more he tried to think of it, the more agitated he became. He told his wife, who urged him to take a deep breath, and when they arrived home, she fixed him a cup of strong coffee with extra sugar in the hopes of sweetening his mood. He was of a mind to call the psychiatrist immediately, but she discouraged him. She held his hands and reminded him that they were doing all they could to assuage their anxieties, and that perhaps he simply needed to distract himself after the long morning. They had plans to see friends that afternoon, and she suggested they leave a little early and take a walk. Maybe that would help.

It did, and he was glad, the following week, that he had not embarrassed himself by phoning the shrink prematurely with complaints. The psychiatrist listened to the husband report on any abnormal thoughts he had had in the past week and then asked what the eyes reminded him of, what they made him feel, and soon he was ready to begin the hypnosis once again.

This session, too, went as well as could be expected, but the damnable tape recorder was acting up and so the psychiatrist had to ask the patient to pause several times in order to double-check that it was working.

There were some pronouncements that day that did not make sense to the psychiatrist: The husband's description of a group of men standing in the road, though he had not really seen them, for he shut his eyes immediately, as instructed, but how? Not with words, no. He knew only that he was being told to close his eyes and keep them so. Furthermore, he described being taken out of his car and carried up a ramp but not feeling his feet on the ground, nor really feeling himself supported, although he knew he was, for his arms were in this position—and here he demonstrated by outstretching them and bending the elbows as if he were a scarecrow—which meant that something or someone was holding him this way.

He next remembered wishing to peek out and see what was happening, for he was very scared and entirely calm at the same time, as if he were both there and not there. When he did finally open his eyes, for only a moment, he saw what reminded him of an operating room, very clean, sky blue, although it was not exactly like the sole real operating room he remembered, from when his tonsils were removed as a child—he did not think of the other room he was in after his injury in the army, for he was unconscious even before the procedure to fix his jaw, having been knocked out by the blast—and although the psychiatrist suggested that the husband was now describing merely a memory or a dream, he answered in the negative, making clear the distinction between the memory of his childhood operation and the place he was reliving in the hypnotic session. He described someone like a doctor, although he did not open his eyes to see who or what it was, being very gentle with him and placing some kind of cup around his groin, after which he was turned on his stomach and something was inserted into his rectum. Neither procedure caused him any pain.

The psychiatrist did not ask for more detail on the procedure the husband seemed to have undergone but instead allowed the patient to continue conveying his story, in which he was quickly moved back to his car, where he and his wife started driving, stunned and giggly, her asking him whether he still refused to believe in flying saucers and him telling her, in between guffaws, that she was speaking nonsense, for such things did not exist.

Of course not.

Of course.

By the time they arrived home, he explained, they had sobered up and agreed never to speak of the matter to anyone, for it was too strange, too far-fetched, but things seemed different after they had slept, and his wife called her sister and related what they remembered of the experience, which included only the drive up until the sighting of the large flying object and the husband running back to the car, and then the arrival at home.

The husband had tried to evict the memory of the night from his mind but had been unable to, as the psychiatrist was clearly witnessing by the patient being there, in the office, on the couch, waking up from the hypnosis as instructed.

He had no more spontaneous memories after the second session but was still relieved that the following week he would be ceding his spot on the couch to his wife.

Those familiar with UFO tropes or abduction lore will recognize in the husband's narrative the infamous anal probe. There have been Freudian readings galore on this particular matter, which clearly holds fascination and some disgust for the overwhelmingly straight, cis, white, and male UFO community—which is not to say that others do not exist within it, merely that they are less visible both online and off and hold fewer positions of leadership within various interest groups.

I mention the husband's experience here only because he did not often share it within the material he approved of releasing, and yet I believe this to be the origin of what has become a key element of abduction narratives, whether mocking or sincere. That the husband's experience, without his knowledge, has become a cornerstone of the popular cultural image surrounding this phenomenon strikes me as, on its own, worthy of attention.

Additionally, there has been much made of the physical bumps that appeared around his groin, which some believe to be a result of the aforementioned cup and others believe to be a mere outbreak of genital warts. I am not sure how to separate the fascination with this physical symptom from the historical demonization and/or fetishization of Black men's genitalia.

Next session, it was her turn. She was invited to sit down, and when the psychiatrist turned the tape recorder on, she remembered something she had meant to ask before but had forgotten, each time distracted by the unfamiliar setting and the anxiety-inducing project they were embarking on—funny, she thought, that the very act of trying to quell anxiety could itself produce it. Having remembered, she inquired about the recordings being made of the sessions and asked whether she and her husband could have them, but the psychiatrist was leery, reassuring her that nothing would be done with the tapes without their consent, but that they would have to discuss the matter of his sharing them at a later date.

She was not entirely satisfied with this answer. How could she know that the tapes might not be used in some paper being written about neurotics or some such, or aired at medical conferences without their knowledge? She was sure she had heard of such cases, or perhaps had only read about them in novels, but still.

It was her nerves talking, she reminded herself as the psychiatrist began his relaxation speech, and next thing she remembered, she was waking up.

But before she awoke, when she was first put into the hypnotic trance, the psychiatrist told her that she would relax, that she would be perfectly calm, that she would remember everything from the trip to Montreal onward perfectly clearly, and she began telling him about it, repeating some of the same memorable details her husband had mentioned, such as the robbery they witnessed there, and the woman at the food stand who insisted that the couple must know French until finally conceding and communicating in halting English.

She eventually began describing the occurrences of the night drive though the White Mountains, how she first noted the strange starlike object, how they stopped to let the dog out and looked though their binoculars. She recalled, too, when the light changed directions, how her husband suggested that whoever was piloting whatever it was saw them driving this way, and she had laughed, asked him whether he had watched The Twilight Zone recently, although she knew neither he nor she had seen it, but they had heard about it, how far-out it was, and the idea that the strange object in the sky was following them seemed, at that point, fantastic.

You may be noticing inconsistencies, how the husband and wife each believed the other was the one who first became scared of or excited about the object. But how often do you remember events differently than someone who shared those events with you? My mother, for example, is convinced that when we went to see the film Men in Black *in the theater, I got so scared of the giant cockroach at the end that she had to take me outside to calm me down. In my recollection, however, it was she who was so disgusted and annoyed at this point in the movie that she said loudly that we'd be leaving, yanking me with her as she followed through on her announcement. Which memory is the true one? Whom does a memory belong to?*

When she described the moment her husband left the car to see the object more clearly, the emotions of that night returned to her and she began to whimper. She was not too afraid when he was with her, but all alone in the car she became more frightened, for what if something happened to him? She could not imagine what she would do, in the middle of the night, on a dark road, her husband lost in an empty field with a pair of binoculars.

But he returned, he returned, and she related the following events calmly until her memory and her nightmares began to close in together.

She wept as she told the psychiatrist that she could not remember anything after that, and he told her she could, she would, and gently, soothingly, ordered her not to be too upset. She explained that she was not so afraid, really, when she saw the beings in the road, but her eyes continued leaking and her voice still broke with sobs. The psychiatrist asked why, and she said she had never been so afraid in all her life.

The psychiatrist understood that she was both afraid and not afraid, and noted how similar this was to her husband's words about being both there and not there as well as how the couple seemed to become upset at the very same moments in their reliving of the night's events, which indicated, if nothing else, that this, strange and far-fetched as it might seem, was the central point of trauma for them both, the origin of their anxiety.

Once again, the psychiatrist reassured her that she was safe now and urged her to dip back into her fragmented memories, which she did, voice trembling still. She recalled then how they encountered people standing in the road, how the car came to a stop. Her husband tried to start it again, but the engine just turned over and over, coughing up noise. She started to weep again and the psychiatrist had to bite down an interruption and take a deep breath so as not to lose patience; he was used to working with World War II veterans suffering from battle trauma and had helped countless young men, some still boys when they went off to war, but women were not his specialty, and their hysterics were not as familiar nor as easy to sit with.

The psychiatrist, realizing he had lost focus, asked the wife to repeat what she had just said, and she did, describing how the beings came over to the car. He probed her about the men's faces, their uniforms, but she could not see them properly in her mind's eye, or could not process what she was seeing. She described being asleep, or thinking she was, wishing she was, believing she was and would wake up any moment now, even though she was walking in the woods, someone on each side of her and a pair ahead, and wondering where her husband was, only to turn around and see him dragged along behind her, his form supported by these beings, who were quite a bit shorter than him, his eyes closed.

She called his name once, twice, three times, but he would not wake. Another figure asked, in what she believed was accented English, her husband's name, and when she refused to respond, the being reassured her that the couple would not come to any harm, would only be given a few brief tests and then sent on their way again. She felt like she had no choice or, more precisely, that it was better—all alone, her husband apparently unconscious, surrounded by strangers—to go along rather than fight back. Surely, this should be something other women understood, and she wondered, in later years, whether this was why the majority of those who tried to refute her and her husband's experience were men. Men had a penchant for ridiculous statements like You could have fought back and You should have run. As if the matter was ever that easy.

Such questions were irrelevant now, though, and she barreled forward, as if, having passed through that memory blockage, her mind was rushing to expel everything it could recall: A clearing, a craft she could not see well, walking up a ramp, being taken into a separate room from her husband despite her objections, and being examined there. She described her eyes being peered at, her ears, her neck and hands and fingers and feet and toes, and equipment seeming to scan or record her, samples of hair and skin and nails being collected with implements she tried to name by the closest analogs she had—something that took a picture, manicure scissors, a TV screen—and finally being asked to remove her dress, which she tried to do by herself before one of the beings attempted but failed to help her, ripping it in the process. She recalled lying down on an exam table and needles being brought over, clumps of them connected to wires, and these devices running over her skin. They were not sharp exactly, but they did cause her to jump when they passed over her knee and ankle and then her wrist as if her reflexes were being tested.

Later, she would wonder at the relative calm in her voice as she related the beings rolling her over onto her stomach and raising her slip and touching her back with the needles. She assumed it was the clinical nature of the experience that triggered her usual response to medical professionals, which was deference, despite occasional mistreatment, for they had saved her life multiple times.

The calm was short-lived. Their time was nearly up, and tears streamed down her cheeks again as she described the final part of this strange and unbelievable examination. A needle, very different from the others, was brought to her navel, and she told them not to put the needle there. But they did, oh they did, they stuck the needle into her navel and she screamed for them to stop, that it was hurting terribly, to please stop, and they did not stop, but one of them told her, somehow, that she would not feel the pain anymore, and slowly it did indeed stop hurting so much, and then the pain disappeared completely and she understood, though she did not know how, that she had been subjected to a pregnancy test. Although she knew, and told them, that this was certainly nothing like that, and then the psychiatrist was telling her to wake up, wake up now, she would feel calm and without anxiety and would forget everything they discussed during this session.

It's remarkable, really, what cis men will do to avoid discussing body parts that make them uncomfortable. I have read men, perhaps a decade after these events, theorize that she was recalling a gynecological exam or a colposcopy, as if she would not know the difference between something going up her vagina or her anus and something stuck violently into her navel. These same men also neglect to consider a psychological explanation, if, indeed, one such is necessary: she was not able to conceive a baby of her own, and even though she had adopted her first husband's children and was warm and loving toward her second husband's sons, her barrenness could have been part of why she read this particular moment and its wrongness as a pregnancy test. For if she was truly being tested by beings from some other planet, might not the potential feelings of inadequacy regarding her fertility have surfaced in that moment? And what married woman of her day who could not bear children was not assumed to be or made to feel inadequate?

Much as her husband had, she felt calm but also vaguely uneasy on the way home from her first session. That week she suffered two nightmares, one of which startled her awake, crying, feeling as if she had just screamed. She rolled over in bed and nudged her husband until he moaned and asked her huskily what the matter was. He drew her close to him and held her, rocking until her breaths quieted and slowed, and in that place between dreams and consciousness he prayed to God for them both to get better, for their troubles to return to earthly matters.

The following week, she told the psychiatrist about these new nightmares, and that she was starting to remember things like men in the road and crying and being scared, although she could not understand, in her conscious state, what could be so frightening about them, nor could she describe the men except to say they did not look like ordinary Americans but odd, somehow, and she thought they may have all been dressed alike.

Curious at the rate at which the wife and husband's conscious recollections were progressing outside of the hypnotic process, the psychiatrist prompted her into a trance state once again.

If the psychiatrist thought that some of what the wife had told him the previous week was far-fetched, this session would leave him even more skeptical. She began in the midst of the physical examination and described the surprise expressed by the beings when she began to scream and cry during the insertion of the long needle into her navel. But then they somehow made the pain go away, and after a few more pokes and prods she was allowed off the exam table and given her dress back. The beings were not finished with her husband yet, and although she was anxious, she began to feel the surreality of her situation and told one of the beings that no one would believe her, no one would believe any of this if she told them about it. The being laughed, or conveyed amusement, anyway, and asked what she knew of the universe. She confessed she knew very little but asked to take some proof of this encounter back home with her. The being allowed her to pick up a big, heavy book whose writing seemed to go in columns rather than rows.

It was unclear how she was able to communicate with the beings, but she could, and in later years she came to believe they spoke to her via telepathy.

She asked about what she thought was a map hanging on the wall, but, after she confessed her ignorance regarding her own planet's place in the universe, the being rolled it up and away. Another being rushed into the room, opened her mouth, and gently tugged at the wife's teeth with long skinny fingers. Why, the being wondered, did her teeth remain firmly inside her mouth while her husband's came out? She tried to explain dentures, how most people who had them were elderly, which confused the beings, who did not seem to understand aging, what a lifespan was, what years were, nor even what time—in the sense that humans understand it—was.

> *Skeptics wonder how and why she was able to communicate with them about things like pregnancy or pain but wasn't able to tell them what time was. But it is possible, across languages, to communicate concepts that varying creatures have in common, while it is much more difficult to communicate abstractions. Consider any pets you have had in your life: when an animal is in pain, it tells you of that pain in a way that you recognize, even though you don't speak the same language or share a similar frame of reference regarding the purpose and sensation of pain. Some animals sense when human beings are in pain as well, don't they? But try to have a conversation with your cat about aging and it is unlikely you will find it satisfying, just as your cat cannot explain what is so fascinating about the smells clinging to the bottoms of your shoes.*

The psychiatrist let her talk, not interrupting as she recalled how she tried to explain to the beings that she would not be useful to them, for she could not communicate what food was, or what Earth was like, or her society. She asked the beings whether they would return and warned that if they should, it would be better if they politely asked people to come aboard rather than going around kidnapping innocents. She wished they would return, she told them, and she could help them find experts to explain everything the beings did not understand. She felt so inadequate, so unable to convey normal, everyday concepts to these entirely abnormal beings, but she was hopeful that taking the book back with her would be a step toward establishing a relationship between humans and whatever, whoever, these aliens were.

This idea filled her with excitement and a sense of importance, so when the leader took the book away she became angry, for the beings had promised she could take something, proof. But they had evidently changed their minds and said it would be better if she forgot everything that happened here. In fact, they said she would forget it, even if she did not wish to, at which point she became petulant and insisted she would not forget it, never, not in a million years, no matter what. Her husband, they assured her, would forget, even if she did not, and besides, neither of them would be believed.

It was no use arguing, she realized, as she was led out of her room and her husband shuffled out of another, and they were escorted back down the ramp. His eyes were still closed, and she became frustrated—had he missed everything? Had he passed the whole experience by with his eyes shut in terror? But perhaps he had not chosen this; maybe they threatened or frightened him.

Now they were back on the ground, and she was invited to watch the craft take off, and she felt so very happy. Had any human on the planet ever experienced something like this? Had they, too, felt this joy, this sense of wonder at the possibilities of what it meant? They were not alone, she now knew, and that was beautiful, and she urged her husband to watch as the bright yellow light rose and grew smaller and smaller, and she got the little dog out of the car and held her tight and murmured that no other dog had ever witnessed what they were both seeing just then, and when the light disappeared and it was again dark, so dark, she laughed aloud and put the dog in the back seat and sat beside her husband, and they looked at each other and smiled and the car started up just fine, and they began to drive.

She told him he surely must believe in flying saucers now, and he told her not to be ridiculous. She wondered whether he was joking but did not ask, just savored the awe. It was like—a blasphemous thought—but it was just like she had seen God.

The psychiatrist asked several times in several different ways whether she and her husband talked about the experience after it occurred, and she told him they had not, no, they had not discussed what happened: going into the craft, being examined, leaving. She could not explain why except that they were forgetting already, or wanted to forget, or needed to. There was a part of her that wanted to remember, but the leader had told her to forget, and she felt compelled to do as he said, although whether she was following this compulsion of her own volition, she could not say.

The psychiatrist recognized that she was describing memory loss very akin to that which could be induced via hypnotic suggestion, much as the psychiatrist would instruct her to forget all that had occurred during this session. But nothing in the experience she described indicated that such suggestion had occurred, for although popular depictions of hypnosis tended toward the melodramatic, the psychiatrist knew how much time and work and repetition it took before a subject was ready to receive such suggestions. The married couple, after all, had spent three sessions with the psychiatrist simply being conditioned. And they were among those who seemed to be especially susceptible to hypnosis. He did not think they were faking, as he had pricked both of them with needles that he told them not to feel, and indeed they had not flinched.

As he considered this, she described the rest of the ride home and getting out of the car in somewhat of a fog and throwing away all the food and drink left over in the cooler in the trunk, and stuffing their worn clothing into the back of their closet, and deciding to take a bath before she went to bed. She soaked and soaped thoroughly and washed her hair vigorously, for she had a vague awareness that, if the beings were indeed from another world, they may have traveled with some kind of radioactive power—nuclear energy was the most powerful kind she knew or could conceive of—and, besides, what about diseases and germs? What had these beings brought with them, and what had they potentially taken after encountering her and her husband? What if they had terribly endangered each other, as the Europeans had endangered the Native Americans when they arrived on the shores of what she still considered, all in all, a great and good land? What if she and her husband infected everyone else and began a great extermination of the human race?

I am, of course, embellishing here, adding curlicues of further thoughts that seem to naturally follow from what was already in the transcripts— which, themselves, are not entirely complete, as the small talk before and after sessions is conveyed in brief summaries.

My own imagination relies, in such instances, on the parts of the couple left behind and accessible to those, like me, who wish to learn more: their own words and the words of those who knew them, whether recorded audibly or written down. I am trying to convey what I believe they were like,

but I also need you to understand that I will never really know. In a sense,
all of this, even the parts based on strictest accounts of reality, is made up.
Just as made up as any story we tell about ourselves.

But that fear, of illness and radioactivity, dissipated, just as the memories of the craft were slipping away one by one, right in front of the
psychiatrist's eyes, for she had been instructed at the start of the session
to relive her experiences exactly as they happened, which included this
forgetfulness descending upon her.

Did she and her husband speak of the events to anyone in the aftermath,
the psychiatrist asked, and she told him how, after getting a few short hours
of sleep, they mentioned to their upstairs tenants that they had seen one of
those flying objects. The wife had then called her sister, who urged her
to make a report to the nearby air force base, which she eventually agreed to
do although she did not believe it was significant enough for all that . . .

But was it?

She relayed how she called the base and, after being transferred many
times, finally spoke to someone who promised that she would be contacted soon. And indeed, someone from the base called back the next day
and asked questions that seemed to be part of a checklist or form and
in addition to that coldness, the air force official sounded so sarcastic
and derisive that she decided she did not wish to talk about it anymore.
It was bad enough to have her husband's mood change every few hours
regarding what they had gone through, swinging between sincere curiosity and annoyed skepticism, almost as if he were fighting within himself.
She did not need some stranger on the telephone making her feel like a
hysterical woman on top of all that.

But her own curiosity was not satisfied, so she did what she had done
about any other bee stuck in her bonnet: she went to the library and found a
book about UFOs written by a retired major, and she read it, and found
on the back cover an address to which she could write, so she did just that
and received a letter in return expressing interest in her experience. A few
days later, one of the investigators from NICAP came and talked to her.

Time was up, the psychiatrist noted, and he stopped her. He began
the process of bringing her back to the present and instructed her not to
recall anything they had talked about. He said she would be calm and

carefree and feel no anxiety when she awoke. She giggled as she regained awareness of the room, of the psychiatrist looking grumpy in his chair, of the smooth leather under her fingers, of the slight pinch in her left heel in the shoes she had bought recently and was still breaking in, of the tightness in her belly that told her she might have drunk too much coffee that morning, and when the psychiatrist asked her why she was making that noise, she mumbled that it was all just so funny, all of this, this life, and he asked how she was feeling and what she remembered, and she laughed again, astonished and a little delighted, for she could remember nothing, nothing at all, and that sure was funny. She told him that her mind was blank and kept cracking up at the oddity of it all, at the idea that she and her husband were seeking professional help for a UFO encounter. Ridiculous!

The psychiatrist, perturbed by her exuberance, informed her that when he wanted her to remember what they had talked about, she would. She thanked the doctor and kept chuckling occasionally, at nothing, all the way home, until her husband was quite annoyed at not being let in on the joke and sat down to deal with paperwork for the rest of the day.

Having established that the psychiatrist was skeptical—and, as you will see momentarily, did not hide this fact—let me pause and consider an alternative.

Let's say there wasn't really a gap of time that night. Let's say that he and she merely convinced themselves of it because they got lost and it was the middle of the night and he succumbed to highway trance while she fell asleep and dreamed of discovering that humans were not alone in the great, wide, endless universe. Let's say their minds, via suggestion from others and then a reflective confirmation strengthened by each of them, created this time gap.

What then?

Does that make the fear they experienced any less real? Was the anxiety and need to understand what occurred any less intense? There is a popular notion that traumatic memories are always sharp, precise as a surgeon's hand wielding a scalpel, and if they're not, then they are at least easily recoverable, tucked away somewhere. But human memory doesn't work so neatly, nor does our experience of the world in general.

The way memory retrieval works is not so different from how imagination unfolds. When we remember a specific event, our mind fills in and tweaks the details, responds to our emotional associations with the memory. We like to believe that our memories are infallible. We like to believe that witness testimony is clear and useful. We like to believe that our most beautiful and most painful memories reflect absolute truths. But more often than not, we embellish. We add onto, subtract, all unconsciously, unwittingly. There is no shame in misremembering, for we can never truly count on memory in the first place.

The unpleasant reality is that our minds are capable of convincing themselves of much, much more than we are comfortable admitting, and the experiences that follow from such convictions can be as real as anything else.

How do we delineate what is true from what is imagined? Do we treat the consequences of delusions, try empirically to disprove them, or do something else entirely?

I do not know.

Do you?

During the husband's next session, the psychiatrist questioned the veracity of his experiences as described under hypnosis and raised the possibility that he was merely parroting his wife's dreams.

Later on, the husband would discover that the psychiatrist sometimes spoke over him and asked leading or confused questions, insinuating that the husband was influenced by his wife or dreamed the experiences himself. But under hypnosis, even though he revealed that he had indeed overheard his wife discuss her dreams—dreams in which appeared some of the same details that she recalled while hypnotized herself—he also insisted that she had never directly relayed them to him. Yes, he had been around when she had described them to others, but he was only half listening, uncomfortable with her eager recollection of nonsense. He had always dismissed them as merely dreams.

And now, under hypnosis, he insisted on the reality of his own experiences, even as he wished dearly, vocally, that they had only been fantasies, for then they would be less frightening.

In later years, when he thought back on these sessions, which by then he had listened to himself, he did not blame the psychiatrist for his skepticism, even if many others, including his wife and his wife's family and mentees and admirers, long after the fact, would do so, and harshly at that. After all, the husband would not have believed the events if he had heard them relayed by someone else. He respected the psychiatrist for pushing back, for trying to figure out whether he was lying or confused, for not accepting at face value such a far-fetched story.

The wife, too, was confronted with the doctor's skepticism during her next hypnotic session, but rather than sowing doubt in her, the questions served only to strengthen her certainty that there was a difference between the nightmares shortly after the experience and the experience itself. She revealed to the psychiatrist that March, on the same day her husband was interrogated as to her influence upon him, how that difference was made clear to her: it had been some weeks after the experience, after she had had those recurring nightmares. One evening, her supervisor at work, K., came over for coffee. The husband had already left for work, and so the women sat comfortably in the kitchen together without worrying about who was overhearing or whom they might be bothering. The wife recounted her dreams to K., and K., apparently exasperated by how thickheaded the wife was being, asked when she would come to terms with the fact that these were not dreams in the ordinary sense but rather experiences she had really had but suppressed.

The psychiatrist found this very interesting and seemed to assume from then on that it was her supervisor, K., who had implanted the obsession in the wife's mind. Yet she insisted, and her husband later did, too, that the obsession need not have been implanted in them by anyone. As soon as they had arrived home that fateful night, or rather, early morning, there was something off, and they both knew it. Was it not strange that even as they discussed the experience with a select few others, they barely spoke of it to each other? They still discussed everything else that came to their minds, for this was a couple who enjoyed conversation, who coexisted as partners and took an interest in each other's doings and thoughts and opinions—but they did not talk of that night in any detail.

.   .   .

In their final hypnosis sessions, the husband and wife were each probed and prodded about the difference between dreams and reality, a tangle that neither she nor he, nor even the psychiatrist, could fully resolve. Although the psychiatrist was clearly doubtful as to the experience inside the craft, the wife was convinced, as the memories accessed during hypnosis surfaced in her daily life, that her dreams reflected the reality she could not accept. In her dreams, the beings appeared to be run-of-the-mill people, whereas in the memory of the events, they looked wrong: top heavy, with large rib cages and heads, big void-filled black eyes, narrow hips and skinny legs, almost like diseased humans, plague-ridden or shrunken with age. The husband could find little logic in the experience but could not claim it was all a dream, for as much as he wished to suppress it, he knew something had happened, and he could remember it all more clearly now, that is as clearly as any other nearly three-year-old memory, which is to say not razor-sharp, but enough to know that it certainly felt real.

It was after these final sessions that the psychiatrist decided to allow the couple to hear the recordings. The husband and wife were doing much better already. In barely six months of sessions, they were reporting lower anxiety levels than at the start. Moreover, the husband's physical ailments were easing—his blood pressure dropping and his ulcers healing—and she was sleeping better despite the occasional vivid dream and was suffering less apprehension. The psychiatrist was pleased with their progress, and recognized that other than this experience, the couple was well adjusted, performing adequately in their careers and personal lives and community endeavors. To find out more about why this experience had occurred to them—that is, in the psychiatrist's way of thinking, why their minds had created and latched on to it—would take a much longer course of treatment, for they would each have to share much more about their lives, such as their childhoods and sexual entanglements and conflict areas with family and friends, and the psychiatrist knew this was not the kind of treatment they were seeking, nor was it clear that they would be able to afford such a lengthy investment.

So the psychiatrist played them the tapes. Hearing their own voices change tenor from the cool monotone shared by most hypnotized subjects to the intensity of their individual terrors was a deeply disconcerting experience, especially as they could not remember saying what they said or reacting how they did. They had been able to recall the specifics of what they recounted during the sessions, because the psychiatrist had ordered them to do so, gradually, outside of the sessions, but the sessions themselves remained shrouded in a lost time all its own. They had exchanged one amnesia for another.

The husband, listening to her recordings, wondered whether he had ever heard his wife in such hysterics during their years together, and could not recall any such time, although he had, on occasion, brought her to ecstasies that produced certain similar moans, a thought that he shook away at once for it was inappropriate. She had her own share of such thoughts while listening to him describe his experiences aboard the craft, for she was quite sure she had never seen her husband's anus, and perhaps had never heard him say the word before that day. Although his description of an object a finger's width being placed into it was clinical and devoid of pleasure, she could not suppress her only association with the idea, which was that homosexuals made love this way, and although sodomy was, she supposed, a sin in the eyes of the church, she had a sudden vision of herself atop her husband, with an organ like his, using it like he did. Yet her thoughts, too, were fleeting and dropped away.

After listening to the tapes, they spoke once more with the psychiatrist both individually and together and came to the mutual decision to discontinue treatment. They had learned, they believed, all they could about the origin of their anxieties, and it was now up to them to decide how to proceed. The psychiatrist, though skeptical, could not tell them with any profound certainty that the abduction had <u>not</u> occurred. Anything could happen, after all, and as there was no absolute proof in either direction, and since they were mature adults with minds of their own, the psychiatrist could not tell them whether to believe in the remembered experience or not.

Before parting at the end of their last session, the couple made one request: that the psychiatrist keep the tapes somewhere safe in case time would come to validate their reality. What if, for instance, in twenty or thirty years, other humans were abducted and were able to bring some tangible proof back? Or what if the beings contacted government officials one day? The couple wished, ultimately, to show they had not been mad.

The husband, in particular, did not like the idea of being considered an eccentric, and even if some few people might always regard him as such now—the psychiatrist, potentially, and those various family members and friends they had chosen and would choose to share the details of the abduction with—he did want the opportunity to redeem himself one day, if their experience should repeat itself.

.   .   .

Their Saturday mornings were, once again, their own to do with as they wished. They no longer took long drives through the White Mountains to search for where they had gone off course that night; instead, they spent their weekends at the beach, in the backyards of friends' homes, or camping. The husband took a trip to Philadelphia to spend some time with his sons, and two weeks later the wife visited her old hometown, where her sister's family lived.

She was able to dedicate herself more fully to her heavy caseload at work and to her secretarial duties for the NAACP. He was able to focus his attention once more on the antipoverty program and his place on the board of directors of the U.S. Commission on Civil Rights. Both made an effort to attend services at their Unitarian Universalist church more often. His supervisor had confirmed that his transfer would occur in several months and that he would be a mail carrier once more, which he and she both looked forward to, for while the job still involved quite a bit of driving, he would be on his feet more and would be able now to sleep beside his wife every night and remain awake during daylight hours.

> *I hope I am doing their story justice, though I know it is not my story to tell. Still, it has been told by so many before me and will be told again so many times after; entire genres of both fictional and nonfictional narratives were born here, from the experience of these two ordinary humans living alongside mystery. Popular culture has turned elements of their memories into tropes; other people have experienced or believe they have experienced similar abductions.*
>
> *It all started here, with the couple's private attempts to understand the stuff of their own nightmares, anxieties, traumas.*

And I wish it all had ended there, with the discovery and acceptance of their truth.

But the story was too incredible, too strange, too new to be left alone. Human beings are narrative obsessed, after all, and we rarely let a good story stay hidden in the shadows for long.

7

Now

The Archivist is trying to meditate, sitting cross-legged on the floor between their desk and the wall, in the space normally occupied by a large paper recycling bin. If what they've been reading is anything to go by, achieving a state of deep relaxation can help with memory retrieval. *Retrieval* is the word the Archivist prefers. They picture a sleek golden-furred puppy bounding across their brain's synaptic pathways, looking for the lost encounter or anything related to it. So far, though, the dog seems to be chasing its tail.

A shadow falls over the Archivist, the bright red of their closed lids darkening, and they snap their eyes open to see their boss standing at their desk, wearing a quizzical smile. The Archivist scrambles up, apologizes, and explains that they thought everyone had gone for lunch. Their boss nods, laughs a little, tells the Archivist they should consider going out, too, it's finally getting balmy. The Archivist knows she's adding another line item to the list of eccentricities she has come to forgive them for over the years. She gives them a hand up, then leaves them to their work, and although the Archivist is mortified by the interaction, neither speaks of the odd moment again.

Collating printed booklets to hand out to the progressive private school children coming to the archive for an educational field trip that afternoon, the Archivist meditates further, only more actively, on the problem of their missing memory.

A few days ago, at the recommendation of the documentary producer—whom they emailed back eventually, feeling beholden to his apology about his intern's behavior—they attended a virtual panel organized by MUFON, the Mutual UFO Network. The speaker was a woman who had attended Slopeside Elementary and who, the producer said, had agreed to be interviewed by him. As she spoke about the encounter, the Archivist was shocked to see the streak of gray in her hair, the crow's feet by her eyes, but knew she must be only a couple of years older than them. Their age has never sat well with them, always feeling like something distant, abstract. In part, it's their body's fatigue, its aches and pains, how these robbed the Archivist of the supple comfort associated with youth. But it's also just another aspect of their strange relationship with time, how it expands and contracts more dramatically than it should.

The woman on the panel spoke of the three alien ships she saw, silver and round, and the beings that came out of them, gray and large-headed and skinny-limbed, and while the Archivist could envision these images easily, they couldn't bring forth any actual memories. They found this, still find this, deeply frustrating.

So much so that they decide, on their way home from work, to mentally gird their loins and give their mother a call. She is in large part why they don't like recalling their childhood, why there are significant portions of it that seem entirely blank. She didn't understand them back then, not that she made an effort to, and still doesn't see what she calls the Archivist's life choices—some of which are not, in fact, choices—as anything to be impressed by or proud of. But she is, in many ways, the keeper of the Archivist's earliest memories. It's been a few days since she's sent them anything about her favorite new conspiracy theory, something about the sky being replaced by a simulation, so they hope she might be in a somewhat less erratic frame of mind.

They get off the train a couple of stops early. What a shame, they think, to spoil such a lovely evening, the earlier warmth still suspended in the air, with their mother's voice. Maybe it won't be so bad. It isn't always. But the knot in their stomach doesn't loosen. The Archivist rips off the proverbial Band-Aid, bites the metaphorical bullet, puts their earbuds in, counts one, two, three, four, five, six steps, and calls.

The four tones before she picks up feel eternal, and in that elongated space, bits of the world come into hyperfocus: a pink curtain fluttering in an open window reminds them of an animated movie they saw once when they were small, with twirling ballerina mice in pink dresses; a dented AC unit sitting on the curb, its vents caked in grime that looks like the black mold in the shower of the apartment they lived in when they were twelve and their mother was dating a tall man with a very small nose; an ancient, abandoned Chevy Bel Air, its color hard to distinguish under the dust and rust.

And then she picks up and the street is just the usual nondescript collection of buildings and trees and cars and sidewalks.

—Baby! she croons.

—Hi, Mom.

She is not the kind of parent who asks her child how they are or what they've been up to. She is the kind who launches into a tale of grievance regarding the synagogue down the street, which attracts too many people taking up parking spaces on the weekends, and which she thinks might occasionally hold meetings of the Satanic Temple, then switches for no apparent reason to reminiscing about a party she attended in the early 1980s where the canapes were just divine, before finally landing on the mundane topic of the pothole in the alleyway behind her building that has finally been filled in.

—That's good, the Archivist says vaguely, but Mom, I wanted to ask something. Remember those couple of years when we lived in New Hampshire with Granny and Granddad?

It's a risk to ask her about this, about the parents who cut her off after this period and took in her only child when they were a teenager needing to get away from her. Their mere mention has set her off at times.

—Sure, baby, why?

Not tonight, though, apparently. A relief.

—Someone sent me a YouTube clip of me talking to this psychiatrist at the school, Slopeside. There was a news story about a bunch of kids who saw aliens during recess, basically, and I guess I was one of them.

—Oh yes! You were darling. I was so proud of you being on TV like that, everyone got to see how cute my _____ was.

The Archivist clenches their fist. Of course that's what she'd value, her child being on the local news, giving her a vicarious fifteen minutes of fame. She would love it if they did the documentary. In realizing this, their resolve not to strengthens.

—But wait, did you believe me? Then, I mean?

—Of course not, it was nonsense! You and your friends made it all up.

Her skepticism is almost funny, considering what she's wholeheartedly believed in the past, but the Archivist knows that while she was always prone to lying, her delusions were never insincere. It stings, though, her pretending they had friends. They may not remember much about their time at Slopeside, but they do know how alone they were there, and at all the other schools they attended over the years of bopping around with her from boyfriend to odd job to boyfriend.

—But the reporter took it pretty seriously, didn't she? And the psychiatrist was from Yale and all. And, like, a lot of people thought something really happened there.

The Archivist doesn't actually know this, but the internet is the internet and they're sure that people like that exist, even if not many.

—Well, it was good TV is what it was.

—So you're saying you don't believe it really happened. That I saw something. Aliens, I mean.

She laughs. One of her prettier sounds, which makes it all the more grating.

—Why, do you?

They don't know. They have no memory of it, but they keep imagining themself as a child seeing what they said they saw back then. The blithe dismissal with which their mother is treating the matter, not to mention the way she treated them back then, makes the Archivist want to cling to whatever their child self experienced. The kid they were seemed so absolutely certain. Down to the insistence on the correct pronoun for the alien who'd communicated with them.

No deeper conversation follows. They let their mother ramble on for another ten minutes, interjecting mhmms and oh reallys as necessary, and by the time they walk into the apartment, they've learned far too much about their mother's recent obsession with geo-engineered skies. They resist the urge to ask her whether she's still taking her meds before hanging up. The trouble, they know, is that even if she is, she has far more access now to like-minded individuals than she did when the Archivist was young. Back then, it was clear to them, somehow, that her paranoias were largely unfounded.

And here they are, hoping to remember what they know is impossible, that they saw aliens during recess three decades ago.

To prove something to themself, or to get the taste of their mother's mind out of their mouth, the Archivist climbs up the fire escape to the roof of the building, which is sloped and technically off-limits. The light pollution means there's not much in the way of stargazing, but they lie on the narrow flat expanse at the roof's peak and look up at the sky anyway. It's cloudless, no chemtrails in sight.

They will someone, something, anything to appear up there, to make them believe in the unbelievable, but nothing out of the ordinary emerges. The Archivist watches the moon rise and wash out the handful of visible stars. Human beings have reached it, stood on it, though not for over half a century. That, too, seems impossible. Minutes, then hours pass as the Archivist watches the lit crescent's progress across the sky, and they wonder how much of that movement is due to its orbiting and how much is their own changing perspective on a coyly spinning planet.

May 4, 1964

Dear Rosa,

I was overjoyed to hear from you last week after so long, and of course I understand about baby Harold. I was half worried all this time that you'd moved and someone else was receiving my letters and finding them odd.

I don't mean to be uncouth, but with how old the baby is I've been wondering . . . is that the reason you got married so quickly last year? I wish you'd told me. I don't know what good it would have done, but what I'm trying to say is that I wouldn't have judged you, you know. The important thing is that your husband is treating you well and that you're enjoying California. How fun that you've taken to nature hiking! All this time I thought what you enjoyed about cheerleading was the outfits and the way everyone, boys and girls alike, was enamored of the head cheerleader, but maybe it was the simple fact of being active!

Don't you feel we're quite old? You have a husband and a son. I have a job and live on my own . . . We're really little women now, aren't we? (By the way, I hope you got the birthday card I sent last month!)

To answer your question, yes, as far as I know Mother and Papa are fine. I don't write to them, but I occasionally call long distance. If it's Mother on the line, I hang up, but if it's Papa, I talk to him some. He sounds almost proud when I tell him about my life. I think he's told Mother I'm all right and alive, but she's as stubborn as I am, so neither of us will make the first reconciliatory move.

Then again, she probably still thinks I'm possessed by the devil.

Speaking of, I'm still seeing Dr. Iverson. It's dull. He wants to talk about my childhood a lot, so you feature heavily. I missed my last appointment, though. I overslept. Mr. Cote gave me an alarm clock for Christmas, and it's been stellar at waking me up, but I forgot that batteries eventually run out. I did manage to get to work when I was expected to after sessions. (I told Mr. Cote that my appointments are related to "women's troubles" and he went positively beet-colored. It was too funny.)

A few weeks ago, I finally agreed to try hypnosis. I fell asleep the first two times, but I guess it worked the third time because when I woke up, Dr. Iverson told me I hadn't been asleep, that I'd been in a trance, and he asked if I wanted to know what we talked about. I didn't. I still don't, and I haven't agreed to try again since. It's too spooky, saying things I have no memory of.

That last story I sent you was also rejected by <u>Amazing Stories</u>, but (!!!) the editor wrote that he quite liked my writing though he thought the narrative rather anticlimactic. I can work with that! (Not that I agree, mind you, about that particular story . . .)

I had the strangest feeling this morning. When I woke, there was some light, but the sun wasn't all the way up yet. I could see my yellow curtain blowing in the cool breeze, and for a moment I was convinced it was Sunday and I was eleven, lying in my old bed, with you on the trundle next to me, and that I was about to get up and sneak out to join Papa for his morning chores. For a flash, it was like I was really back there, as if we were young children and your brother hadn't been sent to Korea yet and Mother was still nice sometimes.

But then, of course, I heard Mrs. Farber upstairs dragging her rocking chair from the stove where she likes to put it at night to stay warm to the window in the east where she likes to do her knitting in the sun, and then I knew where and when I was again.

You know, when people tell me science fiction is silly, I should ask them: Why is it silly to write about time travel? We all do it in our daily lives, floating through memory.

Tell me what you're reading, what albums you're listening to, what you spend your days doing, and what I may send your boy as a gift, please! And more snapshots?

Yours, always,

Phyllis

July 27, 1964

Dear Rosa,

How are you? I haven't heard from you since late May. I hope everything is all right.

Work is the same as always over here, but we make our own fun amid the whirlwind of activity. Here's an example: one of our reporters is on the aviation beat, and he's been doing a series on flying saucers! Some of us had a little bet going. We all knew it'd be a popular series, but we weren't sure in what direction. Which would we get more of: Letters to the editor decrying the waste of space? Or letters to the editor lauding us for taking the phenomenon seriously? Most of the others thought the rationalists would be angry and write in, and a few thought it'd be about even steven. Enid, of all people, and I were the only two who put our dimes on the response to be overwhelmingly positive. And we won! I've enclosed here the last part in the series, which ran today alongside the most complimentary reader notes, but there were so many others. You'll spot the mention of a New England UFO Study Group, and while I'm intrigued by such people, you know I don't actually believe in this nonsense. There are sound reasons for why it's extremely unlikely that visitors from another planet would arrive here. Eminent scientists doubt there could be other sentient life amid the stars at all, and especially the possibility that they'd show up on Earth. I can't help but wonder why some folks dedicate themselves to the so-called study of UFOs ... But I'll stick to science fiction, thank you very much, where I can imagine all sorts of things without needing to stick to unfortunate facts. I prefer admitting that I'm making things up rather than pretending my fancies are real.

There's something else I need to tell you, and I guess I've been avoiding it. I've reread your last two letters many times now, and I suspect you've felt comfortable writing me again only because I was meeting with Dr. Iverson and trying to get over my "little problem." Though I may be jeopardizing any chance of hearing from you again, I must confess that I've decided I'm going to stop seeing him. I've never lied to you outright, not since that one time I fibbed about your necklace, and you knew right away. I won't start doing it now.

You see, two weeks ago, I was in tears when I came out of my session. I'd seen a very beautiful woman on the train ride over and she smiled at me and I smiled back and we just grinned at each other like fools until I felt bashful and looked away. She got off at the next stop, and I looked after her, a little wistfully. Then she turned back and blew me a kiss. I was telling Dr. Iverson all this, and how happy it made me. He disapproved. He worried that I wasn't even trying to get better and said I need to make more of "an effort" to desire men. He was quite impatient with me, and I left feeling rotten.

That's only part of the reason I've decided to quit.

On my way down the stairs, Alice, his secretary, caught up to me. She handed me a tissue and told me quietly that the doctor and his wife were separating and he'd been in a foul mood with all his patients that week, so I mustn't take him too personally. Then she put a manila envelope in my hand.

"There's another way," was what I think she whispered, her breath tickling my ear and neck. And then, more urgently, "Don't open it until you're alone."

I was wildly curious all day, of course, and felt better too. Mysteries can be thrilling that way. I felt the envelope up and down, and it seemed to contain a booklet or magazine. I had the vague notion that Alice must have remembered that I dabbled in writing science fiction, and maybe she was gifting me a subscription, which would have been a very sweet and friendly gesture. (We always chatter a bit before my appointments, and sometimes after.) But why would I need to be alone for that?

When I got home, I found I was right, in a way. It was a magazine, and it bowled me over as surely as the first issue of <u>Weird Tales</u>

I ever encountered. I've included the last page in the book I sent you with this letter. Just in case you're interested.

Yours, always,
Phyllis

August 12, 1964

Dearest Rosa, who will never read this, to whom I will never send this, unless you change your mind again one day. You have before, so I have a morsel of hope, just enough of it to keep in the hollow space under my tongue where it works to keep the bitterness away.

But oh, do I feel bitter. I suppose it doesn't matter whether I tell you. You'll never read this. So there. I <u>am</u> bitter and still very hurt and angry, all these years later, at that trick you pulled after Mother found the books. We got the first one in Portland on that freshman-sophomore field trip, remember? And you, pretending like you'd never seen them, like we didn't read them voraciously together, like you (you!) didn't write to the publisher and order more, like we didn't do all that we did in the toolshed and my bedroom and yours and under the bleachers that one wicked and risky time when we almost got caught. You were there every bit as much as me, but you denied denied denied while Mother beat me like she never had before, not just a slap or a spank but the real thing, with one of Papa's belts, until I remembered I was as big as she was and got up, still crying, and wrested the blasted thing away and threatened to whip her right back. Did word of that ever get out? Or did Papa keep mum like always? Mother certainly wouldn't have told. Not that I believe for one minute that she was ashamed of what she did.

Now you're settled in the grand state of California with a family, and me? I've been here, alone, with you my one tie to a time of happiness. The brave face I've usually worn in my letters was for your benefit, you see. I didn't want you to worry. But I guess you stopped worrying about me a long time ago.

Yours, still, for some reason,

Phyllis

P.S. Because of that ridiculous and tiny measure of hope I still taste, I'll keep these pages. My fantasy is that one day you'll want to hear from me, you'll remember you love me still, and you'll want to know me again and what I've been through.

September 13, 1964

Dear Rosa,

It's been harder to write knowing that I'll never mail these. I'm no good at keeping a diary, and that's what this seems to amount to now. So I'm trying to think of it differently. I'm imagining these are time capsules to be launched into the future, the opposite of the man in that <u>Twilight Zone</u> episode who travels into his own past. Maybe one day <u>I</u> will want to read all this, even if you don't.

Irony of ironies, I've kept seeing Dr. Iverson after all . . . although I really will stop soon. When I missed my appointment two weeks in a row in August, Alice telephoned and left a concerned message with my landlord, who must have gotten the wrong idea because he grumbled that he wouldn't have people calling at all hours to collect unpaid bills. Anyway, after that, I went back. But the more I go the more I realize that it's really to see Alice and work up the nerve to ask her more about <u>The Ladder</u> and how she heard of it and whether she, too, is a lesbian (she must be, right?) and how she knew about me. I've read and reread the issue she gave me so many times that it's getting quite fragile . . . But she's behaved just the same since that day, so I have too. I keep my sessions with Dr. Iverson but haven't told him that I don't believe I can get better.

Or maybe the truth is that I don't want to anymore.

Today was my day off and it was sunny and not too cold, so I decided to take myself out and make the best of it. I went downtown and had lunch and coffee and a fat slice of pie and watched the other diners and imagined things about them. There was one little girl who reminded me of myself when I was that age. Her hair was very short, and I wondered if her mother, too, had insisted on shearing her like a sheep because of lice. I hated Mother so much that summer, which is funny now, because looking at the girl's head all I could think of was how lovely the back of her neck must feel when the wind blows. She was with a big family, and she'd gotten up and was walking in circles around their chairs, running her fingers over the wooden slats on the backs. When an adult smiled at her she'd smile back, but when they turned away, she stuck her tongue out at them. She caught my eye once while she was doing it, and so I put mine out, too, and she looked away as if disgusted. She must've thought me quite old, really, whereas I looked at her and felt like it's been no time at all since I was a child.

After lunch, I went to Filene's and walked around looking at the clothes and the shoppers. I felt pretty fancy being there. I've been thrifty and buying my clothes secondhand mostly, but I decided today that I could afford something new, like trousers. Maybe I'll buy jeans soon. Finally. Can you believe I've been living away from Mother for over three years and still hear her voice in my head? She hated jeans so much, wouldn't even let me try them on, and yours never fit me of course because you're so tall and lean and I'm not. Mother hated when I wore pants of any sort, really. As soon as I grew breasts, she decided I needed to be <u>womanly</u>.

So yes, her voice is still there, but it's fading, if slowly. Quicker in the last few months, since I got the magazine. The woman on the cover looks so normal, almost like a doll, brunette and long-lashed and smiling. She looks like she could be anyone. That she's a lesbian (there's an interview with her inside) is marvelous. If she is, any woman could be. And the articles! They're all about the stereotypes about us (most of which I didn't even know . . .), the prejudice we face, and even medical professionals who believe there's nothing wrong with us at all. There's also news from all sorts of places, New York, Philadelphia, San Francisco, Ontario, about homosexuals standing up for their rights, or trying to.

Anyway. At the store, I wandered into the men's section. I walked along the rows of vests and blazers, some with collars, some collarless. I felt the fabrics—wool, wool blend, rayon, camel hair. The colors were beautiful, too, wood brown and forest green and pollen yellow, cream and onyx. I stayed in the row of pants quite a while, looking at the slim-fit plain weave options. On the other side of the room were suit jackets, vests, cummerbunds, some with jewel-bright linings. I don't think I've ever spent so long in a department store willingly. I kept looking at the mannequins and how dashing they made the clothes look on their wooden frames, no actual men inside.

One of the things Dr. Iverson wanted me to do is watch men when I'm out and about and try to identify what I might find pleasing about them. I've tried, I really have, but usually all I end up doing is looking at their clothes. Polo shirts, single-pleat pants, blue and red and green on the young college men, who also wear a lot of white. Then there are the men in suits with narrow ties and bright socks peeking out from under the somber black or brown suit pants. The clothes themselves are so dapper, unfussy, not to mention comfortable, or at least they look as if they are, and they drape differently than women's. Can a person lust for clothing without desiring the person wearing it?

(Dr. Iverson hasn't been impressed with this cataloging. He asked sarcastically if I was looking to change my career and become a seamstress. I know he was trying to goad me into working harder, but instead I spent the rest of that session thinking about an intergalactic seamstress who travels from planet to planet, dressing the wealthiest and most powerful people, all the while listening to their conversations and memorizing what she can about their homes and reporting back to a group of outlaws who steal from the rich. I'm thinking of trying to work this seamstress into my next Fiona Bridges story. She'd make a formidable foe, I think, and it would be fun to have Fiona square off against another woman.)

Anyway, I guess I was in the men's section a little too long or maybe was wearing an especially befuddled expression, because a broad-faced bespectacled salesman came over to talk to me and asked if he could help. I noticed him glancing at my hands, which must have been to see if I had a wedding band, because then he asked, "A gift for your boyfriend, maybe?"

I almost said no but then realized he'd offered me the perfect cover. So I said yes, and he asked for my boyfriend's measurements. I was trying to come up with an excuse for not having them when I had a flash of inspiration.

"Promise not to laugh?" I asked him. He became very solemn and said he wouldn't. "Well, he's bashful about buying himself nice clothes because he's not very tall, you see. He's actually just my height, and really, he's about my size, only without, you know . . ." I gestured at my chest, feeling every inch of the wire around my ribs.

The salesman was very nice, and showed me some things, and I jotted down the sizes in my notebook and pretended I was going to consult with my "boyfriend" about the options.

Finally, I thanked him and said I'd try to persuade my "boyfriend" to come try things on. I felt bad about wasting the salesman's time, though, so I decided to buy one thing . . . just one, so I could help him make a sale, you know. I chose a beautiful red tie (quite pricey for such a small piece of cloth!) for my "boyfriend" and walked with the salesman to the register. (I'll have to buy pants, women's pants I mean, another day . . . I forgot all about trying to find some.)

At the next till, I noticed the most wonderfully, brightly dressed man, hair grease-darkened and golden. He was gawdy but impeccable, cuff links burnished and catching the light, shoes black and white and gleaming too. His pants were checkered yellow and black, and his shirt was a fabulous blood orange. He had three large boxes piled in front of him, while his clerk folded a moss-green jacket into a fourth and then lifted two more boxes from the floor.

The man said to charge it all, as usual, to a Mister L-something (Lubovitch? Lebowitz? In that region, anyway). I was trying hard not to stare, but I was completely flabbergasted. Imagine buying so many clothes and not even needing to pay for them. Unless he was the Mr. L himself, but he wouldn't refer to himself in the third person, would he? The clerk wondered if Mr. L wanted the clothes delivered to the Beacon Hill or country house, and right around then my own salesman had to get my attention because I was listening so hard that I hadn't noticed it was time to pay.

I spotted the well-dressed shopper again as I was leaving, talking to a young man who looked like a student from Cambridge (there's a <u>look</u>, you see), his collar popped cockily, his penny loafers brand new and shiny. They both laughed and shook hands, and then the blond walked off, swinging the one bag he'd taken with him from the store.

I'm not sure what got into me, but something about his air, about the large sunglasses he pulled out of an inside pocket and put on, the way he kept that bag jauntily moving . . . It wasn't that I found him attractive, not the way Dr. Iverson would consider it, but he did attract me. So I decided to follow him. It was my day off, so why not?

He ambled for ten or fifteen minutes, and I kept needing to stop at shop windows to give him time to get ahead of me. Finally, he reached what I supposed was his destination, a narrow bar with a blacked-out window and a neon sign with its name, Sporters. I'd come this far, so why not go one step farther? I slipped in after him.

It was dim, and for a moment I couldn't see much after the brightness outside, but there wasn't a lot to see. The walls were brick with dark wood paneling, the bar made of the same dark wood. It smelled clean, of lemon soap as well as beer and some sharp cologne. The radio was on, playing a jazzy tune I didn't recognize.

In the gloom, I heard "You lost, miss?" and I think it was the bartender. It couldn't have been the blond man, because he was sitting on a barstool with his back to me, facing an older man with big cheeks and thick red lips, whom I noticed only because he stared at me for a long moment. Then he told the bartender to leave me alone and bring him and Randy their drinks already. I was nervous that Randy would look behind him and realize I'd followed him, and then what would I do? But no, he only moved to light a cigarette.

I sat at the bar as well, turned half toward the door, just in case Randy did look over, and ordered a beer. The bartender looked at me skeptically, which I assumed was because I seemed young. Or perhaps it was because there were only men there. I wondered why none of them had dates. Perhaps it was because of the early hour.

My spine was tingling, and I couldn't figure out why, but then I remembered the last time I was in a bar where I'd been so outnumbered by men was with Cote, where I met that nasty cad who tried to take me to a motel. I finally put the pieces together: I was sitting in a bar frequented by homosexuals! Male ones, I mean. The bar Cote took me to must have been similar. I had been in a gay bar with him then, yes, and just my luck that I met maybe the only other person there who was as clueless as I was! And a rotten one at that!

I drank my beer quickly, feeling tickled and rueful over my newfound understanding, and then went home, just a little bit tipsy. I sat on the stoop of my building and cadged a cigarette off Sam, an elderly Jew who's always going on about boxing and the decline of labor unions. He asked why I looked so pensive. Whether it was the alcohol, the nicotine, or sheer madness, I don't know, but I asked whether he'd ever met a homosexual before.

He got this look on his face, like he was trying to puzzle me out, and then said, "Why, sure I have." I asked him when and who, and he asked me if I was the vice police or something, which made me laugh. Then he told me that his best friend in the war (by which he meant World War I, mind you—he's quite old) lives in Nevada with a man. They're just like husband and wife, he said.

"Did you know he was a homosexual when you first met?" I asked him.

"No," Sam said, then rubbed his jaw and added, "but then again, I don't think he did either."

I may not have many friends in this dratted city, but I have been blessed with good neighbors.

I so wish you could read this, Rosa.

Yours, always, if only in my own memory,

Phyllis

8

Now

———

When the Archivist finally finishes checking the transcriptions of all the letters in the first folder in Phyllis's box, they lean back and sigh, satisfied. It's been nearly three months of stolen moments during which they've come to feel close to this lonely woman. They pull the second folder out of her box and leaf through it, reminding themself of what's there. They leave the typewritten material again and pull out the yellow legal pad pages, which they take to the large scanner.

They place each piece of paper on the glass surface, close the lid, press a button, open the lid, take the sheet off, and repeat. The academic who had reached out about Phyllis finally wrote again and told the Archivist that he'd gone in a different direction and didn't need her materials after all. It riled them up all over again, and they keenly felt snubbed on her behalf. Yet they were grateful. Without the academic's original interest, they might have never had reason to pull Box 23-G out from the stacks.

This doesn't always happen. It's rare, in fact, that the Archivist becomes attached to the research subjects of others. This time, for whatever reason, the scholar's ultimate lack of interest in Phyllis Egerton has spurred the Archivist to greater zeal. They're only scratching the surface, aware that they'll know far more about her once they've finished methodically combing through the bits of her life she left behind, and yet the Archivist already wants her to be a household name. They want there to be a plaque outside the room she used to rent. They want a lecture series dedicated to her life, or a documentary made about her, or at least a wonderfully fat biography.

At the same time, they want to keep her all to themself, to be the keeper of her secrets and the holder of her heart's desires. Which is exactly what they already are, they realize.

Many of the subjects whose writing and belongings are housed in the archive never knew, during their lifetimes, that they would have a profound effect on others. Sometimes, when the Archivist feels the tragedy of this in their bones, they go into the stacks and sit amid the boxes, weeping. Today they ache with the unfulfilled, unfulfillable desire to tell Phyllis how special she was.

And then everything changed. This is where my heart truly breaks for them, not to mention becomes infuriated on their behalf. Still, I have to recognize that without their story's power, without them, who knows what my own childhood confession of strangeness would have wrought. If my narrative had no precedent, if the other kids and I were the first to see what we said we saw—would we all have been condemned to a psych ward, that realm of medicalized madness?

Then again, if there was no precedent, no cultural narrative, would we have seen anything in the first place?

I have no answers. I likely never will.

From the beginning, the couple had shared what happened with others sparingly. Their experience was theirs alone only for the span of a few hours before the wife called her sister or talked to her tenants. But up to this point, they made choices about whom to share the experience with, whom to trust, and even if people were to talk, and people always talk—gossip is a version of storytelling, as timeless as language—it was never loudly enough to interfere with either his or her employment or community ties.

Until the story was no longer theirs.

Before it was wrested away from them, a scene of tranquility, a moment of respite:

The year started out well. On New Year's Day, they went ice-skating, which the husband was better at, although neither was very good, and he and his wife fell over each other and laughed, eventually buying paper cups of cocoa at the stand nearby. They watched her nieces, who had come along, elegantly blading across the thick ice in arcs and figure eights. He drove the girls home afterward, and his wife sat in the back with the eldest while the younger was permitted to sit on the bench seat beside him because she had asked to. He regaled them all with a story about his sons trying and failing to teach him how to roller-skate. The little girl next to him seemed to be trying to imitate her older sister, throwing her head back and exposing her throat in a way that, on a woman, might be seen as flirtatious, but which, on a girl, and this was true of her older sister as well, read as an affectation, a bit of theater. He was reminded of his younger son also copying the elder one, who likely also mimicked other, older boys and men. He tried to recall whether he had ever tried to consciously sound more mature than he was to someone he looked up to and realized that of course he had, even as an adult, certainly when he was in the army. Perhaps it was natural, he thought as the density of houses decreased and the fields multiplied and grew larger in between, for a person to emulate those he admired, or, at least, those he believed that others admired.

After dropping the girls off, his wife moved to the front and watched her hometown receding in the side mirror with a belly full of warm. It had been a good day. She babbled, as she knew she was wont to do, about how much the girls enjoyed themselves.

It was a new moon, and there was nothing twinkling above or below other than the snow where the car's headlights illuminated it, nothing shining other than the chrome of the occasional car rolling toward them, nothing glowing but the orange orbs of streetlamps when they got closer to town.

· · ·

If only it were always thus.

Even though they were both feeling better, less anxious, they kept in touch with the psychiatrist, confused, ultimately, about whether the esteemed doctor could confirm what they now believed had occurred, having learned it from their own mouths, their own hypnotized voices. The psychiatrist had reassured them, early on, that those under hypnosis would not lie, which they understood to mean that whatever was said in that state was God's honest truth. But that was not quite right, the psychiatrist corrected: truth did not mean fact; so even if they were telling the truth as they saw and understood it, it did not mean this truth was objectively factual.

This hedging frustrated the husband, who had deeply disliked hearing his own voice unmanned by such violent tears. He was hoping the emotion yielded a truth he could hold on to, sink his teeth into. His wife also wished the psychiatrist had been clearer on this matter, and, more importantly, wished that now, after everything they had confessed, the scientific man could put a stamp of approval on their whole experience. But she was less distraught by the psychiatrist's flimsy remark that nothing could be entirely ruled out and that everything was, theoretically, possible. That was enough endorsement for her.

The psychiatrist, however, would not delude the couple by openly validating their version of events. He was comfortable saying that, while sightings of UFOs were common enough these days—so common that even he had seen one with his own two entirely objective eyes—still, the abduction scenario was highly unlikely. If it really had occurred, then it was somewhere specific, and as they had not found the place where they were taken, it was more probable that they had fallen asleep on the road, and that the events they remembered were the result of vivid dreams.

But after all the worrying, after seven months of weekly sessions, after letting their minds open to the psychiatrist's methods, after hearing themselves on tape sobbing uncontrollably and as terrified as they could not remember being ever, even once, during their waking life—after all that, neither she nor he could believe that what they had come to recall was not real, not true, not factual.

So began a new wave of weekend drives into the White Mountains.

.   .   .

In other ways, the year was better than the last, and, at first, even with those drives, they were able to put their capture, for the most part, out of their minds, and focus on the things that mattered instead: family, community, church, civil rights.

The husband's transfer had finally been approved and he would begin working as a mail carrier again in September. He was looking forward to it, to the change in pace, to being able to sleep during the night like most ordinary citizens did, and, too, to the exercise he would be getting without any extra effort or time commitment on his part, exercise that his doctor kept encouraging him to do more of. His wife, meanwhile, was eager to share a bed with her husband on a regular basis.

The couple spent winter weekends writing to their correspondents, organizing food drives with their church, and participating in other civic duties, for he was still working with the state's antipoverty program, and, when the season turned and the flowers in Fuller Gardens began to bloom and the maple sugar shacks opened, he received some welcome, flattering news: he was being appointed to the State Advisory Committee to the U.S. Commission on Civil Rights. His wife was terribly proud of him for receiving this recognition, and he turned bashful whenever she told others about it, although he was secretly rather pleased.

All was as peaceful as could be for two hardworking adults with the occasional health issue. And then the journalist called.

The journalist, it must be said, did not have an unusual interest in them in particular. He had been on the UFO beat at his newspaper for some time. I keep forgetting, in my hyperfocus on the married couple, that flying saucer sightings were really very common at this time. Only a year or so before, a farmer in New York had claimed that small men had emerged from a silvery craft to ask him about soil samples and fertilizer before returning to their humming, exhaustless ship and taking off.

There was something in the air, quite literally. Perhaps it was all the lead in the gasoline, or maybe the Red Scare and the wars the United States kept fighting on foreign shores were getting to people. Maybe it was the space race that brought it all about, the idea that mankind could reach the moon, if only via NASA or the Soviet space program. It could have been a symptom of mass hysteria caused by any or all the above factors.

And maybe, just maybe, there really were strange craft flying through the night skies, whether earthly and military and secret, or extraterrestrial, or, as some hypothesize, interdimensional. But whatever the reason

for people seeing what they saw in the night skies, the fact is that they did.
A great many of them did.

It is not surprising, therefore, that journalists were interested in this
phenomenon. Consider the myriad angles they could take! "Air Force
Probe: Canyon Ferry Mystery Flying Objects Still Unsolved"; "'It Went
Zzzzt,' Sergeant Notes in Police Log"; "UFOs Still Flying, Says Saucer
Editor"; "Flying Saucer Seen 1,000 Years Ago." An Arkansas columnist
bemoaned, tongue in cheek, the good old days of early postwar flying saucer
sightings, "when citizens knew their place in the national structure and
there was no nonsense about equal rights, demonstrations in the streets,
wars on poverty, automation, wall-to-wall mink, moon landings, Venus
shots, medical help for the aged, classroom shortages, juvenile delinquency,
'goulash communism,' de Gaulle intransigence, or magic wrinkle remov-
ers for both sexes." An editor's note on a half-page article, complete with
photograph, in a California newspaper explained that although they
"assigned a team to take a new approach to the current rash of saucer
stories," the "assignment went to our whimsical Britisher" and so urged
readers "not to take the resulting story and picture seriously."

UFOs were useful at filling column inches.

So while I am not particularly sympathetic to the journalist, I am
trying to rein in my own bitterness and not cast him as the villain.

I am trying, too, to remind myself that the reporters who captured my
classmates' and my exuberance after seeing something that awed us, and
even the documentarian who hounded me for months, trying to get me to
speak on camera—all of them, too, were just doing their job.

The husband woke up late that afternoon. Still groggy, he stepped out
to retrieve the mail and sorted through it at the kitchen table: catalogues,
which he set aside for his wife; a check from the tenants upstairs; a letter
to his wife from one of the air force majors she corresponded with.

The phone rang, and the voice on the other end asked whether he was
who he was and he confirmed, warily, and asked who was speaking, please.

The journalist introduced himself, his tone measured and distant, and
began to explain that he was writing a newspaper story about the couple's
UFO sighting and subsequent experience and hoped to have their cooperation. The journalist had gotten hold of tapes of the couple's talk at the

UFO study group in 1963 and learned that they had undergone hypnotic therapy. Until that moment, the husband had no knowledge of any such recording, nor did he understand how the journalist learned of their psychiatric treatment. The journalist then suggested visiting the couple on so-and-so a date and such and such a time in order to interview them.

It was this last that set the husband's quiet rage in motion. Curtly, he told the journalist that he and his wife had no interest in meeting, hung up the phone, and began to pace, hands clutched tightly behind his back. The gumption! The presumption! The journalist—the word burned like acid in his mind, corrosive—not only called out of the blue with a startling pronouncement, the intent to write about them, which neither he nor she had consented to, but also then—then!—simply announced the time and day of a visitation that, again, they had not consented to, and expected them to agree? To wait around for the intrusion of their privacy? For that, he was sure, was what would occur, what was already occurring.

Still, it was not the surprise it might have been. Some weeks ago, a friend mentioned that a journalist had contacted her, asking questions about the couple, but as nothing else had followed, the husband had let himself believe the matter was over.

Some corner of his mind that had always known this day might come breathed a sigh of relief that, finally, it was happening, what he had long dreaded, which meant that now he no longer had to live in fear of public attention. Or, so far, the threat of it. But the relief was minuscule and quickly overwhelmed by a wave of foreboding. He did not often give in to pessimism, containing as he did that particularly American sense of attainability, of possibility, of good things being always just right around the next bend in life's long road, but in this moment he despaired. Of course this would happen now, now that he had finally begun to move on, convinced that while his wife might keep indulging her interest in the matter, writing to the various majors and engineers and retired colonels whose acquaintance they had made during the last few years, he, at least, would be done with aliens and spaceships. He still believed in what he now knew had happened, bizarre as it was, but wished to put it away, to seal it in a box in the attic of his mind, from whence he could retrieve it on occasion, could blow the dust off the lid, go through the contents at his leisure but only—only!—when he freely chose to.

When she arrived home, she knew at once that her husband was in a bad mood, for he was sitting at the kitchen table with a full ashtray in front of him. She reminded him as she struggled to pull the key out of the sticky lock that the doctor had ordered him to moderate his smoking or else his ulcers would surely return. He sucked his teeth, irritated, and told her his ulcer was going to come back anyway, now that they were about to become a laughingstock.

She put her purse down with some force, annoyance rising. Her day had been difficult and her throat hurt as it often did, for she was prone to strep and long-lasting colds. She told her husband that if he could not explain himself then he might as well hurry up and go to work because she was not in the frame of mind to play guessing games. So he explained, more tired than angry now, about the call. At first, still standing and clutching the back of a wooden chair, she was excited; attention, in her experience, tended to equal validation, which she craved, though she was not entirely aware of the grip that desire had on her. Yet as she listened, she became frustrated too. This journalist, who did not know them from Adam, wished to write about their private, personal experience, and he had bothered to call them only now, after he had already spoken to other people, including some they knew. What information did the journalist already have? How could they know it was accurate?

The chair legs screeched against the floor as she pulled it out and sat down heavily, feeling every inch of her nearly forty-six years. Her hip ached from the hour spent holding a toddler during a family visit—the boy's blue eyes had stared solemnly into her face as if she might have the answer to why his diaper was wet—and her eyes were tired from paperwork. And now, this. She reached for her husband's hand and told him they would fix this; they would do their best. Besides, she added, she was the one who carried their calendars, social and civic and professional, in her head and she knew they would not be free on the day the journalist planned to arrive anyway. It was the weekend they would be driving to New York to see her adopted stepson and his wife, who were flying in from Japan for a few days.

. . .

The journalist spent the summer months more or less successfully contacting their friends, family, and experts they had spoken to. After finding the couple not at home the day he visited, the journalist sent a letter suggesting another date, which they refused as well. It was then that the husband consulted with lawyers, who said unless the psychiatrist had breached confidentiality in the process, which the esteemed doctor denied doing, there was nothing to be done until after the article came out, and even then they could sue only if there was a clear case of defamation.

So they tried to put it out of their minds.

.   .   .

Previous Labor Day weekends had been times of relative ease, spent outside in someone's backyard or in downtown Portsmouth to celebrate the waning summer and the imminence of the beautiful New England autumn. This year's found the couple back in their car, her parents following with a travel trailer. The day was warm and bright, and the husband had his window rolled down, the breeze tickling his neck pleasantly, while his wife kept hers shut, not wishing to muss up her recently done hair.

Nothing was the same as it had been that night. It was daytime, of course, and the weather was so much warmer, and whereas they had been alone then, they now had family nearby, not to mention Labor Day traffic. Also, the little dog was not with them, for it was ill again.

So the husband was surprised by a chill running down his back when he turned onto Route 3 and then onto Route 175. He had driven these roads countless times before and could not say what was different, only that he knew it was, that something was coming to him. The wife touched his arm, and when he glanced over he knew she felt it too. She spoke softly, tense, and told him to look out for a gravel road to the right. How had they never remembered this before? How had they not realized that it was right here the whole time? No matter. They were here now. They would find the place.

The radio turned staticky, and they exchanged another look. Her skin prickled, her sparse arm hair standing to attention, and she pointed—there, there it was, the gravel road. He turned, downshifted to first, slowed, stopped. Here it was indeed, the place where they had encountered the beings in the road. The trees and their foliage looked nearly the same as they must have that night, for it was the same season. In fact, they were only two weeks from the fourth anniversary of the event, which felt significant. Was there someone out there, they wondered, that had allowed them to find the place now? It felt impossible that after driving these roads for so long, it could be merely random chance.

He pulled over, got out, and she followed suit. While he stepped into the trees and looked up, breathing shallow and quick, she waited for her parents to stop and park too. When they had, she told them that this was it, where it had happened. Her father blinked slowly and nodded, face grave and concerned. Her mother looked scared, alert, eyes darting around as if the beings might emerge from behind any tree.

Although it had never occurred to her to be grateful to her parents for believing her, she did not want, now, to stretch their belief too far by showing them what might be an entirely ordinary trail in the woods, so she asked them to wait while she and her husband investigated a little bit more. Her father said that was fine and turned the radio up. The car filled with brass and piano, a big band jazz piece.

She went back to their own car and turned it on again, even as her husband waited impatiently among the trees, to see whether the static had gone away; it had not. Their radio was not working. Her parents' was. Her heart raced.

Together, they walked down what was barely a path, trampled enough to allow them only narrow passage through the underbrush. Maybe it was a deer track. Maybe it was the wrong spot. Maybe—

But they both knew, even before they reached the strange clearing, strange because there were no trees here, and the ground was covered in a beachy kind of sand that was entirely out of place in the middle of the New Hampshire woods. Their eyes feasted on the reality around them, the place different in daylight but nevertheless recognizable to them both, even to him, who had peeked out from behind his fearful and dissociating lids only a couple of times as he was dragged down the path to the clearing and up the ramp to the craft.

They had found it, the place where they had been taken, and any last traces of doubt they had harbored vanished. What a relief, she thought. Thank goodness, he thought.

> *The discovery came just in time, fortifying them for what was to come, although they did not yet know it. I wish they had been able to find comfort in the new knowledge and leave it at that.*
>
> *Eventually, they would use it as a piece of evidence, one among many, that what happened to them was real. <u>Evidence</u> is not quite the word I'd use to describe an internal sensation, a certainty that can only ever be poorly translated into language from the inexpressibility of intuition and memory. But they and many others did refer to these things as evidence, which is a shame, I think, as instead of bolstering their credibility, it obfuscates it. Imagine, for instance, a child telling you that she's eaten the last cookie, and she knows it's the last cookie because she couldn't reach any deeper into the jar. She presents, as evidence, the crumbs on her lips. But the crumbs prove only that she's eaten a cookie, experienced its flavor and texture in her mouth. There is no proof, until you open the jar, whether it is or is not the last cookie. And, unfortunately, the jar marked <u>Encounters with Extraterrestrial Beings</u> is still on a counter far out of our reach, and it is someone or something else dispensing its cookies to a select few. Besides, the jar's label is only one of several; another label on the same jar might read <u>Collective Unconscious</u> or <u>Dimensional Distortion</u> or <u>Government Conspiracy</u> or <u>Spiritual Realities</u> or, or, or.*
>
> *All of which is to say that this moment would not have needed to stand up to public scrutiny if they had not been outed.*

They were just settling into their new routine as a familiar autumn chill blanketed Portsmouth. The husband was now carrying mail in rural New Hampshire, and she was trying out new recipes. They went out to dinner during the week, just because they could, and both attended evening meetings with the various groups they belonged to, meetings that she had gone to alone before or, more often, had neglected to attend entirely, for it was too easy to choose to stay in with the telephone and television when her husband was absent.

In late October, pumpkins sitting atop stoops and in windows, glorious red and orange leaves falling off the trees and littering the streets, he came home from work to find a gaggle of people standing in front of the house. When he neared, he realized those on the sidewalk were spillover from the group on the lawn. His lawn. As he turned into his driveway, which had been kept clear, he saw the men—they were nearly all men—jostling each other, pointing at the car, at him, notebooks in their hands, and tape recorders.

As soon as he opened the car door, they leaped forward, not quite touching him but pushing each other to try to get as near as they could. They were asking what the little green men were like, what the saucer looked like, whether he had flown in it, whether he thought they were going to invade, whether he feared for his life, what message he wanted to give the Americans from the extraterrestrials, whether it might have all been a dream, whether his family had a history of mental illness or defect, whether he was telling the truth, what did he think, what did he feel, what were they like, what was it like.

He pushed through the voices and the bodies they emerged from, head down, concentrating on the tips of his brown shoes, which could, he thought vaguely, use a polish, as they moved along the trampled grass, which would need a trim soon, toward the porch, which was scuffed and dirty from the excess foot traffic, toward the screen door, which he opened, yanking his keys out of his pocket so that they snagged on a thread. He looked up only when he turned to shut the door behind him, and heard his name, his name, his name repeated over and over again. As the door closed and the volume receded, he felt, for a split second, just as he had that night: like a rabbit over whom the shadow of a hawk has just passed, hoping that if he was still enough, he would not get eaten.

But it was only a moment, and as soon as it passed, he was all business, making telephone calls and trying to figure out what on earth had happened, and when, and how they knew the things they had shouted at him about.

. . .

It was the same when she left her office later, except that she was ready for it, her husband having told her what had happened, and what she was likely to face. The article had finally come out, he told her on the phone, the details tumbling out of him. Worse, it was only the first in a five-part series, and there would be a new piece coming out every day that week. She did the math and chuckled, said that it was a shame Halloween was on a Sunday this year. The timing was so obvious, so dismissive, so insulting: their experience, she suspected, was to be the spooky stuff of ghost stories, fascinating and evocative but not taken seriously, nor considered credible.

He told her that their tenants would track down a copy of the paper, that he had instructed her family and his not to talk to any journalists, that he was going to phone the lawyers again, and when she hung up, her boss stuck her head round the door to tell her that there were reporters crowding in front of the building.

So she left from the back, although some of them had suspected she would do just that and were waiting for her there. She refused to speak to anyone, as her husband recommended, but when she peeled out of the parking lot with more verve than strictly necessary, she felt her belly clench around a little squeal of excitement. Nothing like this had ever happened to her before, and it seemed she was collecting such events, firsts and onlys. She was worried, but there was also something a bit thrilling about it. She patted her hair as she neared the house, preparing to be mobbed again.

So it started. The couple's entrance into public life. My details might be off at times, here and elsewhere, my imagination running away from me, facts getting muddled in my rush to tell the story . . . In other words, I know I'm getting some things wrong, much like the journalist did.

Here are some things I know he misrepresented: he wrote that the couple's sessions with the doctor took place over nearly a year rather than approximately seven months; he made it seem as if the tapes he had acquired, in which she described her dreams, were recordings of recent events, rather than recollections made over two years prior; he gave the sense that she was passing her dreams off as actual experiences, when in fact, at the time the tapes were made, she had only suspected that they might reflect something that really happened, but had no confirmation yet. He did fairly present the couple as being ordinary, responsible citizens, but regardless, no matter how kind the portrait, it was incomplete and conveyed without their consent.

I wonder: Am I any different from him? I'm not entirely sure.

But I do know this: their story has been out there for many years now, has been turned over and over, their words and motives questioned and picked through and, on more than one occasion, ridiculed. I have always felt drawn to those who are ridiculed, misunderstood, shamed, and since I learned of them and their experience, I haven't been able to stop thinking about it. I had to imagine my way into it, into them, as a way of ridding myself of the obsession.

And here we are.

9

Now
___

Spring heats and humidifies into summer, and the hairless cat starts showing up in the Archivist's room. The neighbor, "Ava," must be leaving her window open more often; she, like the Archivist, has no AC unit blocking her access to the fire escape. The Archivist doesn't mind. They have always found comfort in living things that cannot communicate in words. They've long kept a few plants huddled around their room and are often moving them from shadowy corners to the windowsill or outside to get their necessary doses of sun. Even though keeping utilitarian herb gardens is in vogue, none of the Archivist's greenery is edible. They prefer to care for leaves and vines and flowering succulents that simply exist without serving an obvious human purpose. They talk sometimes to these tender growing beings, and now, whenever the cat twines his way into their room, they find themself talking to him as well. He is a fair listener but seems to prefer communicating his own wishes to the Archivist, asking with his movements and reactions to be touched just so. They oblige, and he quickly becomes a semiregular reading buddy, sprawling on their belly and chest for hours at a time.

There is a stack of books on their bedside table now, some recommendations from the documentary producer, whose politeness and patience and professed interest in the Archivist's life has continued to wear away at their resolve to distance themself from the project. The titles reveal their continued obsession: histories of the UFO phenomenon, memoirs about alien abduction experiences, two studies of abductees written by the very Yale psychiatrist who interviewed the Archivist after the Slopeside incident. The cat, all skin and fine hair and wormy tail, purrs when the Archivist reads him passages aloud, which they take to be an expression of his curiosity. Or, perhaps, his enjoyment at feeling the Archivist's voice rumble beneath him.

Pets have never been part of the Archivist's adulthood. Their mother had been excellent with animals, fallen in love with the most neglected ones, the oldest or ugliest ones. When they had stable places to live, she always fed the neighborhood strays, and when she had a job or was with a man who had a job, she fostered elderly dogs that no one wanted and took care of them until they died. The Archivist learned not to get attached, to recognize their mother's projects as doomed from the start. Too many of the outdoor animals disappeared or got run over, while the indoor pets were sure to become sicker, smellier, wheezier, sadder, until their mother took them to the vet to be put down. Even worse was when she didn't, when the Archivist got up in the morning or returned from school to find a stiff, lonely corpse huddled in a corner.

Birds were the one exception to her animal-loving magnanimity. Once, when they were living on the seventh floor of a rundown building whose elevator was nearly always broken, a fat pigeon nested on the bedroom windowsill. Its neck was shimmery, either green or purple, depending on what angle the Archivist tilted their head, just like the holographic stickers everyone had on their notebooks that year. They would put crumbs on the ledge when the pigeon was away and wait for her to come back and eat them. But a few weeks later, their mother, in one of her dark moods, claimed that pigeons were dirty and carried diseases. She opened the window, spooked the pigeon out of her nest, picked up the mess of twigs and leaves and gum wrappers along with the eggs nestled inside, and shoved it all off the ledge. It landed on the dry beige lawn below, eggshells strewn about. The Archivist went into one of their spells after that and didn't talk for several days.

Speechlessness is not a symptom associated with alien abduction, the Archivist has learned, nor are any of the other curiosities marking their childhood and adolescence, like the lengthy bouts of dreaminess, the dissociation from their mysteriously aching body. As for the aching body itself, they do wonder, now. Some people suffer strange illnesses following abductions, and others speculate that some sort of extraterrestrial radiation or chemical is to blame. Could the Archivist's genes have been affected? Could the mutation that disorders their tissue have been triggered or switched on somehow? Their research has, so far, given them no answers, no clear insight into the black hole that is the Slopeside experience. But then again, they weren't abducted, were they?

—No, they tell the cat on their chest, I just communed with an alien, or something.

The cat, happy to be communed with, purrs.

January 12, 1965

Dear Rosa,

I've put off writing you so many times in favor of lying in bed, miserable or bored, or reading one SF pulp after another, or going to the bar and drinking enough beer to make me sleepy while watching the other patrons, or, all too rarely, working on my stories. And now that I've finally decided to write to you—or me in the future—again, I find myself wanting to write everything down, all my thoughts, all my feelings, so that if I die tomorrow, there will be something left of me.

It's an awful feeling, Rosa, to sit alone at night and count on one hand the number of people who would care if you vanished from the earth. I think there's really only two now: Papa and Mr. Cote. Everyone else I know might spare me a thought, but they probably wouldn't mourn, exactly. I imagine Dr. Iverson would miss the curiosity of me, Molly would wonder why I stopped writing her, my colleagues would miss my excellent work (as would Cote, of course, but he'd also miss me), and my landlord would miss the rent. But the people who really care for me in this world are vanishingly few.

I never imagined, when I ran off, how difficult it would be to move in the world all alone. I had dreams that you'd join me, you know. I never told you, because I wanted you to think of it yourself. In hindsight I clearly overestimated what was between us and never realized how easily you could sever yourself from me.

The tie I bought in September is still draped over the closet door. It's beautiful, the red so bold. Sometimes I imagine it's been dyed in blood, although I'm not sure whose. Maybe Mother's. Or my dead siblings'. Or my own menstrual blood, that ridiculous bother that's meant to cement my womanhood, my childbearing abilities. Yet what child will I ever have, the way I am?

(I must write many more stories, Rosa. Future Phyllis. Books as well, and publish them too. I am determined.)

Papa never taught me how to tie a tie because he barely ever needed one. He had one black tie, for church. He kept the knot in it, hung it on a doorknob during the rest of the week. Once a year or so Mother would insist on washing it, and then he'd make a new knot, I suppose, but I never saw him at it.

I pretend to wear mine. I tie it in a sort of bow around my neck, which I hide under my blouse collar, and try to set it on my chest the way that men wear them, and I admire myself in the mirror. But the blouse is all wrong, the collar too round, the fabric too soft.

Next to me right now is a stamped and sealed envelope addressed to The Ladder with my five dollars inside for a subscription. I'm really going to mail it this week. It's a new year, and I've decided to be brave.

So brave that I finally "broke up" with Dr. Iverson. A few weeks ago, I had a fit in his office and started crying. I told him about the magazine (not who gave it to me, of course) and the tie and the bar and how I've been looking at women more than ever, wondering about each whether she might be . . . or she . . . or her. There's freedom in that kind of wondering. It makes me feel less horrid, less aberrant. The doctor tried to be kind, but he wasn't pleased with my disclosures. He must have thought we were making progress; I'd been talking more about home and Mother and work and my ambitions. But the progress, if we may call it that, was in quite the other direction.

He theorized that because I know it isn't the natural order of things to love another woman as a woman myself, I am instead beginning to harbor delusions of becoming a man by dressing like one. His logic goes that, as a man, I would be able to make love to a woman quite naturally.

I'd never thought about it like that before, and we talked about it some more that week and the following several. Is it possible for a woman to become a man? I once pretended it could be, in that story I wrote eons ago, the one I sent to you and shouldn't have, as it was my only clean copy and the earlier scribbles are in one of the mess of notebooks I have piled beside my little kitchen table. (I've rather given up on eating there . . . I usually eat standing at the sink, looking at the sky outside, or else I sit on the sofa and listen to the radio. Living alone does get one out of the habit of table manners.)

I'm not sure that Dr. I. is right, anyhow. Sometimes I do wish to be a man, and then I think, doesn't any woman, really? How could we not when men have the freedoms they have? But perhaps that's not quite the same. Whatever the truth of the matter, I wasn't interested in talking to the doctor about it anymore.

But I did want to keep talking to Alice. So just before Christmas, I told Dr. Iverson that I was finished. Just imagine: I sat there, very calmly, back straight, and told him that I didn't think my desires would ever change and that I no longer wanted them to. Once I started talking, I couldn't stop. I told him I felt most sick in his office, that when I'm out and about and living my life in between sessions I feel sad sometimes and angry and even hopeless some particularly lonely days, but I don't feel ill. My desires may be unconventional but not evil. Desire may at times be harmful, sure—but what harm does it do anyone if I wish to be with a woman? Is there a dearth of women? No. There is not.

I kept talking. I told Dr. I. everything on my mind that I'd never talked about for fear of him giving me some new diagnostic that would make me feel more ashamed or abnormal. He looked rather stunned, I must say, and as I went on a small smile played across his face. Finally, when my torrent of words dried up, he wished me great luck in life and said that although he was disappointed to see me go before we completed our work, his door was always open. At first, I thought that against all odds he might have been proud of me, but then I remembered how often he's pushed me to try hypnosis again, and I can't help but wonder whether he has a professional interest in curing homosexuals and if he's rather hoping that I'll be so miserable without his help that I'm sure to come back.

No matter. I'm through and won't step foot in his office ever again.

On my way out, I dawdled, pretending to look for something in my purse, and Alice, bless her, took the hint and waved in the patient who was waiting. Once we were alone, I told her I wasn't coming back.

"Well, that's wonderful news," she said.

I didn't know what to say. We just looked at each other for a long, long moment, and the radio played "I want to hold your hand . . ." (I've heard nothing but this song for months on end, I swear), and I felt a thrill of excitement. Before I lost my nerve I asked if she'd like to get a drink. It felt like the grown-up thing to say, somehow.

"I can't tonight," she said, "and tomorrow I'm traveling to Pennsylvania for Christmas. How about after the New Year? I'll phone you—I have your number." She smiled a little cheekily—of course she had it, and my address, from the forms I filled out when I started treatment.

I spent Christmas with Cote and some other so-called holiday orphans at the office. We had to work, of course, but we drank champagne and ate pie and had a merry time. But I couldn't stop thinking about Alice, whether she'd really phone.

And—she did! We're going to meet this Friday! At the Charles Playhouse!

I'm all abuzz and in better spirits than I've been in a while. I should try to write something intelligent rather than all this blather. If only I could figure out the last little bit of this story I've been slowly writing, another Fiona Bridges one. The editor at F&SF has sent two more kind rejections, and I know I'm getting closer. He said in the last one that he did like Fiona quite a lot as a protagonist. I think this is the one.

Yours, always,
Phyllis

P.S. Phyllis, old girl, this is becoming rather awkward, don't you think? She hasn't written and she likely never will, no matter how much you wish to hear from her, to know what her little boy is like, how she's getting on. You want to know whether she misses you, and it seems clear that she doesn't.

January 16, 1965

Dear Rosa,

If I were really writing to <u>you</u>, I don't think I'd dare tell you any of what occurred last night.

Maybe it's good, then, that you're little more than a memory, a phantom of a girl I used to know.

Anyway.

Since my last lackluster date with a perfectly nice man (whom I offended by dodging his kiss), I haven't been out on the town on a Friday evening. But last night felt like a welcome and beckoning sort of thing, and I was full of energy when I left my apartment. It was cold, of course, and still is—I'm wearing two heavy sweaters right now—but it was beautiful out regardless, some trees still wrapped in string lights, houses bedecked with now-outdated Christmas decorations. There were plenty of people about, mostly students just back from wherever they went for their holiday break. I ambled from the T to the brick of the Charles Playhouse, walking slower than I usually would, savoring the Friday night mood swirling around me.

Alice wasn't there yet, so I looked at the vivid red poster for the show that's on at the moment, <u>She Loves Me</u>, a musical comedy. I've seen it advertised all over but have no clue what it's about. The poster depicts a woman being held by a strapping man so I'm sure it's a love story, but I imagined it as something else entirely: a woman who becomes weightless, floating the way astronauts are said to do in space, and the hijinks she gets up to. Maybe it's about what's-her-name, Tereshkova, the first woman who went to space! Probably not, though.

I was just getting quite anxious with the waiting when a redheaded man in a fedora and nice suit said my name and held his arm out. I was so surprised that I just put my arm in his before figuring out who it was.

"Alice?" I whispered.

"That's right. But it's Alec tonight, please."

As we walked toward the Playhouse entrance, I looked at the stranger holding my arm whose face was subtly different from Alice's: there was a slender mustache above unpainted lips, the eyebrows were thicker and darker, the voice deeper. She—he? Is Alec just Alice dressed up or someone else entirely? I still don't know how to parse it out.

I asked if we were going to the play, trying to keep my voice steady. I can't describe exactly what I felt seeing Alice, Alec, this way. Some part of it was envy, I think, at the wonderful cut of the clothes, but it wasn't just that. I've always found Alice very beautiful, but it wasn't quite that either. There was a rightness to us, I felt—this woman who was also a man holding on to my arm, me, a woman who sometimes wishes to be manly too. Like we were both—woman, man—and neither at the same time. Which sounds ridiculous, doesn't it?

Well. I just know I was happy, really and truly happy, for the first time in what felt like a long, long while.

Alec was chattering about She Loves Me, which he'd seen, and pointing out the architectural beauty of the lobby, none of which I took in properly. Then he led me down the long, wide stairs. My elation was dwindling, and I was getting very scared. It was illegal, what we were doing. Or rather, what Alice was doing, being Alec. She could get arrested for wearing the clothes he was wearing if anyone discovered her. Him.

Downstairs, Alec ushered me into a nightclub or cabaret. (I'm not sure which, having never been to either.) There were round little tables with two or three chairs gathered at each, and it was quiet, mostly, except for a black man in a tuxedo who was playing a quiet, tender something on the piano.

"It's quiet now, but it won't be later," Alec said. "What's your pleasure?" He sat down across from me, and everything about him seemed different now. I'd seen Alice only in the office, wearing heels

and tight dresses, puttering at her desk or standing to make tea. I
didn't know how she moved in any other situation. Maybe she was
always like this, but it was hard to see how she could be. Alec sat with
his whole body open, looking strong but also languid, like a panther.

"My pleasure? You mean, to drink?" I asked, probably entirely
doe-eyed and flushed. I was scared, still, certain we'd need to flee at
any moment. I'm not entirely ignorant. I know what the vice police
can do, have read the articles about those who get arrested at bars
or clubs, jailed. On top of that they're humiliated, their names and
addresses printed so their family, friends, employers, landlords,
everyone finds out. I didn't want that to happen to Alice-Alec, or to
me for that matter, although I don't know what vice does to those
accompanying the cross-dressed . . .

Alec noticed my trembling. "It's safe tonight, doll," he said.
"We usually know when raids are coming. At least, I do. I have my
sources. Besides, it's much too empty for it to be worth their while.
If they're going to go to the trouble of sending their men to the
Charles, it won't be until after eleven, probably later."

I wasn't entirely reassured, but it's hard to remember that terror
now, in the light of day, when all I can conjure up is the rush of the
evening as a whole.

I didn't know what to say, so I asked about Alec's mustache,
whether it was real hair, and he caressed it and said, with a smirk
and a twinkle in his eye, "Of course. Hair of the wealthy, from the
best barbershop's sweepings." (I'm not sure if that was a joke or not.)

"I'll have a beer, if they've got them," I told him, finally
remembering what his original question had been.

"Very butch," he said, and I blushed at that, too, as he waved a
waiter over. "A beer for the lady, please, and a vodka martini for me,
with a twist, and hold the vermouth."

When the waiter was gone, I felt a little braver and asked, "Isn't
that just vodka in a martini glass?"

"Oh, hush, don't ruin my fun. Now. Why did you decide to stop
treatment?"

"I just don't think he can help me," I told Alec. "Why do you work
for him? You know he thinks I'm sick, for . . . for liking women."

Alec seemed to know all about it. "He's a psychiatrist," he said, as if this was all the explanation necessary. "I work for him because . . . well, believe it or not, I was a bit like you, once. I wasn't so young, but I was alone."

I waited, wanting to hear more, and when he said it was a long story, I told him it didn't matter, that I had all night. Then I wondered if that was rude and was on the verge of apologizing when he squared his shoulders and heaved a big sigh, and began.

Alice is from Georgia, which I knew. What I didn't know is that she has a son there. I could tell this was painful to discuss. Her whole face got tight and lost Alec's brash confidence, but she pushed through and kept going. She divorced young, which was scandalous enough in her town, but her husband was a mean drunk and she could prove it, so the courts granted her the divorce and folks understood.

After that, she met someone, a widow with her own little boy. She moved in with Alice. Neighbors didn't ask too many questions because they were just two young mothers trying to make do, and making house together made sense. Even their families approved, saying it was good for the boys to grow up with a sibling of sorts. No one knew that Alice and the widow shared a bed.

Everything would have been fine, Alice thought, if her ex-husband hadn't decided to stop drinking, but he did. He joined Alcoholics Anonymous and, I'm quoting Alice here, turned into a "self-righteous prick." He badgered Alice, going to her house, asking her to remarry him. When she told him she never wanted to see him again, he began spying on her and the widow. Somehow— Alice said they must have been careless with the curtains—he managed to take photographs of them. I didn't ask what kind, but clearly they were incriminating. Alice was practically chased out of town with pitchforks.

She sounded so matter of fact. He. "Do you do this often?" I asked him. "Talk to women who . . . to people like me?"

He smiled with all his teeth. "Yes, I suppose so. Many of us do, you know. You probably will one day. Everyone deserves a welcome wagon. We're all too alone as it is."

I asked Alec what happened next, how he got here.

Alice had to leave Georgia, so she took a bus and another bus and another and decided to stop in Boston. She thought there was something wrong with her because everyone had been so, so angry back home. She found work as a waitress and eventually, because she missed her son and wanted to see him again, she sought out Dr. Iverson for treatment, exactly like I did.

"You were a patient?!" I was so surprised my voice squeaked.

Alec smiled and nodded. Alice started seeing Dr. I. and thought for a while that talking to him was helping. She let him hypnotize her and she started remembering all sorts of things about her childhood that she hadn't thought about before, like how she used to be a tomboy, how when her father died she didn't have anyone to go hunting or fishing with anymore, and so she stuck close to her mother and sisters and got used to doing ladylike things.

Finally, when she met a man she liked, Dr. Iverson thought she was cured. His secretary happened to be leaving, and Alice was running out of money because the courts were saying that she had to pay alimony now rather than her husband. So she told the doctor that she was a good typist and he gave her the job.

"Who was the man?" I asked, confused now, thinking I'd gotten it all wrong.

He smiled and said, "Alec." Really, it was another lesbian, a butch Bostonian who taught Alice how she could live as she was, a good life, even, as hard as some parts would be.

We were quiet then for a spell. Finally, I asked about Alice's son, and Alec explained that there was no getting the boy back now, no path toward custody. When he's eighteen, Alice will go see him and find out if he'd like to know her.

When I asked about the widow back in Georgia, Alec's face twitched, his jaw clenching hard. "She's dead," he said, and I didn't dare ask anything else.

Soon the pianist was playing a livelier tune than when we first arrived, and more people showed up. Women and men, some wearing very fancy clothes, others in plainer fare. There were all sorts there, darker folk I thought might be Italians or Spaniards, some more Negroes, and everyone mingled. I noticed a bulging Adam's apple on one tall lady's throat, and several rather short men with baby-smooth faces.

I was dumbstruck, thinking about how most or all of the people here were homosexuals, cross-dressers, people like Alice-Alec, people like me. Men were dancing together, women were dancing with women, and even in the dim light it was a sight to see. So many. So many!!!

Alec said that since I hadn't run screaming yet, there was a party at a friend's house we could go to if I was up for it.

"Up for it?" I asked. "I'm a balloon. I'm all the way up there." Because that's exactly how it felt.

Alec paid for our drinks, a perfect gentleman, and led me out on his arm, and off we went to a party filled with women, a few dressed as men like Alec, but all of us, lesbians. I talked, and I laughed, and I drank rather more than I probably should have. I don't remember a single person's name, but I had such a grand time, asked so many questions (the more I drank the more forward they became), and although I have a stabbing headache this morning, I can't believe my good fortune.

I feel so different, Rosa. I don't know how to describe it but—I feel so different. Maybe it won't last, but I am embracing it for the moment.

Sincerely,
Phyllis

September 17, 1965

Dear Rosa,

I've been thinking a lot about war. About violence in general, I suppose. I should be happy. There's so much to be happy about. And I am! But I don't know how it's possible to experience such bliss while so many horrible things are always happening. Does my working at a newspaper mean anything? Journalism is important, I know, but is it enough? Should I do more? How does one go about trying to do more?

These thoughts never come up at work, where I'm focused on going through sentences with a fine-tooth comb. When the president signed the Voting Rights Act into law, for instance, which was objectively exciting, I felt the same working on that story as I felt proofing the one about the new suspect in the coed murders. I think that was the day I started really thinking about how removed I am. Is it normal? It must be. The reporters and editors are all very matter of fact, and while I imagine they must feel something about their work, they never show it at the office.

I worry, though, that because I'm happy, I'll numb myself to the world even further. I have to keep caring, otherwise I don't know what I'll become.

Maybe I'm having these dark thoughts just because I don't know how to let myself feel joy all the way, because it's been so long since I felt it.

Alice won't stay with me forever, I know that. She's a master at mending hearts and breaking them too. Because I know that our love will end—and perhaps because I already know the pain of that kind of loss—I've already made my peace with it. I try to enjoy the time we have. She's friends with many of her former lovers (and now I'm friends with some of them too!), and so I plan to know her for a good long time. But I won't beg her to stay.

And I won't pine. I refuse to. I've done enough of that for one lifetime, don't you think?

Now I'm in a bad, sad mood. I'm going to go work on a story, something about heartbreak during an intergalactic battle and how such a tiny, personal, selfish tragedy can feel as devastating as the most powerful space guns.

Sincerely,
Phyllis

October 25, 1965

Dear Rosa,

I attended my first protest last Saturday, against the war in Vietnam. I've been thinking about you, too, and your brother, and how different and difficult he was when he came home from Korea. I hope he has found his way. I wish I could ask you about him.

The demonstration was both strange and wondrous. Alice suggested we go, and I'm so glad I agreed. It wasn't very large as such things go, we were reportedly a thousand strong, with several hundred onlookers who joined as we marched from the Common down Mass. Ave. Men came out of bars along the way and shouted at the men among us, about why they weren't doing their duty to their country. I wondered how Alice and I would have felt if we'd dressed as men, the way we sometimes do when we go out (not that I'd dare it in broad daylight). Would we have felt included in those hecklers' remarks?

I am in a philosophical mood today, full of questions that I don't have answers to.

What I really want to tell you about, what I wish I could tell the real you, is that my very first published story appeared in this month's Fantastic! I'm thrilled now, but I had some mixed emotions at first. About six months ago or so—hard to believe it's been that long—Alice began asking to read my stories. She's been as wonderful as you once were about encouraging me. She said I'm talented, that I have a marvelous imagination and way with words. So why didn't I have any stories accepted? Alice thought it must be because I'm a woman, but I'm convinced that's not quite right. It's true that most of the SF writers published are men, but then there's Judith Merril, who now edits The Year's Best SF, and Kate Wilhelm and Leigh Brackett and C. L. Moore and all sorts of other women . . . So then Alice, who is thorough and loves nothing more than a project, began reading my ever-growing trove of magazines whenever she stayed over. She noted, quite correctly, that most of the published stories by women star men. And here I am, writing stories with girls and women as the main characters.

She suggested an experiment. What if I turned Fiona Bridges into Fred Bridges, at least for one story, and sent it to a magazine whose editor hadn't already read my work? I didn't want to, and we had our first real fight about it. Fiona is Fiona! Her sex is a key element of who she is. I remember just how Alice looked at me then, the expression of mock surprise she wears when she's annoyed. She asked me whether my sex was a key element of who I am, and if so, why was it that I, like her, found such pleasure in dressing as a man. I had to admit that I suppose I don't think of my own sex quite so rigidly after all. Alice has shared her tailor with me, a sweet gay man, and has helped me pay for the elements of two suits and a few shirts—and I very much enjoy moving about in the world as a man. Not always—sometimes I still go femme to Alice's butch, but other times we're two men about town, egging each other on when pretty women make eyes at us, never guessing that the object of their desire might not be who they think. It gives us a good laugh to buy these heterosexual women a drink or ask them to dance. Sometimes I worry that this makes us no better than the cads who flippantly bed then leave adoring women . . . But Alice says we're only flirting.

I've gotten off track. I finally agreed to try out Fred Bridges. I had to write a story from scratch though—I couldn't bear the thought of just plopping a man into the action instead of Fiona. So he's his own character, although he looks like her somewhat— he's short for a man and has sandy hair and large, slender hands. Fred's the wayward son of a wealthy family on Titan. He's the eldest of several brothers and is set to inherit the family business one day—a transportation operation that sends shuttles all around the Ring Region—but he's determined to be as disappointing as possible so that his parents designate his younger brother to take over instead. His chief vice is gambling. (Yes, I based this on Alice's sometimes consuming love of the races at Suffolk Downs; not that I can complain! She used some of her winnings to pay for those lovely suits.)

The story starts when he wakes up outside a house of ill repute with a splitting headache and discovers he's been robbed. Miffed, he's about to barge into the house and ask the madam about it when he sees a young woman darting into the alleyway. Thinking she's the one who robbed him, he runs after her, only to find himself in the middle of a confrontation between her and several burly men demanding that she hold up her end of the bargain. The woman cowers and Fred steps in, pretending he knows what it's all about—he and Fiona have their swaggering confidence in common, although hers is a little more feral since she's survived alone in a way he's never had to. The woman plays along, and together they buy her some time. Soon, Fred learns that she's a Secret Carrier, a person whose brain has been altered to allow her to store vast amounts of information that can be unlocked only with specific keywords. She has no name and very little sense of self, for most of her mind, including her past, is locked away; she makes her living by ferrying information among governments and corporations and, unfortunately, crime syndicates. But after a recent blow to the head, her keywords aren't working. Fred helps her, of course, and in the process falls in love.

Well, I sent it in, and it was accepted! Soon I'll get my check, too, the first money I've ever made off my writing. When the editor asked how I wanted my name to appear in the byline, I knew at once what it would be: Phyl S. E. Alice isn't the only one with business savvy! I don't want to turn the boys off from reading my story just because I have a girl's name.

It feels wonderful to finally be published, it does, but I can't help but mourn my Fiona and her adventures.

Alice isn't here tonight, and I'm not at hers either. She was vague about where she was going and so I've spent all evening writing to you, Rosa, trying to remind myself that I really will be all right if and when she leaves me. I have my stories. I have my thoughts and my philosophical questions. I also have friends, now, and I think that even if Alice takes up with someone else, I'll be accepted on my own at the parties and bars we frequent.

Then again, she might be doing something perfectly ordinary. Maybe I'm mad, as mad as those people, Mr. and Mrs. Barney Hill, that Luttrell is publishing that weeklong feature about. They claim they were taken into a flying saucer. Can you imagine? Luttrell's been insufferable about the whole thing, crowing like he's gotten the scoop of the century, but Cote tells me to let him be, that it's good for the paper. It's the week before Halloween, after all, and everyone loves a good, eerie story.

Sincerely,

Phyllis

P.S. For my ideas bank: A story about a couple that gets abducted—but really—and disappears for years and then turns up back on Earth and need to contend with no one believing them?

10

Now

———

The archive is usually a quiet place, sedate, so much of its required work occurring on computer screens or in the stacks. Any excitement brought on by new donations or discoveries within the materials tends to be similarly softly voiced, as if bound by the same hush-hush norms of the main library next door. So the Archivist is as startled as their colleague sitting at the next desk over when they exclaim aloud, first with a slap of palm to forehead, and then with a laugh.

Unable to contain their excitement, they apologize and explain that they've just realized who Phyllis Egerton is, that she's Phyl S. E., the science fiction writer, two of whose books the Archivist discovered in a used bookstore ages ago, a novel and a collection of short stories. They had no idea she was a woman, let alone a lesbian. They haven't read her in some time, not since their obsession with '70s sci-fi a few years back, spurred on, then, by the archive receiving the materials of a different queer sci-fi writer, a famous one, but now they can't wait to go home and find her books. They knew they recognized something in her writing, they knew it. Realizing they've been babbling, the Archivist stops themself, apologizes to their colleague again, and turns back to their screen.

But the colleague asks a follow-up question, and then another, and seems interested in the Archivist's discovery as well. She is a self-described supernerd and collects comic books from the era during which Phyl S. E. was publishing, and she does, after all, work at the archive too.

The Archivist rarely talks to her, or to any of their coworkers for that matter, and they feel foolish, now, that they assumed she wouldn't care. They keep conversing for another few minutes, before each returning to their work. The silence between them feels different now, friendlier. It vibrates gently, their bodies in space newly aware of each other's realness.

Still, the Archivist doesn't share the second revelation: that Phyllis worked at the newspaper that outed the couple as abductees. There's something eerie about the coincidence. If that's what it is. After all, the Archivist did become interested in her and in the abductees simultaneously. They hadn't noted the overlapping time periods, but maybe their unconscious had.

How would their colleague have reacted if they'd mentioned this as well? Revealed the depths of their second obsession? Surely, she would have recoiled. There is a difference between reality and fiction, after all. Between being dedicated to the fantastical within the confines of works of art and becoming increasingly interested in its existence in one's own life. It's a difference their mother was never very good at observing. The notion that the Archivist may be sliding in that direction, too, scares them enough to consider giving up the whole endeavor, accepting that they must have made up a kooky story as a kid and leaving it at that.

Consider it, but not make any hasty decisions.

That weekend, sweating even with their shirt off, the cat sitting in the coolest shady spot in the room rather than on their chest, the Archivist finally feels ready to tackle the book they've been keeping themself from reading too soon, the one published in 1966, the one written with the participation of the first alien abductees.

But before they sit down with it, they finally remember to scour their bookcases for the worn paperbacks by Phyl S. E. They find the collection first, *Egalitaria & Other Stories*. Its cover features a generic illustration of a pale, blue-eyed woman with blond hair peeking out from under the hood of her brown cloak, a tear running down her cheek, her mouth slightly open; in the background, a string of covered wagons winds its way through a barren landscape. The Archivist flips it over, but the back of the book is just a three-sentence excerpt from the title story. Inside, at the end, there are a couple of tear-out order forms for other books in the publisher's science fiction catalogue, and then the briefest of bios: "Phyl S. E. is a science fiction writer living in New England." No photograph.

It takes the Archivist what feels like forever to find the novel, and the cat follows their increasingly frantic rummaging with slitted eyes. They finally discover *Bridges of Titan* under the leg of a crooked footstool that holds a few of their plants. The Archivist feels guilty, as if they've personally wounded Phyllis by using her book this way. The cover has a dented, whitened ring on it from the weight of the stool's leg, and the faded circle obscures the upper half of the person illustrated standing next to a small spaceship. The Archivist can see only the bottom of a jumpsuit and a fishbowl helmet held against the figure's thigh. Is the book about Fiona? Or Fred? They can't remember; they read it years ago. They set both books on their nightstand; they'll get to these at a later date. For now, they dry their neck and underarm sweat with a T-shirt from the laundry hamper and sit down with the abductees' book.

So. What happened then? What happened after the couple's story was first co-opted for entertainment? And it was entertaining, make no mistake: the articles about them do not convey a sense of wonder nor curiosity regarding the potential scientific or existential ramifications. Rather, they seem to ask what might cause two normal, middle-class, middle-aged people to claim abduction and aliens and confusion and trauma.

I wonder, sometimes—what if the couple hadn't been so ordinary? Would their story have even made the news if they'd been a pair of gay men, for instance? Or if both had been Black? What if they'd been young and under the influence of the budding hippie culture, hair long and wild, flower-child style? What if they'd been Asian Americans? Mexican immigrants? What if one had used a wheelchair? Would the story have even been approved by the newspaper's editor? I doubt it. Even if the coverage were approved, it likely wouldn't have gotten a five-day arc.

Maybe the same thing would have happened no matter what—but probably not. Still, I am struck by the fact that race didn't play a larger role in the contemporary discourse about them. Their mixed-race relationship was its own kind of alien; in 1960, the year they married, the U.S. Census recorded just 51,000 Black-white interracial marriages, out of over 40 million married couples total. Moreover, most of those marriages were between a white man and a Black woman. That their racial dynamic wasn't discussed more in the articles about them might have been because there was simply no need; their oddity was obvious to readers of their day.

Yet even now, American ufologists tend to avoid sullying their theories with the realities of inequalities, systemic racism among them, in favor of the claim that looking up at the stars should bring us together, whether in fear or wonder. This makes it easier to ignore all the ways humans continue to hurt one another right here on Earth.

It was January again, cold, and the wife was awoken by the doorbell's harsh chime. She groaned but rose and wrapped herself tightly in her robe. The house was warm, she knew; it was the fever making her shiver.

The reporters had disappeared soon after the first barrage, but strangers turned up on the couple's doorstep unexpectedly now, some trying to peep inside, to see whether there was an alien artifact on display, some sign of obvious madness, or maybe a pile of money proving the husband and wife were getting rich off the attention.

When she saw who it was, she opened the door widely and bid good morning to the new mailman, who was holding a sack in his arms and grinning. He handed it to her, wordless, and she stared, unsure what he meant by it. He laughed and took his cap off, scratching his head in a bashful gesture she thought was put on until he finally explained that the post office had gotten so many letters that he decided to bring a week's worth at once, as it was more convenient. Annoyed, she wondered whether that was even legal, and the mailman, seeing that she was not amused by all this, marshaled his face into a neutral expression. She took the sack, gave him a perfunctory thank you, and shut the door.

Almost immediately she was ashamed of herself. It was not his fault, after all, that people from Europe, Canada, and throughout the United States had been writing letters to her and her husband. Their phone had also been ringing off the hook for weeks, and this morning her husband had been kind enough to remove the receiver from its cradle so that she could sleep peacefully for a few hours. But now she was awake anyway, holding a sack of mail, having just been rude to a perfectly pleasant man who had the same job as her husband, a job she knew could be very unpleasant. Her husband had once told her that for some people, he was the embodiment of that infamous messenger, the one who asks not to be shot. He laughed then and so did she, but they had both known it was no joke. He had been yelled at, faced insults and slurs. Dogs had been sicced on him in malice disguised as jest. But he made the best of it, and those incidents were not so common as to make him truly fear for his life; although maybe he simply thought, as most people do, that nothing would happen to him since he was alive and vibrant now, right now.

She rested her burden on the table and then, feeling reckless, turned the sack upside down and let the letters and postcards stream out and into a pile. Some envelopes slipped off the mound and fell to the chair, to the floor. As she tossed the empty sack onto the counter, she was reminded of that strange day, with the leaves. Who were she and her husband, to be cursed or gifted with this bounty of human interest?

Cursed.

Gifted.

Neither he nor she had quite decided which it was yet. Sometimes they talked long into the night, trying to make sense of it all. They had been so intent for so many years on remaining private citizens, worldly in their way and capable of performing their public duties but not apt to go looking for attention. Now there were people who thought they had, some even in their own circles. At least their friends and family stood by them, even if they, too, were a bit baffled.

.   .   .

Over the coming days, as the most recent of her frequent attacks of strep throat subsided, she combed through the letters. The worst, the ones that called her and her husband terrible, awful names, that accused them of fabrication, of deliberate distraction of the American people in service of a Communist plot, these she tore up into little pieces and threw away. It was satisfying, a release valve for the feelings that arose in her when she read such trash.

The others she began to sort, and it was these she shared with her husband every evening after he got home, while they were having dinner, although she did admit that there were some nastier ones that were not worth his time. He was content to let her weed out the missives that would, he knew, confirm the worst of his anxieties and fears: that some strangers out there thought him mad.

Some of the letters were from children, decorated with stickers and drawings, envelopes addressed in a steadier hand by patient and perhaps amused parents. Others were from very old people expressing their thrill at learning about this new and unique experience and its potential world-altering implications. Quite a few were from radio and TV stations, although most of these communicated first by telephone and only then began writing them—another reason it was in poor taste that the mailman delayed the letters, for the couple had been waiting on confirmations and details about appearances they would soon begin taking part in.

They tried to respond to everyone, especially the children and teen-agers who wrote with the most enthusiasm, sharing their thoughts on the future of space travel and the possibility of meeting beings from another planet. Many admitted they were science fiction fans who now read their magazines and books with fresh eyes, wondering what ele-ments of imagination might turn out to be true. She would recommend books when they asked her to, and he would praise their interest in the sciences and encourage them to continue their schooling so that one day they might help the couple learn what the beings had wanted on that September night.

There were soon too many for the wife to be able to weed out all the mean ones, and when, one evening, her husband encountered several letters in the same vein, asking if the couple were entirely sure they were sober and not under the influence of drugs or alcohol during the experience, he crumpled them up in frustration. He wondered aloud why anyone would believe them when the articles were so fragmentary, so incomplete, when he knew that if he had read the pieces about someone else, he would have scoffed, incredulous.

She rubbed his back, trying to soothe him, but really was enraptured with a sweet boy who had written about winning the science fair at his school after reading a book she had suggested to him a month before and thanking her for her help. Her husband had been repeating some version of this refrain for nearly three months, worrying incessantly over what people must think of him now, even as he claimed, on the other hand, that he did not care because he and she had given it a lot of thought, years, really, and had come to the conclusion that what they spoke of under hypnosis was the only viable explanation.

As far as I can tell, neither husband nor wife ever wrote or spoke on the record about receiving any unpleasant letters. But, if you'll pardon my shift in tone, there's no way in hell that they didn't get hate mail.

Maybe it wasn't much. Maybe in 1966 fewer people bothered to respond to things they disdained as the process of doing so took more effort than thumbing a glass screen or typing on a keyboard. Still. That there was none at all? I can't believe it.

But it was in the wife's nature to focus on the positive, and she surely knew there was no point in indulging the critics with a response.

To tell you what happened next, I need to take you back in time for a moment.

In the fall of 1965, F., a nonfiction author of modest success—he wrote a regular column for a well-regarded magazine as well as features and reviews for other publications—was in the throes of researching his newest topic: UFOs. Specifically, the rash of UFO sightings that had occurred in New England that summer, and which would continue for some time. One of the incidents occurred near Exeter, a town in New Hampshire, and among the witnesses was a police officer, who would, F. likely thought, make an excellent, trustworthy character in a story about such far-fetched things as flying saucers.

A local newspaper editor told F. about a couple in Portsmouth who had also had a sighting, which, like the Exeter incident, involved being followed. Although F. was interested, he did not interview them as he had plenty of other material. Indeed, his first piece on the topic would be published in his regular column in October, after which he would be invited to write a longer piece for another magazine, and, finally, a book expanding on it.

The wife, however, had heard of F. through a contact at one of the local police departments with whom she was acquainted as a social worker. She left a message for F., asking that if he were in her city, he should call on her and her husband.

F. decided to telephone rather than visit, and spoke to the wife briefly. She told him about friends and acquaintances of hers who had also seen UFOs in the southern regions of New Hampshire. These were people who had sought her out specifically, having heard the outlines of her experience through the local grapevine, hoping she would take them seriously. She never said so, though, nor did she speak of her own experience; she merely asked F. about his research so far and shared her information warmly.

F. explained later that he believed she deliberately avoided discussing her own experience, which made perfect sense to him when, soon after his own column had appeared, one of his colleagues at the magazine mailed him the series of articles about the couple and asked whether he was planning on including them in the book he was, by now, working on.

Now, back to the present, to 1966.

It took the wife a few weeks, but she finally persuaded her husband that they should at least write to F., who was already working on a serious book about flying saucers in their area. She reminded him that F. was well respected, a real journalist. She hoped, and her husband finally agreed, that F. might help the couple tell their story in its entirety, from their perspective, including, even focusing on, their own reluctance to believe what they had seen and experienced until they had gone through the sessions with the psychiatrist and begun recovering their lost memories.

While they waited for a reply from F., responding to the letters streaming in became almost a full-time job. They spent evenings and weekends on the endeavor, debating whether it was time to create some kind of form letter, deciding not to just yet, neither of them willing to believe that they were becoming public figures who would never be able to personally respond to all the mail they would get in the coming years. But while they tried, they began to note the increase in a certain kind of manically hopeful letter, wherein the writer asked them in all apparent seriousness whether they had seen other planets and what they had looked like; whether they had flown into space and experienced the loss of gravity and what that had felt like; whether the beings had shared any medical secrets or cures to cancer and other deadly diseases, and if so, would the couple please share their knowledge so as to save the letter writer's grandmother or brother or spouse or child; whether they were Christians, and if so, did they think their experience was a sign that the Second Coming was upon them all; and, perhaps bleakest of all, whether the beings they had met would help save the people of Earth.

Neither he nor she enjoyed this line of questioning, for while they wished they had answers to share, wisdom to impart, they had none, and the weight of people believing they did was becoming too much to bear. They had already spoken at one large gathering soon after the articles had come out, and what had struck them then was the sheer number of people who had shown up, as of course the couple's experience was not the only sighting in the area at the time; after all, F. was writing his book about the multitude of UFOs apparently roving back and forth across New England. Yet so many people had shown up that night at the church in the nearby town that, independently from one another, the husband and wife began to wonder at their intense and instinctive desire for privacy, their wish to be left alone. Was it responsible, really, to keep such an event to themselves, to be stingy with what they knew, little as it might be? Perhaps it was selfish to place the comfort of their personal lives above the right of the public to know that, perhaps, human beings were not alone in the universe.

Finally, after responding to letters upon letters upon letters and after hearing back from F., who expressed his interest in interviewing them at length, they decided to ask him to write a book about that night in 1961 and its fallout, a book that would be the definitive account, from their point of view, and would answer once and for all, they hoped, a great many of the questions they were being asked in one piece of post after another. It was, they believed, the right thing to do.

> *Maybe it was also convenient; once it was written and published they would be able to point interested parties toward the book rather than feeling the awful pressure, self-imposed as it might have been, to respond to each letter individually.*
>
> *Maybe they thought, as a surprising number of people still do, that a book could be lucrative, a way to receive something in return for the public scrutiny they hadn't chosen.*
>
> *And maybe, yes, they even enjoyed some of the attention.*
>
> *So? What of it? If two civil servants, on civil servant salaries, thought they might get a little bit of extra income, maybe even enough*

to splurge on a vacation abroad—well, what exactly is wrong with that, and why should that ruin their credibility or imply that this was their goal all along?

Being flattered by others' interest should also not be so suspicious, yet desire for or enjoyment of attention is something that we so often seem to punish, even as we participate in fame by lending our time and language and money to its vehicles.

Is it too pessimistic to believe that humans both revere and reject those they perceive as more powerful—regardless of whether that power is meaningful or real? Somehow, the couple's accounts always sound more cheerful than mine. Were they hiding their true feelings behind closed doors, amid unrecorded conversations? Did they simply choose to keep any evidence of their fame's misfortune or pain out of their archives?

Or is it me? Am I imagining my way into a different story than the one that occurred?

But I've been honest with you from the very start; no matter what I do, no matter how closely I stick to the facts, this story cannot be entirely theirs.

Once again, they spent long hours with a professional. But this time, they were not paying him; rather, the publisher was paying them all, splitting the advance among the couple, their psychiatrist—who had agreed to take part as long as he had a final say over the manuscript, for he had a reputation to maintain and did not wish to be made a fool of any more than his former patients—and F., who was now furiously working on not one but two books simultaneously.

Sometimes they sat together in the couple's home. Other times they wrote letters back and forth, F. asking about some detail, or the husband or wife remembering something they had left out, left unsaid. Occasionally, they spoke on the phone. They enjoyed one another's company and found it easy to socialize together.

I have no definitive evidence as to whether they liked one another, but they did spend quite a lot of time together, spoke respectfully about one another in letters, and kept in touch even after the book—which is generous, careful, well written, and betrays a certain warmth for its subjects—was published.

At the same time, of course, their roles were likely quite clear, and the couple certainly didn't want F. to write the book if he didn't believe them, or at least allow for the option, as they did, that what they remembered happening had actually happened. And F., for his part, must have known this. Was he simply a shill out to make a buck off the trendy interest in UFOs, like those who have always jumped on the bandwagon of public interest? I don't think so. If money were the aim, I imagine he could have written a more scandalous, more lurid, and certainly more sensational book rather than the quiet, serious narrative presented in the final product.

During one of their first long conversations, the husband attempted to convey to F. just how furiously he had tried <u>not</u> to believe what he now believed. He described how absurd he found it that his wife told her sister and close friends about the strange night and the odd dreams; how elated he was at first when the psychiatrist suggested, as he did many times, that perhaps he had been influenced by her dreams, subsuming them into his own memory, for if that was true, then he could put it all behind him; how it was really only hearing his own voice shaking with terror that had convinced him that the memories slowly returning to his mind were true, and not only true but had also left a psychological mark on him that came through in his extreme anxiety.

F. wondered what that change, from skeptic to believer, had given the husband. The question made him laugh, reminding him of the accusations that he and his wife were getting exactly what they wanted, all this fame and money; a silly notion, as they had not even received the small advance from the publisher yet. As for the fame, it had been mostly uncomfortable, an ill-fitting suit neither wished to wear.

The husband did have an answer for F., though. Learning the truth through the hypnotic sessions with the psychiatrist had a great calming effect on him and his wife, he explained, and they had found that the physical and psychological symptoms of their anxious and uncertain years abated steadily. This relief was certainly the most significant thing they had gained, and in its wake was left a different kind of confusion, one that lent them a new wonder for the world, for its possibilities. They had begun, over the last year or so, to visit the nearby planetarium's lectures on physics, space, and the universe, and were enchanted with what they learned, the vastness and all that was still unknown about it, how very like God, who seemed so much like the cosmos, a mysterious presence that was as yet out of man's reach. But unlike God, technology could change that, he knew, and he found his mind opening to the idea that, perhaps, really, there could be life on other planets, in which case it was still improbable but not impossible that his own experience had been true.

But, he reminded F., he had also tried to consider all other possibilities, such as the craft they saw that night being some secret military asset, whether local or foreign. But if that were the case, then what of the odd examinations? And why were he and she, of all the people in the world, in the country, in the state, why were they chosen as specimens? It made little sense to him that an enemy nation, let alone his own, would find use in examining two ordinary citizens. He was no biologist, of course, no expert on such matters, but he knew all human beings were made of the same organic matter, bled the same, and had similar enough psychologies for a whole field to develop around the many neuroses people apparently had in common. No, he finally realized, there was no other explanation as clear as the one they had come to remember. It was wild and far-fetched when first encountered, yes. But, as his wife often reminded him, only some years ago the idea of a television in nearly every home was far-fetched. Not so long before that, the electric light bulb had yet to be invented. Really, when considering any number of items and comforts he had in his own home, it was easy to recognize how rapidly technology could make the impossible possible. And now, men going to space! Perhaps space had decided, in recognizing humanity's ascent toward the stars, to pay the first cordial visit.

The wife laughed a little bit when she overheard or witnessed her husband speaking this way, with his clear and robust ability to ponder a question from a multitude of angles in order to both create in his audience a sense of appreciation over his consideration of every doubt they might have, and to preemptively negate those doubts by addressing the arguments that could be made against his logic. When he caught her at it, he tugged his ear with some embarrassment. He could see what she was seeing—how readily, now that he believed his own experience and hers as well, he was able to use his rather impressive rhetorical capabilities to defend their truth.

For her part, she felt less need to claim her ambivalence. But then again, she also cared less about being thought hysterical; she was a woman and thus used to it.

She did, however, care very much about making a good impression on the eminent astronomer and consultant for the air force whom she was about to meet, a man whose book she had read early in her UFO research. That book had convinced her that dismissing incredible ideas out of hand was less than scientific; science required rigor, time, and a commitment to following the evidence wherever it led.

> *Naive, perhaps, but my sense is that, in many ways, she was. Well meaning, well intentioned, sincere, and also naive. Science has rarely, if ever, been free of politics, or of outcomes required by someone with more power, even if that power is not necessarily nefarious. Generously, because I try to be, I might say that science is often in the service of well-meaning, well-intentioned, and sincere efforts to do something good in the world—but it has certainly never been free of bias, as we cannot escape that aspect of our humanity, although we can, of course, learn to recognize it and give it weight in our actions, our language, our ethical codes.*
>
> *But she believed in the myth that total objectivity was possible, in the sciences most of all; so many people still do. I don't fault her for it; maybe I even envy it, that comfort of certainty, whatever form it takes.*

She was somewhat nervous but mostly excited when, on a winter evening, she and her husband arrived at their psychiatrist's home, no longer patients but partners collaborating and cooperating with F. on the book. After warmly greeting the psychiatrist, his wife, and F., the couple was introduced to the astronomer. Soon they were in the sitting room, drinks in hand and cigarettes lit, recounting the whole experience yet again.

The astronomer would go on to become one of the most prominent former government officials to criticize the task force investigating the UFO phenomenon, the very task force in whose employ he was at the time of the meeting at the psychiatrist's house. After listening to the couple's account, the astronomer asked them and the psychiatrist to explain the hypnotic process more fully, as well as why they all seemed to trust it so implicitly.

One reason, the astronomer was told, was that the couple was, for whatever reason, incredibly susceptible to hypnosis, which made the astronomer wonder whether the aliens had something to do with that receptivity, if, that is, there truly had been aliens. If the couple's minds really had been wiped by extraterrestrials in some fantastic way—and it was fantastic, he was still a skeptic—then might their minds have been permanently altered, leaving them weakened, vulnerable?

The psychiatrist, whatever else he was doubtful about, could confirm the rare ease with which the couple fell hypnotized. The wife nodded as the psychiatrist explained how, when she and her husband came to listen to the session recordings, she had been paying close attention when the psychiatrist began running the tapes, whereas her husband was still in the midst of conversation with the psychiatrist. When she heard the voice on the tape telling her husband—not even her!—to relax, to sink deeper and deeper, she felt herself beginning to. She tried to move, to stomp her foot so that the men would take notice, but she was unable to. When the psychiatrist uttered the final code word, she went under entirely. A moment later—and it really was only a moment this time—the psychiatrist was waking her up, puzzled, listening as she explained what had happened. It was rare, the astronomer learned, that patients reacted so well to a voice and code word that even a recording could trigger them into a trance, but there was no doubt that the psychiatrist had witnessed this occurring to the wife. The day it happened, the psychiatrist instructed her under hypnosis to react to the code word only when they were face to face.

There was another time—and she spoke up now, for after all it was she who was the rare specimen here, she and her husband, not the psychiatrist. There was another time, only a few weeks ago, when she and her husband had been in this very house for dinner with the psychiatrist and his wife, and the men sat in this room and talked while the women were in the kitchen working on dinner. She speculated that the wine had made her a little bit sleepy, and when, somehow, the code word came up in casual conversation in the next room, she heard the psychiatrist's voice utter it and froze. She could not move. Her eyes closed of their own accord. She was powerless. They had not been face to face, but it had been the psychiatrist's actual voice, not a recording, which her brain must have understood to be enough. Then, as now, she thought it amusing, and she explained how, after this, the psychiatrist conditioned her to a different, less common, code word.

.   .   .

The astronomer listened with interest, but the wife suspected the man was not sure what to think of all this. Her husband's knit eyebrows told her that he, too, believed that the astronomer was unimpressed, and seeing her own fears confirmed in her husband's face, she was about to suggest that they stage a live demonstration when the psychiatrist, also perhaps sensing his guest's doubt, beat her to it.

The psychiatrist explained what he was going to do and how he would prove that the wife's unconscious body physically reacted to the hypnosis. The wife lay on a couch while her husband and the astronomer watched from the one opposite. The psychiatrist pulled up a chair and began to hypnotize her. Then the psychiatrist punctured a vein in her hand with a pin and positioned her arm so that the blood, which was flowing swiftly from the burst vessel, would drip down onto a newspaper placed on the floor.

Deeper and deeper she went into the trance state, and the blood stopped its flow, first to a trickle, then entirely. The psychiatrist pointed out that no pressure had been put on the wound, and it was deliberately below her heart so as to allow circulation to continue unabated. While of course it would not have bled freely forever, the astronomer had to admit that the wound clotted far quicker than expected, a process that could not be consciously controlled, meaning that the psychiatrist must really be tapping into her deepest subconscious, even to her autonomic nervous system.

The astronomer felt rather like clapping, as for a magician's performance, but restrained himself, knowing now that it had been no trick. The rest of the evening passed pleasantly, and by its end, the couple knew they had an ally in the astronomer, this U.S. government employee, a scientist, a skeptic who nevertheless believed they were telling the truth.

I have never found the wife on record expressing concern regarding the psychiatrist's power over her. She spoke only of his ability to hypnotize her easily with eagerness, as if the fact that she could go under so fully proved that she wasn't lying about the abduction, or that what she said in the depth of that trance must be objectively true. The same claim of her hypnotizability was later levied against her as proof of the opposite: that she was not only lying to the public but also had lied to her psychiatrist repeatedly as well, perfecting her act. This reading implies that she and her husband masterminded the whole affair, that they paid for their sessions with the psychiatrist, acted consistently throughout those sessions, kept their lie going until a journalist just happened to come across their story and decided to write about it without their cooperation, and then decided to go on the record with a book that could have easily flopped. All of this implies a great deal of time and effort spent on a gamble that was unlikely to pay off.

As I've mentioned elsewhere, hypnosis is still poorly understood, as is the reason why some people are more easily hypnotizable than others, but it is considered an entirely real phenomenon. Migraines are similar, in that there is no clear cause for them. Some people get them and others don't, but they are still accepted as a very real and debilitating condition by the medical establishment.

Wasn't it potentially debilitating how easily she fell under the psychiatrist's sway? Though she wasn't concerned, I certainly am. I worry about what the psychiatrist might have done to her when she was so entirely at his mercy. Clearly, I am a more suspicious character than she ever was.

In late spring, F. showed the couple the introduction to the manuscript, which had to be turned in very soon. The couple noted the mention of scientists who believed that UFO sightings might be an entirely psychological phenomenon, and if that was so, surely the fact that such a phenomenon was so widespread, shared by so many people, was worthy of taking seriously as well. Perhaps, F. posited, even more seriously than if it was purely physical, strictly realistic.

It was an interesting option to ponder, the couple thought, not that they had much spare time to do so. What had started as an attempt to claim back their story and had turned into an interesting experience in its own right was becoming a chore, and they were beginning to feel less attached to the whole thing, unable to keep their focus so narrowly on this one aspect of their life, concerned as they each were with their jobs, families, friends, their community service and activism.

But they had made a commitment to the publisher, and were under contractual obligation to spend six months to a year in service of the book's success and so had to request leaves of absence from their respective jobs, jobs they would never return to in quite the same way again, although they did not know that then, did not recognize or admit to themselves that this was another step on the road away from their formerly more or less conventional lives.

. . .

Before autumn and its flurry of calls with their publisher's publicity department and reams of letters detailing the stops on their nationwide tour to promote the book, before the summer and its conversations with F. and his editor, before the book was even completed, when it was still spring, they saw their psychiatrist one final time—as patients.

I haven't been able to determine precisely when this session occurred, but it is clearly after the couple had already seen their psychiatrist socially. Somehow, despite this, the man still felt ethically sound in treating them again. Perhaps the ethics were different back then, but isn't that the same thing we say about racism in the 1960s? Or sexism? Or ableism? Or homophobia? "It was different back then." As if that's an excuse. As if, amid it all, there weren't also always people who tried to do the best they could, who tried to learn, who tried to be ethical and humanitarian. But then again, a few good apples don't make it safe to pick one at random from a bushel full of bad ones.

People—some, anyway—in my era say that things are better now. The rate of hunger throughout the world has plummeted, for instance, and crime has steadily gone down for decades. And it's true, too, that some things have stayed the same, even if the language and structure they're dressed in are different.

Today I'm thinking about the young queer person in the future who might stumble across this manuscript in the Queer Writers Archive, whichever form it'll exist in then. Will they think my era worse than theirs, or better? Will they be critical of or nostalgic for it? Probably a bit of both.

I didn't intend to talk about time travel, but I'm reminded of something Phyllis wrote, something about how I, the writer, am both in my present—writing—and in my past—inventing. I exist in the future of that past, much like you exist in the future of my present. Together, then, we are all these things: past, present, future. We exist, existed, will exist. We are everlasting.

The wife felt strange being back in the office again, although she was not particularly anxious at the moment, only fatigued due to her harried schedule.

Once she settled into the chair and closed her eyes, the psychiatrist began the relaxation ritual and, as always, she sank into the mire of her subconscious, full of things both ugly and beautiful that simmered under the surface. Sometimes she wished she could access it on her own, poke and prod around it, a garage sale full of personal ephemera, moth-eaten and forgotten or well loved and preserved.

When the psychiatrist asked her, deep in hypnosis now, how she felt regarding the September 1961 experience, she tried to explain that she had accepted that she had gone through something unusual and miraculous and that she was grateful, as harrowing as it had been, but soon the psychiatrist broke in and asked her directly whether what she called memories might in fact have been dreams, dreams she constructed a narrative around. She said no. When the psychiatrist had first presented this possibility two years ago, she had been relieved, even joyous, at the suggestion, and felt calm for several days, until the upsetting images and sensations from the experience began to emerge, confusing her. She had wanted to believe that these images and sensations were nothing but the dregs of nightmares, but she had never had dreams that lingered and left her haunted during the day, and so in trusting her prior experience, she came to accept that the nightmares had really been her brain's attempt at recovering what happened.

Skeptic that he was regarding alien beings, the psychiatrist was inter-ested not in what she was convinced of but rather in the conviction itself, how it had folded itself into the logical and coherent structure of a healthy, thinking mind. What would possess such an otherwise ordi-nary brain to create this momentary break from reality? Was it possible that convictions required an emotional core rather than evidence and common sense? Of course, to an extent, this was obvious: a soldier diving for cover when a child bounces a ball loudly upstairs is having a kind of emotional reaction—the body, tuned to war, recognizes loud noises as bullets and bombs and defaults to adrenaline-filled hypervigilance. The soldier's conviction that bombs are nigh is based on a reality the soldier once lived through. Where did this woman's conviction stem from? Whatever else the psychiatrist believed, there was no doubt that the couple had been through a trauma of some sort, even if it was one disguised by extraterrestrials.

> *Although F. mentions in his book that both husband and wife attended the session that day, I have not been able to find any record of her own conver-sation with the psychiatrist, only a partial transcript of the husband's. Perhaps her session went a little bit like what I've imagined. Perhaps it was nothing like it at all. Perhaps it didn't even happen.*
> *The husband's, however, did.*

When the psychiatrist placed the husband under hypnosis and asked what he felt about the experience, he said that he felt that he had been abducted. Felt. This was the word the psychiatrist clung to, even though the husband was merely echoing the language used in the question. They wrangled over the word, the psychiatrist's soothing, patient voice trying to excavate from the husband an admission that the abduction had not occurred but was only dreamed up, literally, by his wife. But the husband conveyed, finally, that he was more comfortable saying that he felt rather than knew because he still wished for pure skepticism. As he had explained before, both under hypnosis and while conscious, he hated being accused of something he did not do and knew that people thought he was lying. The psychiatrist asked whether, perhaps, it was possible that he had made it up and not realized it, and the husband replied that it was not, and when the psychiatrist asked why, he became unexpectedly agitated. He started breathing quickly, his body became tense, and he exclaimed that he did not like the way they, by which the psychiatrist assumed he meant the extraterrestrials, had put their hands on him. The psychiatrist instructed him to calm down, but the husband repeated that he did not like them touching him and began to weep. He stopped only when he was brought out of the trance state moments later.

It was clear to the psychiatrist then that no matter what had really occurred, the couple were not about to change their minds, were wholly convinced of what they had discovered in this very office.

When the husband emerged into the waiting room, his wife was concerned to see that he was blowing his nose on his blue-and-orange handkerchief, but he seemed as collected as he usually was, so she decided not to mention the matter.

They both shook the psychiatrist's hand and drove home, discussing not the recent session but rather all the things they hoped to get done that summer, from her ambition to plant flowers in the window boxes to his desire to visit his sons in Philadelphia, and from her plans to help train the newly hired social worker so she could feel secure in her replacement during the imminent leave of absence to his looking forward to dedicating more time to his role on the NAACP's New England regional board.

> *Whatever plans did or did not come to fruition that summer, autumn was upon them all too soon, and with it the book's publication. Because they had not written the book themselves, I imagine they did not suffer the sort of nerves authors report experiencing, but there was surely still an air of trepidation, knowing that their whole lives would be available for purchase by any interested party for just a dollar or two.*
>
> *Well. It wasn't quite their whole lives. F. stuck to the elements of the story most closely related to the couple, knowing well that neither he nor she wanted their families to suffer any needless aggravation or humiliation by the press. Their children are barely mentioned, and certainly not by name, nor is the name of either of their ex-spouses printed. Indeed, even the word <u>anus</u> was removed from the transcript excerpts printed in the book, although who made that choice, I do not know.*

Still, there was plenty in the book that would expose them to ridicule, and they worried that they would be greeted poorly or would be seen as a sideshow. But it was too late to change their minds now.

The first leg of the tour began as soon as the book was published. First, they were on a plane to Chicago to be on a WBKB television show; then off to Los Angeles for two more TV appearances; and then a day full of newspaper interviews during which they sat in the hotel's conference room and answered the same questions over and over again. Soon they followed a script, even though they had not planned one in advance; they merely repeated the same words and explanations so many times that they became memorized, nearly exactly. They had no time to see either Chicago, which was cold and gloomy in November, or Los Angeles, which seemed never to be cold and gloomy at all, for they were booked with events and were exhausted by the end of each day, barely speaking to each other as they went through their morning and night-time rituals of first and last cigarettes, of toothbrushes and washcloths and razors and makeup brushes. Then it was on to San Francisco and several radio and TV station interviews, all in one day, then Denver, and next to Philadelphia, where the husband at least felt at home, in this city he had grown up in, where he still had family. Other than Philly, no place they visited on this first tour felt particularly welcoming, even if most people were kind and few made fun of the couple overtly, although the skepticism was on every host's face, every assistant's smirk. As usual, the wife pretended not to notice anything, and, also as usual, the husband carried himself with dignity. While neither of these tactics worked particularly well to make them feel better, what did tend to lift their spirits were the true believers who approached them after a live audience recording or called in to the radio shows or left letters at their hotels. The sincerity of these believers—who ranged from science buffs to housewives to children to, yes, the occasional eccentric—and the excitement in their faces and voices made it all feel worth it, for nearly every one of them had their own strange tales that made little apparent sense, whether it was a UFO sighting or cattle killed in extreme and strange ways or other unexplained phenomena. It was clear to the couple that their own presence was giving these believers a sort of solace, a reminder that, for some, reality is indeed stranger than fiction, and that there will always be things that human beings do not understand.

Their lives became very different once again, only this time it was, in a way, on their own terms. Was it a relief, to have the change arise, for once, from something they'd chosen? Or was it frustrating, because there was no one outside themselves whom they could hold responsible or question? Then again, perhaps it was neither. It was merely the next in a long series of turns their lives had taken since they first met each other all those years ago and sat in white wicker chairs on the porch of a boardinghouse and talked.

II

Now

The Archivist sits in an uncomfortable metal chair, hips aching and bladder filled to bursting. They've had too much beer. Five small tables have been pushed together to accommodate this large group, and the Archivist is seated at the uneven seam between two tables, one taller than the other, their back against the brick wall, several people on either side of them. They feel trapped, unable to extricate themself without a fuss.

This is another recommendation of the documentary producer's, who said he would try to make it as well but hasn't shown up. The Archivist has finally realized why they keep responding to his emails, why they keep pretending they may agree to his request to film them. It's because he believes their child self so completely, so enthusiastically. He believes them more than the Archivist's mother does, more than the Archivist themself. There is comfort in that.

The event is far too up close and personal for the Archivist, but they are doing their best. The woman on their right is twiggy, birdlike, all elbows and angles and a sharp nose beneath large, dreamy eyes, and she's sweating in the closeness of the bar despite the air-conditioning blasting. Her frenetic energy is contagious, and her gregariousness is clearly appreciated by those in her vicinity who rely on her to maintain the flow of conversation. The Archivist tries to be a good listener, to turn their head toward whomever is talking, raise their eyebrows at the right moments and nod or exclaim when appropriate, but they are finding the performance exhausting, and they can't hear well enough over the music and echoes of other conversations to fully take in what anyone is saying.

When, finally, the woman next to them gets up to go to the bathroom, the Archivist seizes the opportunity and follows as the others slide out of their chairs to accommodate her exit. The leader of the group, a white man so utterly average the Archivist will never remember his features later, who claims not to be a leader but merely a facilitator, catches their hand and shakes it. He asks if they'll be back, adding his second hand to the first, his voice warm, inviting, his gaze sincere. The Archivist tells him they might, wanting it to be true, knowing it to be a lie.

On their way home, still needing to pee because the bar's bathrooms were gendered and the clientele seemed unreliably chill about such things, the Archivist considers their outing, deciding that as uncomfortable as it was, they don't regret making the attempt. If nothing else, the meetup has confirmed their suspicion—that most people whose paths have crossed with extraterrestrials are ultimately quite normal, the obsessive eccentrics among them the exception rather than the rule. There were a couple of those, too, of course, and they took up plenty of space early in the evening, but as time went by and the others shared their experiences in turn, it became clear that most simply wanted companionship, a starting point from which to discover further similarities among them. In other words, the Archivist realizes, what they find in the archive, these people find in one another.

.   .   .

The next morning, the Archivist awakens to big black eyes set in a strange, triangular, and grayish face. For a moment, they leave their body, shock and recognition catapulting their consciousness up and out, but then the cat licks their nose, and they laugh. It is a loud sound, so startling in its own way that the offended cat jumps off their chest to the floor, and one of their roommates knocks on the door to ask if they're okay. They choke out a reassurance and put a finger to their lips to shush the cat. Needlessly; the Archivist has never heard the cat meow, which is good, since one of their roommates is allergic and would be furious to find out there's an animal hanging around.

They hear the neighbor clambering out to the fire escape, and the cat shoots out the Archivist's window at the sound of her voice.

—Oh my god, is that where you've been going, you daft animal? No, Amma, not you, sorry, hang on, lemme call you back.

"Ava" grins at the Archivist, who's leaning out, having halfheartedly followed the cat.

—So you're the one he's cheating on me with?

—It's just an emotional affair, I promise, the Archivist says.

Worried the joke will fall flat, they add that they haven't been feeding him.

—Ah, thank you for that, I think that's the only reason he comes back.

—I've been meaning to tell you he visits me, the Archivist begins, but then isn't sure how to continue, because they haven't told her, and they don't want her to think they're trying to steal her cat or anything.

—It's cool, mate. Now that it's warm he won't freeze to death outside. To be honest I just can't keep this window closed. First it was too nice and now it's so fucking hot. I was meaning to get a screen but then he started practicing being an indoor-outdoor kitty and now I feel like we can't go back. Anyway, I guess I shouldn't try to keep him cooped up. He's his own little guy.

—I get that. Well, I like having him here, he's welcome anytime. He woke me up this morning, actually. I thought for a second he was an alien.

The Archivist isn't sure why they're telling "Ava" this, but she laughs and agrees that he looks like one.

—Don't you, Fitz, don't you look like an itty-bitty alien, "Ava" coos.

—Fitz! That's a good name for a cat.

—Oh yeah, I thought I told you his name when I got him! By the way, what's yours?

The Archivist tells her, and asks what hers is.

—Shalani. Actually, not to be weird, but could we exchange numbers? It seems we're accidentally co-parenting this bugger.

It's a compliment, the idea that they could co-parent anything with anyone, let alone be trusted by a neighbor they barely know. Although, they realize, they want to. They'd like to get to know her. It's not only that her shaved head, luxurious armpit hair, and general vibe read as queer. It's also Shalani's friendliness, how easygoing she is. It keeps surprising them, although it shouldn't, since they really know nothing about her. They were wrong about her name, and maybe even her race. The Archivist is assuming now that she must be South Asian and not Black. Or maybe both? Another assumption. Although "Ava" had felt real to them, Shalani is already much more so.

They hand her their phone, and she puts her number in. They text her so she has theirs, and then tell her they should probably get ready for work, and she says she should probably call her mum back. They wave at each other across the short distance.

For hours after, the Archivist feels a warm glow from the interaction. But something niggles at them, something about the way they woke up to the cat's eyes filling their field of vision. There was something familiar about those pools of darkness.

April 26, 1966

Dear Rosa,

A woman ran in the Boston Marathon last week! Can you believe it? When she was asked whether she did it to make some kind of feminist point, she said she just enjoys running. Just enjoys running! Now there's a heroine for you. If that was true, she wouldn't have run the marathon route itself, right? She could have run 26 miles anywhere, at any time, all on her own. But she didn't. She shoehorned herself into the race with all the men, made her point (that she could run the whole course, that the rule against women running because we're "weaker" is hogwash), and then refused to be painted as some kind of protester. I can only imagine the letters to the editor we'd have gotten if she admitted out loud that she ran to prove women can do it.

She's your age, you know, just a year younger than me. Remember how you always ran with the football team during their warmups, egging them on? The other cheerleaders thought you were flirting too hard. One year you had P.E. right before lunch, and you always got to the cafeteria still in your sweaty gym clothes. None of the other girls did that. They all showered and changed first, but you were always ravenous after running around and playing badminton and climbing ropes and whatever else.

I do wonder now whether you avoided showering with the rest of the girls because you were scared they'd know somehow.

That you were intimate with the female form in a way they weren't. I never worried about that. It honestly never occurred to me. I had you, and it wasn't like I was lusting after anyone else. Yes, I knew we had a secret, and yes, I knew there was something different about us, but I was naive. I thought we'd stay together forever and figure it all out.

It's been so long now, but I still think about you all the time. I think about you whenever I see a tall woman with a long nose and small ears, especially when her hair is in a ponytail, and when I see an advertisement with a cheerleader in it, and when I sit on Kathleen's purple velvet couch because purple was your favorite color, and when I first kissed Alice, and when I first kissed Kathleen, and when I first touched their bodies, because their lips and hips and hair were not like yours.

Pathetic, aren't I? In her sharper moods, Alice agrees. Other times, she says no one forgets their first love.

She's wrong, though. You've forgotten about me, I'm certain of it. Even so, I wish I knew what you were up to these days. I wish I knew what your son was like.

But there are other wishes I have a better chance of fulfilling. Fantastic has taken another story about Fred Bridges, and I decided to introduce Fiona in this one by making her Fred's bastard sister. Her mother took her to the Ring Region to protect her from the shame but also gave Fiona her father's last name, hoping she'd get her due from the wealthy Bridges family one day. Eventually, I want to put Fiona front and center again, but I suppose we'll see.

I've started taking a college correspondence course in magazine journalism! Alice encouraged me to try, since I was always saying I could write better copy than some of our reporters . . . She's left me by now, by the way. I knew she would, but it still stung. And then I had a short rebound with Kathleen, one of Alice's friends, another redhead with pink cheeks. I was mortified to learn that I'm not Alice's first lover to have made the leap from her to Kathleen. It suits Kathleen fine, though, because she's not the settling-down type. At least Kathleen told me from the get-go that we'd have a wonderful but brief affair, and she was right.

It's funny. I never thought I'd be lovers with someone <u>before</u> I was their friend, and now here I am, with two friends I've gone to bed with. There's a kind of intimacy with them; we've seen each other in the most compromising of moments, and now we owe something to one another. I don't mean the way the government says homosexuals are dangerous because they can be blackmailed. (Doesn't <u>everyone</u> have some kind of secret they could be blackmailed with? Kennedy had mistresses, didn't he? No one was worried about <u>him</u> being blackmailed.) What I mean is just that there's a rigidity, a polite barrier that I've experienced with everyone I've tried to be friends with (other than you), and it's not there with either Kathleen or Alice.

Yes, I miss Alice as a lover. I try to avoid her at parties once she's started laying her charm on someone. But that pang is nothing compared to the silence I've endured from you.

Phyllis

June 1, 1966

Dear Rosa,

I am in the process of replacing you. Not as a lover—as a correspondent. I've been scouring <u>Women's Circle</u> for notices that seem like a good fit and sending them letters. So far, only one woman has written back. She lives in Maine and she's very prim and rather dull. She reminds me of Mother. I doubt we'll become good friends. Alas! I'll keep trying to find a worthy pen pal.

Meanwhile, I've been toying with this abduction story. I started it late last year, I think, and I picked it up again recently when I was feeling tired of Titan. The scenes I wrote then were terrible, so I threw them out and I've started again. I'm trying to base the main characters off that couple, Mr. and Mrs. Hill, in that they're middle aged and sort of plain, normal, everyday people who don't have any specialized skill sets or knowledge that would make them good subjects for abduction. But I can't quite tell whether the story wants to be serious or funny. There's plenty of humorous potential: For instance, what if they were abducted only to be put in a little house where they're supposed to go about their lives as usual except the walls are all see-through and they're basically part of an intergalactic zoo? Actually, I could make that same concept terribly tragic. I guess I need to think more about what I really want to say, what questions I want to ask with the story. I'll let it percolate some more. Sometimes I wish I had a little being in my head who could sift through my ideas and tell me which were good and which were bad. You used to help me with that, even though you didn't care much about SF. Oh well.

Phyllis

June 5, 1966

Dear Rosa,

I'm no longer quaking with rage, but I'm still upset and writing to you ("you") seems to soothe me sometimes.

Yesterday, Cote insisted I wait for him. I've been leaving earlier on weekends for a while now, since I actually have places to go and people to see. I didn't have plans with anyone last night, though, so I was happy to wait, and I used the time to sketch out some more ideas about the abduction story. I got so absorbed that Cote had to call my name a couple of times when he was ready to go.

We walked to the pub where we sometimes get lunch, and he asked how my correspondence course was going. (He thinks it's swell that I'm getting a degree . . . He must have figured out at some point that I hadn't been entirely truthful about my credentials but has never brought it up directly.) I told him it was fine, and he said that was good and then clammed up. Usually we have plenty to chat about, but I could tell something was going on with him. Instead of sitting at the bar like we usually do, he motioned me to a corner booth and went to get us drinks. It was noisy. The Red Sox were playing the Yankees and, if the groans were anything to go by, losing. I was almost flattered that Cote wanted to sit so far from the bar, where the television is, since he loves the Red Sox. I should have known that nothing good was going to come out of this conversation.

Cote got a Jack and Coke for himself, which should have been my second warning. Instead, I just ribbed him a bit, asked what had him feeling so frisky. He ignored me and asked a question of his own.

"Are you seeing anyone, Phyllis?"

I was stunned. Never, not once, has Cote asked me anything like that. Plenty of people do—Papa does when I call home (I never know if he's glad or sad when I say no), and it's one of the first questions new girls at work ask. But Cote? Never. All this time, I thought we'd had an agreement, unspoken as it was, because we've both had far too many people at the office comment on our single status or try introducing us to their friends. Cote must know that I know he's gay, right? Even if it took me a lot longer than it should have, I did figure it out.

"No," I told him, "but why?" Only then did I have the horrifying thought that maybe I'd read him all wrong and he was about to ask me out after years of pining.

In retrospect, that might have been better.

"How about I set you up with a good pal of mine?" he asked. I was feeling increasingly confused, and he must have seen it on my face because he lowered his voice. I had to lean forward to hear him say that people have been asking questions.

Apparently, Cote's colleagues think I'm strange. The only women who've worked at the paper as long as I have or longer are married and older, their children half- or full-grown already. The young ones like me leave when they get married, or soon after when they have babies. I've been at the paper nearly five years, and I've never even had a boyfriend. When Cote said "strange," I think what he meant was "suspicious."

"What about you?" I asked him. "What do they think about you being single?"

"I <u>was</u> married," he pointed out. I know he was a long time ago, when he was young, but he never talks about her. "So it's different."

I said it was also because he's a man, and he had the grace not to disagree. If he doesn't marry, people think he's either an unrepentant bachelor or a recluse still broken up over his ex-wife. Either way, no one would ever guess Cote is gay. I've heard him call effeminate men sissies, laughing if someone else says it.

It makes me sick, to be honest, but I can understand why he's doing it. He's Irish Catholic, his family's been in Boston for generations. His divorce was quite the scandal already.

Finally, Cote laid it out: the paper is in trouble, and his bosses need to start thinning out some departments in the next few months. Apparently about half the women are on the chopping block. Having fewer, Cote said, would mean they'd gossip less and get more work done. I wanted to slap him. I like Cote a whole lot, and he gave me a chance when he didn't have to, but sometimes he's just as much of a pig as the rest of them.

My job is more or less safe because Cote's vouched for me, so I asked if maybe I could finally be copy chief. He sort of winced and said that he'd try for the title bump but didn't think he could get me a raise. He said I have bigger things to worry about anyway.

To make absolutely sure I understood what he was trying to tell me, I asked, "So what you're saying is that I should be careful who I associate with?"

"I'm saying," he said, "that whoever you're associating with, you should keep it as quiet and private as you can." He grabbed my hand then and quietly said something to the effect of, "Look, there are Reds and Jews and fairies all over the press, everyone knows it, and they may be more or less tolerated, but that doesn't mean that people can go about flaunting it. This isn't New York. This isn't San Francisco. It's Boston. You hear me, Phyl?"

I heard him, loud and clear, and I wasn't sure if I was more furious or scared. It shouldn't be his or anybody's business who I'm seeing or not seeing. How does that have any bearing on my job? It's ridiculous! I asked why he mentioned setting me up and who this pal of his was, and he blushed. He actually blushed!

"Well, he's . . . he's a good friend, a very good friend, and he's willing to help out, for a while at least. He knows how much it'd mean to me to be able to keep you on."

So Cote has a lover, and he's offering him up as a beard. Cote is the closest thing I've ever had to a big brother, and I know I should be grateful. But I can't help thinking that he wouldn't do more if I were discovered and axed for it. He'd just let me go. It's already happened to me once, being found out by Mother, and that was bad enough. I don't think I could take it if I had to leave and make another new life somewhere else. I don't know if I'd bother, really. Maybe I'd just do what Alice's first lover did.

That's certainly not the outcome I want. But needing to hide and pretend and fear for my livelihood or even my life is exhausting. It really is.

I told Cote I'd think about his offer, and he seemed relieved that I understood. We finished our drinks in silence and then he moved to the bar to watch the game and I went home.

I am thinking about it, and all morning I've been remembering how men at the office have asked me out occasionally, and asked who's keeping me from them when I say no. Do they all suspect I'm a lesbian now? I've also realized Cote's offer isn't entirely selfless. He gets something out of it too: a reason to spend time in public with his "very good friend" and me. His lover could finally meet Cote's colleagues, couldn't he? I'd be just as much Cote's lover's beard as he'd be mine.

I wish he and I could talk about all this openly. Instead of that horrible conversation yesterday, I wish we could have talked about something else, like what that actor, Michael Caine, said about Berlin—about there being transvestite joints all over the place. I would have asked Cote if it was true, since I know he was stationed there when he was in the army, and if he'd visited those clubs and what they were like. I would have asked if he thought I might count as a transvestite, or whether it's only men who dress as women. Maybe if I agree to this arrangement we finally could talk about it—we'd have to, right? I wonder what Cote would think of the fact that the way he calls me Phyl inspired my pen name, which I also use when I'm passing as a man.

Phyllis

August 31, 1966

Dear Rosa,

I just finished reading the second part of The Ladder's evaluation of the apparently widely accepted Bieber study of homosexuality and it was a hoot. I almost skipped the first part last month because it seemed like it'd be so dry, but this Dr. Fluckiger managed to make it fascinating. I feel better than ever now about my decision to leave Dr. Iverson. So many things people say about homosexuals are total bunk.

Be that as it may, things have been hard recently. After what Cote told me, I'm scared. He never asked again about his friend, and I haven't brought it up either. It's almost as if I dreamed that conversation we had nearly three months ago. For weeks, I didn't go out at all, although Kathleen and Alice and a couple of others called and invited me to. Then last week, when I did finally go to a party at Amy's house, all the talk was about a riot in San Francisco. Everyone seems to have a friend or two out in California—I almost chimed in to say I did, too, but of course you don't count—and while we don't have the full story, what we heard is bad enough. Apparently there's a cafeteria that transvestites especially frequent, and other queers, too, and the police have been showing up there so often to harass and arrest people that the regulars had enough and picketed. When the police showed up again, someone threw something at them—no one knows what. I heard one person say it was a donut, another claim it was a cup of coffee, and a third insist it was a handbag with a brick inside it, which sounds like a detail too good to be true. Whatever it was, things got hot after that and no one at the party knew how many people were arrested or what's happened there since, but we were all on edge.

That night when I walked home, I was relieved I'd worn women's jeans and a blouse, that I looked like a woman.

On Sunday, Alice came over because she could tell there was something wrong—I left Amy's early that night, and hadn't been out in ages. When she started asking about what was going on with me, the dam broke. I cried and told her everything about Cote and the paper and how I haven't felt this way since before she gave me The Ladder and I began to believe I wasn't alone. She hugged me, tried to comfort me, reminded me that there are things we can do. Earlier this year she went to a conference in Kansas City where homosexual men and women from all sorts of chapters of DOB and Mattachine and other groups came together to try to create a central organization for us to fight for our rights. I could probably get more politically involved, but the queers in San Francisco tried to stand up for theirs and it doesn't sound like anything changed except some of them got beat up by the pigs and not for the first time.

I hate being afraid. I <u>hate</u> it. I want to be the kind of person who can picket, who can proudly say I AM GAY in public and handle whatever the consequences may be. But I'm a coward, and I've worked so hard to have this independent little life. I'm terrified of losing it.

Though I'm already losing it, aren't I? I'm not going out to the bars, to the Charles, to any parties other than that one at Amy's that left such a bad, sad taste in my mouth. Some days it feels like Mother's voice is creeping back into my head. Every time I call Papa he tells me the same thing, that she's joined the church choir, as if it's the only nice thing he has to say about her. Last week I heard her asking, "Who is it?" and Papa said, "No one, just a salesman," and then told me, "No, thank you," and hung up. It was horrible, hearing her voice, hearing Papa call me "no one." He's ashamed of me, and she's forgotten all about me or is at least glad to pretend I don't exist.

I don't know what I'm going to do, Rosa. I don't know how to get my courage back. I don't want to lose my job, but I don't want to lose the rest of my life either.

One bright spot recently has been my new pen pal, Violet. Her advertisement read: "Small town female scholar seeking female pen pals. Interests include books movies news gardening ladders." I think the last word is a kind of code. I hope I'm right, but even if I'm not, it's been so pleasant having someone to write to who writes back (and who's interesting to boot). She recommends books to me, and I send her articles I think she might enjoy. We've exchanged only a few letters so far but she's definitely the best—and fastest—correspondent I've ever had. She lives alone, like me, and has no children but dotes on a niece and nephew she doesn't see as often as she'd like. Alice thinks she absolutely has to be a lesbian, that

I should just ask her if she's butch or femme, but I told her that was ridiculous, especially now that I'm afraid for my job. Imagine sending that kind of question in writing to someone you don't even know! Alice would have taken the risk, I'm sure . . . I suspect she thinks I'm too quiet and wilting. Maybe that's why she left me.

Anyway. Seems like I can't dwell on anything good for very long tonight. I hope tomorrow will feel different, but I can't imagine why it should.

Phyllis

September 12, 1966

Dear Rosa,

I can't stop thinking about this show I watched at Kathleen's place the other night. She's not a science fiction nut, but she knows I am and that I don't have a TV, and Alice probably told her that I've been depressed. It feels good to be cared for, but I don't know what either of them can say to make things better right now. Alice's job is secure, because Dr. Iverson is too wrapped up in his own world and his patients to take notice of her life, and Kathleen doesn't work. She's married to her best friend from high school, Glen, who is gay as well. He's a lawyer and has family money besides. I'd never met him until the other night, actually, because they live on separate floors in Glen's brownstone. He loves SF, too, so he came to watch the show with us, and we got along famously.

It's called <u>Star Trek</u> and the episode was about this spaceship checking in on a married couple who are the only inhabitants of their planet, but one of them, the woman, was killed by a shapeshifting creature who then took her form. It was groovy. We sat around talking about it awhile. I've always been drawn to the idea of shapeshifting. If I could become something supernatural, that's what I would choose, because then I could be anything. (Kathleen said that's cheating, like asking a genie who grants you three wishes for an endless amount of them.)

Of course, the shapeshifter was killed at the end of the episode and was the last of its kind. Even though it's the villain of the story, I couldn't help but feel for it. How tragic, being the last of a species. It reminded me of Leigh Brackett's <u>Shannach—The Last</u>, which is one of my favorites. The creature in that story, Shannach, does terrible things, including enslaving a whole host of humans whose sole purpose is to enslave <u>another</u> group of people to do their bidding and kill whoever tries to run away. That's partly what I love about it: the villains are victims themselves. Even the ultimate villain, Shannach, is as pathetic as he is evil. I nearly went mad with loneliness in this city, with other human beings all around me, but imagine if I were the last person on Earth? The last Homo sapiens? (A homosexual Homo sapiens, har har har.)

I don't want to feel that kind of desolation again.

I'm not going to be afraid anymore.

No. That's not quite right—I can't help being afraid. But I won't let the fear push me back into the closet. I won't. I won't. I won't. I won't. I won't. I won't. I won't. I won't. I won't. I won't. I won't. I won't.

Phyllis

October 25, 1966

Dear Rosa,

I haven't been able to sleep, so I decided to get up and write you. Me. You. Whatever.

It's been quite a day.

I'm looking at what I wrote last time I sat down with this legal pad, the one that is and isn't a journal. I've finally made good on my promise, I guess—if very belatedly.

I hadn't gone out again until tonight. I mean, I've gotten coffee with Alice a couple of times, and I watch <u>Star Trek</u> with Kathleen and Glen every week now, but I haven't gone to the bars on Tremont, or to dance at the Charles, and I certainly haven't tried passing again. I've been jumpy at work, too, not concentrating like I used to. I finally understand what Mother meant when she said she was suffering from "nerves." Three weeks ago quite a few people were fired, just as Cote told me would happen. I felt guilty that I'd kept my mouth shut, like he'd asked me to, and not warned anyone. I might still be next if I'm not careful.

But then yesterday evening, when I got home from work, there was another letter from Violet, and she asked me if I'd ever read Spring Fire or The Well of Loneliness! I read the latter only last year actually, when Alice was absolutely incensed that I hadn't yet. The point is, it's confirmed. Violet is a lesbian. And she asked how I would feel if she looked me up when she visits Boston for a women's academic conference in January. We exchanged photos so we'd be able to imagine whom we were writing to, and she's beautiful, and we get along so famously in our letters that . . . Well. I'm probably being foolish, but I have a little crush on her.

Say what you will about crushes—and all the love songs do, don't they?—but they apparently make me bold. I wrote a very brief response to Violet just to let her know that I'd be delighted to meet and that I'd respond at greater length soon, and immediately went to put on my dark green suit. I greased my hair, I used mascara to give myself the hint of a five o'clock shadow the way Alice taught me, and I took the letter to Violet and went out. I didn't even look through my peephole into the hallway first, which was foolhardy, but I felt so good that I forgot.

After I slipped the letter into the mailbox, I decided to go to the bar Cote took me to all those years ago in Scollay Square. I wanted to be somewhere so big and packed and full of men that nobody would look at me twice.

I was still uneasy the whole way there, keeping my eyes down, tensing every time I heard laughter, just in case I was the object of mirth. When a pregnant woman got on the T and stared I was certain she saw right through me and would say something awful, but then a man across from me got up and gave her his seat and I realized she'd been expecting me to. A gentleman would have, and I had forgotten to be one!

When I got there, the bar was just as I remembered: crowded, mostly with men who seemed straight as straight can be, some with wedding bands on, drinking alone or in small groups; quite a few sailors in uniform again too; and a smattering of men I'd recognize anywhere as queens.

For a long moment, I stood near the door wondering whether to stay or go, but then someone shoved me on their way inside and I found myself walking through the throng to the darkest corner of the bar and ordering a drink in the low voice I practice at home with my plants.

I just watched how the men moved for a while. Awkwardly, gracefully, shoulders twitching, hands gesturing, looking at one another and then away. A swishier one got up and went to the john with a swagger that was somehow both manly and not. Another, face jowly and lined, downed the rest of his beer and followed, a childish grin spreading across his face. I wished I'd brought my notebook, but men don't carry purses, so where would I have kept it? I need to buy a smaller writing pad that can fit in my jacket's inside pocket.

I drank my first beer fast and quickly ordered another, which was probably inadvisable as I soon had to pee. Because I was passing, I went to the men's.

Although I know by now that gay men tend to socialize quite differently than us lesbians, I was still surprised by how many people were in there, standing at the sinks and leaning on the wall opposite, waiting patiently for a urinal or one of the stalls to open up. There wasn't anything too obvious about it, nothing out in the open, but the glances were there, heads cocking at one another's cocks and some grunting from a stall. I was a bit spooked so I turned to leave, but a smooth-faced young man wearing tight jeans stopped me.

"Don't like what you see?" he asked quietly, breathing into my ear. I didn't know whether to shake my head or nod so I did first one and then the other, resulting in the boy—he was definitely younger than me—laughing quietly. "Oh, honey, are you repressed?"

He put his hand on my back and slowly moved it down, cupping my behind and giving it a little slap. I should have found it enraging—and if a man had done that to me any other time, I would have. But I recognized it as flirtation of a different kind, touch of a different kind, the boundaries of propriety blurring in this space where men sized each other up not for comparative strength but for other forms of compatibility. What really troubled me in that moment was that I was aroused. I could feel myself flushing, and he told me, breathing into my ear again, raising goosebumps all along my body, that there was no need for that, that if I had the dough I could have just what I wanted from him. He called me daddy, and I felt my nipples harden under the Ace bandage binding my breasts down.

But then he made the mistake of lightly touching my face and realizing that my simulated stubble was nothing more than mascara. I saw his expression change and I froze. I didn't know what to do, how to move, what to say. He smiled lightly and whispered to me again, something about how he had a reputation to maintain but he wasn't picky and we could work something out. There was a chill between our bodies now, his seduction skills turned off, and I could think clearly enough to say no thank you but could I buy him a drink over the confusion. I felt bad, as if I'd taken business away from him, and that I should compensate him somehow.

He laughed and looked even younger, and I blushed all over again thinking about how my body responded to him. I'm still confused by it—is it because he was lanky and smooth faced, young enough to have an androgynous look about him? Am I attracted to men after all? Or is it that he whispered that way, breathed on my neck, the way that Alice used to? Was it his body that made me respond? His actions? The way he performed those actions? I don't know. My mind is still whirling.

Anyway, he agreed, said he could use a break, and followed me back to my end of the bar. I bought him a drink and soon we were nattering on famously, as if we were two old friends. He pointed out some of the men and told me their positions rather than their names: Norcross Executive, State Senator, Real Estate Mogul. People give false names here, but some were talkative after, and told him more than they meant to.

He estimated that three quarters of the men who frequented this bar were married, and they were his best customer base. He took my hand to see whether I wore a wedding ring and said he should've figured me out right away, my hands were so small. But he'd been looking at my clothes. "Too nice for this place. I thought you might have money."

That made me laugh, of course, as I certainly do not. "No, I'm just lucky to have a friend with a discount on a good tailor."

"So," he finally asked me when I bought him another drink, "why are you here? Are you spying on your man or something?" I could see the curiosity shining in his eyes, as if I might have a juicy story to share.

I asked whether a person couldn't get a drink these days without being a spy, and he said sure, but that it's not every day you see a male impersonator in a bar like this, and that while he's seen a butch or two in his day, I didn't seem to be quite that. I wasn't wearing any leather, for one. That made me laugh too.

"I'm not butch, exactly," I said. "I like to dress this way sometimes. But I'm not a male impersonator—I mean, I don't perform as one or anything."

He asked whether I made it a habit of coming on to gay men and said that I should be careful if so, because I might make someone mad if he wasn't expecting . . . and he cupped his palms in front of his chest.

"No," I insisted. "I didn't come here for that. I didn't realize what I was walking into there. I just had to piss." (I still had to, but ended up waiting until I got home.)

"Then why?" he pressed me. I stared into my beer, thinking. I was starting to get tipsy, and I wasn't sure whether I should trust this boy, or why he was sitting with me—free booze, I guess—or why he was so curious. Maybe it was that I looked young, like him. Maybe he has sisters. Maybe it was just that he could put aside the role he played for a half hour and rest rather than work. Whatever the reason, I decided to tell him everything, how I came to Boston, tried to "get better" with a shrink then embraced being a lesbian, how I was finally happy, and how a few weeks ago the fear came crashing down on me like iron alligator jaws. He was a good listener, which I might have expected, but I'm always surprised when a man is capable of letting someone else talk.

After that, I wanted to hear his story. I had a million questions, most of them probably rude, so maybe it's good that as soon as I asked, "So what about you?" he told me he'd better get back to work. His eyes were darting around the room already, and I wondered—was there someone there watching him, forcing him to do what he was doing? Or was he watching for signs of wealth on the men coming and going, the better to target his next customer? When he hopped off the stool and turned away from me, I couldn't help it—I caught his shoulder and asked him straight out whether he was going to be okay.

"Listen, sister, don't feel sorry for me. I'm just waiting on a rich enough catch so I can retire in style." He grinned then went to the other end of the bar to chat up a gaunt older man.

That was when I realized I'd never learned his name or told him mine. How had we missed exchanging those?

The whole way home, I thought about what he said. How he wanted to find someone rich enough to allow him to retire in style. How different is that, really, from the girls I knew in high school who planned to marry up? Or the girls at the office who get through one day of work after another, marking time until they can be supported by someone else? Are most people content with transactional, loveless relationships? Or does love grow with the fulfilling of one's needs by another's hand?

I'm still reeling from my own audacious bravery tonight. Whether I've broken through those iron jaws completely, I can't say, but at the very least, I've made an effort.

Besides, I have something to be excited about: Violet visiting. Violet in Boston. Violet, beside me. Violet.

Violet + Phyllis

Phyllis + Violet

All right, Phyllis, old girl, you're getting silly now. Go to bed.

November [unintelligible], 1966

Damn it, this is the closest thing to hand, so I'm writing some notes here in the hopes that I'll remember to transfer them to my notebook tomorrow. (I'm in bed and it's late, and I don't feel like getting up.) I just finished reading <u>The Interrupted Journey</u> by John G. Fuller, and I am no longer as incredulous about the Hills as I once was. I mean, I still don't think that there are flying saucers or aliens running about the countryside, but it's a fascinating case nonetheless. I'm rethinking my whole approach to the story I was trying to write. I'm wondering now whether I should try for something in the style of a nonfiction novel, since Capote has proved how popular that genre can be. I'd make up the whole thing but make it <u>seem</u> like it was based on true events and have those events be an abduction and tests and all that.

COPY THIS TO YOUR NOTEBOOK TOMORROW, PHYLLIS!

Now
———

The Archivist has never been interested in academia, per se, although whether this is due to their beliefs about the problematic nature of ivory towers or their sense of being unworthy of such institutions, they don't know. As a result, they don't recognize that their lengthy exchanges with more and less amateur archivists on various messaging boards constitute a participation in the scholarship of their field.

Among these interlocutors is a middle-aged gay man with whom they regularly email about their interests, thoughts, and discoveries. A professor at a large Midwestern university that is home to the first LGBTQ Studies department in the nation, he welcomes the news that the Archivist has found a pre-Stonewall lesbian science fiction writer to add to the relatively small canon of such women. He suggests that they might begin to document these extraordinary figures, their literary lineage, the themes found in their works, and what is known of their lives. The Archivist is impressed with the professor's belief in their own abilities and doesn't recognize that he is encouraging them to begin the process of writing a book, or at least a scholarly paper, for publication.

It's better that they're oblivious to his implied eventuality; otherwise, the Archivist would surely balk. In their return missive to the professor, they share that they have begun a different kind of writing project, one that attempts to explore the lives of the first alien abductees. What the professor will think of this, they can't say, for they barely know themself why they've embarked on the attempt except that it gives them pleasure, their imagination sparking in ways it hasn't in many years. It has dulled the itch of their own unremembered experience.

Distraction is doubly welcome because of their mother, who seems to have aged very suddenly, the occasional selfies she's begun sending them since she got a new phone marked by skin turned papery and limbs grown skinny. She's been complaining of physical ailments, too, her hips hurting, her back spasming, a cold she hasn't been able to shake. Predictably, she's been blaming a variety of things outside her control. 5G. The COVID-19 vaccine. The Satanists down the street putting something in the drinking water. The government weather machine. Et cetera.

None of these paranoias are particularly new, but the fact that her conditions are of mostly normal proportions is. In the past, she's been convinced that she was ill with a variety of cancers, infected by rare parasites, or poisoned by chemicals of one kind or another. That she's experiencing what may simply be the unremarkable reality of an aging body is unsettling. The Archivist has long been physically larger; they surpassed her in height by the time they started high school, and have certainly broadened in the shoulders and grown more muscle and fat since they last saw her face to face. But they've always felt small and uncertain in her presence, and the notion that she might physically diminish enough to change that is hard to fathom.

They recognize that writing about the abductees, imagining their inner lives, is a way to avoid thinking about their mother. Or about Shalani, whom they texted a couple of weeks ago to see if she wanted to grab a coffee or take a walk, and who said yes and she'd get back to them with a good time but hasn't. Or about the documentary producer, who has promised to introduce them to other Slopeside experiencers, specifically those taking part in his film, but who keeps making excuses for why he hasn't yet. Or about the Archivist's body and its pain, its migraines triggered by the barometric changes that come with summer storms.

What they have not admitted to themself quite yet is that on top of everything else, Phyllis's obscurity and their veneration of her have made them contemplate their own mortality, and what evidence of their existence, if any, they might leave behind.

There are some things I haven't told you. But you knew that, right? In imagining my way in, I'm choosing some details to highlight and dropping others. My memory is fallible, as are the memories behind my various source texts. I hold up what I find most interesting, even if that's not what's most important. Or I hold up what I find important, even if it might be uninteresting to you. We're playing a game, you and I, and while I hold the power in the telling, you hold it in the reading. You get to decide what is or isn't real.

As I write this, I watch a plane fly across the velvety deep blue of the sky, one red light on its left wing, a green light on its right, a bright white glare at the front, and I wonder: How would I explain this to myself if I didn't believe in planes, or was skeptical of them? Because really, when I stop to think about it, it seems pretty impossible, doesn't it? Flying metal tubes? Really? I'm sure that somewhere, someone has come up with a far-fetched notion about how planes really work, about how it's all unreal, a fake, like the moon landing, like birds, like the diseases that have and will continue to plague living beings, one way or another. There is always a conspiracy theory somewhere, about someone, about something. Paul's dead, Avril's been replaced, lizard people.

But the thing is: I know nothing about planes, nor how engines or aerodynamics work. The last time I engaged with the field of physics—other than existing in a world defined by its laws—was in high school, and I got a D+. I don't know how or why planes fly, but I've been in one, and it flew me from one place to another, and I know that many people have worked to make sure that planes will not only fly but also get bigger and become a way to travel around the world to see beloveds, to migrate, to explore new places, to have adventures. If some harms occur along the way—harms to the cultures being reduced to refrigerator magnets, to populations shunted away by wealthy expats, to tourists with no street smarts who are parted from their possessions or senses of selves or even their freedoms, to the climate, to the many civilians killed by the bombs that fall from manned or unmanned flying machines—well, yes, all that is true. Would we rather live in a world where nobody had this option? This is not a question I can answer.

My point is this: I do not believe in conspiracy theories, though I enjoy their occasional creativity (see: rocks are actually liquid); I also do not believe in the grandstanding skeptics who sit atop a pile of merchandise they try to sell to the suspicious and the lost and the contemptuous, nor in the self-righteous believers who more often than not hawk their own trinkets to the susceptible and the searching.

Why do I believe the couple?

I can't answer this either. I just know that I do.

Another January. Another drive, this time to a small town inland from Portsmouth on the invitation of its Board of Trade, Lions, and Kiwanis.

There are many topics the couple could have discussed in the car that day: Edward W. Brooke, the new senator representing Massachusetts, for example, who was the first Black man elected to the U.S. Senate by popular vote; as they thought of Boston as their backyard big city, they were proud of its parent state as well. Thousands of unwashed, long-haired, drugged-up young people, not to mention too many misguided older ones, spending time in a park and calling it a protest of something or other; neither he nor she were really sure of what, but they were both amused by the panic with which some of their contemporaries responded to the event. A Black man being democratically elected in the Bahamas as its prime minister. Three astronauts dying in a fire mere weeks before they were set to attempt to land on the moon. The world was so much bigger than him, than her. A person had only to look at the newspaper, at the sky at night, at the view from a mountaintop to admit how impossible it was to comprehend its vastness.

There they were, silent and small, so finite, inside a metal and plastic and rubber contraption whose internal spark allowed its forward momentum, the trees outside their windows curtained in glinting white as if sequined. There they were, perfectly made in God's image, including all their lumps and moles and receding hairline and thinning locks, including their tempers and temptations, resentments and yearnings. There they were, on their way to speak to an audience of ten dozen or more. The Board of Trade, Lions, and Kiwanis thought they mattered, and so they conceded that they must.

In the restaurant where the meeting was to take place, the couple was greeted warmly and taken to a table set up beside a podium at the far end of the room, closest to the kitchen. The wife sucked her cheeks in so as not to be rude about the horrible orange carpet, the spindly chandeliers that looked like spider legs, the brown wallpaper and its visible seams. She would hold the details firmly in her mind and put her husband at ease on the drive home later by bringing up the decor instead of the interest taken in their stories or her enjoyment of the audience's questions.

By now, their dynamic was set. While in private or among his intimates, the psychiatrist and the journalist included, the husband insisted that he believed what had happened with the beings because he simply could not find another way to explain it to himself, but out in the wider world, he spoke more skeptically, determined to maintain his reputation. He refused to sensationalize. His wife, on the other hand . . . she did not exaggerate or embellish, exactly, for she always spoke the truth as they both understood it, but she was more voluble than he, more prone to open speculation no matter how many times he reminded her that some would take her musings to be reflections of sincere beliefs. She did not care; it was not her fault that some people were a little thick, that others willfully misconstrued her words.

After being introduced, the couple performed their well-practiced routine, taking turns describing what had occurred in 1961, what they had experienced after, how psychiatric hypnosis helped them regain memories they had lost, and where they were now, just two people among a rising tide of those calling for a more open-minded scientific investigation of the UFO phenomenon. The audience was rapt, impressed by just how normal the couple was. They answered questions for a good forty-five minutes and there were still hands waving to be called on when the husband finally put his foot down and reminded the audience that it was a school night, as it were, which elicited chuckles and a shuffling of feet as folks tried to push their chairs back to stand up. As the wife retrieved her purse, she thought again of how ridiculous the interior design was. Heavy oak chairs! On carpet! Imagine! Even the most graceful attendees were struggling not to tip their seats over as they rose.

Outside, several audience members caught up to the couple to share their own sightings and ask their own questions, about whether the sex of the beings on board the craft was apparent, for instance, or whether the couple had seen any other UFOs since 1961. He answered sternly in the negative, and his wife remained silent, nodded at her husband's words without repeating them herself. She always thought his response was rather disingenuous but knew that no matter how many strange orbs of light he had seen over the last few years, he would never admit to them being anything other than tricks of the light, the eye, the imagination, or all three. She knew that it would do no good to either of them to bring up her own sightings, never mind the experiments she had been conducting over the last year or so.

. . .

When they began the drive home, the wife stuck with her decision to make fun of the restaurant's ugliness. But when they both fell silent again, the full darkness shielding the shapes of the Earth with its cloak, she mulled over the past year and change, sifting the events into two distinct and separate containers. It was in her nature to categorize things, even mysteries, her strong belief in all things scientific lending a certain pleasure to organizing and clear thinking that came in handy in the extensive administrative tasks her job required.

The events filed into the first box were those that she and her husband considered unnatural but not necessarily alien. There had been that pile of leaves on the table years back, and then, six weeks or so after the articles exposing the couple were published, further oddities accrued in quick succession. Shortly before Christmas that year, she and he had arrived home to find a large block of ice sitting on the morning newspaper the husband had left on the table before work. The paper was dry; the ice was not melting or dripping at all, was more reminiscent of a glass sculpture, bowl-like, as if tipped out of a bundt cake pan. They both touched it, felt how cold it was, the slight moisture that came away with their fingers smelling like nothing, like clean spring water and their own skin. Finally, the husband picked the block up and put it in the sink, stood there staring ferociously at the ice, willing it to melt, and then swept out of the room to check whether anything else was amiss in the house. She took his place at the sink, hoping, too, that the ice would start to thaw, and was startled when her husband came back in and told her to try the hot water tap. Although it took a good deal longer than it should have, the heat gushing from the spigot eventually did what it must do, if the world still followed the same laws of physics that they knew to define their reality. After, she told her family of the incident but no one else—it was too strange, too senseless, and they had destroyed the only evidence they might have had.

Other strange but not necessarily otherworldly events followed. A year before their talk in the tacky restaurant, they had begun hearing footsteps upstairs, sometimes preceded or followed by the hall steps creaking. They had had no tenants that winter, all the units empty, but every couple of weeks, she would find a light on upstairs, and when she went to turn it off, armed with a heavy candlestick that had belonged to her grandmother, she always discovered that either there was no one there or, spookier somehow, the light had gone off on its own. She also heard the closet doors moving back and forth in their metal railings, as if someone was checking their quality, and water running in short bursts from one apartment and then another. She knew her husband heard these noises as well, but he refused to see them as anything other than slight abnormalities in the realm of the ordinary. The sounds could be caused by a bored teenager who broke in, just to show it was possible to do so without leaving a trace. Maybe a wire had become corroded or crossed in the circuitry, making the bulbs turn on by themselves.

The husband was not entirely without superstition: he held his breath when he walked by cemeteries, and he told his sons never to point at a graveyard. But none of this seeming ghostliness—or whatever it was—convinced him of anything other than his and his wife's hypervigilance. When her family began experiencing similar phenomena, he attributed it to their slightly hysterical nature, all those sisters, not to mention the mother and the nieces. And the clicks on the line that his wife and her family were so convinced meant that they were being tapped? Those he was nearly certain were simply overactive, unsettled imaginations at work, for it was surely illegal for their lines to be monitored without a warrant, and a warrant would not be possible unless they were involved in some kind of criminal activity, which they certainly were not. It was nonsense, he knew, and yet still listened for the click every time he used the telephone, just in case.

They agreed that none of this was likely related to their <u>friends</u>, as she had ironically taken to calling the beings after so many newspapers had referred to them as such. Quietly, a slight and self-consciously paranoid idea had taken shape in her mind, and as she sat in the car now, she allowed herself to acknowledge it. It was possible, although not very probable, that she and he were being subjected to psychological manipulation or intimidation by elements of military intelligence who wanted to make sure UFOs remained the realm of oddballs. After all, she had been told some years ago that the air force knew about and studied UFOs but kept their findings away from the public, this being the same public that would surely turn against the couple if they suddenly began discussing hauntings as well as aliens. They could lose all credibility, become a pair of nutjobs at best or hoaxers at worst. Even if they never spoke about the strangeness accompanying their lives, would it eventually sow doubt in their perceptions of their own sanity? She knew that this was an unreasonable line of thinking and tried very hard to strike it from her mind.

> *Another writer imagining them might have allowed the couple to be truly delusional. Telling their story as one of folie à deux would mean writing about the depths of insanity, the mind's ability to completely and utterly believe in something that isn't real. But I've seen what that looks like, and it is not titillating, only terribly sad. Besides, in all the material written by or about the couple, nothing indicates to me that they were this kind of mad, the kind of mad whose distress is nearly unbearable, the kind of mad that breaks hearts.*

The intensity with which his wife was staring out the window concerned the husband. He worried about how seriously she was taking every Tom, Dick, and Harry who called himself a scientist or researcher, and how easily she was giving her time away to the area women, and it was nearly always women, who called every few nights to share a sighting of their own or a feeling of being watched. He knew there was no way to turn back time, no way to gain back the easy camaraderie of the early days of their marriage when everything they cared about and took interest or pleasure in was grounded in present and observable facts. She was involved in all sorts of conversations and experiments he thought ridiculous and tried to keep himself separate from, and while he found her commitment somewhat endearing, an example of her thirst for knowledge and her dedication to her interests, he feared her actions might end up reflecting poorly on them and their well-received book.

Those precise conversations and experiments he was thinking of she sifted into her second mental repository. The previous winter, one of her correspondents had written to ask her and her husband whether they might consider trying to contact the beings, invite them back. She did not know how, but she did share the increase in her sightings. Nearly every time the couple went out at night, they saw a light or orb where it should not be, occasionally stationary but more often moving in erratic patterns. Once, when she was with family at the lake, they all witnessed the strange maneuvers of one UFO that seemed almost to be showing off, and then another joining it, until the two flew off together. Another time, she had seen the rows of windows through her binoculars when she looked at the bright light high up, but when she tried to hand them over to her husband, he backed away, waving his hands in front of him, saying that he believed her, that he did not need to see.

Although she nearly always wrote in the plural first person when she described these later UFO sightings, I strongly suspect, due to the things her husband said in public, that he did not wish to be closely involved in this arena anymore, and while he was clearly comfortable enough with her writing missives on behalf of them both, it stands to reason that just because he was with her during some of these events doesn't mean he was pleased to be there or able to tap into the awe and excitement that were growing in her just as steadily as they were diminishing in him.

Writing back and forth, she and her correspondent—who led a team of several individuals taking an interest in the possibility of communicating with the beings—came to a simple agreement regarding how she might go about it. Every night, at the same hour, she stood on her porch and tried to beam her thoughts out into the universe, repeating in her mind over and over again that she would meet the beings on such and such a date and time at her parents' farm, where there was plenty of space for a craft to land, and that they should knock at the door when they arrived. She reassured the beings that she and her companions wished them no harm, only to obtain some bit of physical evidence and learn more about them. Faithfully, she did this day after day even as her husband poked fun at her, saying she must have taken on Transcendental Meditation out there, or that she was communing with the bats. But as he was attempting to quit smoking, per doctor's orders, the nightly sessions turned out to be useful to them both, since she could smoke and concentrate and think up at the great big sky and he could sit inside without temptation and watch the television in silence, his fingers playing with the lint that seemed to live in each and every pocket he possessed.

She became discouraged as the weeks went on, so when her father called with news, she did not expect it. A cousin who lived a quarter mile from her parents had reported a knock on the door in the middle of the night followed by several more in a repeating pattern. The cousin also saw flashing lights and, when looking out the window, a craft. The wife's heart pounded as she listened to her father and felt something she could not describe, except to recognize that it made her feel good, affirmed. Perhaps she had more power than she knew or was unlocking new parts of her brain. Perhaps—though she was approaching that further end of middle age where it is possible to begin imagining the meaning of <u>elderly</u>—perhaps there was still more to her life, to her development as a person, unexplored depths she might still plumb.

I wonder whether knowing she would live well into her eighties would have changed anything about how she saw herself at this time. Human beings aren't always predictable in our individual actions, though I'm sure some would say otherwise, but we do all share one thing: a knowledge of our mortality. So much of what we do, so much of how we shape the world in our image, relates to how we do or do not consider, question, engage with, or deny our eventual deaths. Isn't a connection to UFOs, empirically real or merely believed (and how distinct is that difference?), divine in some way? Doesn't it expand our sense of life and, as such, lend more meaning to our own?

Regardless of how she felt, what her father shared seemed to indicate progress, and so she redoubled her efforts, communicating more specific directions to her parents' back door, and this seemed to yield success as well, as several days later her mother called to complain about loud knocks that had come past midnight but which went unanswered since no one at the door at that time of night could be good news. Even more exciting was her parents' neighbor, a pilot, swearing he had spotted a round vehicle hovering above the farmhouse that night. She and her family even found an area in the nearby woods that was cleared, some of its trees broken, a charred piece of wood sitting in the middle of the bare patch like an omen.

Several weeks later, after sending the wood to be analyzed in order to learn whether it carried any physical evidence of something extraterrestrial, radiation perhaps, she learned that at least some of these events, including the eerie lone branch, were tricks being played on her and her family by a teenage boy who lived nearby.

If the boy had placed the partially burned piece of wood in the clearing in order to ridicule her attempts at communicating with aliens, then she and her family couldn't have been keeping the experiments as quiet as they claimed they were. Then again, perhaps this was a community in which everyone knew everyone else's business. I have lived in such towns, have witnessed the neighbors exchanging whispers about my mother even when she barely went out, consumed by her paranoias.

Another aspect I'm confused about in my source material is whether it was only the piece of wood that was revealed to be a hoax, or, what seems more likely to me, whether the flashing lights and the knocks on the door were also the boy's doing. I suspect the lack of clarity around this is deliberate, an attempt at saving face.

Just a few months before the talk at the ugliest of restaurants, when summer was contemplating turning into fall, the wife and her correspondent admitted defeat. If she was managing to make contact with the beings, there was no way of proving it. The knocks, the sightings, all of it could be happenstance. If the beings had tried communicating with her, as her correspondent's team advised was possible, she had not recognized it, even though she had been alert, taking note of any repeated flashing lights, patterned percussive sounds, and magnetic or electrical anomalies in her vicinity. Still, there was no apparent method to the madness of chance.

Her husband noticed that her routines had changed again, that she was no longer strictly adhering to a certain number of minutes spent on the porch at a precise time each night, and that she was distracted by other events and happenings. The fall had been kind to them, for once, calm and quiet in a way it had not been for years. The husband and wife had both been able to help out with the Halloween festivities at their church, throw a pumpkin-carving party for the neighborhood, and even plan a couple's costume, which they had never before done, after he bought a rubber mask of The Man from U.N.C.L.E. and she realized she could be The Girl from U.N.C.L.E. from the spinoff that had just started airing.

Christmas came and went peacefully, with less media attention than the year before, and so now, on that January 1967 evening, they both felt almost rejuvenated, despite their each continuing to suffer strange health issues, hers now worse than his as she wrestled with frequent laryngitis and a recurring viral infection.

In this, the couple is not unique: peaceful times come rarely, and are nearly always too short.

In February, the couple learned to their great chagrin that the journalist, F., who had by now become a good friend indeed, had been involved in a dispute at the magazine for which he had been writing a column for the last decade. Whether F. left of his own volition or was politely asked to resign was not clear, but what the couple did know was that the incident was related to F.'s two most recent books, both about UFO encounters, and whether they were adequately reported nonfiction accounts or if F. had simply allowed the sensationalism and public interest in extraterrestrials to guide the work.

Both the husband and the wife were upset by this news, but he in particular. After she read him the article about it, he walked up and down the living room, talking in circles about how outrageous it was that F., a journalist of some renown, who had many years' worth of experience, not to mention the trust of several quality newspapers, was forced to leave simply due to an association with UFOs. He was furious that F.'s integrity and credulity were in question, for this surely implied that he and she would also now be viewed as having that much less integrity or credulity, depending on whether the given skeptic wished to believe that F. was opportunistic and they were nutjobs or that they were scheming attention seekers and F. a fool. The husband had taken such comfort in knowing that F. was established, respected, and now . . .

Still, despite his anxious anger, he sat down with his wife to write to F., and together they expressed their sympathy and asked whether there was anything they could do or say that might help. In an appreciative note in return, F. reassured the couple that they had already lent all the support a writer could ask for because the book was doing well thanks to them, thanks to what they had endured, what they had shared, and how wonderfully they presented to the public.

Indeed, that same month the book went into yet another printing, and the couple began to travel again for radio interviews and panel appearances. Being able to escape New Hampshire's brutal winter was an unexpected pleasure, and they fantasized about moving west, living near the ocean and learning to surf. But of course neither of them meant it, too familiar with the kind of cold that cuts to the quick, that makes a person feel strong for enduring it.

A few weeks after their tour, the wife wrote to a correspondent that she noticed a growing movement among scientists to take the UFO phenomenon more seriously and investigate it objectively, without emotion. Up until now, she knew, these scientists had been too scared or too stubborn, believing the world was as small as what only they could see and measure, as if no one had ever insisted the Earth was flat or that the sun revolved around it.

It gives me a great deal of pleasure that she wrote, in 1967, about how emotional men are, how they attribute logic to their emotion and call it fact, call it objectivity. Say what you will about "things being different back then," but even before a woman like her would have naturally called herself a feminist she saw flaws in the patriarchy. People in the past were no less smart or aware than we are now.

She confessed to the same correspondent that she and her husband were now completely avoiding meeting with UFO study groups and enthusiasts because associating with such spaces would make the couple even more suspect to the scientists they were trying to woo, as it were. While her husband felt comfortable simply sending the study groups the form letter that he and she had finally put together, she preferred to write back personally to those believers, almost as if she knew—though how could she?—that not too far in the future she would end up finding solace and community among their ranks.

It was especially important for the couple to eschew the enthusiasts at the moment because of the next experiment in psychophysics that they were about to embark on with the full support of F., the astronomer they knew, one of the men from IBM they had known for years now, and several others.

In truth, of course, only she seemed to participate in these experiments, while he pleaded, or at least affected, disinterest. But I'm curious. What would happen if I properly included him in this next bout? What if we deviate together and allow him to take a more active stance, one that, as reluctant as he was, might have felt worth doing if only to prove to these various scientific men that it was all nonsense anyway and that despite believing in his experience completely, he wasn't capable of imagining that he and his wife were so inordinately unique that the beings would communicate with them?

Once, as they stood on the porch together trying to beam their thoughts into the darkness above with the new method the scientists had decided upon, one that used a complex system of code words alongside clear instructions in order to leave nothing to chance or coincidence—although neither he nor she could quite grasp the scientists' pretzeled logic—she asked him why he was doing this with her. He shrugged and gestured with his left hand, asking silently for a puff of her cigarette. A puff barely counted. She mused that maybe he wanted to be proved wrong. Maybe he wanted to believe in the possibility that they were special to the beings after all, whatever the reason may be.

But they were so ordinary, he protested, to which she raised her eyebrows and then wiggled them separately up and down. He sighed. It was a sign she used when they were in polite society and someone said something subtly—or not so subtly—racist and neither of them could do anything about it but laugh it off or ignore it. It was always subtle with the people they liked, and sometimes that was worse. Once, after a campaign event for Kennedy, the husband was so frustrated after holding his tongue half the night around Democratic donors that he insisted on going to the backyard to split firewood even though the young bachelor who lived upstairs usually did it, not to mention it was August. That night she had come up with the eyebrow wiggle, hoping it would help him know that he was not alone in the moment, that his restraint was being recognized and lauded. He appreciated the gesture, and sometimes seeing her do it would make him want to laugh, which was a good distraction, but more often than not, he thought it helped her rather more than him.

So when she wiggled her eyebrows now, he understood. It had come up before, of course, the fact that they were an interracial couple. They had been asked a few times whether they thought they were chosen by the beings for that reason. Sometimes the implication seemed to be that aliens surely separate the races in their society as well, usually accompanied by the sentiment encapsulated in the words <u>as God intended</u>; other times the implication was mere practicality, for if the visiting beings had only limited time, they might have wanted to investigate humans who looked different in several ways such as woman, man, white, black, or else, if the beings had been watching the planet for a while, perhaps they wanted to understand why few humans overall coupled this way.

While neither he nor she thought this was very likely, he did wonder whether it was possible that what made them the object of stares in lily-white New Hampshire was the same source of fascination to ETs. This was ridiculous, he thought. He told his wife that it was just as likely that the beings liked the color of their car that night. In truth, what he thought most plausible was that they had simply been chosen by circumstance.

.   .   .

June came and the couple and the semiscientific crew directing their experiment waited with bated breath for the beings to make contact on the selected day and time.

The group had decided to make an outing of it. Some of the scientists set up camping gear the night before, and the couple arrived with their own tent and provisions with which to feed the hungry men who had shuttled out to meet them. It felt like the Fourth of July, though that was still three weeks away. They ate, shared stories, laughed, and had good-natured political debates; they took walks up and down the field when they felt like stretching their legs; one of the scientists brought a small chessboard and played several rounds with whoever was up for the challenge.

When darkness finally descended, a hush fell over the group. They sat around the banked fire as the night grew cooler, and the husband and wife held hands as they watched the starry expanse. They had chosen a place with little light pollution, the better to make the beings feel safe, for it seemed that extraterrestrials did not like cities. Although there were those sightings over Washington, D.C., a dozen or so years back, the husband recalled aloud after his second beer.

His words were the signal to the rest that it was all right to talk as they waited, and so they did, although in soft tones. He allowed himself a cigarette from someone else's pack—that did not count, either, he decided—and let the sounds of his friends and their colleagues and his wife's family wash over him. She sat beside him with a beer and watched the sky intently. When he put his hand on hers, she started, as if she had been in a trance. He wondered again, as he often did, how much he did not and could not understand about this woman, this woman who was his wife, who was an entirely separate entity from him. He guessed she was praying for the beings to make an appearance of any kind, give a light show at the very least. He sent up a prayer of his own, for he would be incredibly embarrassed if they had invited all of these people out to this field for nothing. It felt strange, though, to ask God to send something unearthly to them.

He asked her, quietly, hoping not to involve anyone else, whether she thought that the beings they had met were God's creatures, too, but her sister, who he had thought was asleep, heard him and offered an answer loudly enough so that others could listen in, and soon everyone was talking about whether aliens were or were not godly creations.

Most of the group believed that, if God existed—there were several agnostics among them—then surely the entire universe was created by Him and any living beings throughout would be God's too. But what if, the husband asked, God was only master and creator of their planet, the humans' planet? Even on Earth, he reminded the rest, there were many religions, many different gods. Some survived, while others, like the Greek and Roman gods of myth, seemed to disappear. His wife was surprised; she had always thought him more religious than her, more secure in his faith, but perhaps, she realized now, something had been shaken in him. On the other hand, she reasoned, her husband was also known for asking difficult and provocative questions merely in order to measure the responses of others.

The conversation died again after some time, and as it got late, and then early, some among them climbed into their tents to sleep in shifts, asking the others to wake them up the second, and they meant the absolute split second, that anything out of the ordinary happened.

But nothing did. All night long, he and she stayed awake, until the light began to rise from the east, and she smoked one last cigarette that she buried beneath a rock, and they both climbed into their tent and lay on top of their sleeping bags, since the night felt warm inside the closed space, and tried to sleep.

> I can only imagine the disappointment and, if the husband really was there—which he likely wasn't—the sheepishness they might have felt. After all that waiting, after all the planning, after all the bizarre instructions from the scientific team who, in spite of whatever titles or positions they held, were muddling along in territory as uncharted as the moon . . . after all that, nothing.

They tried again in the waning days of the summer but were disappointed then as well. The team decided to put the experiments to rest. Unless the beings returned and provided hard evidence of their existence or left something behind, there was simply no way to show, beyond a shadow of a doubt, that they existed, let alone that they were able to receive communication from the couple or anyone else.

One evening some weeks later the husband visited an artist friend who shared his love of jazz and with whom he occasionally went to concerts or listened to records. The artist, who knew of the couple's experience, of course—it was impossible, at this point, to meet someone in the area who did not know—suggested making a forensic drawing of what he and his wife had seen that night. The husband agreed and the artist, excited, fetched a sketchpad and charcoal. As the husband described what he remembered, the artist drew, asking whether this or that was right, smudging and refining according to the husband's instructions. When the sketches were complete, the husband rolled them up after glancing at the finished product, and told the artist that he would show these to his wife and that they should all get together for dinner in the next few weeks.

On the way home, the husband wondered whether it might be better to toss the images in the fireplace. They were eerily accurate, he thought, almost as if his artist friend's hand were being guided by something other than his own words. But no, that was ridiculous, he knew, and rejected the idea. His friend was simply talented and he acutely descriptive. As he pulled into the gravel of the driveway, he decided he would show his wife the sketches after all, if only to see how she reacted and gauge whether his memory was correct or whether he had only spooked himself into believing it was.

Her reaction—reaching for her pack and lighting up even though she was trying to smoke outside so as not to tempt him, and then beginning to pace feverishly, staring out the window as if she expected to see something or someone there—confirmed that the drawings were indeed perfect likenesses.

When she calmed down enough to speak, she looked at the sketches again, properly, and asked her husband how they had come to be, and when he finished explaining she decided she, too, wanted to sit with the artist. What might they discover if they both managed to translate their memories into visuals that other people could see? Maybe they could show the sketches to others who had seen beings emerge from craft; surely, if enough of them had seen the same thing, the authorities would have to take the matter seriously.

.   .   .

A few weeks later, the couple visited the psychiatrist for yet another hypnotism session, but this time with their friend, the artist, who would draw up more sketches and later complete color paintings based on them. The familiar ritual commenced, first the wife and then the husband went under, and each was soothingly interrogated by the psychiatrist who echoed the artist's questions.

It was the oddest of all their sessions, the couple agreed later that night as they were preparing for bed. Perhaps it was how far away they were from the experience now. How much longer would there be anything new to recall under hypnosis?

The paintings created by the artist are, to my eyes anyway, strange and not at all helpful. The artist was certainly talented, and his other paintings are still sold today, long after his death, but he seemed to be an expert at landscapes and moody abstracts, neither of which translated very well into the specifics of alien facial features or proportions. In fact, the paintings of the beings and the craft, which I have admittedly been able to see only in black-and-white reproductions, are far from photo-realistic. I don't know if they were meant to be. Yet these paintings and sketches do seem to be some of the earliest images I can find that portray the grays, sometimes called Zeta Reticulans or Roswell Grays, the most common and recognizable images of aliens in pop culture.

I wonder what the couple thought of the artist's work when it was ready. Were they as disappointed as I was, hoping to see something closer to the precision with which their memories had returned to them?

Or have I read the mood of these events all wrong? There is a spirit of whimsy in this affair, something less forensic than creative, and perhaps it was with that mindset that the couple enjoyed their friend's work, recognizing it as the compliment it was, for they had never been muses to anyone before, and even if it wasn't their own faces featured in the art, still, it was their words and memories reworked onto canvas.

There was one other event of note that year. A government scientist who claimed a high-security clearance visited but would not come in, instead waving the couple over to his nondescript brown car parked in their driveway. The husband walked in front of his wife in case there was any funny business, but when he got closer to the scientist, who was dressed in a black suit, a hat, and very dark sunglasses, he stopped worrying, for the man was puny, pencil necked with a nervously bobbing Adam's apple. The scientist asked the couple to describe precisely what the beings looked like, and they complied; as they talked, the suited man visibly shrank away from them.

So they really had been abducted, the scientist murmured in shock, awe, fear, or all three. It was as if, at that moment, the scientist felt the danger he was in. He begged them never to tell anyone about the meeting, got in his car, and drove off in a great hurry.

While she did, obviously, share this anecdote, the wife didn't, as far as I know, ever tell another soul who the scientist actually was.

Does that make the story more reliable? Or less? Then again, nothing in my version of events can be considered reliable. I am trying to hew close to the details I've learned over hours and hours of research, but the very story I'm trying to convey may be centered on a dream, a shared delusion, a reality concocted by the minds of two terrified humans. I believe the couple, I do, and yet I am fully aware that in trying to tell you about them I'm further muddling the line between fact and fiction, between objective and subjective truth.

The space between these, though, strikes me as narrower than I ever imagined. That frightens me, but at the same time, I can't help but love this shimmering border where uncertainty dwells, because it is here that we can live alongside the endless realm we call mystery.

13

Now

The Archivist sits beside their mother, holding her hand, wishing they were anywhere else on Earth, or better yet, off it. She's had one of her episodes, and although she denies it, the doctor told the Archivist that she stopped refilling her prescriptions months ago. The meds control the worst of her paranoias, her delusions, but at a cost. The Archivist can't entirely blame her for wanting a break from the drooling, the head-aches, the gastric distress, the drowsiness. No, they can understand the impulse well enough, but they cannot help being infuriated, exhausted, and resentful. She has again dragged them out of their life and into hers.

It was her neighbor down the hall who called the Archivist, telling them about the wellness check he'd called for, the struggle with the police, her night in jail, and her eventual transfer to the psychiatric wing of a poorly funded public hospital. It is here that the Archivist sits, trying to convince her to begin regularly taking her pills again. They know she will be allowed to remain here for only two or three days; she isn't enough of a danger to herself or others to be kept on beyond that, and there aren't enough resources for her to get long-term treatment anyway. She has to muddle along the best she can, just like she did when the Archivist was a child, just like she has since the Archivist left her two decades ago to move in with their grandparents and then strike out on their own.

She nods, and the Archivist thinks she's taking in their wheedling, but then she jerks her hand away from theirs, calls them by the name they haven't used for many years, and asks why they look like they do. They want to peel off their skin. They suspect she knows exactly what she's doing, that she's taking advantage of her frail-seeming state, even if it's realer now than ever before, to poke at what she knows will hurt them most. They would never say this to anyone else, lest they be perceived as callous for assuming the worst of her, but they've been through this cycle enough times to know that even in her madness she can be cruel and calculating.

They echo her tactic and abruptly change the subject. They ask her to tell them again about their youthful UFO encounter, what she thought of it back then, what they said, how they acted, what the minor media storm that followed was like, whether she enjoyed it. They ask for details, as many as she can remember. She warms to the topic quickly, her eyes brightening. The Archivist recognizes the irony. They've escaped her and her harebrained beliefs, her distorted fears. But they've chosen to surround themself with the papers, effects, and leftovers of people who spent their lives using language to convince and coax and argue. People who spent their lives making things up. People, in other words, exactly like her. Storytellers.

January 4, 1967

Tomorrow I meet her. Violet. She's here already, I mean in Boston, for her conference. It's over tomorrow night and I'll see her then, and she's staying in town through the weekend. On my way to and from work today, I watched the cold, windy streets like I never have before, or at least not since I first moved here. Everything looked new, even though it was gray and damp. Everything had a special shine to it. Violet is in my city.

I don't think I've ever called it that, have I? My city. I suppose it really is by now.

I'm so nervous. I was distracted all day at work, but no one noticed, thank goodness, what with the whispers of a newspaper strike. Here in Boston, in Detroit, in Chicago. Everyone's angry that we're not paid enough, at all levels. I'm certainly mad (not to mention underpaid!), but I'm not about to draw attention to myself, especially with how the paper's finances are looking. Cote's been stressed and smoking more than usual. There was another round of layoffs just before Christmas, which I thought was pretty cruel. I've still got a job, thankfully.

Tomorrow, I see Violet!!! I keep trying to think of something else, but it seems I'm not capable of it, not with this frenetic energy running through me. Even working on my novel doesn't appeal, though lately the thought of being able to rush home to it like a lover has been sustaining me through the anxious aura at work.

I don't think I've written anything here about my novel yet. It's delicious, at least I think so, and I'm having such fun working on it, although I need to keep writing short stories too. It's not that they pay that much, but the extra cash sure is nice, since I'm still paying off the beautiful mint-green Olivetti I finally got a few months ago on installments. Analog accepted a very short humorous piece of mine last week, a version of one I wrote a long time ago, when I first moved here, about a woman whose husband invents a machine that can sift around the molecules in the human body. Well, when I first wrote it, she invented it, but I know my audience better now. Anyway, she decides to test it out while her husband is away, and so she rearranges herself into a man and goes looking for her husband in order to tell him that his machine worked. She discovers him having a romantic dinner with another woman, figures out he's been having an affair, woos his mistress away from him, and never looks back.

But the novel! Well, there's sort of two, the postmodern one (I think I'm using the term correctly) about the couple who get abducted, but that's going so slowly it barely counts. The one I'm actively working on is an expansion of my first Fiona Bridges story, the one none of the magazines wanted. I've been rereading Rocannon's World by Ursula K. Le Guin in order to remind myself that women do publish science fiction adventure novels. If she can, why can't I? Maybe I'll write to her and ask how she went about it.

January 8, 1967

Violet has left. I can still smell her perfume on my collar. I might never wash this shirt, or at least not until the scent fades away. She paid for a car service to take me home from her hotel. Even though all my things are here, my plants and my clothes and my books and my typewriter, it feels lonelier after spending the last three days with someone else always by my side. It reminded me of Rosa, how inseparable we were.

But Violet is nothing like Rosa, nothing at all. I want to memorialize everything about her, build a statue of her in words, but I don't think that's possible. Flesh and blood people can't really be contained in little marks of ink on paper. The magic of fiction, after all, is how characters become real to readers, how we insert ourselves—and our families and friends, our pet peeves, even how we look—into all the blank spaces that hover around the made-up people. When I said that to Violet, she looked so surprised that for a moment I worried I sounded stupid, but she was only impressed, knowing I haven't studied literature in any formal capacity. She has, of course. She's got a PhD in English and is a professor. She's probably the smartest person I've ever met.

Let me start from the beginning so I always remember it.

We'd agreed to meet in front of the Charles, because it's an easy landmark and I wanted to show her the club. I recognized her immediately from her photograph, but it was different, seeing her in motion like that. Her lips were painted red, and her curly black hair was styled beautifully. Her face was pink with the cold, and her eyebrows were so thick and beautiful I wanted to run my thumbs over them immediately. Even though it was the first time we met, I felt half in love with her already. I was dressed femme like she was, because she wrote me once that she didn't like butches. I was hoping to show her how dapper I look in a suit, like Katharine Hepburn, not butch at all, but we never came back to my place.

Violet knew me, too, as soon as she saw me and waved. I ran to her, nearly slipping on a patch of ice. We hugged, like two long-lost sisters, and kept exclaiming "Violet!" and "Phyllis!" and "It's so good to finally meet you in person!" and the like, but when we parted, neither of us said anything for a long moment, we just stared, and I wondered whether we'd made a terrible mistake. Maybe the intimacy of letters wasn't meant to be translated into living reality. But then we both started to say something at the same time, and we laughed, and everything was easy after that.

We didn't go to the Charles in the end. She suggested a walk through the Commons, since it wasn't quite dark yet. Our arms in our coats kept brushing against each other, and even though it was just cloth against cloth, I got goosebumps and felt some familiar clenching. I wondered if she was feeling the same way, but she's such a cool customer that it's difficult to tell. I can't remember what we talked about, I was so focused on making sure I didn't melt into a puddle of desire right there in the park. When it got darker, Vi took me to a very fancy restaurant where I tasted caviar for the first time. I didn't really like it, but I had as much as she did because I didn't want to insult her when she was so excited about introducing me to it. The entrée was all right, but dessert was really the shining standout—we had peach Brown Betty, and although Mother used to make a version of it with apples, I'd never known it could taste like <u>that</u>. Vi had only one bite and then leaned back to watch me eat the rest, which she said she enjoyed much more.

She paid for the meal, and then she gave me her coat and told me to put it on. I was confused, but when she gave me a key and told me to go upstairs and use it, I realized she was actually staying there, right at Parker House! She told me she'd find the washroom, freshen up her makeup, and go to the bar for a drink. Then she'd come up herself with her second key. Later, she told me it was because she didn't want the concierge to notice that she had a guest, a woman no less. This way it'd look, to a casual observer, like she went upstairs and then came back to the bar and went back upstairs. Her coat was bright yellow, and mine was black, so she would carry mine and the hoteliers would think, without looking closely, that I was her. My head spun a little at this scheme. I know she wasn't being paranoid, exactly, but there seemed to be simpler ways to go about it. She's so feminine and classy that no heterosexual would ever suspect she was a lesbian. I suppose she fears for her job even more than I do for mine, since being a woman professor is probably much harder than being a woman copy editor.

On my way up, I couldn't stop staring. I'd never been anywhere so ritzy, and I can't imagine I ever will be again unless it's with Violet. I thought Kathleen and Glen had money, but even they don't stay at the fanciest hotel in town when they travel. And Vi is single, and only 33. I wonder if she comes from old money. She hasn't told me much about her family yet, although I've told her all about mine.

Waiting in her suite was strangely erotic. I couldn't decide whether to sit on the plush couch in the first room or on the high four-poster in the bedroom. There was champagne chilling in a bucket on a counter with one glass and a small bowl of strawberries. I dithered about whether to open the bottle, but it was clearly so expensive that I didn't dare. So I paced, feeling full and warm but also jittery.

When Vi came in, my heart was pounding so hard I think I was actually trembling. I've never experienced that kind of desire for anyone, not since Rosa, but even then, we were so young that half the excitement was about how new everything was. I was attracted to both Alice and Kathleen, of course, but this was something different, it really was. There was an aura about Vi that made me want to kneel, to become her disciple. She stroked my face and laughed at me a little. I think she could tell I was dumbstruck, a doe in her headlights.

She led me to the bedroom and told me to remove my clothes, which I did, and then she looked at me, just looked. I never knew the power a gaze could hold. She walked around me and lightly brushed my skin with the tips of her fingers. We hadn't even kissed yet! But when we did, it was glorious. I am nearly ashamed to say that I moaned in her mouth with just how much I wanted her.

I don't know how to describe the rest. There aren't words enough, and the words I do know make me blush and feel tawdry. Besides, I will never forget that first long night with her, even if everything else this past weekend becomes blurry as the sands of time blow across my life. (Idea: Literal sands of time? A powder of some kind that ages people or makes them young?) Suffice to say, she withheld my pleasure over and over until I begged, and when I attended to hers, I felt as if I were worshipping at an altar. Just recalling the scent and feel of her now gives me a delicious sort of shiver.

We stayed in her suite for nearly the rest of the weekend, except for a walk on Saturday morning. She ordered room service for all our meals, and we drank and laughed and lounged about listening to the radio. We took two long baths together, and the rest of the time I wore the hotel bathrobe while she wore the one she brought from home. It was the height of sybaritic indulgence, and I enjoyed it immensely. We went to bed together several more times of course. I don't know how she was able to put me in such a nervous state when she wanted me and put me entirely at ease when we were eating, laughing at a serial, or reading across from each other on the big couch.

I tried one of the novels Vi brought with her but found it dull and uninspired. She explained to me why it wasn't, really, and although I can tell she must be an incredible teacher, I still couldn't bring myself to keep reading it, so I settled for the magazines, and although some of those were tedious as well, I did love the three stories by a writer named Jorge Luis Borges. They were truly mesmerizing. Vi told me to keep the issue they were in, and I think she was impressed with my taste.

I feel like a bit of a country bumpkin around her, even though I've been living here for so long now. She's so much more refined than I am. I know she's originally from Pennsylvania, and she's been all over the country as well as to Russia and England and even Greece. She has three degrees, a vast store of knowledge about literature, and here I am writing silly little science fiction stories. Vi says she wants to read them, though, so I'll mail her one or two.

This morning, I was nearly inconsolable. I cried as soon as I woke up and saw she wasn't next to me, thinking about how I'd be waking up alone in my narrow bed again from now on. She tried to comfort me, but now that I've had a taste of her in real life, I don't want to rely on letters. She couldn't understand why I was in such a state, and for some reason I didn't tell her about how Rosa abandoned me and later told me to stop writing her.

Finally, when I kept tearing up over breakfast, Violet said she'd fly me out to visit her in Oregon during her Easter break. She was hoping to surprise me with tickets in a few weeks, but I'm so glad she told me now because this way I know for certain when I'll see her next. Just imagine—I'll get to fly in an airplane! I'll see Oregon!

For now, I think I'll go telephone Alice and see if she'd like to get a drink tomorrow evening so I can tell her all about my new lover.

March 8, 1967

I called in sick today. The only other times I've done that have been when I've been running a fever, which doesn't happen often. Mother and Papa blessed me with a healthy body if nothing else. But today I'm simply too angry and upset and fear I'll explode into a hyena laugh or a banshee shriek if someone even looks at me the wrong way, and since everyone at work is walking on eggshells, all of us scared we're next for the firing squad, as Cote morbidly put it, I thought it better to make myself scarce.

Last night, Alice and Amy and I and everyone else who could make it from our Daughters of Bilitis chapter went to Kathleen's, because she has the best TV and a big living room. Some couldn't make it—the ones who have night shifts, the few who are married and keep their lesbianism a secret, the divorced mothers with no one else to watch their kids. But plenty of us were there, squeezed in together, nearly on top of one another on the couches or resorting to pillows on the floor. Alice paced and chain-smoked, listening rather than watching.

The special was atrocious and dispiriting top to bottom. It was commendable, at the very least, that Mike Wallace spoke to some homosexuals who were happy and well adjusted. But much of the report was invested in the fact that we are sick, a smear on society, and shouldn't exist. Wallace made it sound like we're exotic and dangerous creatures, like elephants from India or snow leopards from the mountains of China. We might as well have been aliens from another planet! I was sitting next to Amy, and at one point I felt her arm go rigid, and when I looked at her she was biting her lip and tears were rolling down her cheeks, even though she tried to be still and silent (probably because anyone who tried to speak was viciously shushed by Alice). I was close to tears, too, especially during the long segment with the psychiatrist who spoke of how there was no such thing as a happy homosexual. He saw it as a contradiction in terms. Alice actually hissed from the hallway at that, and I knew she was thinking of Dr. Iverson. I was too.

When it was over some women left pretty quickly, but I stayed to talk it over with wine and beer. We all agreed it was true that some of the gay men we knew were more promiscuous. But as Diana pointed out, plenty of heterosexual men are too! We also all know some homosexual men in monogamous, long-term relationships. So we kept wondering, what is the difference? Why are heterosexual men not called promiscuous when they sleep around? Why didn't Mike Wallace mention that? He's on his third wife himself! Isn't it possible he's a philanderer? Even if not, isn't it simply true that some men—some people, in fact!—are promiscuous while others are not?

I found the clergyman's position interesting, that homosexual urges or desires are not sinful in and of themselves. "Blameless" was the word the priest used, I think. Homosexual acts are sins, he said, but not the proclivities. I wonder if Mother knew that the Vatican held that position when she took the belt to me. I wonder if she and Papa watched the special.

And what of us lesbians? This was my biggest question. I kept expecting Wallace to at least make a passing reference to homosexual women, but he didn't, not once, nor did any of the experts. Alice thought that Gore Vidal alluded to it somewhat—she only came in to watch him because she thinks he's very intelligent and charming, although she hasn't read his books.

Kathleen argued that it was a good thing lesbians weren't mentioned, not if we were also going to be discussed as sick, repellent, hated. Then I think it was Wanda who said the problem was that men can't even imagine our existence, can't understand how women can do anything in the bedroom together. But what about the pulp books about lesbians written by men? If they can imagine us in compromising positions for a novel, especially one meant to be erotic reading for other men, doesn't that mean they can imagine us?

Amy said she thinks that CBS and Mike Wallace are too scared to talk about lesbians on-air lest it give women, dissatisfied with their poorly performing husbands, the idea to try it out with a girlfriend sometime. That gave us all a laugh, which we desperately needed. But on my way home, I felt angrier and angrier thinking about the women I've met who've been arrested, about the nights when rumors of a raid send us scurrying out of the bar.

When I got home, I wrote a long letter to Vi. She must have seen the special, too, I know she has a television, and I'm dying to know what she thought. This morning, I mailed it and then came right back home and called Cote to say I wasn't coming to work today. He asked why, but I was in the hall so I couldn't tell him what was wrong. Finally I asked if he watched CBS last night. He coughed, said he expects to see me tomorrow, then hung up.

So. That's that. I'm furious still but I'm not going to waste the rest of my day on this feeling. I'm going to work on my novel. I can't make Fiona an out-and-out lesbian, not if I want this book to get published, but she isn't going to have a single romance with a man. Men might be her friends and comrades, and they may even fall in love with her. But she will never love them. She'll say she's a widow, and even if I never publish a word about who died to make her one, I'll know that her best friend and first lover died in an accident when she and Fiona were old enough to start working the mines (everyone in the Ring Region is expected to). Afterward, Fiona escaped and started working for herself and the highest bidder. That I know about her life before is enough. It has to be, for now.

June 19, 1967

The newest JFK assassination theory centers around a "highly neurotic and strongly homosexual group," a phrase seared in my mind forever now because, for one, it doesn't really mean anything and, for another, it's one of the last phrases I laid my eyes on at the godforsaken Traveler. I kept trying to tell Cote throughout the afternoon that we should make Max change it or at least explain what on earth he meant, but he could barely look me in the face and kept shooing me out of his office.

I should have known.

Almost six years—over.

At the end of the day, when Cote finally asked to see me, he hemmed and hawed for a while before finally actually saying the words "letting you go," and then he kept repeating how good it was that I'd worked there for so long because my severance pay would give me nearly two months to find another job. Which he was sure I would, especially since I'll finish my degree in a year. Of course, if I don't find work, I won't be able to afford completing said degree.

No. I won't wallow in self-pity. I am an excellent copy editor and copy editors are always necessary. When I finish my degree, I <u>will</u> find work as a writer and editor, too, not just a massager of sentences. I will. I will. I will.

July 6, 1967

Cote phoned this evening. I don't know how but he seemed to have guessed that I haven't been reading the papers at all since I boxed up my few things and left the <u>Traveler</u> newsroom for good. It's still hard to think that I'll never go back.

I haven't started applying for jobs yet, even though Alice has been nagging me to. I've been having a little holiday instead, getting as many books from the library as they'll let me take and sitting at home reading half the day and writing the other half.

I shouldn't have had that third beer tonight. My stomach feels sloshy.

Anyway. Cote said he had something important to tell me, that he hadn't been able to before, and nearly begged me to come to our usual pub. He sounded so sad, honestly, that I couldn't keep freezing him out.

He was already tight when I got there. What had been so important? Two things. First, he wanted to tell me the bad news— that the <u>Boston Evening Traveler</u> was finished and that he was joining the ranks of the unemployed, just like me. He laughed a little at the irony of having fired me so recently, but I could tell he was devastated.

The paper isn't folding exactly, it's merging with the morning paper and expanding its coverage and printing some fancy New York columnists. Cote said he knew our circulation's been declining for years but couldn't understand why. I didn't want to tell him that we both knew our paper was never the best, really. Its prose was purple, its politics weren't exactly either of ours. But it was a good place to work. Solid. Consistent. Until now.

I let him go on for a while about his bosses and his colleagues who'd been kept on. ("Traitors," he called them, and I nearly threw my beer in his face at that, because he would have stayed in a heartbeat, too, if he'd been asked.) Eventually, I asked him what the good news was.

Instead of saying anything, he took out the little notebook that's always in the inside pocket of his jacket and wrote something down and ripped out the page and gave it to me. (Alice would say he's a drama queen, and she'd be right.) He wanted me to tear up the note and get rid of it, but I didn't. I'm pasting it here, because I want to remember that it's possible for things to change:

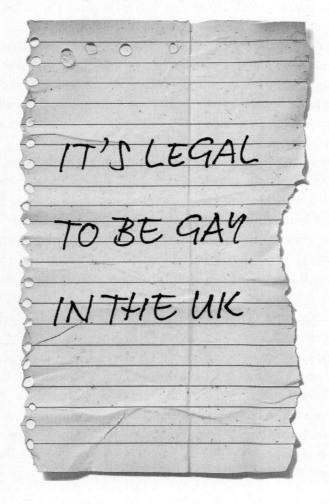

We drank to that. It might not affect us here, but it's something, isn't it?

Why am I so sad now, then? Is it just the alcohol? Is it seeing Cote so clearly broken by losing his job? I don't know. Maybe it'll all feel better in the morning. Mother used to say that, when I was little and in a fight with Rosa or one of the other girls.

Now I'm getting maudlin, thinking of Mother almost fondly. I'm going to bed.

July 29, 1967

Violet wants me to move in with her. That way, she says, I won't need to worry about working and if I absolutely insist on it, she's sure she can get me a job at the college, maybe even at the library. To avoid any untoward questions, she'll tell everyone I'm her cousin and that my parents just died and I need some time to get back on my feet. She says she has it all figured out.

On the one hand, I feel like I should be jumping at this opportunity. Shouldn't I? I had such a lovely visit with her in the spring, even if it was brief. Her home is beautiful, cozy and well appointed and classy. She has a guest bedroom that I could use as my very own office. If anyone asked, we would say that I slept there. We could cook and take walks and read in the evenings with her opera records. (I haven't had the heart to tell her that I find them dreadful . . .) She said I'd be able to read every book on her shelves and continue my correspondence course or I could apply to become a student at the college.

I don't think I'll do that, though. I'd be so much older than the other students, and since it's such a small school, I know I'd stick out like a sore thumb. But otherwise—it sounds perfect. Heavenly.

So why haven't I written her yet to say yes? I keep trying and getting stuck after the first paragraph where I tell her about my day (which she told me she likes me doing, because then she can imagine how I look and act even when we're not together . . . which I find so awfully sweet and romantic).

Maybe it's because she said I could throw away or sell all my things here, even my clothes if I wanted to, and she'd provide me with everything I needed. She gave me some new clothes when I visited her in March, actually. They fit me perfectly, but they felt a little too girly for me, dresses and pastel-colored blouses—the sky-blue sweater especially was odious, and I stuffed it under my heavy winter things when I got home.

And what about my books? She probably didn't mean those. My books are coming with me no matter what. So are my suits, and my Olivetti, of course, and the rest of my clothes, for that matter, because I like them.

That's a silly reason to say no, anyway. She probably got carried away and I can just tell her that I want my things with me. A couple of the DOB gals are Communists and they're always going on about how nobody should own things individually. I actually agree with a lot of their arguments when they get impassioned about it, even if the others roll their eyes and say being a lesbian is hard enough, nobody needs to be Communist on top of that. But I like my things. They're things I've worked hard for. Little treasures of my life here.

Alice doesn't like Vi much, but as Kathleen pointed out, Alice has never met Violet and tends to dislike anyone her former lovers get serious with. Kathleen thinks it's a swell idea, that I should move and live as a kept woman. She's one herself, after all, and loves it. She says it gives her all the time in the world to have lovers, even if those do tend to change as often as the wind, and she's also become quite a good painter, and besides all that she has time to quietly work with the DOB more than some of us. I asked her once whether Glen minds at all that she doesn't work, and she laughed and said that was how it should be, the man goes to work so the woman can enjoy herself. Kathleen has some very old-fashioned ideas sometimes. Anyway, it's not like I'd be taking lovers—I'd have Vi.

I still can't tell whether she's actually wealthy or just splurges when I'm around her. Her house is small, and she doesn't wear ostentatious jewelry, but her clothing is all very fine quality and she did stay at Parker House. Kathleen thinks she must be an heiress of some kind or that she killed a husband a long time ago and got all his money. What I think is that Kathleen reads too many mysteries and sees too many silly movies.

I want to want to accept Violet's offer. I love her, and I miss her terribly. So what is there to quibble about, really? Nothing, that's what.

So I'll accept, and then I can stop circling want ads in the paper and focus on my writing and nothing else. Except packing, I suppose.

The Fiona novel is nearly finished, I think, but I've been stuck on the final few chapters for a while now. First I had Fiona become mortally wounded and get saved by Fred. Then I tried ending with Fiona sitting at her favorite tavern with the six-armed bartender, Mulk, telling him the story readers have just read. But both of those endings felt trite. They tie everything up too neatly in a bow. And I don't think I'm getting across just how hard Fiona's had to fight in order to gain the respect of the Pirate King. Maybe it isn't the ending that's broken. Maybe it's the whole book.

I don't want to start it all over again, but if I have to, I will. This can't be just a silly little adventure story with no depth. Maybe Fiona needs to be more timid earlier on. I can't even remember the first half of the novel anymore. I've been worrying so much about the end.

That's what I'll do tonight. I'll reread what I've written, right from the very start, and take notes. And then I'll write to Violet and tell her I accept.

14

Now

When the Archivist wakes up on their first morning back in their apartment, their brain feels like it's been run through a car wash, plastic bristles getting into the crevices and heavy drying mops smacking the organ from side to side. A brain wash. No, that means something else. There should be a word for this, this sensation of fog lifting. They think about Phyllis's second book, which they had finished soon before they got the call from their mother's neighbor. One of the stories was about a woman reclaiming her mind after years of using it as, basically, a lockbox that ferried secure information for high-paying clients. The Archivist tries to remember how that feeling was described while they scratch Fitz's ears. He showed up soon after they arrived home and opened their window and for all they know might have spent the whole night with them. The Archivist is grateful and hopes Shalani doesn't mind; they so rarely feel chosen.

Their mother, who barely prioritized them while they were growing up, has returned to her one-bedroom, and a social worker will be coming by to check on her for a few weeks. The Archivist was so relieved to be on the train heading away from her that they nearly wept seeing the city coming into view. They weren't even gone that long, only the weekend plus a couple of days of missed work, but as they climbed into bed, all their muscles slowly unclenched, and they recognized how physical the toll had been.

When the cat finally gets bored and gently bites the Archivist's arm, they get up and chivy him out the window. Shalani is there, video chatting with someone in a different time zone, as she often is at this hour, speaking a language the Archivist doesn't recognize. She waves at the Archivist and pulls the bag of cat treats out of its hiding spot under a big stone in one of her planters so Fitz can't reach it on his own, and wins back her pet's affection. The Archivist has decided not to care that she flaked on making real plans with them; she's never anything but enthusiastically friendly when they cross paths with her outside or in the stairwell. People forget things, they know. Aren't they a prime example?

They're excited to go back to work, to Phyllis, eager to see whether the sleuthing they'd begun some weeks ago, trying to track down the people who had donated her items to the archive, has yielded any fruit yet. They're hoping, too, that the hard copy scans they ordered from the abducted couple's archive have arrived. They're even looking forward to the morning and afternoon coffee runs for their boss and colleagues, being able to smile at the cute barista who's usually at the shop on Wednesdays.

By the standards of many, including some of the subjects sitting in the stacks, the Archivist knows their life is small and dull. But in returning to it, they are so filled up that they might just float away.

I keep trying to figure out why I'm writing this. Why I care so much about them. Is it a parasocial relationship? The kind where I, a media user, am in a one-sided relationship with a media persona? Are they media personae though? Does it count if they were more or less coerced into it? Does it count if they're no longer alive?

Whatever I call it, the fact is that I want to commune with them. To hold them close through this act of invention, to honor a kind of truth if not its entirety.

I also want to leave a message in a bottle for someone like me in ten or fifty or twelve hundred years: Keep asking questions. Keep seeking answers. Do it carefully, but keep trying to understand the nature of our species, the spaces where our experiences overlap, the Venn diagrams, the circles, the archetypes of stories, of what moves us.

I don't fully believe that there will be someone like this. I don't really think anyone would care if they did stumble upon these folders and this imagining. But without this imagined future reader, I would never know how to write this. The snake eats its own tail and shits itself out.

This time, the drive was to the hospital. The wife twisted her wedding ring around her finger, its smoothness comforting even though she could barely take it off these days. She was going under the knife again, much as she did not want to. Her body had been invaded too many times, and while it had always withstood the scalpel remarkably well, she was nearly fifty, which was not old exactly, but near enough; she rarely felt it except when ill, as she had been for months now, and while she largely trusted medical professionals, she was still anxious. Would her earthly vessel come through this latest trauma intact? The lump perpetually in her throat, the coughing, the voice that deepened and made some people think she was her husband when she picked up the phone . . . she would be glad to be through with all of this, glad for the polyps to be taken out. But being put to sleep, losing time again, well, that was far less appealing.

At the hospital reception, the husband stood back, let her deal with the particulars of checking in, and once she was taken to her room, he asked a nurse when he would be able to pick her up. He had to go to work, especially since she had transitioned to a part-time schedule and his income was more vital than ever. Yes, there were speaking fees and the book royalties, but they certainly did not make the couple wealthy, despite what some thought. He hoped to pick his wife up later, he explained to the nurse, and would telephone the hospital every two hours from a pay phone, but he left his mother-in-law's number, just in case.

After his wife changed into the humiliating gown, he kissed her and told her everything would be all right, that she would feel better soon. He was confident though he had no qualifications to be, but he simply could not imagine his life without her, his beloved who was sometimes shrill and annoying and nagging but also sweet and funny and curious and rubbed his feet and was the only person he knew who could really and truly understand what had occurred on the strangest night of his life. Being unable to imagine his life without her, he chose not to, and to instead be certain of her renewed health.

She squeezed his warm hand tightly before he left. If only she could bottle his warmth, she could battle the cold, cold rooms of the hospital with it. Her nipples puckered embarrassingly beneath the paper-thin pink-and-white gown, and by the time the nurses wheeled her into the operating room, she was quite ready to be put under the spell of anesthesia, if only to leave her body, its discomfort and fear, behind.

.   .   .

The surgery was only partially successful, and she had to do it all over again a month later. She cried more after the second surgery, the anesthetic being, perhaps, stronger. This time her husband had been able to take the day off work, and he sat by her side as she awoke in the recovery room and watched as she began to sob, soundlessly. He had to remind himself that all the doctors and nurses said that depression was a common side effect of the drugs.

He enfolded his wife's icy hands in his own, brought them to his mouth, and blew on them. She was cold all over, her skin turning bumpy, and he wondered why it was called gooseflesh, for while his former wife had prepared goose, he had never touched its skin, neither alive nor dead, cooked or uncooked, and did not know whether it looked like this. His mind wandered to his uncle's farm, trying to recall whether there had been geese there, and his wife cried, and he let her because he knew that there was nothing he could say or do to make her stop. Finally, when her tears abated and she smiled and opened her mouth to speak, nothing came out. The stricken look in her eyes was so frightening that he thought something must have gone wrong again. But a severely bunned nurse told the wife that she should not even attempt to speak for several more days and that once she did, she should do so very quietly in order not to irritate her vocal cords any further.

His wife, the woman who could speak a mile a minute, rendered voiceless? He could not fathom it, and indeed the days that followed were sad and rather lonely as she communicated via pantomime and impatiently scrawled notes.

Slowly, slowly she was able to retire her hand-waving and scribbles. At first, she whispered, and then, when some amount of life seemed to have returned to them, her vocal cords began producing a louder rasp. But her own specific voice, its former melodious quality, was gone forever.

Did she know, I wonder, that it would never return? Or did her doctors tell her she may keep seeing improvement over time? Doctors like doing that, I've found, making vague and cheery prognoses so the patient and their loved ones can leave their office with that most ephemeral of placebos: hope.

False hope, all too often, and she, well, she seemed to be a trusting person, and she had no choice but to believe her doctors. There was no Dr. Google with which to obsessively research her symptoms; there were no forums dedicated to untangling one's experience of one's body from the pronouncements of professionals.

Another possibility is that she felt fine about whatever might occur following surgery as long as the polyps were removed. Maybe she knew and accepted, going in, that she would lose something irrevocable, irrecoverable. She sounded, I've read, like a heavy smoker for the rest of her life, and while as far as I can tell she was indeed a smoker, I wonder whether she felt judged, especially as smoking became less common, more stigmatized. Maybe she corrected people if they asked how many packs a day she smoked. Or maybe she didn't.

It's hard for me, despite how relatively little I use my own, to imagine the change in her voice having no psychological effect. But she is not me, and she seems to have been capable of rolling with the punches, setting her sights upon her here and now and her future rather than lamenting the past. Yes, it is ironic that the event that determined much of her adult life was what others always wanted to hear about, what I am still attempting to imagine my way into, but as far as I can tell, while her obsession with UFOs continued apace until her death, she wasn't stuck reliving her own experience; she was eager to understand those of others, and to widen the scope of human knowledge.

It was not the last of that year's health concerns.

In late spring, just as she began to feel like she would soon be able to return to work, her husband asked one evening as they were getting ready for bed whether she had gained any weight. She self-consciously peered at her half-clad body, trying to see it from a perspective other than her own. But she had all the same lumps and rolls and softening effects of gravity that had been there for many years already. Her husband was not looking at the usual places where she herself would have noticed a change, such as her hips, arms, stomach. Rather, he was looking at her calves, and it was really only then that she noticed, her stockings rolled down, that they were quite puffy. She sat on the bed and lifted her leg up to examine it, noting at once that the flesh was warm and strangely tight. She poked it, gingerly, almost expecting to hear a sloshing of liquid, but her skin merely whitened briefly at the touch and blotched back to its ruddier pink.

Her husband said quietly that he had read once that swelling in the legs could mean a heart issue, and he kept his eyes averted, knowing that she would look at him with panic or despair or exhaustion, all reactions that he did not have the energy to deal with after his long day. He almost regretted saying anything, but she just sighed and thanked him for bringing her attention to it. She would make another doctor's appointment in the morning.

In bed, he stewed for a while, reading the same page of <u>Look</u> over and over again, his left fist clenching and relaxing repeatedly, until he felt her soft hand on his and allowed himself to put the magazine down. They were not yet fifty, he told her when she asked what was wrong, and here they were, him exercising regularly, popping antacids like candy, not smoking anymore despite desperately missing it, and her doing her level best to give her body the rest it so clearly needed, and yet—it did not seem to matter what they did because the steady march of time kept stomping unceasingly forward. But were they not too young to need to deal quite so much with their health?

She knew what he was asking. She, too, was tired, and a little sad, for she had perceived in recent weeks that her new voice no longer had the soothing quality it had once had, and so she squeezed his hand again, leaned over to kiss him, and switched off her bedside light.

> *Their mortality must have been on their minds, I believe, not only due to their own health issues but also because the wife's father had died that year.*
>
> *It's becoming increasingly clear that fatherhood is a somewhat mysterious concept to me. So: her father died that year, or perhaps the year before, and she and her family likely grieved him, and that is all I know and all I can imagine about the situation. I am aware of how crass I sound. He simply isn't a major character in this story.*

She forgot to make a doctor's appointment, though, distracted by what she had to do at home while she continued to recover from surgery, responding to mail from readers and coordinating the continued speaking opportunities she and her husband were invited to. Whenever she remembered that she should, something else happened to take her mind off it, and in April, when Martin Luther King Jr. was assassinated in Memphis, she and her husband were swept up in the urgency that followed, fundraising, writing letters, participating in a vigil at their church, planning for the next NAACP board meeting and, and, and.

In June, while enjoying the sunshine and warmth on the porch, she was beset with severe chest pains that frightened her enough that she called for an ambulance rather than driving herself to the hospital. When the husband came home from work and saw the note she had left him, he rushed back out, cursing himself for not prodding her again about her legs, for his own exhaustion getting the better of him. He cursed himself doubly as he listened to the radio news reporting that the Poor People's March on Washington, D.C., was much smaller than was hoped for, wishing he and his wife had been able to organize for a larger group from their area to join it. But how could he be thinking about politics at this moment when, for all he knew, his wife might be dying?

His mind felt scrambled, full of worries crashing in one after another like waves. When had he spoken to his boys recently, was the little dog looking unwell again or just old, would the country ever recover from Dr. King's death, would the movement succeed without him, was his own heart going to give out on him, would he survive his wife's death if it came to that, would he need to take care of her mother, was his suit at the dry cleaner's or at home, why could he not remember, was he losing his memory, could he be deteriorating so quickly, how much had he neglected keeping in touch with his family, had he done right by them, and why oh why were he and his wife sickly, and could it have anything to do with the unthinkable, with the event that shaped their lives nearly seven years ago now, had they been marked, were they cursed, were they crazy, was his wife alive, was she alive, would he be able to maintain his grip on what had happened to him without her or would it all crumble under the weight of his inner scoffing rationalist, he needed her alive, please let her be alive.

She was. But her case of pericarditis was bad enough that once she was released from the hospital she was on bed rest for much of the summer. Her widowed mother helped nurse her back to health while the husband went to work until, finally, the wife was well enough that she could return to her own job in a part-time capacity, as well as begin traveling some

distances again for speaking engagements, which provided continued
fascination, for her anyway.

In the car once again several months later, the husband and wife counted their blessings aloud, trying to remind themselves of all that was good in their lives, for the year had been difficult, and they had spent much of it complaining until, finally, they decided that doing so was making things worse than they had to be. So it was that, as they began the fifty-mile drive to a lecture hall, they prayed, in their own way, by giving thanks to God, whatever or whoever He may be, for the many things they did have: each other, a roof over their heads, money enough to be able to afford the expenses incurred by medical troubles, loving families, a supportive church community, the respect of some impressive men of science, the self-confidence and integrity necessary to withstand the ridicule that came from others, the strength of their convictions, and the energy to work toward a world better than the one they were born into.

About halfway through this accounting of good fortune, the husband began to feel a looseness inside his head, as if his brain were swimming around and bumping into the sides of his skull. This was impossible, of course, but nevertheless that was what it felt like, and as he got dizzier, the road shuddering in front of him, he pulled over and asked his wife to drive.

When they arrived, his color was bad, a grayness in his cheeks, and when he tried to get out of the car he stumbled. It was vertigo, he told her, voice cool and collected, as if unconcerned, and although she told him that she would rush inside and explain the situation and then take him to the hospital, he insisted that they go on with the talk, that he would be fine, he just needed some water, maybe a nip of something stronger to sharpen the edges of things. Against her better judgment, she acquiesced, for she knew that no matter how poorly he felt, her husband was a bear about his responsibilities, never reneging on a commitment. Although he leaned on a chair for the majority of their time on the hall's narrow stage, he nevertheless completed his talk with the same firm clarity he always projected when speaking in public.

On the way home, he said he was feeling a bit better, but he was not, and she knew it, having long ago learned what he sounded like when he was lying. She insisted on getting him checked, and he joked—it was a good sign, at least, that he was able to joke—that she was taking him hostage. She laughed and said she was indeed but what a shame that she had not robbed him, too, and they traded such pale quips all the way to the emergency room.

> *It was ultimately a wasted trip, for the doctors couldn't find anything wrong with him other than the high blood pressure he and his own physician already knew about.*
>
> *Was there anything that could have been done that day to prevent what was to come? I wonder how often she asked herself this question later on, or whether she accepted the sequence of events that followed because, well, what else could she do?*

The vertigo did not return, and after the single day off his wife had convinced him to take, he was back at work, and she was, too, and things were almost back to normal.

But the biggest loss that year was not of their own health, but of the only other earthly being who had witnessed what they had. The little dog, Dee, was having accidents at home, and when the wife saw drops of blood in the latest pool of urine, she made a veterinarian appointment as quickly as she could.

It was a bladder infection, and the little dog was dangerously dehydrated as well. They took her home and tried to tempt her with water, with her favorite treats, but she was lethargic and would not drink, nor eat, and so they brought her back to the vet who gave her fluids intravenously, and while she perked up for a day, she was soon terribly weak again.

On Christmas Eve, Dee died, lying on her favorite fuzzy blanket near the small tree they had put up in a failed attempt at cheer.

The wife cried bitterly when the dog took a final breath, and she pet the still fur gently, wishing she could bring back this creature who had been with her and her husband for so many years, who had cowered and shivered the night of the abduction, as aware as the couple that something was terribly wrong.

The husband tried to dig in the backyard, but the ground was too hard, so he finally came back in, face betraying the tears he had wept outside, in solitude, the physical exertion allowing him this moment of release. He held his wife and took in the scent of her hair, which smelled not only of shampoo but also of something else, earthier and womanly, unique to her. He hoped, and said so, that they would suffer no more loss or worry for many months to come, and she whispered a small amen.

15

Now
———

For months, with some guilt for making their room less available to the cat, the Archivist spends most evenings at a dive near their apartment, their old laptop open on the bar next to a beer sweating itself lukewarm. They type, and they type, and they type, and at first the regular bartender looks at them askance for using the spotty wi-fi and ordering only one drink every night, but soon they become such a fixture that she indulgently calls them the resident poet. They tell her they're not, but she just laughs. So they become the Poet to the other regulars, and even though it's wrong, and incorrectness bothers them, the Archivist is pleased by the recognition.

Some nights, they stare at the words they've written until they want to throw the computer into the harbor. At such times, they shut it and, instead, reread whichever documents they've brought with them that night for inspiration. Occasionally, other patrons talk to them, asking politely, or belligerently, what they're up to, what they're writing, what they're reading. The Archivist, whose mother raised them, if nothing else, to be polite to strangers, responds in more or less vague terms, half smiling, trying to bring the interaction to a close as quickly as possible. They feel oddly bereft after such exchanges, as if speaking about their project aloud somehow diminishes it, makes it less solid.

It's the reverse of the childhood memory they're still chasing. Their mother filled in some details that have resonated: the little boy in the video with the cross necklace, Jason Shin, looked familiar to the Archivist because he would come over sometimes with his grandmother, who was friends with their own grandparents; the teacher in the video, Karen Walsh, always let the Archivist stay in the art room after school when their mother was late picking them up; their grandparents were terrified of their grandchild turning out like their daughter and forbade the Archivist from speaking about the alien nonsense at home. These particulars have made the experience feel closer, less out of reach, but whether that's because the Archivist is unearthing something buried or building something new on the spot it once stood is unclear. They wish they had someone else to talk to about it, but the documentary producer has failed to put them in touch with any of the other Slopeside experiencers. The Archivist has finally concluded that he probably never had any of the others on board and was playing a long game with them, trying to wear down their resolve with his friendliness and false promises.

About their project, though, they want to say as little as possible.

They spent several years dating a successful author when they were younger, and she maintained that she was utterly incapable of writing for her own satisfaction. She craved readers, needed the validation of other people's senses engaging with her words. Otherwise, she said, she might as well not exist; to be unread, for her, was akin to being dead. The Archivist found it morosely fitting, once the devastation wore off, that she had broken up with them via a long letter left on the kitchen table in the apartment they had shared in which she explained all the ways she was unsatisfied, all the things she needed, and all the reasons she had decided to exit the Archivist's life. It felt good, at the time, to burn the letter, knowing how sensitive she was to her words' disappearance.

The Archivist thinks of her approach now with confusion. Although they have a precise plan for what to do with their writing, it doesn't involve sharing it with contemporary readers. It barely involves admitting to its existence. Yes, of course, they wish to communicate something, but it is to be a one-way conversation. The kind they have been on the receiving end of for years.

February 15, 1968

Today is my six-month anniversary of living with Violet, and I baked a cake. It's lemon blueberry, two of her favorite flavors, but she barely glanced at it when she got home tonight. She was in a tizzy over a department meeting, telling me all about Howard and Dr. Schultz and Mr. Franklin and the rest of them. It's like a bad drama serial. Maybe I'd be more engaged if I actually knew the players. (I haven't been introduced.) Or maybe not. I never cared much for work gossip, who wasn't talking to whom, who'd slept with whose wife, et cetera.

Vi says she's lucky to be in a relatively small department where everyone still talks to one another (although if Vi is any indication, they also do a lot of talking <u>about</u> one another). But they make her do so much work! She thinks it's because she's the only female tenured professor since Daisy took an offer from Columbia last year. If I never again hear about Daisy and her wonderful position in New York City, it'll be too soon. A few nights ago, when Vi was going on and on about her, I told her she should have asked Daisy to move in instead of me, and I ran to my room like a child. I'm ashamed now, but at the time I felt very self-righteous. I know she and Daisy stopped being romantic years ago, and I need to accept that she's Vi's best friend. I do, usually. I don't think I'm all that jealous by nature. It just seems sometimes that Daisy is the kind of person Vi really wants to share her life with, and I don't measure up. But Vi says she talks of Daisy so much only because they had each other's backs in the department, so it's harder now that she's gone. Well, fine, but after spending a whole day doing what needs to be done around the house and trying to work on my novel, it's tedious to hear again and again about how great Daisy's life must be because she's at such an eminent institution in such a vibrant, international city.

I quite hate New York. No, I'm just sore.

The truth is, I don't like Silver Hills. It's charming and beautiful enough, and while the landscape isn't at all similar, something about it reminds me of where I grew up. Maybe it's how close the farms are to town, or how people seem to be entirely invested in each other's business while also keeping a polite distance. I can't disappear here the way I did in Boston. I never realized how much I'd come to rely on that, on the ability to see so much without being seen myself.

I had to be careful there, too, of course, but here it feels like I can't do much of anything without raising potential suspicions. Vi thinks, for instance, that if I try to get a job, she'll be judged for making her cousin work for her rent. I think it's much stranger, though, to have one's cousin live with one for months on end without spending any time with her in public. It's not that I'm hidden away. I do errands at the shops in town. I take walks in the woods nearby when it's not too cold or wet, although it usually seems to be. The librarian, Christina, knows me well by now and always makes sure to set aside the new SF releases. She says I read more Asimov than the Science Fiction Youth Club.

But Vi and I rarely go out <u>together</u>. We even celebrated her birthday at home, just the two of us. So I wanted to make this half anniversary special, somehow, which is why I was so excited for her to see the cake. She's sitting in front of the television set with her knitting now and letting me sulk. That's what she calls it whenever I insist on spending time in my room alone, even if it's to write rather than brood (or both, as the case may be . . .). She says I have all the time in the world to work and write while she's at the college, teaching, so why do I have to hole up in here when she's home?

Maybe it <u>is</u> childish to care so much about the stupid cake. She took one bite of it after dinner, which I also made, and said it was fair and that she was sure I would make a better one next time. When I was upset she was so surprised, as if she hadn't considered the fact that what she said might hurt my feelings. I suppose she's right, though, since it wasn't the best cake. Something about the texture was off. Too much or too little baking powder, I think. But it tasted very good anyway, and I wish she'd have said something nice.

Anyway. I'm just complaining, which I guess I do fairly often. Vi keeps reminding me, and I know she's right, that change of any kind is hard. After living in Boston so long on my own, it's bound to be difficult for me to live somewhere else. She reminds me also that as a writer, experiencing new things is good for me. Yet I've been having a frightful time writing in recent months. I did publish two more stories, but I don't think they're my best work—more commercial fodder, the kind of thing I know the editors like. It took a lot of work and effort and thought and feeling to write even those pieces, and I'm not saying that my heart wasn't in them. But I want to do better, to write things that excite me, that provoke my own thinking as well as my reader's.

A few weeks ago I started a new novel. I threw Fiona away after New Year's because after I finished reading it aloud to Violet, at her suggestion, I could see from her reaction it was garbage. Just a lot of fluff and fun. But I'm determined to have the <u>right attitude</u> about it, and so I consider it practice for the next book I shall write.

Rather, the one I'm writing already. I'm planning it out more carefully this time instead of just letting the muse take me where she will. I'm picking up the effort I began last year. (Or was it the year before? I need to start dating my drafts . . .) It's the one about that couple that was abducted by aliens. When I told Vi about my idea, how I was thinking about writing it as a nonfiction novel, like Capote, she absolutely gasped. She hates Capote's writing, but she admires his innovation and, as she pointed out, it sold like hotcakes. I'm having the couple be two men, friends (well, lovers in my mind, but I won't say so) who are at university together and decide to drive around at night to see if they can

spot a flying saucer. They spot one, all right, but get more than
they bargained for when they're brought aboard. Then they
vanish for months. That's where the book starts, really, with the
investigation into their disappearance, the cops and parents and
school administrators and everyone spouting theories about what
happened, and there's a big argument about whether to declare
the young men dead in absentia. In the middle of that drama,
they reappear and don't know they've been away for so long.
That's about as far as I've gotten. I'm trying to figure out what
happens next, whether they start remembering things from when
they were gone. I think they will, but they'll be able to talk about
it only to each other. When they try to talk to anyone else about
what happened, they'll forget all about it again.

Well. Anyway. Now that I've cooled out, I better go cuddle
with Vi and apologize for my mood. I shouldn't ruin the whole
anniversary just because I'm a mediocre baker.

March 29, 1968

My, my, my! We're having some excitement in Silver Hills! Violet's
hating every minute of it, but I'm having fun. She's only seven years
older than me, but she acts like such a dour old dame sometimes.

Some army general is supposed to come give a speech here
next week about the history of American military might, from the
Revolutionary War up to Vietnam, and a student organization,
DEMO, Democratic Education Minus Oppression, is staging a
sit-in on the lawn of the university president's house. I took a walk
on campus today while Vi was teaching so I could see it without her
getting her panties in a twist about my hanging around there. It's
been years since I yearned for this kind of campus life, but seeing
all those young people holding signs and chanting about how they
didn't want warmongering military officials on campus was inspiring.

It was easy to tell who'd been there since yesterday morning
when the protest started because they were the group at the center,
sitting on a big picnic blanket and looking more rumpled and tired.
There must have been at least two or three hundred others gathered
around them. I could see some leaving their book bags with friends

and running to one of the buildings to get something or maybe to use the bathroom. And others arrived with Tupperware containers filled to bursting with food from the dining hall.

Would I have joined them if I were a student here? I like to think so. I can imagine myself being the bearer and re-filler of coffee thermoses. Violet's got a big red one she takes with her to school every day after making her own coffee to her exacting specifications, and she bought me my own (green, to match my Olivetti!). Yes. I think that if I were nineteen again and in college, I'd take part and help keep everyone awake and energetic.

But it's easy to imagine what I'd do when I don't have to do it. When no one expects it of me.

Vi thinks it's all a tremendous waste of time. Protesting, picketing, the whole nine yards. She's skeptical of anything other than voting, really—she thinks political action of any other kind is mostly messy, a public disturbance, a nuisance, and most importantly it takes people away from other things they could be doing. Like homework for her classes.

She says that the war is none of our business because we regular people obviously don't understand what's going on and need to trust those in charge. This baffles me a little bit, and I've tried to tell her that there's plenty we do know—I used to read the war reports on the wire service every day at work, after all—but she didn't seem interested, really, so I stopped.

I guess I know what she means. Kind of. After all, neither of us is related to anyone in the army, and most of the students and professors are staying out of it. And, Vi likes to joke, it's not like we mind having fewer men around . . . I like men fine, though, as friends, and besides, I don't think it's funny to joke about all those people dying. I still remember Papa talking about friends of his that died in France and Germany during the Second World War. People keep saying a draft is coming because the military needs more soldiers, and I think that's just horrible.

How can anyone, even a government, force a person to pick up a weapon and shoot someone else? Maybe I'm naive, but I don't understand how Violet can't see that people killing one another is unequivocally tragic. No, that's not fair. She must know it's terrible. She just thinks that she has no control over it, and so it isn't her business.

Honestly, she's probably mostly annoyed because quite a few of the English majors are at the sit-in and her classes have been poorly attended. I think she should join them, to show solidarity. It would make those kids look up to her even more. They'd never turn in a paper late again. But Vi thinks I'm being as silly as they are when I say things like that.

I suppose I am. Silly.

I love her very much, of course, but sometimes I wonder whether it was a good idea, moving to Oregon so quickly. It's not that I feel underappreciated exactly. Vi loves having me around, I can tell. Even on afternoons when she comes home exhausted from teaching and student conferences and meetings all day, the way she looks at me when I brew her tea and rub her feet makes me feel warm inside. And I'm getting better at both cooking and baking because she has such high expectations that I do my best to rise to the occasion. That's a good thing, right?

Kathleen and Alice, bless them, have been active correspondents since I moved. They keep saying they're worried about me, especially since they found out I gave up on the Fiona novel I told them so much about. But the new novel is going well, I think, and I keep reminding them (and myself) of that. Alice still doesn't like Violet, and so I mostly just tell her about odd things I see and ask her opinion about this or that piece in The Ladder. She keeps saying I should move back. In almost every letter. I guess she misses me, which is a pretty satisfying feeling. It's not like she wants me back or anything. I've just never been missed before.

Kathleen is less snooty about Violet, but because she's also more vulgar, she's told me that if Vi still satisfies me in bed, that's half the ball game right there. Well, in that case, I've won half the ball game with a big lead! Vi would have a conniption, thinking about what would happen if Kathleen's letters were intercepted and she was found out. Anyway. Kathleen thinks she's being practical, that if I have a good time in bed and a woman who pays my way, I needn't want for anything else, at least not until my novel is finished, published, and making me barrels of money. At least Kathleen believes in me!

I hope the students don't give up, and that they make it until tomorrow so the general can see how many people are opposed to his agenda. But there's rain in the forecast, and I imagine that might put a damper on things. Ha ha. Oh, Phyllis, go to bed already, you're getting punchy.

April 10, 1968

Everything feels wrong and I barely know what to do with myself. It's the middle of the night and I can't sleep. Vi kept holding on to me in bed and it felt good but then the boozy fog would lift for a moment, and I'd remember everything and feel almost slimy.

My head is aching from all the wine, but it's more than that. The spinning is also more than the alcohol, I'm sure of it. My mind is reeling, making everything feel uncertain, as if I might touch the wall and find it giving beneath my hand. It's as if I've been plopped down into another world where everything is a little bit different, like a fun house mirror, and I'm not quite sure of the rules here. (Yes, yes, Phyllis, of course that's an idea for a story, but for Pete's sake, why can't you for once focus on what's happening right now rather than immediately trying to make a story of it? Was Violet right when she said that everything is some kind of fairy tale to me? That I don't deal enough with reality? Is that true?)

Vi and I finished nearly two bottles between us. It was for our one-year anniversary (we decided we were seriously together when I visited her here last March), a bit belated because she's had so many student conferences and committee duties and so so so much grading to do the last couple of weeks. But tonight, finally, we honored the occasion. I made her favorite roast beef recipe and bought a raspberry tart from a bakery she likes and got the Merlot she's partial to and remembered to shut the curtains so that we could have a romantic candlelit dinner without concern. Everything started out so well too! She was gracious and impressed and moved that I made things special for us, for her.

I don't even know how or when exactly things turned south, but it was sometime after we heard the hourly news on the radio, when we were having the tart and wine in the living room, and she was knitting, and I was reading the new PKD novel. The broadcaster talked about the protests in Pittsburgh, where Vi got her doctorate. She got peevish and said something about "those hooligans." I asked her what she meant, and she started going on and on about the Reverend King, how he always said he was so peaceful but now he'd gotten himself killed and with him dead, the rest of <u>them</u> were returning to their baser selves.

She didn't seem angry at first, more rueful and impatient, as if the protesters were children being naughty. My ears got very hot while she was talking, which happens only when I'm very, very angry. (The last time was when Cote laid me off.) I asked her what she meant by <u>them</u> because although I suspected she meant Negroes, I couldn't quite believe what was coming out of her mouth. She said she meant exactly that, Negroes, although she used an uglier word that Molly told me long ago never to say. (I should write Molly . . . I don't remember which of us dropped the correspondence, but I haven't heard from her in ages. How horrible of me to think of her now because of this.) Vi said nobody should be surprised by "their" violence because it's in "their" nature. She spoke with such dripping disdain that I felt like I was looking at a stranger. I'd only ever heard her talk this way about her department chair, an amiable Irishman whom she hates because she thinks he's frivolous and doesn't take his job seriously enough. But even when she speaks of him, she doesn't sound quite so . . . ugly? Yes, ugly. With her face flushed with wine she even looked ugly as she went on about how "those people" should be muzzled with a strong hand—I remember the phrase because it's a mixed metaphor, the kind Vi rails against—and that LBJ should do something about "them."

I didn't know what to say, how to argue with her. It made me think about that CBS report last year, how Mike Wallace sounded dispassionate even while talking about how disgusting and reviled we all are. But then Violet's tone got more and more heated the longer she went on. It was as if something was coming out of its shell, like she'd been inside a pristine and well-wrapped cocoon and what was emerging now wasn't the butterfly I've always thought her to be but something poisonous and wasplike. When she trailed off the music was back on the radio, and I tried very hard to calm myself, because if I try to argue with her while I'm upset she says I'm being irrational and childish.

Finally, I asked her rather timidly how she could say those things about Negroes when people look at lesbians and think we're horrible, degraded, sinful, monstrous creatures who need to be fixed or put away somewhere or "dealt with," as she'd put it. She rolled her eyes at me and told me not to be so dramatic. All we have to do, she said, is keep our heads down and stay quiet and we'll be fine. If Negroes kept their heads down and stayed quiet like us, she said, they would be fine, too, but they insisted on making trouble.

I keep thinking of an interview with a Negro woman in The Ladder a year or two ago. She was the head of the New York chapter of the DOB. Odds are Vi's precious Daisy even knows her. Ernestine something, her initials were E. E., like E. E. Cummings, but I can't remember her last name (and anyway, it was a pseudonym)—she said in the interview the editors did with her that the gay rights movement needs to incorporate tactics from the black civil rights movement. Things beyond picketing in skirts and suits once in a blue moon. She mentioned civil disobedience, marches, electing homosexuals to office. It makes sense to me. The civil rights movement has been quite successful, hasn't it? At least, the Civil Rights Act passed, and schools and buses, etcetera, aren't supposed to be segregated anymore, and that's not nothing, right? I feel too stupid and uneducated about things like this. I should really change that.

The argument's kept going in my head. I know if I told Violet about Ernestine and about civil disobedience and protecting our own like the Black Panthers do . . . if I tried to bring any of that up, she'd ask me why I don't mind incidents of violence on our own shores but am so opposed to the war in Vietnam. It's not a fair comparison, for many reasons, and besides, governments can be wrong both abroad and at home. But I get tongue-tied. I don't know how to argue with her properly. Maybe I'd try to say that the Vietnamese don't deserve our gunfire just like Negroes don't deserve police beatings. Queers are also on the wrong end of a baton far too often, and we don't deserve it, either, or to be scared for our lives and livelihoods whenever we go to a bar in the "wrong" clothes. I know I'm not as smart as Vi is, and I'm definitely less sophisticated and worldly, but I know when right is right and wrong is wrong.

Seeing Violet like that, drunk and bigoted as if her mind had shrunk to the size of a pea all of a sudden, made me start to wonder. Has she always been like this? I think about how she hadn't wanted to go to the Charles when she first came to Boston. I had told her in my letters about how everyone there was copacetic, how it felt like a little paradise with men and women, black and white, all getting along and dancing and laughing. I thought it was beautiful. But then Vi didn't want to go there; she wanted to take a walk and go to her hotel. Then she didn't want to come see my apartment in Roxbury. Had I told her about my Negro neighbors? The Jewish ones? About the T'iens' laundry and their funny little girl who did her homework at the counter and was always making bubbles with her gum? I don't remember what I told Vi anymore. She burned each of my letters after she responded to it, so I can't even check. I wonder how that little girl is doing. Grace, her name was, in English anyway. Her parents called her something else. She was just a tiny thing when I first met her, and I saw her grow to be nearly a teenager—she might be one by now. It hasn't even been that long, but Boston feels a lifetime away.

Maybe things will feel better tomorrow. Maybe I just need some sleep. Maybe Vi will regret everything she said once she's not so drunk.

April 11, 1968

Violet has a wicked hangover. She yelled at me to stop typing so loudly this morning because her head aches. I brought her aspirin and water and tried to be very gentle with her, but she's in such a mood that there's no talking to her. I didn't sleep well, either, and my head hurts, too, but you don't see me taking it out on anyone. So instead of working on my novel, I'm back to thinking myself in circles about last night.

The question is: Am I going crazy? Is Violet always so horribly bigoted, or am I taking everything she said too seriously? (Although how else can I take it?) Was she just being nasty because she was drunk? I don't know what to do, what to think.

Well. That's silly. What I think is that I missed or ignored something I didn't want to see. How can I feel so blindsided but also realize that the signs have been there all along? Did I know it, unconsciously? Dr. Iverson was always talking about that, how the unconscious knew things your conscious mind wasn't ready to face yet.

She's always been very, very worried about us being found out because it could, no, it would end her career. But I didn't think she was what Alice calls a self-loathing lesbian. The precautions Vi insists on are maybe more extreme than the ones Alice and I took in Boston. I mean, we were careful, of course we were, it's not like we were parading around the Common holding hands and shouting about free love. But Vi is so terrified of being found out that she gets The Ladder mailed to a postbox the next town over. It wasn't until I visited her over Easter break last year that I realized that all my own letters went there too.

I keep turning it over and over in my mind: Vi seems entirely content being a lesbian, and she certainly doesn't pull back in the bedroom. But she also seems to think there's nothing wrong with how we have to live. I've never heard her complain about how ridiculous it is that we can't be out for fear of our jobs and reputations. Is she disgusted with herself? With us? So much so that she can't, or maybe won't, see the parallels between our plight and those of others? It's so glaringly obvious to me that my own situation (being a lesbian, being a woman) helps me feel for others facing adversity.

I assumed all gays and lesbians were like this. Alice has always said I'm naive. I guess she's right.

I thought Vi just didn't want to lose what she has, and that's why she never complains about how we have to pretend that I'm her cousin, that we aren't lovers. Her wealthy family's quite happy to keep supporting her in addition to her salary, as long as they don't have to know or hear anything about her "lifestyle" and as long as she always visits them alone. They call her the family's old maid, because every respectable family has one. Vi's fine with that, with how they ridicule her. It's almost like she doesn't know any better. It's true she's been sheltered, in her way. She went from her fancy Connecticut boarding school to Vassar to the University of Pittsburgh and then here. But she <u>must</u> know better. She's told me how it's been an uphill battle, and it's true there are so few women who get PhDs and professorships. Shouldn't she want it to be easier, then, for other women, whatever their color, to do what she's done?

Yet her favorite students are the boys. She only tells me about the boys. The girls, she says, are dull, there to find a handsome man to marry. Surely that can't be true of them <u>all</u>, can it?

I feel like water endlessly circling the drain, wondering how I could have missed these aspects of her. She said she's going to vote for Nixon in November. Nixon! How did I ignore that? I just thought she . . . I don't know what I thought. I didn't, I suppose. No, Phyllis, take responsibility, you chose not to think of it. Didn't I?

I wish I hadn't let her make love to me last night. Even after she changed the subject and started talking about <u>Middlemarch</u>, which she teaches every spring, she still made me feel so odd and small and stupid. When she rose and drew her fingers along my neck, I felt like a dog at her heel, and when she beckoned, I followed.

Later

She's up now and whistling out in the garden where she's doing some weeding. She barged into my room earlier and told me I could use the typewriter again, that she was feeling better. She asked me what was wrong, and I didn't know what to say, so I just told her I'm tired.

The truth is, I feel like I'm coming out of a dream. A warm, lovely dream where everything between us was perfect, where I finally found a love to replace Rosa, someone who wanted me right there, next to her, all the time. Except she doesn't want me with her most of the time, does she? She wants me at home, cooking dinner, because I don't have a job anyway. But I wanted a job. I wanted to be able to pay for my journalism course myself, but instead she paid for last semester, and this one, and told me to focus on my writing. Writing she thinks is beneath her. She never wants me on campus or with her anywhere. She's ashamed of me.

My whole body is vibrating, like something is going to explode out of my skin. A scorpion, maybe. Or a roaring lioness. Alice always said that Vi seemed hateful, even though nothing I told her about Vi seemed to demonstrate that. I thought Alice was jealous or sad that Vi wanted me to leave Boston, but maybe Alice saw something I didn't? It doesn't matter. I'm the one who should have seen it, and I'm the one who didn't.

It's almost Easter, and Violet and I are supposed to go driving around the American West together during her break. She wants to visit Nevada and Utah and Arizona and maybe get all the way to New Mexico and then come back. I don't think I can manage it. Not after last night. Not with the revulsion I feel crawling up my throat.

It's nearly dinnertime and I haven't made anything. Damn.

April 13, 1968

Well. I've done it again. I've run.

I have a suitcase, a carpetbag, my Olivetti, my notes about the novel and the pages I've written so far, and a few of my favorite books. I left everything else at Violet's.

I'm a coward. I know it. But I didn't know what else to do. I didn't know how to speak to her about being upset. About thinking she was someone different from who she was all along.

My only excuse, I suppose, is that I was scared of her. I was scared she'd convince me to stay, that I'm being crazy. She's only struck me once, the evening I came by her office on campus unannounced and she sent me away mildly. At home, later, she told me I couldn't traipse around campus or there'd be questions. If I enrolled as a student, it would be different, but I didn't want to be a 26-year-old freshman, so things had to be this way. She apologized profusely after she hit me. She even cried, said she was so scared of something coming between us. And she never did it again. No, I'm not afraid of her hurting me like that. Only of her making me feel like I don't know my own mind.

Still, I'm a coward. She already booked us rooms in Nevada and Utah. I wonder if she'll still go. I know she'll be furious when she reads my note. She'll think I'm so ungrateful.

She'll be right.

I should have talked to her.

I shouldn't have run away like a child.

It's too late now, though. It's done and I'm at the Greyhound station in Portland. I hitched a ride here from a young man in a convertible, a student at the college, and now I need to get on a bus as soon as possible.

I could buy a ticket for only as far as St. Louis, Missouri, and there are about a hundred stops between here and there (half of them going the wrong direction), but the agent said I'd be able to make my way on another line from there.

April 14, 1968

I'm in Bakersfield, California. There's a crick in my neck from sleeping against the window and my hands are chapped from all this dry desert air. I was hoping to take my mind off things by working on a new story, but every time I tried, my handwriting got so shaky with the bus moving that I got nauseous. I can read, thank goodness, or I'd have gone mad.

It's Easter. There are children here dressed in their Sunday best, fresh from church, running around the station while their parents look at their watches impatiently, waiting for a bus that's running late, I guess. Mother loved Easter. She thought it was the most joyful holiday of the year, better even than Christmas, because it was all about <u>re</u>birth. It gave her hope of some kind.

Or maybe she just liked it because she could start eating meat again after the Lenten fast. She never made me do it, though. She said that because I was a child, I could give up sweets. I told her I'd rather stop having meat and keep my candies, and she said that was exactly the point. You were supposed to give up something you cared about.

I'm not going back to Violet. I can't. All yesterday and this morning, I've been thinking, putting things together, trying to see our life together like Alice or Kathleen might have if they knew the specifics, the peculiarities. I started to see all the ways she's discouraged me from my writing, how she didn't want me to get a job so I could be her little housewife. How did I give up my independence so fast?

Or am I just making excuses for why I left so that I don't look back later with regret? I keep crying. It's nearly my time of the month. Am I just being unreasonable then? Suffering from the irrationality that comes before the blood?

I have until the day after tomorrow, when the bus reaches St. Louis, to decide where to go next. I thought I'd go straight to Boston, but seeing these children, thinking about Mother . . . Maybe I'll go to New Hampshire first. Something about leaving Violet has made me want to go home, or what home used to be, where Rosa and I were, well, Rosa and I. Hugging Papa would feel good. And Mother, well, we'll see I suppose.

Why are human beings cursed with feelings? Wouldn't we be better if we were all like the Vulcans, creatures of logic?

I am all questions and no answers.

April 20, 1968

I thought Mother would have thrown all my things away at some point over the last seven years. Seven years! Yet my room smells exactly the same. It's a little mustier, since Mother said the door's been closed for a long time, but there's still a hint of that awful perfume I started wearing when I turned 16. The bottle must be here somewhere.

I'm sure I'll find it. I'll have to. It seems I arrived here rather fortuitously. In a sense.

Papa is dead. It was a cerebral hemorrhage, very sudden, although he held on for nearly a week in the hospital. He wasn't able to speak anymore after, but he was awake on and off, and Mother sat with him and held his hand and he would stroke the inside of her palm with one finger. After a couple of days, she realized it was the same way each time. She says he was making the shape of the letter P̲ on her palm, over and over. Even though her name also begins with a P̲, Mother is convinced he was asking about me.

I feel awfully guilty and terribly sad. I never called Papa from Silver Hills. I should have, I meant to, but I never did. Mother didn't know how to find me. I'm a bad daughter. Mother's basically admitted as much, saying I should have come home years ago, but I can't bring myself to be angry at her. She looks so . . . old. She's still beautiful—she was always beautiful—but she now has white streaks in her brown hair, and the lines on her face are deep, grief stricken. It's been nearly three months since Papa passed, and I can see how small her life has become. She hasn't stopped going to church, but her freezer is full of TV dinners, the kind she would never even bring into the house when I was a girl. It looks like she's been using the same mug over and over again, bits of stone from our old kettle dotting the bottom. I gave it a proper wash last night. She seemed surprised at how clean it was this morning but didn't say anything.

She hasn't talked much at all. When I got out of Mr. Bernhardt's truck (he spotted me having lunch in Concord when I arrived and offered me a ride), everything looked the same, but I was shaking like a leaf. Mr. Bernhardt mentioned Papa's death during the drive, thinking I knew already, and if I weren't so shocked, I might have asked him to drop me off right then so I could hitch back to Concord and get on the next bus to Boston. I guess it's good I didn't.

Mother must have heard the truck in front of the house because she came out, and when she saw me with my things she clutched her hands to her chest and started crying. She stayed right there, the door to the house open behind her, until I came near enough to touch and then she grabbed me and held me. She didn't say she missed me or that she was glad I was back. She didn't apologize. But she hugged me so hard I felt the swollen knuckles of her right hand pressing into my spine, her sobs moving her chest up and down. "Your poor papa," she kept saying. "Your poor papa."

Once she calmed down, she made tea—with a tea bag, another thing she never used to put stock in—and we sat quietly in the kitchen for a while. When she did finally speak, she told me how Papa died, about him tracing a <u>P</u> on her palm, about how my coming back was a sign from God, that He has forgiven her. I think that's as close as I'm going to get to an apology.

Over the last few days, I've seen how much the farm has deteriorated. Mother has already sold most of the animals—the pigs are gone, and the cows. The chickens are still here, but it looks like she's been letting them fend for themselves, mostly. She says she's going to sell the house and the land soon and go live with her friend Celia, another widow with too much space to knock about in. They'll keep house together and live off their husbands' life insurance. "Until one of us croaks," she said. I can't tell how serious she is about this Boston marriage arrangement, and I don't know how much money Papa's insurance left her or whether it's enough or how much she can get for the house. But she doesn't seem to want to discuss the specifics, at least not yet.

This morning over fresh eggs I made us—the hens sure were happy that someone checked their nests!—Mother asked how long I planned on staying. I wish she'd admit that she needs my help, but her asking at all is something. I said I'd stay until the house was ready to sell. She almost smiled.

She's said nothing about Rosa, and I haven't asked. I've said nothing about Violet or Alice or anything about my life in Boston, and she hasn't asked. For now, I'm all right with that.

It's quiet here. I forgot how quiet. Vi's was quiet, too, I suppose, but not in the same way. It didn't feel peaceful there. But here . . . it does.

I'm going to set up my typewriter now and try to flee this confusing world for a little while. But despite it all, despite knowing that I'll never hear Papa's voice again, that I missed his death, that my mother is aging before her time and might need more help than she's letting on, despite the mess inside my head and my heart, there's a small something brewing in me. A warmth, almost a joy, at being here, in my room with my yellow curtains, with the bed where I dreamed teenage dreams, with the ugly cross on the wall that still bears the curse word I scratched into the back after some bad fight with Mother. Knowing that Mother is somewhere in the house. That we are under the same roof.

16

Now
———

The Archivist has tracked down the two donors who are responsible for Phyllis Egerton's papers finding a home amid the stacks they care so deeply for. One they haven't managed to contact yet, her digital footprint so minuscule they're not even sure she's still alive. The other, though, has written them back, and although he says he's too busy for a phone call, his lengthy missive betrays his need to process what he knows, and doesn't, about his mother and the woman she loved.

Harold, Harry these days, is a man in his sixties, a union electrician not yet retired, living in California with his wife, an elementary school teacher. He has three children, he tells the Archivist. The elder two are married with kids of their own, the younger a bit lost, coming up with a big new plan for the rest of her life every few months. His father has been living in a care facility for the last decade or so with increasingly severe Alzheimer's, and Harry is glad that his mother, who passed in the late 1990s, never had to see him this way. Harry discovered the letters when he and his father were going through her things in the months after the funeral. As soon as he saw them at the bottom of a shoebox, tied together with twine so tight it bit into the paper, Harry knew, somehow, that he needed to keep them from his father. That night, alone, reading what he could of the letters, he was astonished. His mother, Rosa, had mentioned Phyllis once or twice as a dear childhood friend who, don't you know, became a published writer, how grand, and whose three books she kept on a shelf in the living room alongside her husband's spy novels. But never, not once, had she mentioned anything about what she and Phyllis once shared.

At first, Harry was angry, thinking his mother's character was being maligned, her personality tainted. The Archivist's stomach clenches at the notion, but the sensation dissipates as they read on and learn that Harry's wife talked him into a different frame of mind, one that saw the potential tragedy at hand. Rosa had kept the letters for decades, after all; Phyllis must have meant something to her, even if it wasn't what she herself had meant to Phyllis. A few years later, when his youngest came out and became interested in LGBTQ history, Harry learned about the QWA and decided to donate the letters.

The Archivist, who began weeping toward the end of Harry's email, blows their nose. If anyone were to ask them what they were feeling just then, they would not know what to say.

. . .

Later that night, they sit outside with Shalani, the third or fourth time they've made a plan to meet there but the first time that's for longer than a cigarette. They share a bottle of wine a co-worker gave her as a going-away present. She's leaving and has been interviewing people to take over her lease for the last few days. Her aunt's longtime boyfriend left, claiming he couldn't stand the caretaking, that her illness was smothering him, and Shalani is going to move in with her and help out, a prospect she doesn't seem to find onerous.

—It's not like she even needs all that much, honestly. I mean, she has bad days, but she's really up and down, you know?

The Archivist doesn't, but they listen to Shalani talk through her nerves. She's been in the United States for years now and is more anxious about fitting in back in England than she is about living with her aunt.

—Why did you move here in the first place?

Shalani covers her eyes with her palm.

—It's so embarrassing. I moved to be with an American girl I met at uni. To my hypocrite parents' eternal disappointment.

—Why hypocrite? Why disappointment?

—You never pussyfoot around, huh, always go for the hard shit.

It's true, the Archivist thinks, and shrugs. They've never been good at small talk, although they've tried. They always try.

—Anyway, hypocrite because they met at uni too! At Cambridge, because they were all fancy and shit. And before you ask, Shalani adds, my mum's Tamil and from Sri Lanka, my dad's Black and from Michigan.

—I wasn't going to, they say.

Shalani raises her eyebrows and quirks her head like she doesn't believe them, and while the Archivist really wasn't going to ask about her racial makeup because that would be weird, they had wondered. Shalani seems to want to move past it.

—Anyway, that's why I can work in America, I have a passport.

The Archivist nods.

—What happened with the girl? they ask, instead of pointing out that Shalani didn't respond to their question about her folks' disappointment. The thought that she has disapproving parents sours their own pleasure at confirming finally, too late, that she is indeed queer.

—She dumped me after like six months, but by then I was hooked.

—On the U.S., the Archivist states, incredulous.

—Nah, man, on how you people act when I talk! Do you know how much tail I get just for having an accent? Can't go back to being one of the horde now. I'm spoiled.

She laughs, and the Archivist does too. She's not wrong about American Anglophilia.

—Right, but really what happened, she continues, is I met someone else and then I was already getting my certification for work once we broke up, and then I just, like, stayed. I was gonna apply to veterinary school this year but then that asshole left Auntie Sirima and, well, here we are.

For the first time the Archivist sees how brave a face she's putting on during all of this, leaving her life here for another one there.

—It sounds hard, they say, moving to take care of her.

Shalani shrugs this off, pours the last of the wine into both of their mugs.

—It's gonna be fine. Tell me about you, tell me about that woman you've been researching, what's her name, Frances?

—Phyllis, the Archivist says.

They tell her about Phyl S. E.'s third book, which they finally found a used copy of online, and how strange and wonderful it is, more openly queer than her other published work. Shalani asks if that's why she never had another book come out after, and the Archivist shakes their head, says it's possible but they don't know for sure.

And then the wine is finished and they're both a little buzzed and the autumn night has very suddenly turned chilly.

The Archivist wants to tell Shalani that they wish they'd started hanging out earlier. That they'll miss her, even though they barely know her. That they think she's cool and pretty and interesting and they wish they had a chance to learn more about her. They think they might actually do it, tell her, but then she yawns, one of those that stretches in the middle, and she says fuck and scratches at her scalp through the short hair that has grown in, and says she should go to sleep.

Instead of saying any of it, the Archivist asks her when she's going, and she tells them the date, and they say they should meet out here again before then, and she agrees, and they stay outside and think about how nice it is, knowing that there's someone so close by who enjoys spending time with them.

Before the Vietnam draft lottery began, before the debut of Sesame Street, *before the Tate-LaBianca murders, before the moon landing, before the Stonewall Uprising, a couple was driving together, once again, through the White Mountains, unaware that their experiences would have such an enduring effect, cementing a set of tropes and motifs into the collective (un)consciousness of generations to come . . .*

They knew how to be quiet together, these two. Always, from their beginning, they knew the comfort of shared silence, the blessed voiceless quiet that lets in the rest of the world's noises and gives a body room to experience its many senses. Hours they had spent in one car or another over their years together, visiting each other before they were married and then, once married, driving around the East Coast and New England to visit friends, to speak, to camp, to do what many a red-blooded American with a modest income could, which was travel and see the sights and smell the scents and taste the delicacies.

But they also knew how to be loud together, these two, and this late night, driving home from a speaking engagement three hours away, an event that had gone well and culminated in a lengthy dinner at a local restaurant, this late night together, full of food and pleasant company and the effects of flattery and excitement not yet worn off, they were exquisitely, joyously loud, and a bit punchy, the hour having grown later than they expected. Perhaps they knew to nurse the giddy adrenaline lending them energy in order to remain awake for the rest of their drive home, or perhaps they were not at all considering the reason for their good humor, just bathing in it, but regardless of their self-awareness or lack thereof, they were indeed enjoying each other's company.

The husband was behind the wheel, sending the wife into near hysterics with his hammed-up mimicry of Frank Sinatra, and although in normal circumstances this trick would likely cause far less mirth, it was the kind of night where everything clever seems brilliant, anything funny becomes hilarious, anything tender becomes the stuff of epic romance. When her laughter resulted in an undignified snort, his own redoubled, and so they egged each other on, their fun making them feel younger than they had in years, or perhaps not younger, exactly, so much as more in touch with that ageless thing that sits inside every living, breathing human, the sense of innocence and play that is forced to lie dormant in the world of grown-up concerns like jobs and politics and money and mortality.

There was nothing in the sky that night, nothing but stars, so many stars that, once they had both calmed down some, the hilarity slowly seeping from their bodies, she asked him to pull over at a rest stop and turn the headlights off.

It was a dark stretch of highway, no dwellings nearby, and the night was still but for the rustle of leaves in the winter wind. They leaned together on the car's trunk and fixed their gazes on the heavens. They could see the Milky Way, awesome and impossible to really grasp, the plurality of so many stars so close together, the knowledge that each of those stars was a sun, like their own, their light arriving delayed by many human generations over, their lives as ancient as what the couple called God.

He felt full in that moment, like he had as a child after eating so many wineberries from the wild bushes that grew on his uncle's land that it seemed that his tongue and teeth and gums might be forever coated in tart red sweetness. Opening his mouth now to the cold air, he shared this memory with her and heard the smile in her voice when she responded, asking him what else he loved to gorge himself on as a child, what else gave him that feeling of perfect satiety, and he told her and echoed the question back at her, and she told him and on they went, recalling childhood flavors and sights and sounds, the memories rising up their throats. When their fingers and faces began to numb, they broke from their reminiscences and returned to what they had expected to be the warmth of the car, except that of course they had turned it off and she had foolishly left her door open, so the inside of the vehicle was just as frigid as the air outside. It took many miles of road before the heating finally began to make a difference and they stopped shivering.

They were both more subdued now, but not because they were thinking about anything following them, flying above them, about the beings that might descend from that beautiful milky sky, about the mess such beings could make in the lives of humans. No, they were subdued only because they were tired, and chilled, and because they had had a pleasurable night that turned nostalgic in their conversation.

At home, they indulged in that most honeyed of adult privileges, late-night desserts, and ate a slice of peach pie each with a scoop of vanilla ice cream, giggling like teenagers doing something naughty, and then fell into bed without even brushing their teeth, feeling comfortable, loving, loved.

They deserve a good night, the best of nights, the most comforting of nights. They deserve this and so much more, and I hope that they had it. I so deeply, truly, desperately hope that they did. I hope that my imagination doesn't hold a candle to the kind of gladness and goodness and joy they felt. I hope that they never needed me to tell their story in this way; I hope, ultimately, that my effort is misguided, selfish, and that they had everything they wanted and needed in this life.

But no, that's not quite true either. Of course I want my version to be necessary, or if not exactly necessary then at least acceptable. I want to imagine a world in which they would appreciate my interpretation of them, or at least see the respect and love with which I've tried to imbue it.

I am trying to remind myself that as much as I want this story to be an expression of my love for them, an attempt to see their full humanity with its good and bad and petty and dull moments, they might not have read it this way if they found it nestled in these folders in the archive. I am learning to accept—because I must—that this is ultimately my story. Not theirs. That, being a wholly separate person, my telling of the story has colored it with my own sensibilities.

Still, I hope this story might be ours in some cosmic way, mine and theirs, theirs and mine. They will never be able to tell me.

Unless, of course, they somehow communicate with me from beyond the grave—but I don't believe in such things, haven't grown up in a tradition or a culture that allow me to believe in such things.
   Then again, they did not believe in aliens until one night in 1961.
   Perhaps there's hope for me yet.

On their last day together, he kissed his wife in the driveway before they each got into their own cars. As she backed out, she noticed that the snow, which had been coming down gently all night, was picking up so that the bare asphalt where their cars had sheltered the ground quickly acquired a fresh white carpet. As a matter of course, she turned the radio on as she drove. She had gone only a few miles when she heard the announcement about the descending storm, which the weatherman was calling the worst in years. Offices and businesses were closing, and drivers were being told to stay off the highways, to go home or find indoor shelter. So she turned around and plodded back the way she came, slower now as the visibility decreased and the other cars moved more carefully, their occupants growing tense as their wheels began to slide.

When she got back home her mind was finally free enough from the immediate effort of staying safe to worry about her husband, whose job was rather famously not to be deterred by rain, snow, or gloom of night. She hoped he had remembered to put on the extra pair of socks she had left on the bathroom counter for him and went to double check, only to find the thick rolled-up ball still sitting there. She felt especially wifely as she shook her head at no one and contemplated the ways in which men, even grown men who had raised two children, seemed so uniquely incapable of taking care of themselves.

But before she was even able to put the socks back in the drawer, she heard the intended wearer call her name and returned to the foyer to find him grinning at her, shaking off the snow dusted on him between car and front porch, and laughing when she lifted up the bundle in her hand and shook her head again, this time at him. He had gotten almost to the highway when the newscaster announced that all government offices in the region were to be closed as well, which was monumental, for in all the years he had worked for the post office, he had never had a snow day, never, not once.

Neither of them had had a proper breakfast before leaving that morning, only a slice of dry toast to soak up the strong coffee, and so now, while he changed out of his uniform, she began to cook them eggs and sausages and English muffins heated just slightly so that the butter she spread thickly on them would melt into the nooks and crannies, and fresh coffee, of course, with just a little bit more sugar and cream than usual, as a treat.

They ate slowly, trading sections of the newspaper that had been delivered before the storm warning, sipping their coffee, each knowing without needing to say it that the day would be a good one, a reprieve from the drudgery of work or the expectations of social engagements with anyone outside their own twosome. While she did the crossword puzzle, he put down the obituaries he had been glancing at and let his gaze fasten and then unfocus on the brightness outside the window, until a shadow cut through the bleached space and brought him back from the daydream. He became curious about the dark shape flitting by again and rose, approached the window, a small bell in the furthest corners of his mind beginning to tremble with remembered alarm, but no, it was just a bird, and then another one, and another.

His wife joined him, and they watched for a while as the birds in their backyard flew around and around when they should, the couple agreed, have been finding dry spots where they could keep warm, but they were out there nevertheless and perhaps, she ventured a guess, hungry. Exclaiming, her husband pulled a bag of birdseed from the back of a cupboard, having just remembered it was there, and she laughed in surprise, for she could not think of a more perfect activity, in that moment, than the two of them standing on the covered back porch and feeding the birds.

In reality, it was bread, not birdseed. I forgot that she had specified, in her account of this last day, what exactly they had fed the birds. I mean to say that I had forgotten this, but I just checked, and she did indeed write that it was bread, not seed. Should I change my detail? No. No, because birdseed paints a more beautiful picture than breadcrumbs, the way it scatters more pleasing to my mind's eye. Or maybe, really, it's my knowing that birds should not be fed bread that has caused me to make this alteration.

I have agonized over such mistakes, such presentist intrusions of mine, and could do so again now. But I keep trying to remember that

I needn't explain myself to you—which means, I suppose, that I am still trying to explain myself to myself.

When they got too cold, the wind having whipped itself into the kind that cuts to the bone, they returned indoors, and before she had a chance to feel the listlessness descend upon her as it sometimes did when she did not want to but felt she should be doing something useful like writing letters or going over case files, and before she had a chance to suggest some activity like this to him, he threw an arm around her shoulders and pinned her to his side in a teasing, almost brotherly sort of way and challenged her to a game or two of pool, say best out of three. She poked him in the stomach and wriggled away, protesting that he always won anyway, he was so much better, and he said he would play with one hand tied behind his back. Although she knew he would do no such thing, she relented, and soon regretted it, for they discovered the basement was freezing cold.

He wrapped his own sweater around her shoulders and ran upstairs to get some wood for the fireplace, which he then proceeded to efficiently stack and light. As the room warmed, it smelled deliciously of Christmastime, a season they both loved but which had been spoiled this past December by the death of their beloved dog. For a moment, she felt the grief well up in her, and she told him that she missed Dee. He hugged her and said he did, too, but she soon pushed him away for she did not want to spoil this beautiful day with sad memories and told him to prove to her just how good he was.

He won two games handily and began showing off with trick shots that bounced one ball over another or drove three into pockets in quick succession while she clapped and whooped and even attempted a cheerleader dance where she tried to spell his name with her arms, which could not quite be done. They were both laughing when very suddenly he clapped a hand to the back of his neck.

She asked what happened and he explained, puzzled, that it felt like he was just stung by something, like a hornet, which was impossible, of course, as it was not only winter but also the middle of a snowstorm, and they both would have noticed, heard and seen it, if such a large insect was flying around. As if in a dream, he moved toward the stairs and began to ascend but on the second or third step he stumbled, and instead of getting up, remained on his hands and knees as he climbed the rest of the way, which she found especially eerie as she could not remember ever seeing him on all fours.

He was able to walk to the couch when he got up to the main floor, but after sitting there for a moment he slipped to the ground, surprising himself, and her own heart began to beat faster as she watched it happen, her husband falling out of his seat as if it were buttered beneath him. She always knew what to do during her own health crises and how to take care of him when the doctor gave him new orders for lowering his blood pressure, but she was unable to move or think until, lying on the floor, he told her in a small voice that something was very, very wrong, a fact that was obvious and that should have set her in motion already. He told her she had better call an ambulance, and fast.

Lying there, he felt like a felled giant amid furniture that seemed to be getting smaller and farther away. Had he ever, really, been prone on the floor this way, looking at the room from this angle? He knew these were not the kinds of thoughts he should be having and recognized that what was happening to him may be unthinkable, as unimaginable as flying saucers, but no, those were real. None of that mattered right now when he was on the ground and far, far away from the sky and all that was in it, and so he focused on his wife's voice calling the hospital and thought, reassuringly, that he would be fine very soon. It seemed an eon before she was back in the room, and another small age before she crossed it and lifted his head gently and pulled at the upper half of his body so that he would be partially in her lap. Her hands were soft on his smooth face, freshly shaved only a few hours ago. Her murmured chatter filled his ears comfortably, and he thought he might drift off to sleep.

She noticed that his eyes, his beautiful brown eyes, were unfocused, one of them lazing a little, but she tried to stay calm, knowing that it would not help him to feel the distress radiating off her person. She was convinced that humans were like dogs or horses in that way, able to sense the reek of fear and agitation in their loved ones. The snow was so thick by now that she worried she would not hear when the ambulance arrived, but she did, its engine roaring and quieting, its doors clanging open. Here were people who would be able to do something. When they knocked, she yelled for them to come in, that the door was unlocked, but kept her gaze fixed on her husband, who had become alert at the sound of new voices entering the room.

The ambulance crew were men her husband knew, evidently, having seen them at church or meetings or somewhere else about town, but nothing and no one seemed familiar to her in that moment except her husband's face, her mind unable to expand beyond his comfort or lack thereof. The paramedics joked around in that gentle tone that people used when dealing with the very ill, and they checked his pulse and blood pressure and moved him onto a stretcher. They asked him why he had not driven himself to the hospital, strong man that he was, suggesting that maybe he was scared of an itty-bitty snowstorm like the one raging outside. The banter pleased him, and although he knew he would never have been able to drive in his current state, storm or no, he did feel a little better as he asked them why he should bother driving himself when he had such fine chauffeurs.

She held his hand the whole way to the hospital and was glad to see that the admitting doctor was a former college friend of hers, a jovial sort of man she felt she could trust. Since her husband's blood pressure was normal and he was breathing comfortably, the doctor felt there was no need to put him on oxygen and declared that he would be all right soon. The words filled her with hope. She repeated them, willing the fog in her mind to recede.

The husband wanted to agree, to say he really was going to be fine, but he was distracted by the doctor asking for his birthday, which he confidently shared, only to realize from the expression on his wife's face that he must have given the wrong answer. He concentrated, furrowing his brow but only moving the right side, and tried to remember what he had said so he could correct it, but when he opened his mouth next, it seemed he was in a different room, no longer in the admitting area. He tried to speak, to reassure his wife, but the words coming out were in the wrong order and his tongue felt very heavy, as if injected with something at the dentist.

Seeing him fading in and out of consciousness, waves pulling at a shore, and hearing the way his speech was becoming garbled, she felt the fog rolling back in on her, thicker than ever, and her body going numb. She pinched the inside of her wrist, and, determined not to be useless, began to bustle about, telephoning her husband's primary doctor who was too far away and unable to come in with the weather being what it was but who recommended another physician who was closer and whom she managed to reach. When that doctor arrived and examined her husband all over again, vital signs and everything, she learned that what she had already suspected was indeed what had occurred. A stroke. Not only a stroke, but a bad one, a cerebral hemorrhage, she was told. Her husband had a very small chance of full recovery, though it was more likely that, if he survived, he would be left in a vegetative state.

A chill ran down her spine. Her husband's father had been left brain-dead in such a way for a long time after a stroke of his own, albeit one that occurred much later in life, and she knew her husband did not want to live in that state no matter what. They had, of course, had conversations like this, as married couples who take the time to draw up wills and think of the future are wont to do. While she felt that her life was sacred enough that she wanted to live it for as long as possible, he took a different approach, for he had a horror of losing such a degree of control over himself. She knew, too, that he hated being a burden to anyone, which she thought was silly. Human beings were all burdens to one another, that was what caring for others meant, but she understood his more pressing fear, the notion that he might become trapped in a body that did not do his bidding, able to hear what was being said to him, as some people said comatose patients could, but unable to respond. He did not want to be caged inside a mind that could not ask for its own quick death.

When the doctor touched her shoulder, her whole body seized, star-tled, for she had not realized how long she had been sitting there, holding her husband's limp hand, fingering his wedding band. The doctor said she should go home, there was nothing more to be done, that he, her husband, was in a deep coma now, that he was already dying and would not wake again, and that with the storm being what it was, she should go, and someone would call her when he died.

She kissed her husband one last time, and left.

I have been thinking about his last moments, her last moments with him, for a long time. Why did she leave? Why didn't she stay by his side until he died? Was it a dissociation, or an inability to stand seeing him without breath and soul and life in his body? Was it sheer practicality, knowing the storm might go on and on, and that her being stuck in the hospital would

do no good to anyone? Was it understanding that she truly could do noth-
ing there, that her husband was no longer inside his flesh, that he had fled
it already? Was it the shock at being told shortly before that he would be
fine, only to witness his quick descent toward death? Most likely, it was a
mix of factors, but whatever prompted her decision to leave, I know down
to the marrow of my bones that it was not a lack of care, love, or devotion.

And what of him? What could his last thoughts have been? How
aware was he of what was going on at the end? Did he have any last
words, or were those lost amid the bustle of nurses and doctors and IVs and
whatever other noise was occurring around him? I hope he knew, before
the end, that he was loved.

When she arrived home, trembling, she realized she had not dressed
well, that she had been cold on the way to the hospital and at the hospital
and on the way home with the nurse who kindly agreed to drive her. She
put the kettle on and began to make phone calls, bearing the bad news
of her husband's imminent death to his family, his friends, the minister,
and finally her own family and friends. Only when her best friend asked
what the whistling was did she realize that the kettle had been boiling and
boiling for the last however long it had been, the water long gone by the
time she removed it from the stove, its bottom blistered black.

The kettle had preceded his arrival in her life, and staring at it felt like
looking into her future, a place where he would never again be. It was this
that finally broke the sturdy rod of stubborn pragmatism propping her up.
She sat heavily in a kitchen chair and let the tears come.

Soon her best friend arrived and put a new pot of water on and brewed
tea, and it was only a little later that the minister came to sit with her,
and it was only minutes after his entrance that the phone rang, and she
knew, somehow, she knew that it was not a family member or friend or
co-worker. She knew it was the hospital. It was twenty after seven, and
her husband was dead.

She had begun the day a married woman enjoying an unexpected holiday with her husband, and now she was alone, a widow, grieving.

The events that followed were what might be expected when a beloved dies.
There were phone calls to make, funeral arrangements to be figured out,

people to bring together to celebrate and mourn the life of a man dead far
too young, a man in his prime. I've read about those days, her recollections
that news of her husband's death broke into the programming of some TV
channels, the many important people in government and the military and
the sciences who attended his funeral, and more meaningfully the USPS
workers who came to see him off and the Portsmouth NAACP chapter that
shared food and space for people to gather after his body was put to rest.

There were strange and eerie events that followed his death, too, objects
appearing where they shouldn't, noises haunting the apartments above
again, and she wondered whether the beings were trying to communicate
with her or else someone from a covert intelligence agency was trying to
threaten her so that she wouldn't become loose lipped without the sobering
presence of her husband. There was the night when she saw a bright object
following her from Kingston to Portsmouth, which hovered above once she
stopped the car, got out, and thought as hard as she could up at the object
and the beings inside it that her husband was buried back the way she
came, in Kingston, and she knew she had managed to communicate this
when it moved back and forth above her, as if in acknowledgment, before
flying off toward the cemetery.

But none of those events included him, and it is their themness that
I've been interested in all along.

Her life went on, of course, but it seems to me it was never the same.
Rather than attempting to return to a life that involved the beautiful
mundanities of provable reality, she dove deeper into her ET interests,
believing too much for too long, willing others to find the proof she
so badly wanted, making a career out of rehashing her experience with the
beings and attempting many times—and occasionally semisucceeding—in
making some kind of contact again.

Over time, she was trusted less and less by the more credible investi-
gators of UFO phenomena, but she remained an integral part of the lore.
A complicated legacy so typical of the women we choose to remember: the
mother of a narrative that has remained with us for decades, she was
also discounted, deemed excitable and overeager or, perhaps worst of all, a
manipulative liar trying to make headlines.

But where others might see an attempt by a foolish woman to grab the
spotlight again in her later years, I see grief. She could not bring the man

she loved back to life, but she could keep him in existence by continuing to tell and retell and live and relive the trauma they had gone through together, processed together. If she kept telling their story, kept finding new ways to approach it or see beyond and around it, if she could keep sharing her experience with those who shared theirs with her, well, then he was still there, in a way, and she was not so alone.

What happens to a story when one half of its primary driving force disappears?

What happens to the storyteller?

These are the wrong questions, but I don't know the right ones. I only know that, decades after his death, decades after hers, I grieve for them. I keep them alive just a little bit longer, so that I, too, am not so very alone.

17

Now

The Archivist is still asleep on a weekend morning with Shalani's cat, Fitz, nestled in between their torso and their arm when their mother calls them. She sounds lucid, sharp, and they can tell, even in their sleepy state, that she has been taking her meds. The cat meows. It is only the third or fourth time the Archivist has ever heard him do so, and their mother demands to know when they got a cat, why hadn't they told her. The Archivist explains that they didn't, that it's the neighbor's, and that this neighbor moved out a few weeks ago and left the cat with them because taking him to England would have been too much of a pain and potentially traumatizing. Their roommates begrudgingly agreed to let them keep Fitz, as long as he stays out of the allergic one's room. Their mother goes on a lengthy diatribe about the rise in allergies, asking who is responsible for the weakening of the human immune system if not big pharma or the government, but then pivots, as she sometimes does, into a coherent lecture about how to keep an indoor-outdoor cat as safe as possible. The Archivist takes mental notes: They should buy a collar with a bell and a thick sweater to keep on Fitz during the cold months. They should ask Shalani for his chip information and keep a bowl of water always full on the fire escape in case he gets stuck outside. They thank their mother. It's a nice moment between them, a rare one.

She had a reason to call, she says, which was that she forgot about something that had happened during that period of time just after the

Archivist and a bunch of other schoolchildren saw aliens and flying saucers behind their school. The Archivist sits up, spilling Fitz onto the floor, and listens hard, the glass rectangle of their phone screen growing hot against their ear.

For several days after the sighting, their mother tells them, the Archivist kept talking about the people they saw inside the UFO. Not the aliens, which they had described as grayish and large-headed and thin-limbed and black-eyed. No, not them. There were, they insisted, people peeking out from the open door of the silver capsule, a middle-aged Black man and a very old white lady, holding hands. None of the other children had seen this particular couple, although some had seen other humans inside the craft, people who resembled their deceased grandparents or imaginary friends or favorite cartoon characters. The Archivist asks why these details weren't in the reporting of what happened, and she says she doesn't know, that maybe it was just too weird. She asks the Archivist if this sparks their memory, and they say no, but they thank her profusely for calling anyway, for sharing this with them. She sounds surprised at the warmth in their voice and tells them she loves them before they hang up. The Archivist is so taken aback that they repeat the words in response. It's been years since either one of them has said this, and the Archivist isn't convinced that she or they mean it, but it's a nice gesture.

The cat jumps back onto the bed, demanding to be pet. The Archivist massages his ears. What their mother says they saw makes no sense.

Could it be? No, surely not. As much as they want to believe in something bigger than themself, they can't, not quite. Not yet, anyway. There is still, they suppose, time.

READERS RESPOND

Dear DOB,

I have been an avid reader of THE LADDER for many years now, but this is my first time writing to you under my own name. I have sent you a few of my short stories over the years, and you have accepted two of my science fiction romances (see "The Rise of Lady Mars" and "She Fell from the Stars," both in 1969 issues), which I deeply appreciate.

I am writing today on quite a different errand. I have always appreciated this section of the magazine, as it has allowed me to witness time and time again the variety in our midst, the way our thoughts do not always run parallel to one another, even if we all share certain affinities. I am so grateful for all that THE LADDER has done for us lesbians over the years, and I confess that like many others I am heartbroken to know that this next issue will be its last.

Instead of shedding tears in print, however, I wanted to share another romance, a real one this time, in the hopes that, if you print it, other women will find it encouraging and remember not to give up on themselves.

Two years ago, in 1970, I joined a Daughters of Bilitis group that was traveling from where I live to New York City in order to join in the march commemorating the anniversary of the events of June 1969 at the Stonewall Inn. The day was a great success, and it was an exciting time, walking arm and arm with other gay men and women, telling the world of our existence without shame and insisting on our equal rights.

I had not eaten for several hours and was growing faint with the sunlight and sweat when a woman approached me bearing a sight for sore eyes: a plastic bag with a big sandwich inside it. She said I looked pale despite my developing sunburn and that I should eat something. We split what ended up being a PB&J, and perhaps it was the childishness of the meal and how it reminded us both of our girlhood school days that allowed us to talk so freely. Or perhaps it was the mood of the day, the solidarity we all felt with our fellows. Whatever the reason, we became fast friends over the course of the afternoon, and by day's end, I was quite nearly in love with her.

Although Jane—that is her name—claims that she was not so quickly infatuated with me, the fact is that we are now lovers and she and I live together. Jane is bisexual, a widow, her husband having died in the still raging and unjust war. She was raising her four-year-old daughter on her own when we met, and now I am becoming a second mother to this child, who grows more lovely and wise every day. Both Jane and I love her dearly and have vowed, much like any married couple would, to raise her to be a good and honest woman with the strength of her convictions. We are proud of her, and she sits on Jane's shoulders at most of the antiwar rallies we go to and hefts a big sign with her small hands. She knows, even at such a tender age, what it means to lose someone to war.

What do people say about us? Usually, they don't ask many questions. A benefit of living in a city, I have learned, is that it is easier to be ignored by others. Most folk have too much to occupy their minds to pay close attention to their neighbors, beyond the occasional exchange of gossip. When they do ask questions, we avoid giving direct answers, explaining only that I moved in to help Jane with her daughter some time after the death of the girl's father. Jane is a painter and has long run in rather bohemian circles where plenty of people accept us, and I have been an active member in the DOB for several years and have my own safe social circle as well. However, I am currently working for the United States Post Office, writing and proofreading manuals, and being a civil servant, I have to keep our secret rather more guardedly at work. But I have decided that should my sexuality be discovered and cost me my job, I will join the ranks of those currently attempting to fight for our right to equal employment in the courts.

Before Jane, I experienced many a heartbreak, and thought some days that the organ would never be mended enough to open itself up to another. But then there was Jane.

Without THE LADDER, I don't think I would have ever been brave enough to live as a lesbian. Which means that without THE LADDER, I would never have met Jane. I hope this story, with its happy ending, will remind the editors of all we readers owe you, and will remind readers that we are worthy of love and a life lived as our full selves.

Phyllis E.

18

Now

—

The Archivist sets Phyllis's box on the shelf, in its proper place. They finally found Phyllis and Jane's daughter, Aimee, who happened to be living in a suburb of the city. Aimee visited the QWA a few days ago to see her second mom's papers. She had never known that Phyllis's unpublished writing was kept anywhere; Jane had neglected to mention before her death that she'd sent her wife's things to the archive, and for years Aimee had assumed that either she or Phyllis had thrown it all away. She cried, looking through the papers, and told the Archivist how grateful she was to know that even though Phyllis had never achieved the kind of long-term, sustaining success she yearned for, she was still going to live on in a way, through the archive.

The Archivist pats the box, says goodbye to it, glad that they are alone in the dusty stacks, able to complete this little ritual without judgment.

They walk two aisles over, to the most recent boxes and folders, those belonging to contemporary writers and thinkers, most still alive. They left their own papers there before putting Phyllis's box away and now they pick them up and flip through the stack. It's a foolish endeavor, perhaps, but it's done. Before they left for work, they had the cat, whom they've renamed ET with Shalani's blessing, leave a paw print on each of the stuffed folders, using nontoxic vegetable ink that their tattoo artist roommate gave them. Now they put all three folders in a narrow box, and write their name on the side with the thick black marker that unites the labels across the archive. They pat this box, too, before striding back to the office and to their desk.

They will have a new historical obsession or two soon enough, they suspect. And who knows, they think, aware of the hubris involved in such a notion. Perhaps one day, they will be someone else's.

. . .

It's a day of letting go. The Archivist decides that night, before they go to sleep, to try one last thing to remember the Slopeside experience they first learned about over a year ago. They do some googling and find a vast array of guided meditations claiming to help with memory recall. They click one that has a quarter million views, and a man's gentle voice emanates from their phone. He recommends using headphones, so they find some old earbuds. They sit in a lotus position and then, because no one is going to be impressed with this feat of their otherwise unimpressive flexibility, and because it hurts more than it used to, they remove one foot from a thigh and sit cross-legged like a normal person. They listen.

An itch distracts them, and then a cough, but after a few moments, they let the man's soothing voice wash over them, and they focus on the time and place they want to remember. Slopeside Elementary. Being nine. Third grade—no, fourth. The trees and bushes at the back of the school, down the hill that in winter became a perfect sledding spot for the littlest kids.

Slowly, slowly, they breathe and follow the instructions, and breathe some more, and feel their body relaxing around them. They begin to feel another itch, but this time it's internal. A tickle, as if something is slithering across the floor of their mind, emerging from the darkness and into the light.

It feels miles away at first, and the concern over its distance makes it feel even farther, impossible to reach. But the Archivist keeps listening to the voice in their ears, keeps breathing, commands their eyebrows to unfurrow and their shoulders to let go. The thing snaking forward grows closer, a thread of bodily memory. The grass crunched by hundreds of feet; the private place between a prickly bush and a thick-trunked tree where they often went during recess to be alone and daydream or read a book; the unusual light piercing their hiding spot; the humming.

Eyes. Black eyes. No pupils. Shiny and wet. Unblinking. Eyes that should be terrifying, so foreign and inhuman. But they're not. They're ... compassionate? Yes, and wise. They're set in a face that isn't what a face should look like. There's no nose, just two flat slits. There's not really a mouth, just another gash that seems to flutter open and closed without the rest of the face moving. A foreign but intense care radiates from those eyes.

—and now return to the present, the man in the video says.

Startled, the Archivist's eyes snap open. Forty-five minutes have passed. They lie back and stare at the ceiling.

Did it actually work? Did they actually remember something from that experience? Or did they just want it to work, and so their brain conjured up an image? A set of images?

They will never know.

But maybe, just maybe, it doesn't really matter.

ACKNOWLEDGMENTS

Before I get to the thank-yous, I want to acknowledge that any misrepresentations of or factual errors regarding real places, time periods, or people—and any mistakes in general—are entirely my own.

There are many, many people to thank (some of whom don't know I exist but whom I feel compelled to acknowledge anyway), so let's get started.

Thank you to Mike Cahill, to whom this book is dedicated, for always listening to podcasts while making dinner, for letting me interrupt you with incessant questions even when I come in halfway through an episode, for indulging my increasing fascination with Barney and Betty Hill, for getting me scanned archival material for my birthday and books by John E. Mack and Jacques Vallee for Christmas, for cheering me on, for materially and emotionally supporting me, and for generally being the best partner.

Thank you to *The Last Podcast on the Left* for episode 169, which introduced me to the Hills and their story for the first time.

Thank you to these books and their authors: *Delayed Rays of a Star* by Amanda Lee Koe, *Meet Us by the Roaring Sea* by Akil Kumarasamy; *Confessions of the Fox* by Jordy Rosenberg; *Before All the World* by Moriel Rothman-Zecher; *Greenland* by David Santos Donaldson; *My Autobiography of Carson McCullers* by Jenn Shapland. Reading and thinking about your books helped me believe that I could write this one.

Thank you to Emeline Dehn-Reynolds, Morgan Wilson, and everyone at the Milne Special Collections and Archives at the University of New Hampshire for housing the Hills' papers and helping me access them.

Thank you to John G. Fuller for writing such a compassionate account of the Hills' experience in *The Interrupted Journey*, and to Kathleen Marden and Stanton T. Friedman for sharing further details in *Captured! The Betty and Barney Hill UFO Experience*. Thank you to Sarah Scoles for your excellent book *They Are Already Here*. Thank you to everyone at the Robert S. Cox Special Collections and University Archives Research Center at the University of Massachusetts Amherst Libraries for the scant yet fascinating material from the NAACP Portsmouth Branch. Thank you to the Lesbian Herstory Archives for introducing me to the magic of archives in the first place.

Thank you to Angela "Overkill" Hill, Barney Hill's granddaughter, for interviewing your dad, Barney Hill III, about his dad, Barney Hill Jr., on your podcast, *Ceremonial Weigh-In*. May you win all your fights!

Thank you to Eric Marcus and the *Making Gay History* podcast for teaching me so much, for letting me hear the voices of my queer ancestors, and for introducing me to the Daughters of Bilitis, Phyllis Lyon and Del Martin, *The Ladder*, and, in particular, Ernestine Eckstein. Thank you to Joan Ilacqua, executive director of the History Project: Documenting LGBTQ Boston, for meeting me, being a wealth of knowledge, and for sending me *Improper Bostonians: Lesbian and Gay History from the Puritans to Playland*. Thank you to Elizabeth Lapovsky Kennedy and Madeline D. Davis and your book *Boots of Leather, Slippers of Gold*, and to Marcia Gallo for your work on the history of the Daughters of Bilitis and *The Ladder*. Thank you also to Alex, Kate Dickson, Neal Z. Shipe, and Kelly Wooten at the David M. Rubenstein Rare Book & Manuscript Library at Duke University; to the One Archives at the USC Libraries; and to Devin McGeehan Muchmore at the GLBT Historical Society.

Thank you to the sci-fi writers—the women and queers especially—in the 1920s–70s; your stories and novels helped me imagine Phyllis into the world. In particular, I'm indebted to Leigh Brackett, Samuel R. Delany, Ursula K. Le Guin, Judith Merril, C. L. Moore, and Leslie F. Stone. Thank you also to the scholars whose books introduced me to some of these and to other women in early SF: Lisa Yaszek, Patrick B. Sharp, and Eric Leif Davin.

In addition to the wonders of the Internet Archive (which houses so many old science fiction and fantasy magazines) and Newspapers.com,

GeneaologyBank, and the TimesMachine (which provide digital access to historical newspapers), I visited approximately a million random little websites while doing research, which was a good reminder that there's still some good internet to be had outside the silos of social media. Thank you to the history bloggers and amateur archivists out there.

Similarly, thank you to the used bookstores—especially the Iliad Bookshop and the Last Bookstore—for the delicious smells, the occasional cats, and the preservation of so much good old stuff for me to rummage through and discover.

Thank you to *Hearts of Space* and Stephen Hill for the music, the vibes, and the voice.

Thank you to all my professors, peers, friends, and colleagues at the University of Nebraska–Lincoln. Special thanks to: Jess Poli, for spending hours and hours over two or three semesters reading this book with me, and for loving Phyllis best from the very beginning; Ava Nathaniel Winter, Katie Marya, and Isaac Essex, for having various longwinded conversations with me about memory, trauma, queerness, imagination, and teaching; Timothy Schaffert, of course, for believing in this book so early on, and to the rest of my inimitable dissertation committee—Hope Wabuke, Thomas Gannon, and Emily Kazyak—for reading, making incredible comments, and also for passing me and making me, officially, a doctor. Special thanks again to Hope Wabuke for hooding me at graduation—it was an honor.

Thank you to Abigail Ellery for the love, the cuddles, the smokes, the time, the smile, and, of course, for fixing my fan.

Thank you to my incredible Tin House teacher, Megan Giddings, and to my fabulous and hugely talented Tin House cohort: Helen Armstrong, Dana Fang, Yalitza Ferreras, Anu Kandikuppa, Jennie Evenson, Eliana Ramage, Miranda Sanchez, Kristin Sherman, and Kaj Tanaka. Thank you for letting me cry that one time.

Thank you to Gerre in Chula Vista for the perfect little studio where I spent ten days watching old movies, reading out-of-print science fiction magazines, and writing—and thank you to my family for gifting me this little self-led residency. Thank you to Kyle Hobratschk, Nancy Rebal, David Searcy, Lou Michaels, Adrienne Lichliter, Alysia Nicole Harris, and everyone involved in the Corsicana Artist and Writer

Residency, where I finished the first draft of this book; and thank you to my fellow residents Virginia L. Montgomery, José Morbán, and especially Tricia Park, for sharing time, space, and laughs. Thank you to Gil Soltz at the Yefe Nof Residency for the beautiful home which, when I first stepped inside, made me cry because it smelled exactly like my grandparents' house.

Thank you to Nancy Sexton at the Muse Rooms for accommodating me and for the lovely space, and thank you to Peter Wacks for the conversations and smoke breaks.

Thank you to early readers: Jess Poli, again; Sharon Holiner; David Henson; Rachel Cochran; Gabrielle Korn; Katharine Coldiron; Orin Posner; Langston Epps; Jazz Paquet; Mike Cahill, again; and, of course, my first reader always, Andrea Paymar, the best Ima who ever was.

Thank you to my family—Ima/Andi again, David and Dani and Libby, Michelle and Vero, Jay and Nancy, and all the cousins at various degrees of removal—and thank you to my in-laws too—Mike, Deb, Marty, Cosette, Brendan, Staci, Hudson, Nora, and all the aunts and uncles and cousins—for being enthusiastic supporters of this very strange career I keep trying to maintain, in which I make things up and write them down. Thank you to various cats: Margaret Catwood, Jane Pawsten, and Abigail, as well as Fitz, for the name, and Bayshan, for not minding that I only used your brother's.

Thank you to my friends, writers and not—there are many of you from different eras of my life—for the conversations, the inspiration, the critiques, the gossip, the camaraderie. Some of you are mentioned above already, but additional special thanks to Kit Haggard and the spreadsheet group; the Slutty Jewish Babes group, Gabrielle Korn, Irina Gusin, and Alana Hope Levinson; my co-editor, colleague, and dear friend Stevie Seibert Desjarlais (and James, and all the animals too); Jean Lee for the walks and talks and our mutual flurries of texts; Katharine Coldiron for the 1950s and '60s movie recs, the history lessons (that I request!), and the fellow Star Trek enthusiasm; Joshua Langman for the fonts and friendship; Celia Laskey and Ruth Madievsky for separately being some of my first new friends in L.A.; Nico and Jules Byrne for movie nights and brunches; Mariko Tamaki and Heather Gold for latkes and long talks; Ben Ehrlich for coffees and kvetching; and Brian Morton, still, again . . .

I am wealthy in friends, and I'm grateful to each and every one of you, including those I haven't listed.

Thank you to my agent, Eric Simonoff, who told me to keep going when I wasn't sure, and to his assistants Jessica Spitz, Criss Moon, and Grace Blaxill, for being the kindest communicators and readers.

Thank you to my editor Mo Crist at Bloomsbury, for not only wanting this book and seeing what it was doing and what it could be, but for taking me along with you when you moved. Thank you to Barbara Darko, Tanya Heinrich, Gleni Bartels, Patti Ratchford, Alona Fryman, Suzanne Keller, Laura Phillips, Rosie Mahorter, Olivia Treynor, and everyone else at Bloomsbury for a truly lovely acquisition-to-publication experience. Thank you to Carla Bruce and Amelia Possanza at Lavender PR for your excitement, dedication, and work.

There are many people who are no longer with us whom I wish I could thank, but the only ones that I feel like I can't close this book without acknowledging are Barney and Betty Hill, without whom large swaths of our world and the stories we fill it with would be very different.

A NOTE ON THE AUTHOR

ILANA MASAD is a writer of fiction, nonfiction, and criticism whose work has been widely published. Masad is the author of the novel *All My Mother's Lovers* and is co-editing the forthcoming anthology *Here For All the Reasons: #BachelorNation on Why We Watch*.

A NOTE ON THE TYPE

Janson is the name given to a set of old-style serif typefaces cut by the Hungarian punchcutter Miklós Kis in the Netherlands in 1685. This crisp, upright, and compact face represented the height of the Dutch Baroque typographic style and was incorrectly attributed to the Leipzig-based printer Anton Janson until the 1950s. The revival printed in this book was designed for hot metal casting by Hermann Zapf for Monotype in 1954 and digitized for Linotype under the supervision of Adrian Frutiger in 1985.